# Finding

# Delaware

## Bree Wiley

Cover Design by Bree Wiley

Cover Photo by Yuri Arcurs

First edition 2024

Paperback ISBN 979-8-218-49489-6

# CONTENTS

# FOREWORD

Taylor and Huckslee's story deals with some dark and heavy themes. For those of you who would like to know what you're getting into, please refer to the CW list in the back of the book.

Though the characters start as seniors in high school, all sexual acts take place when they are of legal age.

Please, please always remember that your mental health matters and your experiences are valid. The world is a brighter place with you in it, and you are loved.

**Note:** While I know it's highly unlikely for Berkeley and the University of Utah to face off in football during the national championships, some creative liberties were taken for the sake of the story.

This is, after all, a work of fiction.

# SOUNDTRACK

Romance Is Dead – Parkway Drive
Panic Switch – Silversun Pickups
Lip Gloss And Black – Atreyu
DRAG ME DOWN – Breathe Carolina
Routines In The Night - Twenty One Pilots
Dethrone – Bad Omens
Rain – Sleep Token
Lost In Yesterday – Tame Impala
The Emptiness – Alesana
Hollywood's Bleeding – Post Malone
Killing You – Asking Alexandria
Bad Blood – Bastille
Something Real – Post Malone
Too Much – Pepper
Like This – Breathe Carolina
The Bad Touch - Bloodhound Gang
Sunflower – Post Malone, Swae Lee

Blackout – Breathe Carolina
i apologise if you feel something – Bring Me The Horizon
Royal We – Silversun Pickups

# Part One

# HUCKSLEE

## AUGUST

"**M**otherfucker!"

The word explodes from my mouth as the wheel of an ugly yellow dirt bike clips mine, sending me skidding sideways in the mud. "Taylor, you fucking fuck!"

My wheel wobbles when I over-correct, the back end of my bike fishtailing toward the asshole next to me who's popping a wheelie in the middle of the goddamn race. Taylor whips his helmet to the side, losing balance when he sees me careening toward him, his front wheel hitting the ground hard as he jerks to the right, trying to avoid our inevitable crash. It's useless—the terrain shifts, and the track curves into a bend, sealing our fate.

Pulling the clutch, I press the front brake just in time for my back fender to tap him and bail, letting go of the handlebars to sail through the air. The sound of my bike scraping against dirt makes my damn ears bleed as I silently pray it doesn't crush me into dust.

The air punches out of my lungs as I hit the ground and roll, flipping like a rag doll until a hard body stops me. Strong arms wrap around my shoulders, slowing my momentum while our bikes halt mere inches from us.

"You son of a *bitch*." The arms unwrap from around me before yanking off my helmet. My dirty blonde curls, drenched in sweat, stick to my forehead as I gaze up dazedly into Taylor's blazing blue-green eyes. His full lips curl back in a snarl, and his fist clenches, drawing back with palpable fury.

"Not the face!" I shout, but it's too late.

Skin meets skin with a sickening crack, my lip splitting from the force of the blow. Taylor shoves me down into the dirt, his fists pounding my sides and forearms as I raise them in defense. His shaggy black hair is wild, billowing in the breeze as he rains down punches, and I desperately try to grab his wrists to stop him. Another racer whizzes by, narrowly avoiding us as we grapple furiously on the track.

"What the hell, Fuckslee?"

"Your wheel clipped mine, dude!" Gritting my teeth, I brace against a blow to my kidney. "You fucking showoff!"

Seriously. Why can't I have *one* race without Taylor Tottman popping wheelies or doing tricks off the jumps?

We're here to race, not put on some damn show. But he does it.

Every. Fucking. Time.

A few more racers fly by, screaming at us to get off the track as one of them pulls up next to us. My head rocks back when he hits my brow, pain exploding behind my eyes. Bucking my hips, I try to dislodge him since I'm broader, but his lean build gives him a speed I can't match.

"The wedding, man, the wedding!" I holler, thinking it'll get him to ease up, but it only makes him angrier.

"Fuck you, you sissy bottom bitch."

His fists connect harder, and I whip my gaze over to the racer next to us, who's pulling off his helmet. Christian, Taylor's best friend, climbs from his bike before yanking Taylor off me.

He drags him back, allowing me to breathe and process the fact that I just crashed my bike two laps before the finish line.

Dark sky blankets above, stars drowned out by the bright lights of the track. It's a clear Utah night, summer heat making my motocross gear stick to my skin. Pulling off my racing gloves, I sit up with a wince. Everything fucking hurts. Taylor's attack made my ribs ache, and slamming into the ground when I crashed definitely bruised my shoulders. A trickle of blood rolls down my busted brow and lip.

Great. Any chance I had at getting home without my dad knowing I'd snuck out has just gone out the window. All because of Taylor.

Shooting a glare at him as he and Christian lift his bike, a painful groan escapes my lips when I stand. My two-stroke lies a few yards away on its side, and Taylor's eyes follow me as I move toward it.

"I swear, Huck, if you fucked up my bike, I'll ruin you," he spits venomously, but I roll my eyes. He's been threatening me since the ninth fucking grade. I'm over it.

"It would be your own goddamn fault." My muscles scream in agony as I lift my bike. "Who the hell pops a wheelie around a corner?"

Luckily, when I test the throttle, everything seems okay. It runs fine, but a deep gouge along the radiator shroud has me clenching my jaw. Yep, I'm in deep shit. Dad is going to be pissed.

As I wheel myself off to the side, something Taylor said snags in my brain, and I turn to glare over my shoulder as I blow a curl out of my eyes. "Did you seriously call me a sissy bottom bitch?"

Christian's thick brows rise into his hairline as he glances at his best friend, whose beautiful smirking face makes me want to punch it.

"Tell me I'm wrong," Taylor snickers, a challenge dancing in his eyes that he knows I can't rise to.

And that's what pisses me off the most—he *knows*. But I'm tired of fighting with him. Every day has been a fight for the last three years, ever since that day in PE when I fucked up. When I misread the signs of our friendship so thoroughly that I handed him a weapon to use against me.

And use it he does—with precision. So, instead, I turn away, shaking my head as I prepare to slide back on my helmet, hiding the red splotches of embarrassment staining my cheeks. His cruel laugh makes me pause.

"That's what I thought. Run home to your daddy, fairy boy."

My helmet hits the ground along with my bike as I come at him. Christian steps between us to hold Taylor back, and I can't help the pang in my chest every time I see them together. Best fucking friends. Inseparable. Exactly what I'd hoped Taylor and I would be until I screwed it all up.

"Let's chill out, guys," Christian grumbles, his long brown hair falling over his shoulders, but I shout around him instead.

"Soon, he'll be your dad too. Show some respect!"

Taylor's nostrils flare at my words, his eyes widening into a sneer. Mentally, I brace myself for what's coming. After three years of taking this shit from him at school and on the track, I know whatever he's about to say will feel like a gunshot to the chest. It always does.

"Bro, stop," Christian warns, hands on Taylor's shoulders. It does no good.

"Fuck you," he snarls, "and fuck your pedo bishop father."

Fury unlike anything I've ever felt burns in my veins, white-hot. The world goes red. Christian raises his palms and steps aside resignedly, knowing his best friend just signed his own death warrant, and I fucking launch. My arms wrap around Taylor's midsection as I take him to the ground, a yelp clawing out of his throat when my knuckle splits against his front teeth.

"Don't you *ever* say shit like that about my dad again!" I scream, hitting him wherever I can bruise skin. It's an accusation of the absolute worst kind, completely unfounded, and part of me can't believe something so horrible even came out of his mouth.

But another part of me can because this is Taylor fucking Tottman we're dealing with—the boy who lied our sophomore year and told the entire swim team I'd shit in the pool. (I did not.)

The same motherfucker who just last week had the football coach convinced I was addicted to porn and had me hauled into the counseling office for an evaluation. (I am not!) *This motherfucker.*

"Keep my father's name out of your dirty mouth!" My punches keep landing, and Taylor does nothing to fight back. He turns his head to spit blood onto the ground, laughing mockingly. I swear if it weren't for Christian hauling me off him, I would have murdered his ass.

My dad doesn't deserve that, especially not after what's coming tomorrow. More than that, my dad is an all-around genuine guy. Yes, he's the local bishop, but he's well-known in our small Utah town, and everyone loves him. He'd give the shirt off his back to someone in need without question.

"Let it go, Huckslee." Christian puts a hand on my chest and firmly but gently pushes me back. "Just let it go."

"No, fuck off, man."

A wheeze comes from the ground as Taylor slowly climbs to his feet, blood staining his teeth when he grins. He's gripping his side, his motocross gear dirty and torn. If this had been a certified race, the officials would have been here by now, tearing us a new one. Luckily, we didn't jeopardize anything since someone organized this little night race on social media.

"Go home, Huck." Taylor spits onto the ground again, and Christian pushes me back more forcefully this time.

"He's right, *hermano*. You both need to go home. The wedding, remember?"

*Right.* The fucking wedding.

Hitting Taylor with a glare that I hope haunts his fucking nightmares, I pick up my bike and helmet, yanking on my gloves with two quick tugs. Then, I roar out of the track, kicking up a dirt storm in my wake.

The motorsport park is a few miles outside town, in the middle of nowhere, so I ride fast, wishing I could feel the wind on my heated skin. My racing gear covers every inch of my body, protecting me in case of a crash like the one earlier. Sometimes, it leaves no room to breathe, and right now, it feels suffocating. The vibration from my bike makes every bone ache, and tomorrow weighs heavily on my mind.

I ease off the throttle as the Gville town sign comes into view, not wanting to get caught out after curfew. Technically, my bike isn't street legal, but I've lived here all my life, so I know the shortcuts.

The town isn't large, with a population of around twelve thousand, and I fly through fields and side streets quickly enough. Once within a few blocks of my neighborhood, I cut the engine and make the rest of the journey on foot, removing my helmet with a slight wheeze.

Fucking Taylor. I wait for the rage to hit me again as I think about him, but all I can muster are the coiling remnants of exhaustion and regret. Every single day for the past three years has been a struggle to get out of bed, knowing he waits at school to punish me for being me. For liking what I like. For ruining our friendship. I've held this secret in my brain since I was nine, letting it rot me from the inside out. The first person I ever shared a little piece of myself with threw it back in my face.

And I'm just so fucking tired.

The houses I pass are large and beautiful, with manicured lawns and swaying trees. My childhood home comes into view as I round a corner, red brick, and white columns at the end of a cul-de-sac. Besides being a Bishop, Dad's also a realtor and bought the house when Mom was pregnant with me. The three of us lived here happily until two years ago, when it was just me and Dad. Until now...

Pulling up to the side door next to the garage, I quietly sneak inside and park my bike where it's supposed to sit. After tossing the rest of my gear onto a workbench, I step up to the door leading into the house and swear under my breath when I find it locked.

*Shit.*

I had explicitly left it unlocked so that I could sneak back in. Dad must have locked it while getting a drink or something.

"Fuck you, Tay," I mutter as I rummage through toolboxes, searching for a screwdriver. Obviously, Taylor isn't to blame for the locked door, but blaming him makes me feel better anyway.

Pushing curls out of my eyes, I insert the screwdriver into the bottom of the lock and turn, using a paperclip to scrub the pins inside the keyhole until I hear it click open. A breath of relief leaves my aching lungs. I'd only picked a lock as practice, and this is the first time I've actually done it to get inside anywhere. My best friend Logan's uncle, Devon, taught us how to do it a few months ago. He's cool, only five years older than us, and loans out his four-wheeler whenever he visits from college. Solid guy.

As quietly as possible, I step into the pitch-black kitchen and softly shut the door behind me, throwing the deadbolt into place. Intending to grab a water bottle from the fridge before heading upstairs, I barely make it five steps before I'm blinded by the overhead lights flooding the kitchen, and I freeze.

Dad stands in the doorway to the dining room, arms folded and eyes narrowed behind the glasses perched on the edge of his nose. His short blonde hair is a mess, as if he'd been running his hands through it.

We stare at each other silently for a moment before I straighten up, flashing him my practiced grin.

"Hiya, Pops."

"What the hell happened to your face, Huck?"

Oh, he's mad. Dad hardly ever swears, and when he does, you know you've messed up.

"I, uh...crashed my bike?"

It comes off like a question, and he lifts a brow before rounding the kitchen island to open the freezer. Pulling out an ice pack, he stands before me, the bottoms of his plaid pajamas swishing against the polished marble.

Handing it to me silently, he simply stares as I place it against my swollen lip. His expression tells me he knows there's more to the story.

And he's not going to ask twice.

"...plus, I sorta got into a fight."

He breathes out slowly through his nose, still watching me with brown eyes that match mine. "With who?"

I wince, teeth gnawing at my cheek. "Okay, don't freak out, but...Taylor."

"Maisie is going to be so pissed," he murmurs as his lids close for a brief second, and inwardly I cringe at the mention of her name—my soon-to-be stepmother.

Sure, I've met her a handful of times over the last six months they've been dating, and yes, she's nice in that *I'll only be dealing with you for a year until you go off to college* sort of way, but something always feels off about her. But maybe that's because of my history with her son.

Dad walks over to the farmhouse-style sink, grabs a washcloth from the drawer, and runs it under the water. "Come here."

There's a disapproving note to his voice that has me hanging my head, silently cursing myself as I shuffle over to him so he can clean the blood off my face.

Great. He's upset with me.

*I'm a shitty son. I'll never be enough.*

"Who started it?" he asks after a pause, and my eyes flick at him warily.

"Does it matter?"

"I guess not." He tosses the rag into the sink before crossing his arms again. "Who won?"

A grin breaks out on my face, splitting my lip again, and he grins back. But it's gone in a flash when his smile changes into a stern frown.

"You know you're grounded until probably graduation, right?"

A scowl furrows my brows as I glance down at the floor. No way in hell am I going to tell him the reason why I punched

Taylor, not when everything is going to change tomorrow. All that would do is make things even more awkward than they already are.

"Why her, Dad?" I mutter, poking my tongue at my cut lip. "Out of all the people in this shitty town, why did it have to be her?"

"Language!" His cutting tone has my head snapping up, and even though we're the same height, his eyes make me feel like a child again, being reprimanded for falling asleep in church. "We've talked about this, Huckslee. Maisie will be your stepmother tomorrow, and Taylor will be your brother. You'll share a bathroom and living space. You've had weeks to adjust to the idea."

I cringe so hard that I feel it in my soul.

Dad's brows jump. "What happened between you two, anyway? Not even a few years ago, you were friends."

Yeah. *Were*. Almost more than friends...

He continues his lecture in my silence. "Well, get over it, whatever it is. And no more fighting. Do you understand me?"

In another lifetime, maybe.

"Yes, sir." I salute him with a forced cheesy grin that has him rolling his eyes, excusing me off to bed.

As I take the stairs two at a time, closing myself in the bathroom I'll be sharing with my high school bully tomorrow, I can't help but think: Just one year. One more year of hiding, and then I'll be off to college, away from Taylor and this stupid town for good.

# TAYLOR

I think Fuckslee cracked a rib.

And the real kicker is that it wasn't even during the fight. His shoulder slammed into me when I caught him before our bikes splattered his ass all over the track.

Fucker. Should have let the bikes smash him. But then, who would I mess with every day?

A haggard breath leaves my lungs as I ride into Arbitrary Hills trailer park, my head tipping back to watch the metal arch pass over me.

Man, fuck this place. Not just Arbitrary Hills but the whole ass town in general. Only good things here are the biking trails and Rhonda at the smoke shop on Vine Street, who never IDs me because I smile and wink at her.

That's it.

Well, and Christian. And Salem. *Maybe* Matty and Xed. But that's really it.

Revving my engine, I hiss beneath my helmet at the burning in my chest as I floor it past Old Man Jones's place. I know I woke him up, and the reaming he'll give me for it tomorrow puts a grin on my lips. I hate that old fucker, but I love to watch him scream. His face turns purple, and his eyes pop out. Shit's hilarious.

As soon as I get a lane over from where the trailer sits, I bring the bike to a halt in someone's front yard, snickering at the way my wheel tears up their small patch of grass. The list of people I'm pissing off tonight keeps growing—including Christian, which really irks me.

*"You took it too far, dumbass. Huckslee's dad is a nice guy."*

My teeth grind as I walk my bike between fences, recalling my best friend's words. Yeah, well, if the good Bishop Aaron Davis was a nice guy, he wouldn't be marrying my piece-of-shit mother. Or forcing me to live with them. With *him.*

The thought of Huckslee has my chest wrenching, like always, but it has nothing to do with the cracked rib. Fuck, I wish I could leave him alone sometimes. He makes it so easy to rile him up, though, and honestly, I really don't want to stop.

His dark, glittering eyes and blonde curls flash in my mind, those full lips of his red from where I punched them, and a sick rush of satisfaction almost steals my breath at the memory.

I did that. I made those lips swell. I made those dark eyes water. I left my mark on him.

*Me.*

The backyard of my father's single-wide enters my vision, and I stop to take a pack of cigarettes out of my pocket. Pulling one out, I flick my BIC and light it, inhaling deep, even as sharp pain shoots through me. My head falls back against a fence, and I take in the bright stars dotting the sky, breathing out smoke.

Tomorrow's going to suck major ass. Whether it'll suck more than my current living situation remains to be seen. Sure, being closer to Fuckslee has some irritating form of anticipation coursing through me—I'd get to make his life hell from the comfort of my own room now—but the thought of being near my mother makes my skin itch worse than being near the asshole currently passed out drunk on the couch inside the trailer.

I can count on one hand the number of times I've seen my mother over the last ten years, but suddenly, now she wants to be a parent? Yeah, fuck off with that shit.

I finish my smoke, putting the butt out on the side of the trailer before rolling my bike over to the padlocked shed. After slipping it inside, I cross to the front where I left my bedroom window slightly cracked. Gripping the ledge with my hands, I grimace as I pull myself onto the windowsill, biting my tongue to quiet a whimper. Fuck, everything hurts. Other than the cracked rib, my nose is clogged with blood, and I'm pretty sure my left eye is starting to swell shut. Seems Huck left his mark on me, too.

Ignoring the weird flip that thought does to my stomach, I swing my legs into the room, intending to drop down silently, when the twisting motion of my torso has my rib twinging so painfully that my muscles give out. I fall from the window, landing on the floor beside my bed and, unfortunately, the cat. She yowls at the top of her little lungs and launches into the shelf above.

"Shhh, quiet," I hiss, breathing hard through the pain. "Lasagna, you asshole."

The little orange ball of fur knocks over everything in sight, junk clattering to the ground before she runs from the room, shoving my door on her way out so that it swings and hits the wall behind it.

With a flinch, I hold my breath and wait. Maybe he didn't hear it. Maybe he's so plastered that nothing short of a bomb going off would wake him. Maybe pigs will fly because five seconds later, I hear his shout from the living room as the springs in the couch squeak.

"What are you doing, boy?"

*Goddammit.*

Rising from my crouch, body shaking, I yank a duffel out of my closet and start pulling every shirt I own off the hooks, stuffing them into the bag.

"Packing." My voice is slightly weak against the throbbing that's radiating through my ribs. It's too hot in here, too muggy, so I unzip my motocross jacket and leave it dangling at my waist as I cross to my dresser, where I snicker at the punching bag in the corner that has Huckslee's picture taped on it. So what if I like to imagine it's his face that I'm punching the days between school and motocross? Does that seem obsessive? Maybe. Don't give two fucks, though.

I stuff every pair of boxers and socks I have into the bag, along with several baggies of weed I've yet to sell, when the pungent odor of whiskey stings my nostrils. My nose automatically wrinkles as I take in my father leaning against the doorway, a bottle of Jack in one hand while his other scratches at the gut hanging over his dirty sweatpants. A dangerous, glassy gleam glints in his eyes.

Fucking great. Drunk *and* high. Always a winning combination.

"Who fucked up your face?" he grunts, swigging from his bottle, and I turn back around to continue gathering my shit.

"Fight at the track."

He grunts again. "Who was it?"

I pause, weighing my words before shrugging with a wince. "Huckslee Davis."

"Did you kick his ass?"

There's a lethal undertone to his words that has me seeing red, and I brush past him down the small hall toward the bathroom. "What the fuck do you think?"

While I may get violent with Huckslee because I'm forced to, the thought of anyone else touching him pisses me off. He's mine to torment. No one else's.

Before I can enter the bathroom, a hand wraps around my arm with so much force I swear I feel something crack, and I'm whipped around to face my father. He steps into my space, close enough for me to gag at his whiskey breath. "Watch how you talk to me, boy."

Tears prick my eyes from the way his fingers tighten around my bicep, and I blink them away rapidly. This isn't the first time he's grabbed me like this or even laid hands on me, but I know that whatever I say right now will either escalate or defuse the situation.

"Okay, sorry. Jesus."

His grip tightens so hard that my knees nearly buckle, but finally, he lets me go with a hard shove into the bathroom door, a whimper bubbling out of my throat when the knob hits my sore rib.

I hate him. I fucking hate him.

With my back to him, I mask a sniffle, grabbing my toothbrush and toothpaste from the mirror before stuffing them into my bag, along with deodorant and the electric razor I shave my balls with.

"What time is the wedding?" Another swig off that bottle has my jaw ticking, and I move on to get my things from the shower, ignoring the soap scum that lines the tub.

"Noon tomorrow."

He scoffs loudly and turns away, finally leaving me alone in peace. Once he's gone, I study myself in the mirror for a minute.

God, I look like shit. My black hair is sticking up with grease and sweat; one eye is bloodshot, and the other is beginning to blacken. Blood crusts my upper lip from where Huck bashed my nose, which is definitely starting to bruise.

Dropping my gaze to my arm, I scowl at the ring of bruises already forming from my father's fingerprints. At least with the other marks covering my body, I won't have to hide myself in the locker room after football practice. I can blame my appearance on fighting with Huckslee, just like I always do.

After I've gathered everything I need from the bathroom, I tip-toe back to my room, glancing at the state of the living room and kitchen. Empty beer bottles line the stained carpet, and a mountain of dishes are in the sink. The whole place reeks, but I stay away as much as possible. My father is a fucking slob.

In all honesty, I can see why my mother would get sick of this life and want to leave it. What I've never understood, though, is why she couldn't take her seven-year-old son with her.

Entering my room, which I always keep clean and organized, I freeze when I find my dad staring at my punching bag in the corner, at the picture of Huck taped to it. Dread prickles my skin, and I swallow hard when he turns around with a sneer.

"Is that why you're in such a rush to leave?"

*No, I'm trying to get away from you.*

"Huck's an asshole," I scoff, going to my bed where Lasagna knocked over my books, quickly stuffing my copies of *Ender's Game* and *I, Robot* into the bag. "We're enemies."

He takes a long pull off his bottle. "But you didn't always feel that way, did ya?"

Memories invade my brain, images and feelings from a day three years ago that I've done my damndest to bury deep, and I bite down on my tongue so hard it bleeds.

*"Let's sneak under the bleachers, Tay."*

*"Hell, no. I heard they found a cougar under there last week."*

*"Aw, are you scared? Need me to hold your hand?"*

Suddenly, my father is in my face again, snarling with contempt. "Remember who owns your bike, boy. Don't forget."

How the fuck can I when the name of his mechanic shop is plastered all over the side of my helmet? When he constantly reminds me every day that his shop sponsors me, which I desperately need in order to enter the amateur races hosted by the motorsports park? When the ticket to my fucking freedom—a two-year scholarship to the University of Utah—rests in the hands of me winning those damn races with that damned bike?

"You wouldn't have racing if it weren't for me, you little shit stain."

"I know." Zipping up my duffle, I shake out of his grasp and approach the door, feeling him follow close behind. The bag is too light, but it's everything I own.

"I don't like the idea of you living under the same roof as that faggot."

I stop in my tracks, rage licking up my spine at his slur. I hate that fucking word. No matter how much shit I sling at Huckslee, I'd never call him that.

"Huck's not a faggot."

It's a lie. I know it is. But something in me feels the need to protect his secret despite the way I constantly call him out on it. As I've stated, he's mine to fuck with.

Shouldering the duffle, I cross the living room toward the door.

"Where do you think you're going?"

"I'm staying at Salem's," I bite out, even though I have no intention of going to my girlfriend's house. We're on a break because she's dating Brad Hanagin. I'm really going to knock on Christian's window and ask to crash on his floor, but I'd rather my father not know that. He'd just make more nasty comments about shit that isn't true. Shit about me.

"Take the fucking cat with you," is all he says before he disappears into his room, slamming the door.

Searching through the mess, I find the orange ball of fluff chewing on what looks like a chicken bone near the back door and scoop her up.

"Let's go, Lasagna." Kissing her soft head, I stuff her inside my duffle bag. "Don't piss on my shit."

She immediately starts purring, and I sigh heavily with a wince as I make my way toward my bike around the back of the house. Christian's allergic, but maybe Salem's family can care for her or something. Not like my father will do it once I'm gone.

*Just one more year*, I think desperately as I start my bike, waking the whole trailer park but not giving a fuck. The Bluetooth from my helmet connects to my phone, and 'Romance is Dead' by Parkway Drive blasts in my ears.

One more year, and I can pay off my bike and leave this hellhole for good.

# HUCKSLEE

"**S**mile for the camera, boys!"

The flash of a camera blinds me, and I blink rapidly to clear the dark spots in my vision, my cheeks sore from the pleasantly fake smile I've had plastered on my face since we pulled into the church. I really hate weddings.

"Come on, boys, smile," comes a shrill voice to my right, doing nothing for the headache I've had since this morning.

I turn to grin at Maisie, my new stepmom. She looks lovely, dressed in a white satin gown that sparkles and pools at her feet, the black hair she must have given Tay curling around her shoulders. Something's off about her, though. Something cold and withdrawn.

She has the same blue-green eyes as Taylor, which remind me of the ocean in summer, except her gaze glints with disapproval. They even share the same features—a delicate nose, and high cheekbones—but I think his lips must come from his dad because hers are thin, whereas his bottom lip juts out, puffy and juicy enough to bite.

*Dammit.*

My fist clenches as Dad pushes us shoulder to shoulder in front of the curtained backdrop, posing as one big happy fucking family. Except for Taylor, who's had a permanent scowl on his beautiful face all morning. He's hardly said two words to anyone, other than a few mumbled sentences to my dad when we'd gotten here earlier.

Today had almost been a disaster, and of course, it was all thanks to Taylor fucking Tottman.

We were supposed to be at the church by eleven, but ten-fifteen had rolled around, and he still hadn't shown up at the house. Finally, by ten-forty, he'd peeled into the driveway on his bike holding some scrawny orange cat. I'd just tossed the creature inside the house before shoving him into my Honda Civic.

Driving him hadn't been my idea, but I was trying to get back on Dad's good side before the next race, so I'd gritted my teeth and put up with the thirty-minute awkward drive, Silversun Pickups filling the silence. The only words he said to me were how 'gay' my music was, but I'd just turned it up and ignored him. He hadn't said anything else or even looked my way, which was odd.

Now, here I stand in the reception hall, trying my hardest to keep my eyes off him. Despite the swelling in his face that matches my own, he looks fucking fantastic in his black tux and red tie, dark hair looking softer than raven's wings as it falls over his brow. His skin is paler than usual, but I chalk it up to the satin jacket washing out his tone. It makes the bruises peppering his face stand out, which had made his mother's eye twitch when she'd seen him.

"Smile, boys," Dad says as the camera goes off again. Maisie frowns in disappointment as she looks at her son. He's still scowling.

Their relationship seems...strained, to say the least. According to Dad, Taylor's father had custody of him for the last few years, and he and his mom are trying to repair their relationship.

Looking over at him, I do a double take, noting the tension in his shoulders and strain lines next to his mouth.

"What's up with your face?" I mutter, sweeping my gaze across the heavily decorated church.

He glances at me sideways. "You punched it, jackass."

"No, I mean the death glare you've been sporting all morning."

He just ignores me, and for some insane reason, I find that even more irritating than his usual snark. It's as if he's entirely different around his mom, and I don't know if I like it.

Dad claps us both on the shoulder. "Alright, enough photos for now. Why don't you two get something to eat? Huckslee can introduce you to some of the fam," he adds with a brow waggle, and inwardly, I groan.

Taylor simply nods, mumbling as he walks away, and Dad frowns after him.

"Not much of a talker, is he?"

I open my mouth to tell him something's wrong because the Taylor I know loves the sound of his own voice, but Maisie interrupts me.

"Oh, he's probably stressed with the move and all." She waves a hand, brushing him off with an eye roll. "He's never done well with change."

That sounds wrong. I've never seen the asshole exude anything other than rock-solid confidence in any situation, but since she's his mother, she'd know him better than I would.

"Go make him feel welcome, son." Dad gently pushes me forward with a shove. "Show him off to everyone."

For the umpteenth time today, I grit my teeth. Three years spent being tormented by this shithead, and now I have to play nice? It's not fucking fair.

Weaving my way through round tables covered in white cloths, I find Taylor in front of the dessert table, staring down into the cheesecake bites with a grimace, looking uncomfortable as hell. As crazy as it sounds, I kinda want to see that usual cocky smirk on his face again.

"Seriously, what's up with you?" I ask as I take a spot beside him, surveying the room. A pinkish glow illuminates the hall from lanterns strung along the ceiling, vases of red and yellow roses adorning each table. A tall figure waves at me near the buffet—my best friend Logan—and I wave back.

"Why do you care, Fuckslee?"

Ignoring his taunt, I shrug my aching shoulders. Why do I care? I really shouldn't. If anything, I should be getting joy out of his misery. Lord knows he's caused me enough of it to leave a lasting impression. And yet, as I watch him shoot daggers down at the cake with his eyes, I can't help how my stomach twists with sympathy. I've never seen him like this before. It's unnerving. Is the idea of living with me really that bad for him?

28

Leaning in close, I try to keep my voice light. "That glare is reserved for me. You're giving it to everyone else, and I'm jealous."

Squinting incredulously, he narrows his gaze. "You flirting with me?"

"Uh, negatory," I scoff, even though I feel my cheeks heat. "Just trying to wipe that constipated look off your face."

We glare at each other before he surprises me by huffing a laugh, followed by a wince. Grabbing his side, he mutters something that sounds suspiciously like *fucking prick*, but before I can tell him to say it with his chest, a hand lands on my shoulder.

"You look dope, dude," Logan laughs as he turns me around, humor dancing in his honey-brown eyes. "Like freaking James Bond or something."

"Yeah? You like this shit?" I grin at my tux before glancing around to ensure Dad isn't nearby to hear me swear in church.

"At least you get to look sexy. Well, other than the busted face." He looks down at himself with pursed lips. "I'm pretty sure this is the suit I wore at my great-aunt June's funeral."

"No, that one was blue," I chuckle, just as someone steps into my periphery.

"Thought this thing was for family only." Taylor stands next to me, glaring up at my best friend, who's a few inches taller than us. Logan's brows raise, and he looks at me perplexed, running a hand through his chestnut brown hair.

"Logan *is* family." I jerk my thumb at him. "His dad and mine go way back. We met when we played youth soccer–"

"I don't need to hear your dating story." Taylor cuts me off with a sneer, and I stiffen, glancing sideways at Logan. He doesn't know my secret, and I'd prefer to keep it that way.

Logan moves in closer, eyeing my new stepbrother with something like disdain. "You really want to start a fight at a wedding, Tottman? Inside a church?"

Taylor smirks, turning away, and just when I think he'll leave us alone, I'm being dragged away with his hand wrapped around my wrist.

"Hey, what the hell, man?" I look over my shoulder at Logan, who mouths *what the fuck*, and I throw up my free arm in an *I don't even know* gesture. I'm pulled over to the nearest table, where Taylor drops my wrist and crosses his arms.

"Let's get this shit over with," he mutters. "Introduce me to your family."

To be honest, I'd rather lick a light socket than do that. Something about presenting my enemy to my closest relatives makes my skin crawl, but seeing as I have no choice—Dad's good side, remember—I do as he asks.

And it's fucking weird. Because I've grown to know the asshole version of Taylor over the last few years, but as all my aunts and uncles and cousins ask him questions, he's actually, like...nice? Really nice. And polite.

He answers every question with a small smile, albeit fake, but there's no trace of venom in his tone. Not when they ask about school or football, his college plans, or if he's got some-one special in his life. My ears perk up at that last question, even though I know his answer. He and Salem Vaughn have been dating since ninth grade.

The only time I see him clam up is when my grandmother on Dad's side asks him if he's been baptized, to which he replies with a strained *yes*. And when she asks if he'll be joining us for church on Sundays from now on, he gives her a calm, non-committal answer. I can tell he's uncomfortable, so I steer him away from the conversation.

The weirdest part of the night, though, is when he introduces me to his mom's side of the family. There aren't as many of them as on Dad's, and though they all seem like great people, the way they look at Taylor confuses me—as if he's a stain on their carpet or something. Even his own grandparents stare at him like he's a stranger, making me wonder how strained his relationship with his mother must be. They ask me all the same questions my family asked him, though they seem less enthused, and after that, the introductions are over.

Thankfully.

When I leave to sit with my best friend, though, Taylor parks himself at a table all alone, and fuck my conscience, dammit. Questioning my sanity, I slide into the seat across from him, immediately regretting it when he snarls at me.

"Go sit with your boyfriend, Fuckslee."

"He's not my boyfriend," I hiss through my teeth, "and shut the fuck up. You look pathetic sitting here by yourself."

"I don't need your pity." His ocean eyes snap up to mine, full of fire, the brightness of his irises driving me insane.

Blue *and* green, blue *or* green. *Pick a fucking color.*

"It's not pity. I'm trying to get ungrounded by playing nice with you. Don't flatter yourself."

He seems to relax at that. I hadn't realized he'd gone stiff.

31

The rest of the evening is spent in a strange, amiable silence as we ignore each other on our phones while everyone laughs and dances around us. The cake gets cut, the speeches are said, everyone sends off Dad and Maisie with a toss of rice, and finally, the most uncomfortable night of my life comes to a close.

At least, until Dad says, "Take Taylor home and give him the tour, son," before stepping into his Prius to take him and his new wife to the airport for their honeymoon.

That's when it hits me. I'm going to be cohabiting with Taylor fucking Tottman, alone, in my house, for a week.

And the thought just makes me want to disappear.

The drive back home is as unbearable as the one to the church, but only because Taylor grabs my aux cord without asking and immediately turns on his angry music, making me want to rip my ears off. Upon pulling into the driveway, he gets out without a word, grabs his duffle from the backseat, and stomps up the front steps of the wrap-around porch, waiting for me to unlock the door. Some small creature immediately starts screaming at my feet when I flick on the entryway light, and I stare in shock at a raggedy-looking orange cat.

"No one else could take her," Taylor mumbles as he bends down to pick her up, and then I remember how he'd pulled up this morning with her in his bag.

Right. Apparently, we have a cat now. Dad will be thrilled.

"We can run to the store later for cat stuff," I say as I lead him into the foyer. A mahogany staircase rises before us, leading up to the second level, living room on the left, and dining room on the right. Taylor takes in everything—the cream-colored walls and swirling lights that dangle from the ceiling. He looks less than impressed.

We cut through the dining room, where a large table sits with eight seats, tall-stemmed calla lilies taking up the center. Maisie's favorite flower, I guess, according to Dad. I walk into the kitchen but stop when I see Taylor eyeing the photos that line the mantle above the fireplace.

"Cute." He snickers at a picture of me with the Easter bunny when I was five, and I roll my eyes.

There are other pictures, one of Mom and me on Halloween when I was Buzz Lightyear and another of a family vacation to the beach in California, where Mom's parents live.

He picks one up. "These all gonna go in the trash now that Maisie is moving in?"

"What, no," I frown, noting how he calls his mother by her first name. "Why would they?"

He shrugs, staring at the photo momentarily before gently setting it down. "You look more like your dad."

A chuckle leaves my throat. "Yeah, I know. Same hair color."

"But not the curls, though," he replies softly, skirting by me into the kitchen. I cast one last glance at the picture of my mother, long curls blowing in the wind as she smiles at the camera, the sun glowing off her dark skin and a calm ocean behind her.

"Yeah. Not the curls." There's an ache in my chest as the memories of the day we lost her two years ago threaten to pull me under, but I shake my head quickly to dispel them.

Not right here. I will not fall apart in front of Taylor.

"So, does being a Bishop pay bank or something?" he calls from the kitchen, and I clear my throat to steady myself before following him in.

"No, Bishops don't get paid. It's voluntary only. Dad's still a realtor. Guess that's how he met your mom, she's a receptionist at his brokerage."

Taylor shifts the cat into his other arm to open the fridge, the entitlement of the act making my fists clench. Technically, this is now his house, too, but my brain is taking this invasion of my space as a threat.

"Figures," he mutters, slamming the door shut. "Not a drop of booze in sight."

"Well, my dad is a Bishop, so...no."

He scoffs before turning away, and I follow, unsure what to say. The vibe he's giving off right now reminds me of an animal stalking its cage. I don't want to provoke it.

His eyes light up for half a second when he spots the eighty-five-inch flat-screen in the living room, but he deflates instantly at the painting of Dad and Maisie hanging on the wall. Some artist friend of Dad's made it for them, but it always gave me the creeps.

Leading him up the stairs to the second level, I start down the hall. "Your room's the one at the end." But then I hear the hinges groan from my bedroom door, and I spin around to see Taylor's form disappear into my room. "Hey! What the hell?"

Quickly following him, I stop inside the doorway to see him snickering up at the mini statue of Cloud from Final Fantasy sitting on top of my trophy case.

"This your crush?" He snorts, and I choose not to respond because, well...yes.

"Get out of my room, Taylor."

Instead, he drops his cat on my unmade bed and studies his surroundings, taking in the sports posters and medals lining the walls. My shoulders are tense as hell while I watch him, my jaw tight enough to crack a molar. This is *my* space, and he doesn't belong in it.

His fingers brush along my desk, where the sketchpad I doodle on rests beside a pile of colored pencils. "You still draw?"

"When I have time." I shrug with an exasperated sigh. "Can I please show you your room?"

Before I can register what he's doing, his hand is on the drawer handle of my nightstand, and he's yanking it open.

Momentarily, I'm stunned because *what the actual fuck?* Who does that?! But when his hand reaches inside, I lunge at him, planting my hands on his chest as I shove him back into my bookcase. A few die-cast cars I'd made with Dad clatter onto the ground at our feet, and I'm in Taylor's face before he can even blink.

"What the fuck is wrong with you?! Haven't you ever heard of personal space? Get out of my shit!"

He flashes me a Cheshire grin. "Don't worry, bro, I wasn't going after your lube. What's this?" An orange pill bottle shakes in my face, and I blink, still pissed off at him for snooping. And yes, if I'm being honest, completely mortified at the bottle of lube he saw sitting in the drawer. He'll definitely find a way to use that against me later. Pun unintended.

"Lortabs," I grit through my teeth. "From when I got my wisdom teeth out in May. I never finished the prescription."

And what does this motherfucker do? He opens the bottle, pours a pill into his hand, and swallows that sucker down dry right in front of my God-given eyeballs. Just rawdogs a pain pill like candy. My face must reveal my shock because he simply winks before looking at something over my shoulder.

"You like Dethklok?"

What the fuck is happening right now?

I follow his gaze to where my Metalocalypse poster hangs above my bed and nod stiffly. I have several Dethklok shirts I wear to school regularly, but maybe he doesn't notice the clothes I wear like I do with him.

*Well, of course, he doesn't*, a little voice in my head reasons. *He's not attracted to you.*

Taylor simply hums, pocketing the pill bottle as if it belongs to him before scooping the cat up from where she's chewing on one of my shoelaces near the closet.

I follow him down the hall, feeling slightly dazed at our interaction, to be honest, because he's throwing me through a loop. He only glances at the bathroom briefly before pushing open the door to the room that's now his, which used to house all of my and Dad's sports memorabilia. We had to move it all down into the garage and let me tell you, I was not happy that day.

Right now, the space is pretty sparse. A full bed, nightstand, dresser, and an empty shelf line the walls. Other than that, it's a blank canvas for him to decorate as he wishes. My attention catches on the duffle bag he tosses onto the bed.

"Is that all you brought?"

Some emotion flickers across his face, but it's gone before I can process it.

"I left the rest at my father's place. I'll only be here a year, anyway."

Right. That makes sense.

"Your new home, Lasagna." He kisses the cat before dropping her onto the floor, and I can't help but laugh.

"Lasagna? Why not just call her Garfield?"

"Because I'm not a basic bitch like you." He unbuttons his tuxedo jacket, shrugging out of it as I'm about to respond with some witty comeback when my mouth slams shut. I'm across the room instantly, and he blinks in surprise as I grab his arm.

"Who the fuck did this?"

Dark bruises line his arm, almost black, peppered along his bicep. I can make out the impression of fingerprints against his skin, but before I can inspect them further, he's ripping his arm from my grip.

"You did, asshole." He shoves me back violently, those blue-green eyes blazing, and a sick feeling churns in my stomach.

"I did that?" Honestly, I don't remember grabbing him that hard, but last night's kind of a blur where the fight was concerned. I remember tackling him to the ground and hitting him, but...Jesus. Yes, he's got bruises covering his face from my fists, but for some reason, the ones on his arm make me ashamed. Make me want to puke.

Do I regret attacking him? No, not after what he said about Dad. Honestly, the fucker had it coming, but the fact that I could inflict that kind of damage on someone makes me want to throw myself off a cliff.

"Huck, stop," Taylor says suddenly, his voice rough. I meet his gaze, but he looks away with a hard swallow. "Look, I deserved it, okay? They're just bruises."

Just bruises. Right.

We stand awkwardly silent for a few minutes, unsure what to say. And even though I know I have no reason to feel guilty, it's starting to claw at my throat. So I quickly clear it and say, "Change into your moto gear and meet me downstairs."

Without giving him a chance to respond, I leave his room and return to mine, changing from the tux into clothes meant for dirt biking. Ten minutes later, I watch from the bottom of the stairs as he descends with his hands in his pockets, looking for all the world like he'd rather turn around and nap.

Too fucking bad.

I hurt him, even if he deserved it. What separates us is that I actually feel bad about it, so I need to make it right.

"I'm really not in the mood to ride, Huck," he mumbles, confirming my suspicions.

"We'll see." I jerk my chin toward the kitchen, gesturing for him to follow, and roll my eyes when he sighs heavily in annoyance.

Must be a bad day for him, though, or a good day for me because he follows without putting up much of a fight.

We round the island and cross over to the back door, where we step onto the covered deck accented with patio furniture, a brick-oven grill, and a lidded hot tub. Before us sprawls the back lawn, and I exit down the porch steps to cross it.

Behind the backyard, several acres of land make up Dad's property, which is divided by a fence. When we cross through the gate and onto the field, I glance over to see Taylor stop short as he takes in what I'm showing him, a grin pulling at my cheeks when his eyes almost bug out.

"Ta-da," I say lamely, throwing my arms out wide.

"You have a dirt bike track in your backyard." He huffs a dry laugh, raising his face to the darkening sky. "Of course you fucking do."

Yeah, I do. It's not the prettiest track in the world or the biggest, but it's mine, less than half a football field in length and complete with jumps.

"This used to be a pasture for the horses," I explain as I lead him further. "My mom trained them for a living. But after she died...well, horses were more her thing than Dad's, so he sold them and had this track made for me."

"Money really does buy happiness," he mutters, and I stiffen but force myself to ignore the comment.

What Dad did for me was a mercy. I was drowning after Mom's death, spending every day at the motorsports park trying to outrun the grief, and he wanted me to have a space of my own to do that. Yeah, we're well-off, but that doesn't mean my dad hasn't earned his living or loves me any less because of it.

Turning toward him, I freeze when I see the look on his face. There's a smile on his lips, excitement shining in his eyes as he takes in the track, and it reminds me of that day in PE three years ago when I thought I'd get to see that look on his face forever. I didn't realize until this moment that I'd missed it.

"You wanna go for a ride?" I ask hoarsely, low-key wanting to keep that light in his eyes for as long as possible.

He throws me a sideways glance, lips turned down. "With you?"

"Yeah, why not? This can be like neutral ground or something. A fake place. Like...Delaware."

"Delaware?"

I shrug, raising a brow at him. "Have you ever heard of that city? I don't even know where or if it exists."

Taylor's eyes nearly bug out of his skull. "Delaware is a *state*, dumbass."

I knew that. I just wanted to see if *he* knew that.

"What?!" My jaw drops in faux surprise. "See what I mean? How do we know it's even a real place? Seems fake to me."

"The people that live there would disagree with you," he huffs, gazing around us. "So, what, this track is a land of make-believe or some shit?"

Nodding, I do my best to toss him a megawatt grin. "Exactly. Out here, nothing has to exist. No fights. Just us. Just Taylor and Huckslee." Like I wish it could be. "What do you say?"

He seems uncertain, eyeing the track eagerly as he considers it. My heart starts to thump wildly in my chest.

*Please say yes. Please.*

After a silent moment, he steps away, slamming a wall between us. "I'm not playing pretend with you, Huck."

"Suit yourself." I shrug again, walking away to hide the disappointment I'm sure is plain on my face. Which is confusing as hell because why the fuck was I wanting to hang out with him, anyway? With Taylor Tottman?

Two days ago, he filled my backpack with milk while sitting behind me in the library, ruining all my homework.

Thankfully, that stunt had gotten him banned from there for the rest of the year, but after all his bullshit, what possessed my mind into thinking we could spend any amount of time together in peace?

I'm glad he said no. Really. Not irritated by it at all.

After grabbing my two-stroke from the garage, I bring it back to the track, pulling on my gloves before thumbing the throttle. I'm about to start it up when the sound of an engine reaches my ears, and I turn just in time to see Taylor fly by on his awful yellow bike.

"That's cheating!" I yell, laughing when he grins over his shoulder and flips me the middle finger.

Something warm floods my chest, an emotion I can't place, and as I race after him, a dangerous thought bounces around my brain.

Maybe, at least for the next year, things will be okay.

I couldn't have been more wrong.

# TAYLOR

## OCTOBER

Huckslee's staring again.

I can feel his eyes burning a hole in the side of my face.

Coach is debriefing us in the locker room after our football game, praising everyone else while telling me precisely what I did wrong, and I wrap my arms around myself. As the quarterback, it's always my fault when something happens that Coach doesn't like. It doesn't matter whether we won or Matty failed to stop a touchdown not once but *twice* tonight; I'm wrong for not passing to Huck when he was open. Which, admittedly, was on purpose just to piss him off.

Casting a glance in his direction, I find his gaze still on me, and I scowl.

He's been different since his eighteenth birthday last month.

A small chuckle leaves my throat when I think about the ramen restaurant his dad took us to, Huck's favorite one apparently, and how I dumped an entire bottle of hot sauce in his soup when no one was looking, just to see his eyes water and his face turn red. As sick as it was, I loved seeing the tears stream down his cheeks.

It had been fun until Maisie started asking him about his dating life, and I had to watch him shut down. He'd immediately thrown on a mask, turned into a fucking robot, and pulled away from me the rest of the night. It bothered me more than I'd like to admit.

Finally unable to ignore the weight of his gaze any longer, I turn to meet his dark brown eyes with a sneer. If it had been months ago, the old Huckslee would have dropped his gaze from mine, but ever since his birthday, he's been bolder. More outspoken, more...aggressive, for lack of a better word. It's almost like he's challenging me to do something, but I can't figure out what.

Raising my finger, I point directly at him before pumping my fist in front of my mouth with my tongue in my cheek, the universal sign for sucking cock. His brows lift, and he lowers his head to type something on his phone.

I snicker to myself until my own phone goes off in my pocket. Pulling it out, I silently read the message from an unknown number:

> Unknown: Did you just offer to suck my dick?

What the hell? I glance up to see him staring across the locker room at me expectantly, his lips slightly parted.

> Me: How the fuck did you get my number? And no, I gestured that YOU suck dick.

> Huckslee: You're just jealous that I'm not sucking YOUR dick.

*Yeah, okay.*

It's on the tip of my thumbs to type out *you couldn't handle this dick*, but that crosses a line, and I'm not gay. So instead, I say:

> Me: How'd you like your shampoo this morning?

Peeking over at him beneath my lashes, I catch sight of the blood draining from his face as he begins typing furiously.

> Huckslee: What the fuck did you do to my shampoo Taylor?

With a smirk, I pocket my phone and point a finger gun at him before grabbing my gym bag to hit the showers. His angry shout at my back puts a wide grin on my face. I didn't do anything to his shampoo, but I like watching him squirm. It's been the highlight of these last two months, especially living with Maisie.

The grin falls off my lips at the thought of her. In some ways, it's been worse than living with my dad. At least when I was in Arbitrary Hills, I could wait until he passed out on the couch before sneaking off to hang with Christian and the guys. But apparently, Huck's grounding carried over to me, too, because his dad is always *there*. I hate it.

The constant questions—how was school, did you do your homework, how are you feeling—make my brain feel zappy and my palms sweat. The way he asks makes it seem like he actually cares about the answers, unlike Maisie, who seems more put out than anything when she has to be a mother. I can tell she only tries for her new husband's sake, especially when she's forced to sit beside me in church every Sunday.

*Feeling's mutual, Maisie. I don't want to sit next to you, either.*

I finish washing up, throwing on a clean shirt before leaving school and heading toward the parking lot where my bike is parked. I'm not supposed to ride it around town, but what's one more fine from the cops for my father to add onto everything else I owe him? I like the freedom of having my own ride.

"Tottman!"

A familiar voice pulls me out of my thoughts, and I stop next to where Christian straddles a red dirt bike, his girlfriend Tatiana on the back.

"What up, Totillo," I greet with a grin, reaching out to bump his fist. We've been best friends since kindergarten when he'd always end up in the lunch line before me because of the closeness of our last names.

He pulls me in for a noogie. "Congrats on the win, fucker!"

"Yeah, congratulations," his girlfriend purrs, flinging blonde strands over her shoulder as her eyes dip down my body, but I pointedly ignore her as I shove Christian off me.

"Thanks, man. We partying tonight or what?"

"Fuck yeah." He dramatically looks around before leaning in closer. "The foam pit is fixed."

I whoop out a laugh, pumping my arms. "No fucking way!"

"Yep. It's all set up for us, homie. And my mom's working a double, so we've got all night."

*Yes.* I need this.

Christian's mom supervises a mattress factory two towns over, and she's always bringing home defective strips of foam they can't use. We'd filled an old above-ground pool with the pieces years ago to jump our bikes into. But shortly after the wedding, I'd overshot during a flip and landed my bike on the rim. Not only did I fuck up the pool, but my axle too.

And that had been a fun conversation with my dad.

Absently, my hand comes up to rub my ribcage as I think about the day he pulled me out of school and hauled my ass to his shop to fix it myself while he screamed at me the entire time. And then he kicked me so hard, I'm pretty sure he re-cracked my rib because weeks later, it still aches at times. I'd started a fight with Huck that night at the track just to be able to explain the bruises.

*We don't fight at the track, asshole! This is Delaware!*

Fucking no geography knowing dumbass.

Ever since that week when we had the house to ourselves while our parents were on their honeymoon, things have been awkward between us. He caught me in a vulnerable state with all the shit going on, and I was nice to him. We bonded over Lasagna—the cat, not the pasta. Things got weird. Not like, in a gay way, but we shared some emotions about our moms, and the intimacy of it made me feel nauseous.

A pit opens in my stomach when I think about the night we watched a movie together.

*"What are you watching?"*

*Huckslee jolts from his place on the couch, scrambling to pause the movie with Lasagna and a bowl of popcorn in his lap. Even in the dim light of the living room, I can see how nervous he is, and I'm not gonna lie—it's kind of adorable.*

*"I-I thought you were staying the night at Christian's,"* he stammers, frowning over where I'm leaning against the archway, and I shrug nonchalantly.

*Staying the night with my best friend had been the plan. I should still do it. But after spending a few hours doing jumps and getting high in his backyard with the guys, I just wanted to see Huck without being scrutinized by our parents or peers.*

*"He's busy," is all I say, shoving off the wall to grab my cat and plop down on the far end of the sofa. "You didn't answer me. What are you watching?"*

*Huck's silent for a moment, blinking over at me with a frown on his face, and the way his shoulders tighten tells me he really doesn't want to share what movie is paused. With a smirk, I reach over and pry the remote out of his sweaty palm, little jolts of energy skittering over my skin when our fingers brush and push a button to bring up the title screen.*

*"Across the Universe?"*

*"It was my mom's favorite," he grumbles, nervously running a hand through his curls. "She was a huge Beatles fan, and we used to watch it at least once a month. And I know you're gonna say some shit about it being a musical, but don't, okay? It's just a comfort thing. I didn't even know you'd be here tonight, or I wouldn't have even—"*

*"You're fucking cute when you're flustered," I blurt out, cutting off his rant, and my smile grows when his lips part at my words. His dark eyes widen, twinkling like a starry night*

sky as he flounders like a fish for something to say. I enjoy the sight for a few more seconds before pressing play. "I've never seen this one before."

He scans the side of my face, completely taken aback, but I curl into the arm of the couch with Lasagna and focus on the TV. He's still tense like he thinks I'm going to make a joke about his dead mom's favorite thing, and I hate the way my stomach revolts at the thought. I can be a cruel bastard when I have to, but that would be downright unforgivable.

Plus, in all honesty, the movie isn't half bad. Pretty trippy, which is great because I'm stoned as fuck right now.

After a bit, Huckslee eventually relaxes, settling into the cushions, and we fall into a peaceful silence. He even passes the popcorn bowl to me at one point, offering to share his snack, which I accept even though I'm not the biggest popcorn fan. Any excuse to keep 'accidentally' bumping my knuckles with his, I'll take.

Between the high I'm riding and Lasagna purring on my lap, I must have fallen asleep because sometime later, when I crack my eyes open, the title screen is back on again.

I'm lying on my side, stretched out on the couch, my head inches from Huck's thigh, and...his fingers are in my hair, playing with the strands.

His movements falter as he inhales sharply, both of us freezing, analyzing the situation. When I make no effort to get up, Huck slowly resumes massaging my scalp.

It's lovely. Different. Soft. I like it. My entire body relaxes, and I'm asleep again within minutes.

When I wake once more, hours later, I'm alone. The TV is off, the house dark, the couch cold.

After that, I stopped messing with him for about a month. Then, there were more bruises to hide, and whatever cease-fire that Huck and I had seemed to reach crumbled to pieces. Even when I'm not living under the same roof as my father, I can't escape.

"Hello? You in there, *hombre*?" Christian's fingers snap in my face, bringing me back to the present, and I flash him a sheepish grin.

"Sorry, what were you saying?"

His brows furrow, a slight look of concern on his face. "I said my mom's working, so we have all night. You sure you're up for it?"

Opening my mouth to assure him that I definitely fucking am, a voice cuts me off from behind.

"Up for what?"

Shit. I hadn't even heard him sneak up on us.

"Fuck off, Huckslee," I mutter in annoyance, not even bothering to look at him as I jerk my chin to my best friend. "Let's go."

Jesus, just like his dad, he's everywhere. I used to dream up creative ways to piss him off on the weekends when we didn't have school, but now that I can easily ruin his day from morning until night, I just want my space.

Christian raises a brow, glancing between Huck and me curiously before thumbing his throttle. "Meet up at my place to get ready. Party starts at eight."

I nod as he starts his bike, Tatiana's eyes soaking me up when he pulls away. She mouths *see you tonight,* and I scowl.

After they're far enough in the distance, I pull out my phone to send her a text before getting onto my bike.

Me: You gotta stop eye fucking me, or he'll know something's up.

Am I a bad friend? Probably. Do I feel guilty? Christian slept with Salem three months after she and I started dating, so no. Not that I ever held any ill feelings toward them. It was a one-night thing—they both got it out of their systems, and that was that.

"You're going to a party?"

For the second time in five minutes, I'm pulled from my thoughts as I blink over at Huck standing beside me. His curls are damp from his shower, flopping to one side of his face, and his forearm flexes as he pushes them back.

"What about it?"

"Can I come?"

I stare at him blankly for a few minutes, debating it. "Doesn't your daddy give you a curfew?"

"We both have a curfew," he drawls, rolling his eyes. "And they're going on a date tonight."

Even better for me.

"Nah, no pussies allowed. You're not invited."

Whatever he replies is drowned out by my engine, and I do a burnout, my back wheel smoking before speeding away.

This party is starting to get out of hand.

And not in a fun way.

Everything spins as I fly through the air, my bike beneath me. My legs leave the seat when I bring them up to wrap around my arms, tapping my feet together in a Heel Clicker, rotating my body around and around until I land with an oomph upside down in soft foam. It's a collision that isn't pleasant but not painful either. Nothing like the bone-jarring impact of landing a bike on hard dirt after a jump.

"*Ay Dios mío*, that was almost three backflips!"

Damn. Almost? I'd been aiming for three. Only issue, though, is the world's still spinning even though my body is not.

Crawling up through the foam, I claw my way to the edge of the pool and haul myself up over the lip just in time to rip my helmet off before projectile vomiting onto the ground. It stings my throat, the taste of Kraken rum burning my nostrils along with whatever the fuck I ate earlier to soak up the alcohol. Clearly, it hadn't worked.

"Nasty, dude." Christian yanks me out while our friends Matt and Xed fish my bike from the pit, laying me on the ground, and I flop over onto my back.

There are people everywhere. The house that Christian lives in with his mom and five siblings isn't the biggest—it's a small two-bedroom, one-bath near the edge of town. However, an empty parking lot backs up the yard, so it's perfect for when we want to do tricks off the ramp we built and have a few friends over.

Well, in this case, more than a few.

'Drag Me Down' by Breathe Carolina thumps from someone's shitty speakers, shouts ringing out from a game of beer pong near the back door. Groups of people are scattered throughout the lawn, and a fire pit is burning in an old barrel, where everyone is tossing their trash. Some of them I recognize from our high school, and some I'm sure are from the next town over.

"You good, Tay?" Christian's sweaty face appears in my swimming vision, and I flash a sloppy smile with a thumbs up. My stomach still churns slightly, but throwing up made me feel ten times better.

He chuckles, reaching down to pull me to my feet before slapping my chest. "That's what I'm talking about! My turn."

On unstable feet, I watch a group of our football buddies help lift Christian's bike onto the top of the house, and a disbelieving laugh bubbles out of me.

*Fuuuck*, I can't believe I just jumped off of that while shitfaced. Can't believe we secured the ramp to the *roof.* It's why he'd wanted me to come over early. Not only had it taken hours to get the ramp safely secured, but we'd needed to make sure the angle of the pit was just right so that we didn't splatter ourselves all over the grass. It was reckless as hell, but I was powerless to resist when Christian came up with his ideas.

My best friend takes his place on his bike on the ridge of the roof, revving the engine. Using the downslope as an advantage, he guns it toward the incline, wheels catching air. Pulling back, he lets go of the handlebars to throw up two middle fingers as he backflips once. Twice. Three fucking times before landing upright in the pit.

"FUCK YEAH, MOTHERFUCKER!"

The crowd erupts into cheers as everyone swarms the pool, me included, and I'm reaching in to yank him out by his shirt as a massive grin splits his face.

"You did it, you crazy asshole," I shout ecstatically, pulling too hard so that we topple over onto the ground, taking Matty with us and thankfully missing my pile of puke. An elbow hits my rib, and I wheeze, shoving Matt's massive linebacker body off of me.

"You two are fucking insane." His dark blue eyes dance with laughter as he falls onto Christian. "That was terrifying."

"The adrenaline rush, though." Christian pushes him back, making me wince when Matty's entire body weight crushes me, but he's pulled off in an instant when his best friend hauls him up.

Xed grins down at me, green hair spiked into a mohawk, his ring-covered fingers pulling me to my feet. Another engine revs, getting our attention, and we watch someone else jump from the roof, whipping their bike to the side before landing in the pit.

*This* is what I fucking live for. Heart-pumping, gut-wrenching tricks and jumps that make my stomach fall out of my ass. Yeah, racing is fun, and I need to compete to get my professional license eventually, but free-style motocross is what lights my soul on fire. The reason I breathe and the only part of this place that makes dealing with my father worth it.

Because when I win that race at the end of the school year and get my scholarship, I can register for the national championship finals. And when I win that? I'll go pro, baby.

Me and Christian. This shitty town will be nothing but a memory for us.

A hand grips the back of my neck as someone shakes me out of my thoughts, and my best friend's hazel eyes come into view. "What's going on with you, Tay? You're ditzy lately."

"I'm not ditzy, I'm drunk." I wiggle out of his grip. "Anyone got a smoke?"

Xed pulls a pack out of his leather jacket pocket and hands me one, lighting it when I put it to my lips. Running my hands through my hair, I inhale deeply, feeling heated and feverish despite the slight bite of fall in the breeze.

"Shit. Valerie alert." Christian whacks Matty on the chest, who groans before ducking behind me.

"Don't let her see me."

"You're built like a fucking tank, man. Everyone here can see you."

Right on cue, a nasally feminine voice calls out his name, and he swears under his breath before taking off toward the parking lot to hide behind someone's car.

"You can't run from love, Matty," Xed hollers, snickering as our friend's ex-girlfriend hurries after him. I feel slightly bad for the guy. Valerie's gorgeous, but she's fucking insane.

Seriously. She cut his breaks one night when he tried to break up with her.

"Must be a full moon or something, cuz the bitches are out." Christian points a finger behind me, and my stomach does a weird flip until I see Salem leaning against the side of the house with Brad, their lips locked in battle. Something like disappointment has my shoulders drooping, which just confuses me. Who was I expecting to see?

*A certain mop of blond curls, maybe...*

"You want me to kick them out?"

"What?" I turn back to Christian with a smirk, puffing on my cigarette. "No, why would I?"

"That shit really doesn't bother you?" Xed asks with narrowed eyes, and I shrug.

"Not really."

"Tay and Salem are, like, weird," Christian laughs, rubbing the back of his neck as I roll my eyes.

We're not weird; we just don't hold each other back from unfair expectations. She does her thing, I do mine, and then we meet in the middle when we can. Sometimes we fuck, sometimes we don't. We're easy. It's complicated to explain to people, so I don't even try half the time. Love that girl to death, though, and I'd go to war for her in a heartbeat.

"So what do ya say, man? One more jump?" Christian waggles his brows at me, and I huff a chuckle around my cigarette before dropping it into someone's half-empty beer bottle on the ground.

"Hell yeah. Gimme a minute to take a piss."

Leaving them to talk amongst themselves, I stumble across the yard, weaving around people toward the backdoor as my eyes jump from group to group, searching for something I can't place. The chances that the only bathroom isn't occupied are slim, so I aim for the narrow space between the garage and the house instead.

My feet come to a halt when a deep, familiar laugh reaches my ears, and my head whips toward the burn barrel, where I see Logan standing around, chatting with members of the swim team.

A rush of satisfaction courses through me, and I immediately start looking for Huck. If Logan's here, then he can't be too far behind. A bit of excitement tingles up my spine, which is weird, but I tell myself it's because I can't wait to pick a fight with him as I head in the direction of his best friend. For nearly two months now, the fucker has been constantly at my side between school and home. I told him he wasn't invited tonight, but he didn't listen.

Because he enjoys fighting with me, too.

"Where is he?" I cut off whatever Logan was saying, and he faces me with a seething glare, animosity rolling off him. He's probably still pissed at me from my own birthday party three weeks ago when I threw a firecracker into the hot tub that he and Huck were sitting in.

"Where's who?" His jaw clenches, hands fisting at his sides, and I wave my arms irritably.

"You know who. Huckslee. I told him he wasn't invited."

Logan tilts his head. "He's at home."

*Fuck*. For real?

I immediately feel myself deflate as I turn away.

Well, shit. So much for a fight tonight.

A frown pulls at my lips the longer I think about Huck.

Why is he at home when his best friend is here? The two are almost as inseparable as Christian and me.

It's not like he has homework, it's a Friday night. When I told him he wasn't invited, I'd been half-lying because I wanted him to come anyway so that I could watch him—

My brain scratches to a screeching halt.

Why the hell do I care where Huckslee is?

I told him he couldn't come, so he didn't. And I don't want him here.

Because he's a pain in my ass, right?

*Pun unintended?*

What the fuck, brain? *Yes*, the pun was unintended. Because I'm not fucking gay.

The space between the house and garage comes into view, and I squeeze into it, thankfully finding it empty. It's big enough for me to stand with my shoulders touching each wall, and I'm about to unzip my pants when a small pair of arms wraps around me from behind.

"I've been wondering when I'd be able to get you alone."

*Ah, fuck me.*

"Tatiana." I turn around so that I'm facing her, and the moment I do, her lips are on mine.

Inwardly, I cringe. Not only because I threw up earlier but the scent of her skin against mine is making me ill right now. She trails a line of kisses down my neck, her hands pushing under my shirt to run along my chest.

"We gotta make it quick, lover," she whispers, grinning as she drops to her knees.

The fact that I had to piss ten seconds ago is forgotten when she starts unbuckling my belt. Her fingers pop open the button on my jeans, reaching inside to pull out my soft cock, and she jerks it until I harden slightly.

Leaning against the wall, I close my eyes as she works me, but something's off. Her hands feel too small, her grip too light. And when she wraps her lips around my shaft, even the tentative flick of her tongue sets my teeth on edge. A whine leaves her throat at my half-hard dick, but when I open my lids to stare down at her, it jumps painfully to full attention at the dark brown eyes looking up at me.

Because they're her eyes, yes, but they're also *his*.

No. That's not the reason. It's just that I have a girl on her knees for me. It has nothing to do with that. But I keep staring down into those eyes, my hips beginning to move against her tongue as I tangle my fingers in her hair. And even that doesn't feel right, the dry, straight strands sticking to my skin.

*Unlike silky soft curls, which would feel amazing.*

No.

I pump myself inside her mouth harder, pleasure vibrating my body as I grip her head in both my hands. She moans around my cock, her eyes fluttering closed, but I command her to keep them open. And fuck, the tears glistening in those brown eyes are almost enough to have me spilling my load down her throat.

She's whimpering as I fuck her face, but the sound is too high. Too breathy. Too *feminine*, so I slide my cock deeper to hush her up. And still, I watch those eyes, imagining a bigger, muscled body connected to them. It feels wrong, but in my drunken state, it's the wrongness about it that's getting me off right now.

My balls tighten when those tears finally spill over, trickling down her cheeks, and I'm coming before I can hold back.

Hot cum fills her mouth, seeping out the sides of her lips as I milk my cock on her tongue until she's taken every last drop.

Only then does a breath gunshot from my lungs, burning my throat. *Jesus fucking Christ,* what just happened?

Tatiana blinks up at me with watery eyes as I tuck myself back into my jeans, makeup tracking down her face, and I notice how her hand shakes as she raises it to wipe her mouth.

"Fuck, are you okay?" Reaching down, I gently grab her arm to help her up. "I'm sorry."

She grins, about to respond, when her eyes catch on something over my shoulder. They widen in shame and fear as she pulls from my grip, and my spine stiffens.

*Fuck.*

I feel his presence behind me before he even speaks.

"What the fuck is this shit?!"

I whirl around in time to see my best friend's fist flying toward my face, and then pain erupts as everything goes dark.

# HUCKSLEE

I hate these pills.

Swirling lights from the speaker reflect on my ceiling, melding into an explosion of color and sound. 'Routines In The Night' by Twenty One Pilots echoes softly around the room, the melodic beat helping to ease my pounding skull and racing heart.

These pills always give me a headache. To be honest, I don't know if they even work. I try to calm my breathing as I lay on my back on the bed, hoping the darkness of my room and the meds will lull me to sleep.

Dad doesn't know about them, and neither does Logan. I'd made the appointment as soon as I'd turned eighteen, no longer needing parental permission to see the doctor. Hiding it only makes the anxiety worse, though.

I have everything a kid could ask for—a loving father and an amazing best friend who's always there for me. I live in a fancy house and have a car, plus a potential football scholarship as long as I keep up the hard work.

So why do I always feel like I'm fucking drowning?

*Because you'd lose it all if they knew who you really were,* a voice whispers in my head. And I can't tell it that it's wrong.

There's a part of me that fears coming out to my dad and Logan. Because they're religious, and this is Utah. Sure, I have people at school I hang out with at lunch. I get along well enough with everyone on the football team, but none of my friends at school are really anything more than that—school friends. Logan and Dad are the only two people I care about, and the more I feel like I have to pretend with them, the more messed up my head gets.

Having my fucking enemy in my house at all times doesn't help with that, either. I feel like I'm constantly on edge, waiting for something to happen, like a fight or one of his shitty pranks. Keeping a steady eye on him at all times is giving me ulcers, I swear.

And it makes me so damn tired. I can't sleep, can't relax. The need to act like I'm the happy-go-lucky kid everyone believes me to be is exhausting. Something has to give. I don't know how long I can go on like this. I just want it to end.

With a heavy sigh, I roll onto my side and close my eyes. In all honesty, I didn't even want to go to Christian's stupid party. I only asked if I could come to keep up appearances.

Hide that I'd rather be here, in my room, miserable and alone.

I want to sleep. I really do. But who knows when Taylor will be home, and even though my door is locked, I don't trust that asshole. Just last week, he tied a string outside my room, and I tripped over it first thing in the morning. And then put saran wrap under the toilet seat so that I pissed all over myself. Not to mention the constant gay jokes.

Fucking prick. The only time it seems we aren't at each other's throats is when we're racing on the track in the backyard. In Delaware. Which isn't often these last few months, almost like he *wants* to be a douchebag to me.

Well, except for that week when he first moved in.

Tucking my fist beneath my chin, I force my body to relax as I remember that morning after the wedding.

*There's a soft scratching at my door, drawing my focus from the comic strip I'm trying to draw. Listening intently for a moment, I hear nothing, so I return to the artwork in front of me. I rarely get time to draw anymore since summer is usually my only reprieve. Once school starts, all my time is filled with football, swim team, motocross, and church shit. The motocross, I enjoy, but the rest of it? Let's just say that the thought of my freedom ending has me in a sour mood this evening.*

*The scratching comes again, followed by a loud meow and a low chuckle that sends goosebumps over my skin. Putting down a colored pencil, I stand and stretch. After I showed Taylor the track and we'd raced last night, we'd gone to the store to buy supplies for his cat. It had been weird because he'd actually been tolerable to be around, but I chalked it up to the effects of the second pain pill he popped before getting in my car. After that, I'd spent the rest of the night and all morning in my room. Having him here is throwing me off. I'm not sure how to handle it.*

*A thump hits my door, and annoyance has me huffing as I throw on some pants before checking on the noise. Upon stepping into the hall, I look down to see Lasagna chasing a red dot. Taylor sits on the floor just inside the doorway of his room, holding the laser pointer for her, a black tank top hanging off his lean frame depicting an image of MewTwo and Beerus from DragonballZ locked in a space battle. He's also wearing sweats, his bare feet tucked beneath him, dark hair mussed as if he'd just gotten up from a nap.*

*My heart leaps when his gaze meets mine, his forearms bulging as he flicks the laser pointer. A crooked grin curls his lips, but it doesn't reach his eyes.*

*Fuck, why?*

*Why does he have to be so gorgeous?*

*"Hey," he says, watching me sit cross-legged in front of my door.*

*"Hey." I look away, avoiding the ring of bruises that I caused on his arm. The sight of them still makes me feel like throwing up despite the ones on his face. We sit quietly, watching Lasagna go crazy for the red dot.*

*Taylor is the first to break the silence, clearing his throat. "What are you up to in there?"*

*His eyes flick over my shoulder, but I ignore his question, instead holding out a palm for the toy. "Can I try?"*

*He tosses it to me, and I catch it midair, chuckling at Lasagna as she jumps to try and catch it herself. She's really a cute thing, albeit scruffy. Her pupils nearly consume her amber eyes, little chirping noises twitching her whiskers when I point the dot at the ceiling.*

*"How old is she?"*

*"Eleven." He pauses for a beat. "Maisie got her for me a year before she left."*

*I turn to him and see his cheek resting on his fist, hair falling into his eyes as he plays with the string of his sweats. There's something heartbreakingly sad about his expression, the way his shoulders curve forward as if he'd curl in on himself if he could.*

*I don't know if it's the wedding or the pain pills, but I've never seen him this way before, and I don't know how to respond.*

*"I'm sorry," I reply softly, bracing for the inevitable lashing he's sure to give me. 'I don't want your pity' or 'fuck off' are sure to follow, but after a solid minute of flinching...they never come.*

*He shrugs, not meeting my eyes. "My father is an asshole. He was abusive to her, so I get why she left. I don't think she ever wanted to be a mother. I just..."*

*He trails off, but I can hear the words he's trying to say.*

I don't get why she had to leave me, too.

*Lasagna continues to meow as I sweep the light over the wall, another awkward silence settling over us. He shifts uncomfortably, almost like he's going to leave, but something in me desperately wants him to stay, to keep this open flow of communication between us after so many years of cold cruelty.*

*So I open my mouth.*

*"That picture downstairs that you were holding yester-day," I start, "the one of my mom at the beach? It's the last vacation we took before... before she died. The last time I truly saw her healthy." Taylor slowly settles back down on the floor, and I take that as a cue to continue.*

*"She was diagnosed with breast cancer shortly after my sixteenth birthday. I guess she had a lump for a while, but she ignored it because she didn't want to bother anyone." I scoff, even as my throat closes. "Can you believe that? To be so sick yet worry about how it will affect everyone else? Anyway, by the time she finally made it to the doctor, it had metastasized. Spread everywhere and took over most of her organs. In little under two months, she was just... gone."*

*It's quiet in the hall, and I don't think Taylor's even breathing. I keep swinging the laser around, though I'm not seeing it. I'm reliving the worst year of my life.*

*"At first, I was angry. So fucking angry with her because how could she? Dad and I needed her, but she ignored her health like that? I thought it was selfish. Like she somehow let the cancer spread on purpose. For a long time, I felt like it was my fault. I must have done something, right? For her to have wanted to leave us like that?"*

*"You did nothing wrong, Huck," Taylor murmurs, and I give a jerky nod.*

*"I know that now. But at the time, I couldn't see it. I was... consumed by grief. And it was worse for my dad, but he had to put all his effort into keeping his teenage son from falling apart." I laugh bitterly. "Church was always hard for me, but it was impossible after that. How could a God exist when diseases like cancer take away good people? People who are kind, faithful, loved by their communities, and all-around good."*

*My voice cracks at the last word, and I swallow hard, falling silent to collect myself momentarily. Taylor says noth-*

*ing, but I can feel his eyes on me. I don't meet his gaze, unsure if I could handle what I'd find there.*

*Inhaling a shaky breath, I keep talking. "Anyway, I didn't mean to make this about me. Now that I've had time to come to terms with my mom's death and some therapy, I understand that she did the best she could. She was only human and thought she was doing what was best for Dad and me. I'm sure your mom felt the same way. Maybe leaving you with your dad wasn't the right choice, but she thought it was better for you at the time. For whatever reason."*

*Fuck, I didn't mean to get all sentimental. But those words from my therapist helped me, and I hope they'll help Taylor, too. Even after everything that's happened between us, I can't help wanting to take away his pain.*

*I toss the laser across the hall to him, and he picks it up, turning it over in his hands. When his eyes lift to mine, I feel like I've been hit in the chest at the anguish I see beneath their depths.*

*"Sometimes bad things happen, Huck." He sighs deeply. "And God has nothing to do with it. Sometimes, shitty people are just shitty people."*

My phone dings loudly over the speaker, alerting me to a new text, and I flop onto my back with a growl of frustration. Sleep is a cold, hard bitch these days.

With one eye open, I unlock the screen to find a text from Royce. Sitting up straight, I'm suddenly wide awake, excitement quickening the blood in my veins.

Royce: Hey :)

> Me: Hi (: What's up?

I lick my lips, leaning against the headboard to make myself comfortable. Royce is a guy from another school nearby. We'd hit it off during a competitive swim meet at the start of the year. In more ways than one...

> Royce: Oh, just bored. Thinking of you ;)

> Me: Yeah? What about me?

> Royce: Remember your birthday ;p

> Me: Of course

How could I forget? We'd finally agreed to hang out near the reservoir the night I turned eighteen. Things had gotten heated, we'd kissed...and for the first time, I'd known what it felt like to have my dick in someone's mouth. In a *guy's* mouth.

> Royce: I want to do it again sometime...

> Me: Mmm, me too. It felt so good.

> Royce: I'm glad you liked it. I was nervous lol you're huge

Well, if that isn't an ego boost.

> Me: You did amazing ;)

In all honesty, the blowjob felt mid. Not that I had anything to compare it to because, well, I don't. But his tentative nature and teeth made getting off a little tricky.

I'm not going to say that, though.

I'm not a complete asshole.

*Unlike someone...*

His following text is a picture of himself from the chin down, torso on full display in a low pair of briefs, and my cock twitches in my boxers. He has a lean swimmer's body, all toned muscles and dark brown skin. No hair, obviously, because of swimming. And though I'd prefer a little, the sight of his next picture, which outlines his hard dick in his underwear, has mine rising toward my belly button.

> Royce: Send me something to keep me company. I'm lonely ;D

Pulling my cock out, I press the record button as I slowly stroke myself from base to tip. Some low-fi pop song filters through the speaker, and I meet the tempo with my hand, pleasurable waves clenching my muscles with each slow pass.

Ending the recording, I hit send when the front door slams shut, echoing throughout the house. My breath catches as I scramble to pause the music, listening for Dad and Maisie in case they're back from their date.

Instead, all I hear is a grunt and a series of thumps as someone tumbles down the stairs.

"What the fuck?"

With my phone still gripped in my hand, I tuck myself back into my boxers and launch off my bed, yanking open the door just in time to see Taylor lying at the bottom of the stairs, grumbling into the tile.

As I climb down the stairs toward him, my phone immediately drops to the carpet. "Did you just eat shit, dude?"

He raises his head and squints at me, licking his lips, a dark bruise blooming on his cheekbone. "Where've you been?"

My hands grip him under the arms as I haul him up. "Did you break your face on the steps?"

"Nah. Christian clocked me," he laughs hoarsely, burying his face in my chest with a deep inhale.

"What? Why?" I pull him up the stairs, struggling against his weight as he leans on me. I'm not exactly weak—football and the swim team keep me fit. But the way he's putting his full weight on my shoulders has me fighting to stay upright.

"Caught me with my dick down Tatiana's throat." His glassy eyes narrow as he glances at me sideways, and my brows shoot to my hairline.

"Seriously?"

"Yeah. S'okay, though. I punched him when I caught him with Salem. We're solid."

Well. That's...fucked up.

"You guys seem like great friends," I mutter sarcastically, tugging him up the last few stairs.

His answering chuckle brushes along the crook of my neck, his breath smelling like smoke, liquor, and vomit.

"Christian's m'best friend. I love that guy so much."

His speech is slurred, and I fight a smile when we step onto the landing. "Okay, Romeo. Let's get you to bed."

We barely take a step before I feel his body go rigid against me. He stops with such force that I lose my grip on his arm, spinning around to find his eyes laser-focused on the ground. It takes me exactly two seconds to figure out what he's looking at, but it's too late.

"Who's fucking dick is on your phone?!"

I feel all the blood drain from my body as we dive simultaneously. Like an idiot, I'd left the phone unlocked when I'd dropped it to the ground, and the video of me playing with my cock is on repeat. I almost have the phone in my hands when Taylor yanks me back at the last minute, climbing onto my chest. We battle for a short second before it's in his hands, and my throat closes in terror.

Fuck.

"Give it back, Taylor!"

"Aw, lil' Hucksie's got a boyfriend." He sneers down at the screen, thumb swiping as he no doubt reads through my messages.

I grab for the phone again, but he lifts it out of reach. "Give me back my fucking phone!"

"This what gets your dick up, bro? Who is this guy, anyway?"

Digging my heels into the carpet, I lift my pelvis and rotate until I have him pinned on the ground beneath me. He tucks the phone against his chest, snickering as I try to pry his arms apart.

"Give me his number." He wriggles beneath me, trying to free himself. "I'll show him what a *real* cock looks like."

"I doubt his phone can even zoom in that far."

Taylor blinks, lips twitching before his features twist into a nasty scowl. "Tell me, does the good Bishop know what his precious son does in the middle of the night?"

Whatever anger I felt completely dissipates as ice forms in my veins.

"No. And you can't say anything, Tay."

"Oh?" His lips curve, a cruel glint darkening his blue-green eyes. "I think this will make a great conversation over breakfast."

My hand strikes out to wrap around his throat, squeezing as I lean down toward his face. "You say anything to my dad, and I'll tell Coach about the weed you sell in the second-floor boys' bathroom."

*No, no, no, no.* This isn't happening. My heart is like a battering ram in my chest, threatening to break from my ribs and leap onto the floor.

Taylor snorts, flashing his teeth, and I've never wanted to knock them out more than this moment. "You think I actually give a shit about football? Try again."

"Then I'll tell your mom," I shout desperately, still clawing at his fingers with my free hand for the phone.

He curls upward, so close that our noses brush as he laughs in my face. "Nice try. She could give two shits about me. You got nothin' on me, Fuckslee."

My vision goes red. He hasn't used that name since I asked him to stop. For once, I thought he'd be decent and care about someone other than himself, but I was wrong. Taylor fucking Tottman is a selfish piece of trash, and if he tries to take me down, I'll make sure he crashes and burns along with me.

"You're wrong." Leaning all the way forward, I flatten my body to his, lips brushing the shell of his ear. "You say anything, and I'll tell everyone about the kiss."

He shudders, an audible swallow flexing his throat as his hands grip the front of my shirt. "What kiss?"

"You know what kiss."

Taylor goes boneless beneath me, releasing my phone, and I pluck it from his palm while my cheek brushes against his. "Remember the one we shared under the bleachers in PE three years ago? When I told you that I liked you, and you–"

Before I can finish, he throws me to the side with such force that my forehead splits open when it hits the door jamb. Searing pain blurs my vision, white spots dancing in my eyes. I blink rapidly, realizing after a moment that I'm pinned on my stomach with a knee pressed agonizingly between my shoulder blades.

Taylor's harsh inhale echoes off the hallway walls as he pulls my arm backward until I yelp, something wet trickling into my eyes. The scent of his liquor breath stings my nostrils when he twists, bending my elbow unnaturally until I hear something break, and I bellow into the carpet.

"You ever bring that shit up again," he hisses, "I'll fuck you up, Huckslee. I mean it."

The venom in his voice makes me quake, my lungs struggling to expand from the total weight of his knee on my back, contorting my arm like he wants to rip it from my body. Real fear sluices through me as the seconds tick by and the longer I struggle to breathe.

Finally, the weight lifts. Sharp, burning pain shoots up my forearm when Taylor releases me, and I crawl to my knees with a wince. Cradling the aching limb against my chest, I dazedly look up at my stepbrother. He stands above me, glaring down with such hatred that I'm rendered speechless.

"Keep your fucking queer hands to yourself."

Those words cut me to the bone, hurting deeper than the gash on my brow or the twisted arm. His lips curl with disgust before he whirls toward his room, slamming the door behind him. Tears that were welling behind my lashes spill forth, soaking my face as sobs wrack my body. I try to move my arm, but pain shoots up to my elbow, and I can't.

I can't move. I feel like I can't breathe. All I can do is sit here and cry.

Like a fucking weakling.

# TAYLOR

I fucked up.

Like, astronomically fucked up in a way that I can't fix. I feel it the moment Aaron pounds on my door the following day, waking me up to utter words that have my chest caving in around me.

"I'm taking Huck to the ER. He broke his arm."

Fuck. Me.

I'm out of bed within seconds, despite the immediate spinning in my head from the alcohol and the ache in my cheek from Christian's fist. "I'm coming with."

He nods, telling me to get dressed and to meet them downstairs. Dread is locking my muscles, but I push through, throwing on my Lamb of God hoodie without even thinking about it until Aaron's lips thin in the foyer, but he doesn't comment.

And Huck...God, he looks like hell. He's cradling his arm against him, curls falling over his brow as he keeps his head bent. He won't even look at me. There are tear tracks on his reddened cheeks, and though that usually satisfies me, right now, it only makes me feel sick.

We file into Aaron's Prius, both of them taking the front while I crawl into the back. I feel eyes on me, and I meet Aaron's gaze in the rearview mirror. There's something there, an anger or a disappointment that I can't puzzle out, but it has my throat closing with guilt.

Did Huck tell him what happened—what I did to him?

The hospital comes into view, and shame wars with disgust in my bones. Disgust at myself for losing control like I did last night. For turning into *him*. Between what happened with Tatiana, the fucking video of Huck stroking his goddamn cock—which had done things to me I'd rather not think about—and his mention of what happened between us years ago, I'd just...snapped. Fucking lost it.

But there's no excuse.

We get to the emergency room, and Aaron checks Huck in. After a few tense minutes of waiting, a nurse finally pulls us back. Huck hasn't said a word, which only sets me further on edge. I try to catch his eye but only notice the bruised cut on his brow, and the self-hatred ravaging my mind grows.

The door opens, revealing a doctor with a deep voice and a curved nose.

He asks what brings us in today, typical doctor questions, but what Huck's dad says has my brain screeching to a halt.

"He says he broke it because he slipped down the stairs this morning."

*No, no, no,* fuck that.

A memory assaults me, of a night when I was fourteen and I sat in a similar room with a similar doctor, telling them that I broke my hand in three places because of a dirt bike accident while the reason for the injuries stood there looking like the most concerned father in the world.

I'm not him. I am *not him.*

"I did it," I blurt out, cutting off the doctor as he discusses Huck needing x-rays, "I broke his arm."

Everyone's attention snaps to me, including Huck's. His dark eyes meet mine, a crease forming between his brows. The swollen, puffy skin beneath his lids has my jaw clenching.

Without taking my gaze off Huck, I explain what happened. "We fought last night, and I was a little too rough. It was an accident. I...I didn't mean it."

I really didn't. Not to break him, at least. God, I'm gonna puke.

Aaron removes his glasses and exhales slowly, pinching the bridge of his nose.

"You smell like a distillery, Taylor," he mutters, and my pulse races.

Will he kick me out? Send me back to my dad's, away from his precious golden boy and fancy house? Deep down, I know I deserve it. But the thought of living back in that trailer...not that it matters, because Dad still controls me even when I'm not immediately under his thumb. But at least for a moment, the constant beatings have lessened.

Maybe it wouldn't be so bad. I could spend all my time at Christian's like I did before. If he'd let me, that is. After decking me, he'd said we were solid last night, but I still saw the hurt in his eyes. What if he finally decided he was over my shit and dropped me? Who would I have, then?

*Shit, shit, shit.*

"It was my fault." Huck's raspy voice brings me out of my spiraling thoughts, and I raise my eyes to find him watching me with an unreadable expression. "I started the fight. Taylor just retaliated."

I know that's a half-truth because I was the one who wouldn't give him back his phone in the first place. I pushed him too far. But he pushed me first.

Aaron glances between us, rubbing the scruff on his chin.

"I'm sorry, Huck," I choke, pushing every ounce of sincerity into my words because, fuck, this shouldn't have happened. I should have been in control.

Huck nods, dropping his gaze finally, and the doctor takes him away for the X-rays.

Aaron and I wait alone in the room, tense silence weighing heavily between us, and when they come back, the doctor confirms a hairline fracture in his forearm. He'll have to wear a splint for the next two weeks, but after that, he can continue swimming as long as the X-rays are good. No football for at least six weeks, which isn't so bad since the season is almost over. After that, they'll perform more X-rays to ensure the fracture has healed.

What kills me, though, is the fear in Huck's voice when he asks if this will fuck up his chances at a football scholarship, and I feel like the biggest piece of shit on the planet. The doctor tells him that if he doesn't push himself and everything heals properly, he'll return to playing in no time, so there's that. An hour later, we're leaving, and Huck has a fresh splint with a painkiller prescription. Aaron speaks quietly once we're in the car, me again in the backseat.

"I'm very disappointed in both of you."

"I'm sorry, Dad," Huck says, and I mumble my apologies.

He looks at his son, "I told you before the wedding to fix whatever grief you two had with each other, Huckslee, remember?"

"Yes, sir."

That black hole in me opens wider, threatening to tear me apart because Huck had fucking *tried*. That day at the wedding, when he'd sat with me. Showing me the track, trying to hang out with me, to be fucking nice to me, but I was a selfish asshole, unable to let something go that happened when we were kids.

We're almost adults now, for Christ's sake. No, we *are* adults. We're both eighteen and here I am, messing with him like an adolescent. Things need to change.

"You are both grounded until further notice," Aaron states firmly, turning to look at me from the front seat. "School, practice, church activities, then home. That's it. No motocross."

*What the fuck?*

Rage ignites in my blood, white-hot. All my earlier sentiments of being an adult leave the vicinity as I scoff incredulously. "You're not my dad."

Huck visibly stiffens in his seat, waves of anger rolling off him.

Aaron's lips thin, his dark eyes flashing as he turns around. "That may be true, but you live under my roof and will abide by my rules. And your mother agrees with me."

Goddammit.

I know I deserve it. Hell, I expected to be kicked to the curb for hurting Huckslee, so I know it could be worse, but taking motocross from me? Seriously? Winter's coming, and I only have a few weeks before it's too cold to ride. There isn't another official race until the spring, but still. The one fucking thing I live for, and now I can't even enjoy it?

Yeah, I'm pissed off.

"I'm not doing church stuff anymore," I mutter, throwing my hood over my head as I glare out the window.

He's been making me go for months now, but I'm done with that shit.

There's a pause, and I'm expecting him to push the issue, but instead, he gives me a calm *that's fine*, which makes my anger dissipate in a puff of smoke. Ugh, why does he have to be such a good guy? It seriously makes it hard to hate him. Maisie, on the other hand...

She's standing on the porch waiting for us when we pull into the driveway. Her hand rests on my shoulder when I try to pass her into the house, stopping me, but I refuse to meet her eyes.

"I raised you better than this, Taylor," she hisses, reigniting my fury, and I yank myself out of her touch.

"Actually, you didn't raise me at all. *He* did, so what did you expect?"

I'm through the door before she can grab me again, and I ignore her when she calls my name, taking the stairs two at a time before locking myself in my room. My head is throbbing, nausea churning in my stomach from the leftover alcohol and the look on Huck's face.

But I don't want to think about it all right now.

So I pull a joint from my bedside table, slide open my window, and light it, inhaling deeply until the paper is ash on my fingers. And then I shove my headphones in, 'Dethrone' by Bad Omens filling my ears, before diving under the covers to shut out the entire world.

After hours of silence from Huck, I finally break down and text him.

Me: Hey. You awake?

It's just after midnight. Besides the awkward dinner Aaron forced us to sit through, we'd both been holed up in our rooms all day. Of course, Huck had talked with his dad, but he ignored my presence. I'd sat there with my head down, purposely not meeting Maisie's covert glares. When I tried bringing up a conversation with Huck, he either didn't respond or directed his answer at his dad, and it drove me fucking nuts.

The last few hours have been torture.

Not even the music blasting in my ears could distract me from the video replaying over and over in my head of Huck's girthy fucking dick, so I tried to occupy my time by doom-scrolling social media. All that resulted in, though, was me stalking my stepbrother's profile, searching through his friends list for whoever this 'Royce' guy is that he's sending nudes to.

I try to lie to myself, thinking I just want to make sure Huck is safe and not getting catfished or something, but the reality stares me in the face, and I can't ignore it—I'm fucking jealous. And I have no goddamn right to be.

I need to talk to him, to make this right even though I have no clue how the hell to do it. Yes, we've fought plenty in the past. We've aimed fists at each other and bruised each other, but this...this went beyond that. This was brutal and angry, and the words I'd said to him...

Like a floodgate bursting open, memories from that day in eighth-grade crash into me like a giant wave.

*"I think I'm gonna be sick."*

*Slowing to a halt, I bend over with my hands on my knees, trying to catch my breath while Xed laughs at me. Checking over my shoulder to make sure our PE teacher isn't watching, I flip him off with a scowl. I hate running the mile. This shit sucks.*

*"It's not even that bad, you puss," Xed snickers, barely breaking a sweat under the midday sun, and I scoff as I straighten.*

*"You run track and field, dude. This is easy for you. My legs feel like jello."*

*He only grins, punching me in the shoulder before jogging ahead, leaving me in the dust.*

*Whatever. I'm walking the rest of the way. I'll take the point. Wouldn't be the first time I've gotten lunch detention, anyway, plus it's not so bad. They make you eat in a room beside the tortoise enclosure, and I get to watch the turtles move around. Not a punishment if you ask me. They're cute, with little heads and tails that wiggle like a puppy's, which is kind of interesting—*

*"Hey."*

*A shadow blocks the sun, dragging me out of my thoughts, and my stomach does some weird, somersault thing when I see Huckslee walking next to me.*

*"Oh, hey, Huck." He's new this year; I guess his parents homeschooled him until now. And he also rides dirt bikes, so we've been hanging out more. We also have two other classes, but he's usually with his friend Logan.*

*"You tired?" He eyes me sideways, curls a mess around his face, and I have to clench my fists to keep from reaching out to touch them. Honestly, it's a problem how much I want to do that. It's wrong. Boys don't touch other boys' hair.*

*"Yeah, man, I hate that they make us do this. The only time I'll ever be running is if someone's chasing me."*

*He snorts before looking behind him, checking for the teacher. "You need to take a break."*

*Yeah, right.*

*"I wish."*

*We walk silently before he lightly touches my arm, drawing us to a halt.*

*"Let's sneak under the bleachers, Tay." He jerks his chin to where they sit a few yards away, and I widen my eyes at him.*

*"Hell, no. I heard they found a cougar under there last week."*

*"Aw, are you scared? Need me to hold your hand?"*

*I open my mouth to swear at him, but then his palm drifts down my arm, and his fingers curl around mine, suddenly making it hard to breathe.*

*"Come on."*

*Next thing I know, I'm being tugged off the field toward the bleachers quickly, and he doesn't drop my hand when we climb under them. Neither do I, for some reason. Though I should, I really should. My dad would flip if he saw this.*

*"Well, no cougars." Huck turns toward me with a grin, dark eyes glittering, and I can't look away from him. We've never been alone before, usually surrounded by friends or peers, but here it's quiet. Dark. Close.*

*His gaze drops to where I'm biting my lip, and the fingers holding mine flex. "So, I saw you hanging with Salem Vaughn in homeroom."*

*"Uh, yeah," I swallow hard, finally tearing my gaze away. "She's cool. Hot, too."*

*He shrugs in response, shoulders dropping slightly, but when he goes to pull his hand from mine, I tighten my hold, not ready to let go.*

*"She's not really my type."*

*"Oh, yeah?" I lick my lips, mouth going dry when his eyes track the movement. "What's your type then?"*

*My heartbeat thumps wildly when he steps closer, backing me against a metal beam.*

*"Not Salem, that's for sure."*

*"Then what?"*

*There's something in his eyes that I don't understand as he dips his head, breath brushing over my ear. "Can I tell you a secret?"*

*In the back of my head, I hear my father's voice telling me to say no and back away, but my mouth responds before I can stop it.*

*"Yes."*

*His chest moves slightly, curls tickling my skin. "I think my type is you, Taylor."*

*"M-me?" My voice comes out embarrassingly high, but I'm too shocked by what he just said to care.*

*"Yeah," he nods, searching my gaze with his own. "Is that okay?"*

*No. This is wrong. Boys shouldn't like boys. My dad is going to kill me.*

*But my mouth isn't connecting with my brain. "Yeah...that's okay."*

*His face lights up, and it hits me how close we are. His body warms mine as we clasp our hands tightly. From this distance, I notice how soft his lips look, all puffy and pink. I picked up on it before but always shoved the thought aside because it felt wrong to think something like that about another dude.*

*But something must be wrong with me because no matter how much I try to tell my limbs to stay still, they don't listen. Instead, my free hand raises to tangle in those curls I've been dying to touch, a hum leaving me when I find them as soft as they look. Huck's breath catches as he cups the back of my neck.*

*Alarm bells are blaring, warning of danger, but I'm too distracted to listen.*

*Instead, I pull his head down and press my lips to his.*

A notification snaps me out of the memory, but it's just a message from Christian. Checking my thread with Huck, I see he's read my text but hasn't responded, which means he's awake and ignoring me. So I throw on some clothes and leave my room, taking a deep breath before knocking on his door.

"Huck? It's me. Taylor."

*Duh, dumbass.* Pretty sure he knows.

"Look, can we talk?"

Seconds go by, and there's no answer. But somehow, I can sense him on the other side of the door, listening.

"Okay, you don't want to talk. I get it. You don't have to, but please open up."

His muffled voice reaches me through the wood. "What do you want, Taylor?"

I open my mouth, then shut it. Because what do I want? His forgiveness? No, I don't deserve that. To explain? I can't, not really. Not without telling him about my father.

*Would it be the end of the world if he knew?*

No, I shut that thought down. The last thing I need is Dad in prison, and my sponsorship lost. It's my only hope of leaving this place behind.

So I clear my throat and say, "I want to see you."

Fuck, that sounds gay as hell and clingy and so damn stupid, but it's the truth, so I just roll with it. A full minute passes without a response, and the word *please* leaves my lips softly, almost like a whisper.

Finally, the door opens.

My breath catches at the wary, guarded expression that meets me on the other side.

"What?" He spits the question flatly, so void of emotion that I cringe.

"I just..." My voice trails off as a slight shock rolls through me, the look in his eyes unnerving my system. Their depths are empty and lifeless as they bore into mine. I've never seen him look so cold before.

His jaw tightens the longer I stare until he starts to swing the door closed. "Leave me the fuck alone, Taylor."

Shooting out a hand, I prevent it from closing at the last minute, and Huck visibly tenses. His pupils dilate, an emotion finally flashing in his irises, but I feel like I've been gutted when I realize it's fear. He's standing there staring at me as if I'm a wild animal poised to strike, and that's when I know that he thinks I'm going to start a fight.

He's fucking *afraid* of me.

That has my heart dropping like a stone. I never wanted him to fear me.

"Taylor?" A frown pulls at his full lips, and before I can stop myself, I find my hand reaching out to him slowly. Ever, ever so slowly, until my palm slides against his, fingers tangling together.

"Come on." Gently, I tug him out into the hallway, his frown deepening as he lets me lead him down the stairs.

The feeling of his hand in mine is foreign, setting off little alarm bells in my brain that say this is wrong, but I don't let go. Because I want to show him, for some insane fucking reason, that my touch isn't always painful. He doesn't pull away, either, so I take that as a win.

It's not until we have to put our shoes on near the back door that I drop his hand, and the emptiness I feel at the absence confuses me. It sends a flood of irritation through my chest, old habits to lash out against the unknown rising to the surface, but I force myself to shove all of that into a box and nail it shut, bury it in a hole. I'll always be hot-headed—nothing can change that. But making other people pay for my issues is coming to an end. I'm determined.

"Where are we going?" Huck finally asks when I lead him out onto the back porch. Cool October air bites into my skin, colder than usual, promising future snow. I use it to ground myself, close my eyes, and take a deep breath.

"The track."

"But I can't ride," he answers sadly.

"I know." Turning toward him, I meet his eyes with my own. "But I want to talk to you, and you don't trust me right now. So we're going to Delaware."

# Huckslee

Taylor's hand found mine again somewhere between the house and the backyard, causing my brain to short-circuit. Half of me wonders if I'm hallucinating. The anxiety meds and pain pills must be scrambling my brain because there's no way Taylor fucking Tottman is holding my hand right now.

*What do you want, Taylor?*

*I want to see you.*

*Please.*

His palm is warm in mine as he leads me onto the track, and he squeezes before letting go. Moonlight shimmers down from a clear night sky, giving his dark hair blue hues under the stars. His teeth dig into his bottom lip as he glances at me sideways, uncertainty rippling across his features. It reminds me of the night after the wedding when we opened up to one another, and I can't force myself to look away.

I should be furious with him. Hell, I *was* furious with him. Last night, I sat in bed and cried until the sun came up. When

I couldn't handle the pain in my arm anymore, I knocked on Dad's door to tell him I tripped. The whole time, I was cursing Taylor in my mind, wishing every bad thing on him I could think of, even coming up with ways to make him feel what he made me feel.

But then, he surprised me at the hospital by telling my dad the truth. And yeah, I'm pissed at him for it because my dad ripped into me for lying to him, but Taylor told the truth. And then he apologized. An honest, genuine apology, too. Not a fake one, for Dad's sake. Still, I was pissed at him. Not in the 'I want to hurt him' way any longer, but definitely in the 'he could disappear and I wouldn't give a shit' kind of way.

Then, the motherfucker knocks on my door, shakes me to my core by grabbing my hand with a tenderness I didn't know he even possessed, and now here we are—standing in our neutral zone because, for some reason, he wants me to trust him.

What is happening right now?

"Look, Huck," Taylor starts, running a hand down his face before looking up at the sky. "Last night was wrong. And I'm so fucking sorry."

He swallows, throat flexing as his eyes meet mine. There's a question in them, a pleading like he wants me to forgive him, but he doesn't ask. I don't know what to say because he's right. It was wrong and probably the shittiest thing he's ever done to me—the worst he's ever made me feel. So I tell him that.

He nods slowly, glancing away. "I know. I could blame it on a shitty night and the alcohol, but that would be a cop-out."

"What set you off?"

Sighing deeply, he tugs at his hair. "I don't... I don't know, man. It's hard to explain. I don't really understand it myself."

"So let's talk about it," I say quickly, desperately wanting to understand because Taylor is so rarely this candid with me. "Maybe I can help?"

A nervous laugh leaves his throat. "I don't think so."

"Why not?" Stepping closer, I place myself in front of him, looking down into his eyes with raised brows. "Why do you hate me so much, Taylor?"

His tongue darts out to moisten his lips. "I don't hate you, Huck. Not even close."

"Then what? Why have you made my life fucking hell the last few years? Was it because of what happened in eighth grade? Because if you didn't feel the same way—"

He tenses immediately and backs away, causing me to stiffen as well. Multitudes of emotions war across his face—guilt, anger, apprehension.

"I told you not to bring that up again," he grits through clenched teeth, his hands fisting like he's physically holding himself back from taking a swing.

"Why? Because you kissed me? Because you liked it?"

An almost pained grimace hardens his features. "Don't."

"Or what? You'll break my other arm?!" With a scoff, I turn away. "This is pointless. I'm fucking done trying to find something good in you. Your friendship would have been enough even if you didn't like me that way, but I'm just a fucking queer, right? And God forbid you associate yourself with a faggot—"

"Shut the fuck up, Huckslee," he growls, cutting off my words.

Before I can process what's happening, he's spinning me around and crushing his mouth to mine. It's like an electric shock to my senses, the feel of his soft lips sliding over mine like velvet.

"What are you doing?" I murmur.

Taylor laughs, a husky, breathy noise that shoots right to my dick. "Silencing your bullshit."

His fingers snake up the side of my face, curling into my hair, and a gasp fills my lungs. He takes advantage of it by slipping his tongue inside, gliding against mine, tasting of mint and nicotine. My arms wrap around him, palm coming up to cup his jaw, the kiss messy and sloppy in the best way.

It's nothing like the sweet ones I've shared with Royce. No, this is desperate, needy, almost frantic as I hold him against my chest, grinding our bodies together, all of my neurons firing at once.

A low groan rolls from his throat before he rips himself away, our breaths loud and ragged against the quiet night air. We blink at each other for a few moments before his dazed eyes drop down his body, and I catch the tented bulge in his sweatpants before he quickly turns around.

"Fuck."

Looking down at myself, I notice my own cock at full mast, the tip too close to peeking out of my waistband for comfort, so I reach down to adjust it before glancing up at Taylor. He still stands with his back to me, hands on his hips.

Nerves have me tensing as I watch him, waiting for the explosion to happen. "Tay?"

"Just gimme a minute," he says, rubbing a hand down his face before it tangles in the hair at the base of his neck.

We stay like that for a while, facing away from each other as we wait for our dicks to go down. The situation would be funny if it were anyone else, but Taylor's temper has repeatedly proven to me that he has a short fuse, so I hold in my laugh as I wait.

And wait.

And wait.

Finally, after what feels like twenty minutes, he exhales slowly. "I need a smoke after that."

He covers his eyes, and I can't hold it anymore. A snorting laugh bursts out of me, shaking my shoulders, and Taylor turns around with wide eyes, looking like a deer in headlights. His baffled expression only makes me laugh harder, and he flashes me a grin that shows off a crooked incisor.

"Don't be an ass," he chuckles, blushing as I shake my head.

"Sorry. Your fucking face. I swear."

His smile slowly fades, his tongue darting out to lick his lips as he glances away. Something in his expression shifts—a slight change that raises my hackles.

"Huck, that was..." He squints, gazing off at the track as he tries to find his bearings. What comes out of his mouth takes me entirely off guard. "That was a mistake."

Those words hit me like a punch to the gut, stealing my breath. I stare at him incredulously, mouth agape. He sighs heavily when his eyes find mine again before raising them upwards. "Don't be like this, man."

"Like what?" Is he serious right now? "Like you've kissed me not once, but *twice* now, and both times you've taken it back?"

"I shouldn't have lost control like that," he grumbles, everything he's saying like a vice around my lungs.

"Yeah," I agree, the anger in me rising again. "And I should have known better than to trust you."

His head snaps up, hurt flashing in his eyes as he steps toward me. "Listen, let me try to explain."

Shaking my head quickly, I spin around to head back toward the house, "I'm done with this. Done with you. It's too fucking confusing, and I'm tired of it."

"Huckslee." His hand grips my non-splinted arm tightly. *"Please."*

The desperation in his voice stops me in my tracks.

Pausing for a few moments, I nod once, not turning around. Cold fingers slip down my arm, running from the crook of my elbow to my wrist before falling away. It's a touch that sends goosebumps over my skin.

"Look, my father is an asshole," he says haltingly, and I exhale in exasperation.

"I know, you've said that before."

"Shut up and let me talk, Huck."

My jaw feathers at the corners, molars grinding, but I stay silent.

"As I'm sure you know, my dad's shop is my racing sponsor. Without his backing, I wouldn't have been able to enter the competition for the scholarship next year. Plus, he owns my bike. Whatever prize money I get from winning goes toward paying it off, not to mention all the tickets and fines I've gotten from...well, from being me."

*Okay, and your point?*

It's on the tip of my tongue to say those exact words, but instead, I hold back as Taylor continues.

"He's an old-fashioned guy, my father. Very set in his ways. One of the reasons Maisie left him. Let's just say he has very particular opinions on a woman's place in the household." He huffs a humorless laugh. "So, you can imagine his thoughts regarding...unconventional relationships are very outdated."

At that admission, I turn around to see Taylor's bright and open eyes on my face, pleading for me to understand. His teeth work his bottom lip again—the lip my teeth were biting on.

"Unconventional," I repeat slowly, trying to understand what he's saying.

"Yeah. As in...relationships that aren't strictly of the 'male and female' variety. And he's very vocal about it."

Understanding dawns on me, loud and clear. "So your dad is homophobic."

Taylor nods grimly. "Yep. With a capital 'H.'"

"He's where you get it from, then," I add, somewhat resentfully, and Taylor's eyes flash angrily.

"I'm not my father," he snarls, whirling away as he starts to pace, "and I'm not a homophobe. I have nothing against gay people."

"Just me, then?"

Another punch to the gut from this guy. How many times am I going to open myself up to him so that he can hurt me?

"*No*, Huck," he growls in frustration, halting his pacing to meet my gaze. "Look, if my dad had any kind of suspicion that I was gay, he'd take away my sponsorship. He'd take my bike.

Any chance I had at getting that scholarship would fly out the window, and I need that scholarship, man."

"Are you?" I ask quickly, snagging onto only one part of his speech, even though I know what he's trying to tell me is important.

He blinks. "Am I what?"

"Gay?"

"Fuck no," he snaps, and I rear back at the intensity in his tone. Taylor notices immediately, growling again as he resumes his pacing. "I don't know, Huck. I don't think so."

The way his dick reacted to our kiss earlier tells me otherwise, but his sexuality isn't my concern. I have enough issues with my own sexuality, thank you very much. Yes, I'm in the closet, but I don't lie to myself about it.

Breathing slowly, I reach up to pinch the bridge of my nose. "So why don't you just find another sponsor?"

"Tried that. No one will take me. I'm a bit of a bad influence. Not like you, golden boy," he smirks. "Plus, when my father found out I was searching for someone else, he got...upset about it."

The way he winces when he says that last part has a sick feeling churning in my stomach.

"Did he get violent with you?"

"What?" Taylor's eyes widen as they snap to mine, and he quickly shakes his head. "No, no. Nothing like that. He's just unpleasant to be around when he's angry. That's all."

Like father, like son.

I relax slightly, taking him at his word, and he surprises me by stepping forward to grasp my wrist.

"I *need* that scholarship, Huck," he says again, eyes burning into mine with such intensity that I find myself drowning in their oceanic depths. "I'm not good like you. I don't have the potential of a full ride or wealthy parents. I really don't give a shit about football. Motocross is my life—the only thing that matters to me. And with the possibility of college, I can actually leave this place and make something of myself. So you see, don't you? I can't risk losing everything."

"Okay, I get it," I grumble, because really, I do. I understand. We are similar in that I don't really care about football, either. But I'm good at it, and it offers me a chance to leave this town for good. So I get it.

What I don't get, though...

"So tell me why you turned into such a jackass," I demand, pulling my wrist from his grip. "After the eighth grade. Why did you hate me so much?"

Taylor sighs, covering his eyes again with a hand.

"I was a little...obsessed with you," he admits, grinning sheepishly, and I hate how fucking cute it makes him look. "Even more so after we...kissed. My father kind of caught on and made some comments, pretty much told me that if he caught us hanging out again, he'd take my dirt bike away."

I go still. "Your bike?"

He's kidding, right?

"Yeah. So I pretended to hate you even though I didn't. And I guess, over the years, it just kind of became easier to lie to myself, too. Because I...we couldn't be anything. We can't be anything. To each other."

A roaring fills my ears, the blood in my veins close to boiling. My cheeks heat with shame and embarrassment.

"Are you telling me," I start slowly, trying my damnedest and failing at keeping my voice calm, "that you spent the last three fucking years torturing me because you didn't want your daddy to take away your precious bike?"

His eyes widen at my tone, nearly bugging out of their sockets as his face twists into a sneer. "Fuck you, Huckslee."

Oh, I'm mad. Beyond mad. I'm fucking fuming. Everything comes to a head, all the times I sat in detention because of something he did. All of the bruises and all of the lunches spent eating alone in my car because he tripped me one too many times in the cafeteria. The rumors, the hurtful slurs, that time I had to go to urgent care because he somehow got the combination to my locker and slipped Christian's pet tarantula inside, causing me to fly into a panic attack. He'd overheard Logan telling the science teacher I had arachnophobia and thought it was fucking funny. All of the times I wished I could disappear, all of the misery and hate. Over a goddamned dirt bike.

"God, I'm so fucking stupid." I laugh humorlessly as I turn on my heel, heading back toward the house. "Despite all the shit you've done to me, I pined after you for years. *Years*. You really couldn't care less about anyone but yourself, Taylor."

His voice comes from close behind as he follows. "You can go fuck yourself with your judgment, asshole."

I spin around so fast I almost get whiplash as my hand wraps around his throat. Yanking him to me, I put myself so close to his face that our noses brush.

"*Me?* Judge you? How many times have you called me names because of my sexuality? Or my grades, or my clothes? I'm the golden boy, right? With the rich daddy? Or am I the fucking sissy bottom bitch, fairy boy queer, Taylor? Because I can't keep it all straight anymore."

"I'm s-sorry." His hand grips my wrist as I squeeze.

"I don't want your apologies! I want you to take back all the damage you've done to me. Can you do that?"

He wheezes against my hand. "Would...if I...could."

The whites of his eyes begin to darken, veins going blood-shot, and some sick part of me likes the sight. To see him be the one struggling to breathe for once, powerless to do anything about it but drown like he made me feel over and over and over again.

There's an addictive rush of power that comes from having someone at your mercy, and I'm living for it. Living for the way he dangles in my grip.

And that's when it hits me like a fucking brick that Taylor isn't fighting back. He's literally standing there, letting me choke the life out of him.

Immediately, I drop him, his knees hitting the ground with an audible crack. Inhaling sharply, he bends over to cough into the dirt, massaging his throat. When he raises his head to peer up at me, I notice a slight bluish tint at the corners of his mouth, and all my anger just...vanishes into thin air. A bone-deep exhaustion takes its place, so draining that my own knees threaten to buckle.

"Just stay away from me, Taylor," I sigh wearily, rubbing my temples before turning toward the house again. "Leave me the fuck alone."

This time, he doesn't follow.

# TAYLOR

## DECEMBER

S now has finally arrived in Utah, and I hate it.

A blizzard rages outside the cafeteria windows, so thick it obscures the entire football field in the distance. Thick flakes swirl into a heavy maelstrom, practically blowing sideways from the wind—perfectly matching my sour mood. Snow means no motocross, and no motocross means pissy Taylor. Not that I'd been able to ride since October. Still, saying goodbye to my two-stroke this morning as I covered it in the garage had felt like a funeral.

A deep, rolling laugh pulls me from my wallowing, and I turn to glare across the cafeteria at the source of the laughter. He's been eating lunch here more often now that I've stopped messing with him. At first, I liked it. The opportunity to observe him from a distance was too good to pass up, but lately, the sight of him has been grinding my gears. The impulse to go over there and say some shit or do something to piss him off is intense.

Old habits die hard.

Huck laughs again, grinning at something Logan says next to him, and I feel my scowl deepen. He snorted at me this morning when I put my bike away, which was the only reaction he'd given me in weeks. Logan shoves Huck playfully on the shoulder, and I feel like I'm going crazy because I want to take his arm off for touching my stepbrother.

"What did he do this time?" Christian snickers, following my gaze over to where Huck is sitting.

I give him a blank stare. "Nothing."

"Then why do you look like you're about ready to kill him, bruh," he laughs, digging into his lunch, and I force myself to look away from Huck before I do something I can't take back. Again.

"You'd look like this too if you'd been grounded for two months."

Xed sits next to Christian at the table, followed by Matty, who plops beside me. "Aaron still hasn't let you off the hook?"

Shaking my head, I push my food around on my tray. Nope, the Good Bishop is sticking to his guns about this whole grounding thing. It's been a dull few months, that's for sure. Mainly because I've been trying to do like Huck asked and stay away from him, but it's been so fucking hard. Especially after I got a taste of him.

I've tried to bury the memory of that disaster of a night at the track, but it won't give me peace. It just runs on a loop in my head, the feel of Huck against me and the shit I could have said differently. Logically, I get why he didn't understand. He doesn't know the whole story, after all. But there's a toxic side of me that's screaming *how fucking dare you walk away when I opened up to you, motherfucker.*

To him, it's just a bike. An object or something fun to pass the time with, but to me? That bike is everything. Not only is it my ticket to freedom but a reprieve from the shit my father slings at me.

I wince, rubbing my aching collarbone as I think about what he did to me on Thanksgiving a week ago. Maisie had forced me to spend it with him since I hadn't seen him in a while. She played it off like a good parent, but I know it's because she didn't want me ruining her perfect family holiday. Thank fuck football season is over, so I don't have to undress in front of the guys—I can't blame the injuries on Huck anymore.

"Earth to Taylor, helloooo?" Xed waves a hand in front of my face, his green-tinted Mohawk catching in the light, and I blink as I realize there's a heavy body leaning into my side, nearly pushing me over.

"Seriously, Matthew?" Shoving him off of me, I grimace when the movement causes my rotator cuff to twinge. "You have no semblance of personal space, my guy."

Matty laughs, righting himself before overcorrecting and shoulder-checking the person beside him. "Sorry, my bad."

"It's not his fault." Xed switches the orange juice on his tray for Matt's energy drink. "I'm convinced he body-swapped with a golden retriever at birth, and the poor thing doesn't know what to do with all that muscle."

That's likely the truth. Matt's the biggest, clumsiest person out of all of us, constantly tripping over his own two feet.

Luckily, that doesn't carry over onto the field. It's like his body knows how to defend a ball because he's a beast when it comes to the defensive line. A small chuckle leaves my throat at the thought. He's definitely a dog trapped in a human body.

"You missed the Symbiotic show on Friday," Christian says around his food, and I groan as I cover my face with my hands, irritated at missing one of my favorite bands playing live.

"I fuckin' know, man. This grounding thing is killing me."

"My *tio* is taking me snowmobiling New Year's weekend. Maybe you can ask to be let off early for good behavior?"

"Yeah, maybe. I'll try."

God, I fucking hope so. I've been a good boy. Real good. And I need something to take my mind off the current subject of my obsession, sitting ten feet away, smiling at his best friend like he has no care in the world.

My eyes drift back over to him reluctantly. He looks good. Got a haircut, so the curls are shorter on the sides and longer on top, falling over his forehead. My fingers twitch against my fork, remembering how soft his hair felt when I ran them through it. His teeth on my bottom lip, stiff muscles pressed against my own, and then the confusing way my cock hardened when he had my throat in a death grip—

No.

*No, no, no.*

No.

I will *not* pop a boner in the middle of the lunchroom. Absolutely not.

Mentally, I shove those thoughts inside the box that's beginning to overflow in my mind and bury it again for later.

Because I'll *definitely* be thinking about that again later, in my room. With my hand down my pants.

Fuck, I need to get laid.

As if someone up above heard my plight, a small shoulder bumps into mine, and a familiar feminine body squeezes in between me and Matty.

"Hey, Taytortot." Salem grins up at me, her gray eyes glowing against the reflection of the snow-covered windows.

Returning her grin, I feel myself relax in the presence of my second best friend. "Sally Mal. What's shakin', babe?"

She laughs, tossing her long red hair into a messy bun on the top of her head before leaning in and pressing a kiss to my throat. After weeks of no human contact, the feel of her lips on my skin has my dick perking up almost immediately, and I stifle a groan. With this one gesture, she's telling me that she let Brad go, and now it's my turn again. See what I mean about our relationship being easy? This girl just gets me.

Throwing an arm around her shoulders, I lean in, pressing my nose against her hair. She always smells fantastic, like lilacs or some shit, and it always calms me down. Salem is the only soul on the planet who knows about all the shit with my father, and only because she witnessed my near mental breakdown over it one night a few years ago. She saw the worst parts of me and stayed, which is more than I can say for some people.

Speaking of one of those people...

I feel his attention burning a hole in the side of my face, and I turn to meet Huck's stare. A frown pulls at his lips, his gaze bouncing between Salem and me, some form of anger burning in his irises that I can feel from here. The sight gives my sick and twisted brain an idea.

Keeping my eyes locked on Huckslee, I turn Salem's face and plant a kiss on her lips, cutting off whatever she'd been saying to Xed. She purrs, relaxing into me, her mouth parting to grant my tongue access. It's slow and sultry, nothing like the desperate frenzy of kissing my stepbrother, and though her lips are as familiar to me as my own, the kiss lacks any real heat. But that's okay because the way Huck's jaw visibly tightens as he watches us tells me I've achieved my goal.

Turning back to Salem, I find her gazing at me with narrowed eyes, and I break the kiss with a grin. "What?"

"Who are we making jealous?" She looks around the cafeteria, searching for whoever I'd been staring at.

Debating for half a second, I decide to tell her the truth. "Huckslee."

Her manicured brows rise as she snaps her eyes to Huck, who's glaring at us from across the room, and she smiles broadly as she waves at him. "Not who I expected, but it's hot, and I'm down for it."

Fuck, this is why I love her. Salem is always down for anything.

"So what did Huck do to piss you off now?" She asks. Christian laughs when he catches the end of our whispered conversation.

"That's what I asked, too."

I frown at both of them. "Why does everyone think he did something to piss me off?"

He did. But they don't need to know that.

Salem shrugs as she pulls my tray over, grabbing the fork out of my hand. "Doesn't he always?"

Ain't that the fucking truth.

Glancing back over at him, I find his attention no longer on us. He's staring down at his phone, smiling as he types away, and it's my turn to glare. Who the fuck is he talking to? Who has him smiling like that? Is it the Royce guy he was texting months ago? The thought makes my blood boil. I still haven't been able to find whoever he is on social media, though maybe I should recruit Salem for the job. Girl could work for the FBI with her investigative skills, no joke.

Pulling out my phone, I type out a quick message.

> Me: Who are you texting?

And then I sit back and wait. Only a few minutes pass before his head snaps up from his phone, and he briefly locks eyes with me.

It's been months since we've even talked to each other in person. I sent him a few texts after the night on the track, which he ignored, so this is the first time in weeks that we've broken our weird stalemate. I even started staying late in the gym, lifting and performing drills Coach makes us do in the offseason to avoid awkward dinners with Aaron and Maisie. Since Huck is still on light duty for his arm, weights are out of the question, so I usually get the gym to myself late in the evening after everyone else goes home.

My phone vibrates, and I grin when I read his text.

> Suckslee: Mind your fucking business.

I send him a pouty emoji, followed by a crying one. He reads it and doesn't respond.

> Me: No sexting at the lunch table, young man.

His responding text comes through immediately.

> Suckslee: What makes you think I'm sexting?

> Me: You're a dude. I'm a dude. We only smile at our phones for nudes.

That rhymed. I'm a poet, and I didn't know it.

> Suckslee: You're so off base, it's ridiculous.

> Me: But I hit a home run, right? You are talking to someone?

He doesn't respond, and I peek under my lashes to find him blinking at his phone. Joining the conversation with the guys, I wait for him to say something else, but he never does. So I text him again.

> Me: Is it that Royce fella?

Instant response:

> Suckslee: I don't see how that's any of your business, Taylor, just like who you suck face with in the middle of the cafeteria isn't mine.

My stomach flips, thumbs flying over the screen.

> Me: Saw that did you?

> Suckslee: The whole lunchroom saw it. Get a room next time.

> Me: Just admit that you were watching me, Huck.

Suckslee: Why? Because I'm gay so I'm always looking at you?

I shoot him an annoyed glance.

Me: No. I watch you too. It's okay.

He reads it but doesn't respond. I wait and wait, becoming engrossed in Matty's discussion with Salem about their AP Psych class. By the time the lunch bell rings, Huck is gone. And I'm still left on read, surrounded by friends but feeling lonelier than ever.

# HUCKSLEE

D eep breath.

I inhale, expanding my lungs to total capacity before diving beneath the water. Pumping my legs, I glide from one end of the pool to the other before coming up for air. 'Rain' by Sleep Token reverberates around the quiet pool room from my Bluetooth speaker, keeping me focused while I swim my laps.

Winter break officially started today, and everyone's gone home for the week. While some would feel spooked in an empty school alone, I find it calming and peaceful. It's like the world has finally stopped turning for a moment, and all that exists is myself.

I've always felt more at home in the water than on a football field.

Once, during sophomore year, I begged my dad to let me drop football and focus on the swim team, but he shot me down. Said that football was more of a team sport and it would be good for me to learn how to cope in a team environment and learn to share. Like it was my fault he and Mom chose to homeschool their only child until the age of twelve. And it's not like I'd been wholly isolated—they'd put me in tons of youth church sports. Really, I think Dad just thought that football looked better on a college resume.

Diving back down again, I swim another lap, pushing my body until I hopefully become so exerted that I'll fall right into sleep the moment my head hits the pillow. The anxiety pills stopped working, so I'm trying something new, but the painkillers ran out. Not that I need them anyway; the latest x-ray shows good progress on my arm. It's healing nicely enough that they took off my splint, but I still can't lift or do anything to compromise the bone.

I just wish I could sleep. Something is brewing under the surface, steadily rising inside me each day. My mask is slipping. I snapped at Logan this morning, and the way he looked at me as if I'd lost my mind made me want to jab a fork into my neck.

It's all because of Taylor. I've been hyper-aware of his presence since that night at the track—everywhere he fucking goes, I feel it. In the house, at school, in the gym, running drills. And even though he hasn't messed with me in months, I find myself waiting for the rug to be pulled out from under me. Like, I'll wake up and find a severed horse head in my bed or something. It's the type of apprehension I can't shake anywhere but alone in the pool, knowing he's home and not waiting around a corner to fuck with me.

Like kissing Salem in the cafeteria three days ago and then having the audacity to ask me if I'm talking to anyone. Like, what the fuck was that about? Which I am, for the record. And yes, it's Royce. Though we've only hung out the few handfuls of times I could sneak out of the house. I usually meet him down the street in his car, and then he drives us somewhere to fool around. It's been nice. He's a fun and sweet guy. The only issue is, well...I can't get myself to kiss him anymore.

Putting my mouth on his dick seems to give me no problem, but the thought of anyone else on my lips other than my fucking stepbrother makes me nauseous. Which is why the sight of him kissing Salem sent me spiraling. Cue the mental breakdown.

As the song on my speaker rises to a crescendo, the water ripples with a splash, startling me. I sense him before breaking the surface, and I come up for air in time to see Taylor's dark head of hair swimming toward me. Pushing my goggles onto my forehead, I grit my teeth as he draws closer. His eyes lock onto mine, more green in the pool's reflection, and he stops several feet from where I'm treading water.

"You're not allowed to be here," I clip, irritated that he's invading the small space of peace I've found in months.

He scoffs, dipping down until the waterline touches his jaw. "What, like swimming is illegal now?"

"Technically, yeah. It's after hours. Pool's closed."

"You're here," he points out, shaking water from his ears, and I track a droplet running down the side of his neck.

"I have permission from the swim coach. Doctor says it'll help me get my arm strength back."

Taylor merely hums before twisting around, moving into a breaststroke. I watch the sculpted muscles of his back work as he swims to the other side of the pool before kicking off the edge and swimming back. Goddammit. Being half-naked with him in a pool is the last place I want to be right now.

So I ignore him, putting my goggles back on and continuing with my own laps. We pass each other in silence as he does the same, and I try to keep my eyes from gravitating toward him every time he flashes his abs. And fail miserably. Honestly, he's a good swimmer. His form is near perfect. No part of his arms or hands come back past his shoulders when he sweeps them to the side; on the glide, his hands and feet touch like they're supposed to. Truly magnificent. It isn't until he stops to look at me curiously mid-stroke that I realize I've been floating here staring at him like a creep.

Clearing my throat, I pull my goggles off and fling them onto the ledge. "Looks like someone paid attention in swim team after all."

"Sure did, Captain," he grins, mocking me with a salute.

"So why'd you quit?"

His grin fades, eyes darkening before he looks away. "Wasn't my thing."

Now, that feels like bullshit. He wasn't on the swim team for long, maybe half a semester, but he showed up for every practice and every meet. Of course, I'd done my best to stay out of his way, so I don't remember much, but I do remember seeing joy on his face in the pool that wasn't there during football. It was the same joy as mine.

But I don't call him out on his blatant lie because I really don't give a shit. Whatever internal stuff he's going through is none of my concern. It's not like he's ever cared about what I go through. So I turn to swim toward the ladder that'll take me out of the pool, planning on leaving him here alone to drown, hopefully, but then I remember that Coach gave me the key. So I can't.

Fuck.

"Is there a reason you're here," I growl irritably, turning around to jolt with surprise when I find him inches from me, close enough to feel the heat of his skin. Sneaky fucker.

"I was lifting late." His eyes search my face. "Saw the door to the pool open. Figured I'd investigate."

"Well, it's just me." My voice is rough when I respond, watching the reflection of the water shimmer in his eyes. "So you can leave now."

He swallows, moving closer, and I tread backward to keep the distance between us.

"Is that what you want?" he asks softly, licking his bottom lip. "For me to leave?"

*Say yes. Say yes*, my mind screams at me, but when I open my mouth, no words come out. I can only float and stare as his gorgeous face moves toward me. Our chests brush and my breath hitches, his eyes intently holding mine when he leans in close enough for our mouths to barely touch.

"I don't think you do," he whispers, gazing at my lips. "I think that you want me to stay."

But I don't. *I don't.*

My nerve endings feel like they're on fire when his fingertips brush my biceps, trailing over my shoulders and leaving molten lava in their wake. He presses himself against me, cupping the back of my neck, and I can feel when my heart jumps as if it wants to leap out of my chest and into his.

Warm breath caresses my face. "Say it. Say you want me to stay, Huck."

No.

"I don't." It comes out breathless, barely audible over my speaker, so I raise my voice louder. "I don't want you to stay."

It sounds unconvincing, even to my own ears.

Taylor tilts his head, studying me for a moment before a slow, wicked grin forms on his face.

"Liar."

Somehow, my body knows what's coming before my brain does.

I breathe in just before he shoves me under the water, his hands gripping my shoulders. Struggling against him, I kick out my legs, but we're in the deep end, and it's useless. He holds me down until my lungs begin to burn, nostrils stinging from the chlorine I accidentally snorted. Just when I think he's going to keep me there until I pass out, he yanks me to the surface.

My lips part as I gasp for air, and suddenly, Taylor's mouth is on mine, breathing life into me. He crushes my body to him, gliding our tongues together with such fervor that I'm breathless again when he pulls away and shoves me back under. Punching through the water, I try to hit his torso, to wriggle out of his grasp as terror ices my veins, but I'm weak from months of inactivity due to the splint.

I start to spasm, desperate for oxygen, spots filling my vision.

And then Taylor is there again, emptying his lungs into mine as if our very existence depends on each other. He tastes like chlorine and bad decisions, but damn if I don't find myself sucking on his bottom lip like it's a lifeline.

When he pushes me under again, I don't fight it. I let the waves pull me down, closing my eyes and relinquishing to the darkness that has clawed at me for years. It's euphoric. Weightless. A high I'll never find again but continue to chase for as long as I live.

It's easy to give in like this. Easy in a way that's addicting.

Our bodies slide together when Taylor lifts me, holding my shaking frame as he dominates my mouth. Any strength I had disintegrates, the struggle for air taking everything out of my aching limbs. If not for his strong arms keeping me afloat, I'd sink to the bottom and cease to exist.

His lips leave mine to trail kisses along my jaw, down my neck, until his teeth bite into my throat, and I hiss at the pleasure that shoots down to my aching cock.

Taylor chuckles into my skin, pressing his hard length against my thigh as his tongue traces a line up to my ear.

"I've dreamt about this," he murmurs, nibbling on my earlobe as his hand palms my dick outside of my swim shorts.

My attempt at a scoff comes out like a gasp. "About drowning me?"

I've never been so exhausted and turned on in my life.

"Yeah," he laughs, smiling against my face. He starts to jerk me slowly through my pants, and I groan, dropping my forehead to his shoulder. My own hand slides to his crotch, rubbing him like he's doing to me, equally delighted and annoyed to find how much bigger he is than me. It's not fair.

Taylor's hips thrust against my palm, seeking friction while his teeth work my lobe. I'm also moving, albeit less animatedly, thanks to the oxygen deprivation, but it's not enough. I need more. And I must say it out loud because Taylor hums before his hand slowly starts to ease its way under the waistband of my shorts.

"As you wish," he breathes, and my body jolts the minute he wraps around my cock. It hits me like lightning, filling me with heat, and I raise my head to capture his lips as he works me in long, languid strokes. Before long, we're both panting while I writhe against him, fucking his fist as the water sloshes around us.

God, he feels good. Not just his hand on my cock, but his tongue as it lazily plays with mine, the curve of his ribs where I grip him, using his body as leverage to thrust myself into a frenzy. In the way his free arm braces me behind my back, keeping me upright.

"So fucking good," I groan into his mouth, and his smile is almost enough to send me spilling over the edge.

"Let go, Huck," he says, kissing down the line of my jaw. "Give in for me."

So I do.

Three thrusts later, I come apart in his hand, moaning as I bury my face into his neck. He jerks me completely dry, stroking my cock until every last drop of cum is spent. We cling to each other for a long moment after he tucks me back into my shorts, his cheek resting against my hair while mine continues to take up space on his shoulder.

I feel like I've just run a marathon.

As the orgasm high starts to fade, I begin to notice the burning in my throat and the heaviness in my limbs. My eyes are exhausted, struggling to keep open. Taylor's body is warm against mine, steady, an anchor holding me in place as I feel like I'm lifting into space.

"We can't stay here, Huck," he murmurs, but his voice seems far away as if he's on the other side of the pool instead of in my arms.

Tightening my hold on him, I keep him pressed against me, knowing I've responded, but I don't hear it. I don't feel it. A numbness works up my body, seeping into my skin and bones. His lips are in my hair, whispering words that no longer register because sleep has pulled me into its dark, sticky web for the first time in months.

And I don't ever want to leave.

# TAYLOR

Huckslee snores. *Loudly.*

Like a bear starting a chainsaw, or whatever that saying is.

Cracking open an eye, I nudge him irritably with my elbow until he finally quiets down, and then I try to go back to sleep.

Five minutes later, he's snoring again.

With a sigh, I roll onto my back and resign myself to staring at his ceiling. There's a snowstorm outside, so the room is dark even though it's late morning. Whatever shitty playlist he'd been listening to last night still plays quietly from the speaker I'd barely remembered to take with us from the pool.

*Fuck.* The pool.

Memories from last night come pouring back, and I shift to adjust my morning wood. To be honest, I hadn't planned on nearly drowning my stepbrother and then jerking him off when I found him yesterday. But life's a lot easier to deal with

117

if I go with the flow instead of fighting it, so here we are, I guess.

In Huck's bed. With a massive boner at the memory of the sound he made right before he came.

Jesus. What the fuck had I been thinking?

Well, that's just it. I *hadn't* been thinking, had I? Not with the right head, anyway. One look at Huck's glowing skin and damp curls was enough to push me into insanity, apparently.

What's wrong with me?

He mumbles something in his sleep, moaning low, and I feel it go straight to my balls.

I'm horny as fuck right now. Did I like what I did to him last night? Hell yeah. Hottest experience of my life. Never given a handjob before, but the way he turned to putty in my hands tells me that I did just fine.

If the roles had been reversed, though? If he'd been the one to slip his hands into my pants instead?

Pulling my cock out, I stroke myself slowly next to Huck's sleeping body, imagining his hand instead of mine. I picture him gripping me, his lips on mine like I was the answer to his salvation. A bead of precum forms at my tip, and I roll my thumb over it as the fantasy in my head changes. I see Huck on his knees now, kneeling with my cock in his mouth, those big brown eyes looking up at me while I thrust into his throat—

The asshole chooses that exact moment to let loose the loudest snore I've ever heard in my entire fucking life.

Growling in exasperation, I tuck myself back into my sweats before yanking the pillow out from under his head to smack him with it. "Shut the fuck up, Huckslee."

He snorts, slowly opening his bloodshot eyes. "Taylor?"

His voice is low and husky from sleep, doing nothing to help the situation in my pants right now.

"Morning, princess," I smirk at him, watching as he rubs the crusties from his long lashes and slowly sits up. He blinks around the room dazedly, confused as hell, and I bite my lip at how adorable he looks. Of course, he's still in his swim trunks because dressing him in jammies was way too much for me.

"What are you doing in my room?"

*Trying to get off, which you rudely interrupted.*

"I *was* sleeping," I drawl, "but your loud-ass snores woke me up."

He stares at me blankly, and I can almost see his gears turning beneath those tousled curls. "You slept in my bed?"

"Well, yeah. You were pretty out of it last night when we got home. Wrapped your arms around me like an octopus and wouldn't let me leave."

Bit of an exaggeration, but it's true for the most part. He had my hand in a vice grip and kept mumbling *don't leave* in a way that seriously freaked me out. I only meant to stay with him until he fell asleep, but I ended up passing out myself not too long after.

A frown pulls at his brows. "Got home?"

"Yeah. From the pool."

The look he gives me makes it seem as if I've sprouted horns, and a sick feeling churns in my stomach.

"What pool?"

"What do you mean?" I sit up quickly, my heart kicking up in my chest as I scoot closer to him. "You don't remember the pool?"

He shakes his head quickly as if to clear it. "The last thing I remember is texting you in the cafeteria."

What the fucking fuck.

"Are you serious right now?" My hands fly to cup his face, pulling down his bottom lids to look at his eyes, real fear closing my throat. "That was four days ago, Huck."

Shit. Shit shit. This is bad. Did I cause some kind of permanent damage?

Bile rises in my throat as the pulse pounds in my veins. The room spins, and I do weird shit, like check his gums and feel his forehead. I don't even know what I'm looking for, but panic is seizing my lungs. The corners of Huck's lips twitch when my fingers find his pulse point, and I pause when a grin slowly spreads across his face. Before I know it, he's doubling over in a fit of laughter.

"You motherfucker." Shoving him in the chest, an exhale of relief makes me weak. "I thought I scrambled your brains or some shit."

"You deserve it for nearly drowning me, bitch." His shoulders shake with chuckles as he wipes the corners of his eyes.

Christ.

Falling backwards onto the bed, I cover my face. Honestly, last night could have been bad. Fuck's sake. Next time I try drowning him, remind me to do it when we're near the vicinity of a bed and not in a fucking high school.

"Hey." He leans over me, pulling my arms from my face, and I can't stand the way my chest aches at the warmth in his eyes. "How did we get home?"

"Um...I drove you."

He blinks. "In my car?"

"Uh-huh."

"Do you even have a license?"

I grin sheepishly up at him. "Nope."

"*Fuuuck.*" Huck hangs his head, curls falling into his eyes. "I don't even remember leaving the pool."

"Yeah, about that." I bite my lip with a wince. "Don't be surprised later when your dad gives you a lecture about the dangers of taking pain pills while swimming."

His eyes snap up to mine, shoulders tensing. "Are you fucking kidding me?"

"You were super out of it, man. I had to come up with something."

He opens his mouth, dark eyes flashing in what I'm sure is anger before they zero in on something near my neck. His fingers pull down the collar of my shirt.

"Who the hell did this?" he demands, brushing a knuckle along my collarbone. I already know he's seeing the bruises my dad left when he held me in place on Thanksgiving, drunkenly screaming in my face for burning the food he'd forced me to make. With everything happening, Huck must have missed them last night in the pool.

Clearing my throat, I shrug as nonchalantly as I can. "Matty. The other day, he was excited about something and grabbed me a little too hard. No big deal."

The lie burns, but it flows off my tongue so smoothly. I've perfected this art over the years, though Huckslee is usually the one I'm blaming.

His nostrils flare as he looks at the bruises, pupils dilating in what I can only describe as pure rage. His jaw ticks at the corners, and for some reason, it looks like he's really fucking bothered by it.

"Hey," I reach up, pressing my thumb into the crease between his brows, "it's fine. It was an accident. Matt's a big doofus who doesn't know his own strength."

It's honestly the truth. As a kid, he got so excited about holding a baby duck that he accidentally squished it. His sister made me promise never to tell.

Huck is quiet for a moment before he leans down, closing the distance between us as he touches his lips to my collarbone and fuck. My barely deflated cock swells to life.

"I don't like seeing someone else's marks on you," he whispers into my skin, pressing soft kisses over my bruises like I'm some precious thing that requires care. It's something I'm used to getting from a girl, but from a guy? From Huck? The way he's trailing his hands down my chest, worshiping my throat with his tongue...it's completely different. Foreign. Uncharted territory.

My shirt lifts as his fingers push beneath it, running over my abs, and I squirm, breathing out a laugh. He raises his head to peek at me curiously.

"Ticklish." I bite my lip, and he gives me the brightest smile. It's so different from the strained, fake one I'm accustomed to seeing, lighting up his entire face. I'm slightly mesmerized when he kisses his way down my sternum.

"You didn't get to come last night." His teeth sink gently into my hip, forcing a groan out of me. My pulse quickens when his hand palms my cock outside my pants, rubbing firmly, deliberately, with slow strokes that I chase on a thrust. The tip of his tongue flicks out to lick the skin on my lower abdomen, and I almost come right there, swear to fucking God.

It's when his fingers tease the waistband of my sweats, though, that everything shifts. He tugs slightly, attempting to pull them down to release my cock, and immediately I clam up.

My father's voice roars through my head, every hateful word cracking my skull like a thunderclap. All of his threats shove to the surface, the fear of getting beaten to death and my bike taken away tangibly potent. His murderous face flashes in my mind's eye, gripping my arms when he threw me from the front porch at twelve, and I can't.

*I can't.*

"Wait, Huck." I grab both of his hands, halting his movements. "Stop. Stop"

"What's wrong?" His eyes snap to mine as he goes still, brows creasing in concern.

I moisten my lips nervously, my brain a puzzled mess. "I just...don't want to be touched...by you."

*Fucking hell.*

That last part wasn't on purpose.

Hurt flashes across his face, swiftly followed by anger, and he's off the bed before I can even process what the fuck I just said.

"No, Huck, I didn't mean—"

He retreats to the furthest side of the room near his closet, crossing his arms over his chest as if to protect himself from some metaphorical blow, and it feels like I'm inhaling glass.

"You don't want me to touch you," he repeats flatly, eyes growing colder than I've ever seen them.

Quickly rising from the bed, I face him with my palms up. "That's not what I meant."

"Explain it then, Taylor."

My lips part and then close. Part again. Nothing comes out because I don't even know what's happening in this fucked up head of mine right now. Everything's jumbled, thoughts and feelings as confusing as the next.

"Fucking say something," Huck snarls, and my self-control snaps.

"I don't fucking know," I yell angrily, and he grimaces as it echoes throughout the quiet house. "Okay? I. Don't. Know. I'm not... I've never done this type of shit before, Huckslee. I'm not like you!"

"Like what?" he spits frigidly. "Gay?"

"YES!"

*God-fucking-dammit.*

He scoffs, glaring at me incredulously. "What's your thought process here, Taylor? Enlighten me. Touching a dude's dick, jerking him off, isn't gay, but having *your* dick touched by another dude *is?*"

Is that it? Is that why I feel like I'm on the verge of a meltdown right now? It doesn't feel right...but nothing else makes sense.

"And what about kissing a guy?" Huck continues, seething at me from the corner while I feel strapped to a runaway roller coaster, and it's on fire. "Because your tongue was pretty far down my throat last night. Is that not gay?"

He's making valid points. I know he is. So why does it feel like the air is being siphoned from my lungs by a vacuum? Why does my heart feel like it's trying to climb into my throat?

Last night, when I touched Huck like that, I didn't even think about it. It felt like it came naturally to hold and kiss him like we were just two ordinary people sharing a moment. So I know, I *know* it's not the kissing part that's freaking me out right now. It's my fucking dick, apparently. Is he right? Does the thought of another guy touching it make me disgusted? The idea of him?

No.

So, what the fuck?

"Get out, Taylor," he snarls, and I blurt out the only thing I can think of.

"I've got a girlfriend."

He blinks, downright flabbergasted. "What?"

I swallow, glancing away. "I'm dating Salem. We broke up for a while, but we're back together now, so..."

It's a shitty excuse, but it's the only one I've got right now—at least until I figure out my shit.

He stares at me silently for a few minutes, his eyes jumping back and forth between mine.

Eventually, he turns his back to me, facing his closet, hands running through his hair. "Just...go, Taylor."

The defeat in those three words feels like a knife to my chest. I don't want to go. What's happening with my dick right now may be confusing as hell, but one thing for sure is that *I do not want to leave.*

"Huck..."

"Get the fuck out!"

Flinching, I step toward the door, stopping only once to look back at him, pleading silently for him to meet my gaze. He doesn't. So I leave without another word, the door softly closing behind me.

# HUCKSLEE

Taylor is smoking weed in the house again.

I can smell it, wafting down the hallway. Usually, he opens his window, but he's probably drunk. He's been drinking all week.

Shaking my head, I lean back over my desk as the sounds of laughter from downstairs filter up the stairs. Dad's annual New Year's Eve party is in full swing, the one night out of the year when he indulges in wine. Since it's the first year with Maisie, her friends are over, too. He invited us to come down and play board games, but I wasn't in the mood. Neither was Taylor.

Glancing over at my phone, I resist the urge to pull up his message thread. He's been texting me all day like a drunken idiot from his bedroom, but I haven't responded. Focusing on the panel for the comic I'm working on, I try to block out the memory of what he did to me in the bathroom yesterday, but it's been at the forefront of my mind since I opened my eyes.

*Steam from the shower fills the bathroom, thick and heavy. The heat from the water feels good against my skin as I stand under the spray, letting it roll off my back. It soothes the slight ache in my arm that's been present ever since Taylor held me under in the pool. I know I should be worried about it—fractures can be delicate. But the pain has been serving as a reminder this past week that what happened wasn't in my head.*

*Tipping back my chin, I run my fingers through my wet curls, closing my eyes as I remember what it felt like when Taylor touched me. Everything has been so confusing between us. We've barely spoken since I kicked him out of my room, and the few times I've caught him in the kitchen or passed him in the hallway, he's been plastered. Dad ungrounded us for the Winter break, and Taylor spent Christmas at his dad's, plus a day in the mountains with his friends. Not having him here was a welcome reprieve from the chaos of feelings that cyclone inside me whenever he's near.*

*Five months ago, his status in my life was clear. Public enemy number fucking one. Then he kissed me on the track, which threw me for one hell of a loop. Still, he was the bad guy—my bully. But then...*

*I don't fucking know what he is to me anymore. Everything changed that night in the pool, at least for me. For him? He made his intentions clear the morning after when he cringed at my touch. What happened between us altered my fucking brain chemistry, but to him, it was a game. Another way to mess with me.*

*Pounding on the door breaks me out of my thoughts, and Taylor's angry voice invades the bathroom.*

*"Huckslee! Open the fuck up, man. You've been in there for forty-five minutes!"*

*Are you kidding me?*

*"Go away," I growl, reaching for my body wash, but the banging intensifies.*

*"I'll kick the door down, dude. Swear to God."*

*I can hear a slight slur to his speech even over the shower, and with another growl of annoyance, I leave the water running as I step out. Wrapping a towel around my waist, I yank the door open to see an irate Taylor standing in the hallway with his arms folded, his dark hair a mess. He's wearing a new shirt with a zombie unicorn holding a severed arm in its mouth on the front. He wears the weirdest fucking t-shirts.*

*His eyes take in my bare torso, sweeping from the V in between my hips up to my neck when I swallow. It's a slow perusal, and the way his cheeks slightly flush sends a flow of blood to my groin. When his eyes jump up to mine, they're glassy and unfocused, his pupils blown out.*

*"I need to brush my teeth." He rushes in almost frantically, and I grimace when the smell of whiskey hits my nose. "Maisie's making me help decorate for their stupid party."*

*And he needs to hide the alcohol on his breath. Right.*

*Turning around, I make my way back toward the shower. "Make it quick."*

*He scoffs, but I ignore him as I close the shower door and whip off the towel. My cock is semi-hard now at the nearness of his presence, and as I wash my body, all I can think is, thank fuck for frosted glass. I hear the cabinet open, and the sink turn on, so I tune him out while I wash my hair.*

*Several moments later, the shower door opens, and I spin around in shock to see Taylor stepping over the lip of the tub, fully clothed.*

*"What the fuck—"*

*His mouth slams into mine, and for a moment, all I can do is freeze. His arms wrap around my neck, sealing us together as his tongue brushes the seam of my lips, seeking entry.*

*I know I should push him away because he's drunk, and our parents are home. And he's my stepbrother, and he's dating Salem, and he's Taylor. There are a million reasons why this is wrong.*

*So why does my mouth part for him, a groan leaving my throat at the first touch of our tongues? Why do my palms come up to cup his chin, tilting it to give myself deeper access while he holds on to me for dear life?*

*Why do my eyes sink closed as I savor his taste—mint with the slightest trace of whiskey left?*

*Why is this happening to me?*

*My teeth catch his bottom lip, pulling a whimper out of him. He thrusts against me, and I can feel his hard dick inside his basketball shorts rubbing against mine. The friction is delicious, little zaps of pleasure skittering across my shaft with every roll of his hips. We devour each other, entangling and melting together until his ending and my beginning fuse.*

*He moves backward until he collides with the shower wall, bracing himself between it and my chest. When I open my eyes and pull back to breathe, the expression on his face almost sends me to my knees. He looks fucking wrecked, lips swollen and jaw red from where I gripped him. His eyes look more blue in this moment, darkened with anguish and brimming with...*

*Tears.*

*My heart skips a beat.*

*"Touch me," he whispers desperately before I can speak, pressing his lips to mine. "Touch me, Huck."*

*But I hear the uncertainty in his voice. His body stiffens, and his fingers twitch nervously against my neck, almost like he's forcing himself to do this. It feels like a kick in the chest.*

*"You're drunk, Taylor." I go to pull away, my face hardening with disgust at myself for letting him play me like this again, but his hold tightens, and he presses his face into my shoulder.*

*"Please, Huckslee. I need you."*

*"Let me go."*

*He shakes his head, hair tickling my chin, before grabbing my hand and placing it on the waistband of his shorts. I try to back away again, but when his fingers wrap around my cock, any fight left in me goes out the window.*

*"Do it," he whispers, kissing the side of my neck as he strokes me slowly. "I want you to do it."*

*So I give him what he wants, despite every warning bell blaring inside my head. Despite the sinking feeling in my gut screaming at me that this is a bad idea, I slowly slip my hand into the hem of his shorts and wrap myself around him.*

*And fuck, he's enormous. Bigger than what I initially thought when I'd felt him with just material separating us. He gasps against my wet skin as I work my hand from base to tip, running my thumb over the slit of his swollen crown. He hisses, shuddering, but doesn't raise his head. Doesn't pull away. So I take that as my cue to continue, jerking him inside his shorts while he jerks me. Our heavy breaths fill the shower, both of us fighting to keep our groans quiet. His tongue darts out to lick his lips, brushing against my throat, and I decide that I want those lips on mine before I come.*

*However, when I pull back to lift his face to mine, what I see stops me completely.*

*Taylor's lips are tight, his eyes squeezed shut, and his brows furrowed as if this is physically painful for him. And right at that moment, I realize that his cock is going soft in my hands.*

*I'm on the other side of the shower in an instant, my back pressed against the opposite wall, embarrassment flooding my cheeks.*

*"Wait, Huck—" He steps toward me, shame filling his eyes, but I hold up my arm in a defensive gesture as I shake my head.*

*Am I that ugly to him? Is my touch so revolting that it makes him look like he wants to vomit? My stomach churns at the thought.*

*"Leave," I try to snap, but it comes out hollow. My throat feels like it's on fire.*

*"Please, Huckslee, I don't—" He thumps the back of his head against the wall twice. "I don't fucking get it."*

*A harsh, disbelieving laugh leaves my mouth, realization dawning on me. I don't need to ask him what he doesn't get because I already know. I've been nothing but an experiment to him, a test subject to quench his curiosity. He used me.*

*Maisie's voice comes from the bottom of the stairs, and we both freeze.*

*"TAYLOR! Did I say five minutes or five hours? Get down here now."*

*"In a minute," he shouts back, his eyes watching me cautiously.*

*Pointing my finger toward the door, I bare my teeth at him. "Get out. For good this time, Taylor. Touch me again, and I'll hurt you."*

*Because I will, so help me, God. I'm done being his punching bag. For almost four years now, I've dealt with this.*

*He opens his mouth as if to protest but thinks better of it when he meets the resolve in my eyes. The outrage. The pain.*

*Nodding resignedly, he licks his lips slowly as if to savor my taste one last time before stepping out of the shower.*

*"I'm sorry, Huck," he whispers, then he's gone—leaving me to pick up the pieces of myself in his aftermath, like always.*

Raised voices draw me out of the memory, and I blink into my sketchbook. My neck is sore, fingers cramped where they held the colored pencil in a white-knuckle grip.

Jesus. How long have I been sitting here like this?

Another string of angry voices comes from behind my door, this time much closer, and I frown as I turn in my seat, listening.

Maisie's shrill shout hits my ears. "I will not live under the same roof as another drug addict!"

What the hell?

"It's fucking weed, Maisie, not heroin," Taylor snaps in reply, and my breath catches.

Oh shit.

More words are exchanged between them, drowned out by the dread now pounding in my ears, and when I hear Dad bellowing loudly, I'm off my seat and out the door in the blink of an eye.

"You will not talk to my wife that way!" Dad is shouting into Taylor's open door, face red, and I don't think I've ever seen him look this mad. Maisie is beside him, equally as enraged.

"I will not have this in my home, and if you continue to act this way, you will leave."

I stiffen, confused about what the fuck is happening and wondering how the hell I'm supposed to stop it.

"I don't want to fucking be here anyway," Taylor shouts back, shoving past my dad into the hallway. He doesn't even look at me as he passes, so I catch him on the arm when he reaches the stairs.

"What happened?"

I don't know why I ask. It's pretty fucking obvious his mom smelled the marijuana just like I did and came looking.

"Get off me." He rips his arm from my grip, speech as slurred as it was yesterday, and I'm frozen on the stairs in bewilderment as I hear the front door slam shut. It echoes loudly through the quiet house, making me realize their party must have ended while I was lost in my head. Had it struck midnight already?

"Dad, what's going on?"

"Go to bed, Huckslee." Dad is leading Maisie down the stairs, and I can't help but notice that he looks more upset about what just happened than she does. There's an odd glint in her eye, something close to relief. It sets me on edge.

I follow them down into the living room. "Did you just kick Taylor out?"

Maisie answers, her thin lips pursed, "he needs to understand that there are consequences for his actions."

"I'll not have drug use or abusive language in this house." Dad takes off his glasses to scrub a hand down his face. "We gave him multiple chances."

"What? When?"

They've caught him smoking before?

Why didn't I know about it?

Dad gives me a weary sigh. "It's late, Huck. Go to bed."

"But..." I feel so completely lost right now and unsure how to feel. "What about Taylor?"

He stares at me for a long moment. "Give him the night to sober up. I'll call him in the morning and see if he's ready to have an adult conversation without slinging insults."

My blood boils instantly. "He *insulted* you?!"

"Go to bed, son."

There's a finality in his voice that has me spinning on my heel and heading back toward my room, head swimming.

When I reach my room, I open Taylor's texts to send a message.

> Me: What the fuck did you say to my dad?

He never reads it.

And the hatred I'm feeling at everything he's done festers. So I text him again.

> Me: You know, my dad's done a lot for you that he didn't have to. You treat him and everyone around you like shit. Maybe you should just stay gone.

He never reads that message, either.

Looking back, I probably should have taken his silence as a warning. Taylor never ignores my texts. But I'm so done with him, and all of his bullshit that I take one of my meds to calm the thoughts that are opening a black pit inside my head, ignoring the feeling in my gut that's screaming *something is very, very wrong.*

Hours later, after falling into a restless sleep, Dad throws open my bedroom door, startling me awake. He flicks on the top light and rushes in, a phone pressed to his ear with panic in his voice. "Huckslee, did you give Taylor your car keys?"

"What?"

Quickly jumping from my bed, I pull down the blinds to look down into the driveway. Sure enough, my Honda is missing.

"Huck." Dad's hand lands on my shoulder, and when I take in the alarm in his eyes, it feels like the ground just opened up and tossed me into free fall. "Son, there's been an accident."

# TAYLOR

## MARCH

"**I** need you to give me something here, Taylor. Anything."

*Unlikely.*

With my head resting against the plush back of a sofa chair, I keep my eyes trained out the window. It's only light flurries today, soft flakes drifting down lazily to mix with the slush already covering the ground. It's still snowing in March, can you fucking believe that shit? Winter in Utah is temperamental. Some years, the snow starts in January. For others, it doesn't stop until May.

For the sake of the race next month, I sincerely hope this shit stops by then.

"Taylor, are you listening to me?"

*Trying not to.*

I hear a heavy sigh and roll my head to peek at the woman sitting behind a stylish black desk. She's rubbing her temples, pink lips pursed. Clearly annoyed with me.

"Do you know why you're here?" She asks, pulling the wool cardigan tighter around her to ward off the chill in the room.

"Because I'm forced to be," I mutter, feeling around my jacket for a pack of smokes out of habit. There's none there, which irritates me further. Ran out two days ago and haven't had money for more.

"Court ordered, yes," she agrees, nodding her head of peppered brown hair. "And in order to eventually pass these sessions, Taylor, you actually have to talk with me."

Which is fucking bullshit. All of it. How a judge can force someone into shit like this should be illegal. I tell her as much.

"No, what *you* did was illegal," she says firmly, "which led us here. Now, we can talk about what happened, or I can tell the judge you refused, and you can spend some time in a cell."

My brows raise slightly as I give her a look. Fuck kind of therapist is she? Aren't they supposed to be all light and rainbows and shit?

"Let's start with the holidays." Doctor Hart picks up a pen and flips open her notebook. "How was your Christmas?"

"Fantastic," I snap sarcastically, facing the window again. "How was yours?"

It really wasn't, but that's not unlike any other year, so what else is new?

"Mine was great, thank you for asking. But we aren't talking about me. Did you get any gifts?"

Fuck, I really need a cigarette.

"I guess."

"What gifts did you get?"

Squinting over at her, I scoff. "Weed. Obviously."

*Thanks, Christian.*

She flashes me a smile. "Obviously. And from your parents?"

"Socks and a bath towel from Maisie. Nothing from my father."

*Unless you count the knuckle sandwich he gave me.*

"Is that normal for them?"

Rolling my eyes at the atypical shrink question, I shrug and return to the window. "It's...whatever."

Honestly, it's the first Christmas gift Maisie had gotten me in nearly a decade, so there's that. The bath towel was soft, at least.

"Anything from your stepdad or stepbrother?"

My throat closes at the mention of Huck, and I grit my teeth as I shake my head. I can't bring myself to tell her about the brand-new motocross jacket Aaron picked out for me.

"Now, let's talk about what happened on New Year's Eve."

*Let's fucking not, Doc.*

Blowing a dirty strand of hair out of my eyes, I let my head fall back against the cushion to gaze at the ceiling. "You wouldn't happen to have a smoke, would you?"

Duh. Of course, she doesn't.

Doctor Hart raises a thin brow and sits back in her seat but says nothing, waiting for me to start the conversation.

"Not much to talk about. I got caught smoking weed in the house, and the Good Bishop kicked me out. That's it."

Five months. I made it five months before he gave up on me, too.

She taps her pen before writing something down. "Bishop Davis kicked you out, or your mother did?"

"It was a joint effort," I respond with a sneer.

"According to the police report, you and your mother fought. Is that correct?"

Fuck, this woman's nosy.

"Not really a fight. We yelled at each other."

She glances up. "Is that not a fight?"

"No. A fight involves fists. We had an argument that she blew out of proportion because she never wanted me there in the first place."

"What makes you say that?"

My head pushes back into the cushion again. "Because. She had no interest in my life up until she remarried. It was his idea to make us all live under one roof in the first place."

"So you were estranged?"

Nah, nope. Not talking about my shitty childhood. If I'm forced to talk, I'll talk, but only about the shit I need to.

"Look, I argued with Maisie, and then Aaron told me to leave. That's what happened. Happy fucking New Year."

I'm not going to mention the fact that I called Maisie a cunt. Or that I yelled *'fuck your church, fuck this house, fuck your family.'*

I fucking lost it, okay? After what happened the morning after the pool with Huck...I pretty much spent the entire week of Christmas break high and drunk off my ass.

"So you borrowed your stepbrother's car," she prompts, and I can't hide my flinch.

"Yeah."

I didn't borrow Huck's car—I *stole* it with the spare key I took the night I drove him home from the pool. But like the fucking saint he is, he told the cops that I had permission to drive it, probably getting himself into trouble in the process.

"And where did you go after you left?"

Swallowing hard, I stare down at my hands folded on my lap. "To my Dad's place."

Biggest mistake of my life. One I'll regret until the day I die. Absently, I reach up and touch the scar that now lines my face from brow to cheek.

The therapist continues. "Tell me what happened."

"We fought."

Understatement. He beat me within inches of my life because I provoked him like a fucking idiot. Poked the sleeping bear, if you will.

"Fought?" She looks at me with a knowing smile. "Not argued?"

Shit.

You got me there, Doc.

"Things got heated," I admit, shrugging it off, "words were exchanged. I left."

"And then the accident happened."

"Yep."

'Accident' isn't the term I'd use for what happened. I knew full well what I was doing. I just didn't understand how bad it would fuck everything up.

"You wrapped your stepbrother's car around a tree, Taylor. Ended up in the hospital for a month. You could have killed someone."

"No shit, Doc," I snap irritably, my patience thinner than usual these days. "That's why I'm here, isn't it?"

I hadn't even been inside the car. But shifting into neutral and a steep incline had done the trick. It was the only thing I could think of to explain the injuries. But I'd also been drunk, high, concussed, and in massive amounts of pain, so looking back, I hadn't been in the best state of mind.

"Let's go over your injuries." She pulls out a manilla folder and flips it open. "Multiple broken ribs. Ruptured spleen. A head injury."

Her eyes flick up, studying the scar on my brow. Yeah, none of that was caused by a car accident. Just dear old dad. They had to wire my jaw shut for six weeks, and eating through a straw got old real quick. I'll forever be thankful for Christian's mom—that lady is an angel for taking care of me. I broke down in the hospital and finally told my best friend everything about the shit with my father, and I'm pretty sure he told her, which is why she's been so good to me.

"You had to have been going pretty fast. What was the fight with your father about that affected you so much?"

A harsh, bitter laugh exits my mouth. "That's the thing, Doc. It doesn't take much with him. He's a drug addict with a temper. Just breathing wrong is enough to flip his switch."

"Is that what you did?" She folds her arms, crossing her legs at the ankles under her desk. "Breathed wrong?"

No.

To be honest, I don't even remember what started the fight.

I remember leaving the house pissed off at the world, pissed off at myself because Huck wouldn't talk to me, and that's all I fucking wanted him to do.

I remember being confused and jumping into his car because my fucked up brain thought that maybe he'd come after me for it.

Pulling into Arbitrary Hills is a solid memory, but after that, it gets blurry. I'm pretty sure I went straight to the fridge when I got into the trailer and gunshot two beers, which pissed off my dad. And then it just...escalated from there. I blamed him for Maisie hating me and for fucking up my head; he blamed me for her leaving us. Shit hit the fan real quick. Then I left before he could kill me and just...drove. Drove until I couldn't handle the pain anymore.

As they say, the rest is history.

"Have you spoken to anyone in your family recently?"

*Maybe it's best if you just stay gone.*

"Nah." I glance at the clock, realizing with relief that this hour of hell is almost up. "Don't want to."

Maisie and Aaron were at the hospital in the beginning, mainly to answer questions from the cops when they ran the plates and found out the car didn't belong to me. As for Huck...

I haven't seen or heard from him in three months, not even when I was lying in a hospital bed recovering from surgery. Christian, Salem, Matty, and Xed were the only people who came to see me. The only people that matter, really. For what it's worth, Aaron did try to visit, but...I refused to see him. Couldn't bring myself to look him in the eye.

Since my fuck up had to happen, unfortunately, after the age of eighteen, Maisie and my father have no legal responsibility to get me out of trouble. This shit all falls on me, which is why I'm here—in court-ordered therapy, on probation, pissing in a cup three times a week. Oh, and four hundred hours of community service.

Ain't life fun?

My only saving grace in all of this is the fact that Huckslee's lie essentially saved me from prison time due to auto theft. And I hate the feeling that leaves me with.

"I hear you haven't been back to school?" Doctor Hart continues to write in her little notebook, not looking at me. I shake my head.

"Decided to drop out. I enrolled to get my GED."

Honestly, it's fine. School was never my strong suit, anyway. I was barely passing enough to skirt by, mainly going just to escape. See my friends. Antagonize Huck.

I hate how much I miss him. Hearing his dumb music from the bathroom when he showers every night, his messy curls when he comes down the stairs first thing in the morning. Seeing him in the halls at school, watching him at football practice. Fighting with him. His voice. The kisses...

I hate it even more that I admit to missing him at all.

The urge to glare down at my dick is strong. *So you could get hard at the thought of him touching you, but not when it actually came down to it?* Make it make sense, motherfucker.

"So, what do you say, Doc?" I rise from the chair and stretch as the clock strikes the hour. "Do I pass your little test? Can I go now?"

She gives me that sweet smile that pisses me off, flipping her notebook closed before folding her hands on the desk.

"You're free to go. I'll see you next week for session number two."

*What the fuck?*

"I've done my three sessions," I argue angrily, but she shakes her head.

"No, Taylor. We met two previous times, and you sat in silence until the time ran out. It doesn't count unless we talk. See you next week."

Fuck my fucking life.

# HUCKSLEE

## APRIL

C hilled wind penetrates the material of my Carhart, sending shivers through my body.

Though the sun is out and the snow has melted enough,
winter still refuses to release its icy grip. Lifting my hands to
blow warmth into them, I gaze out over the lake in front of me.
The waters are calm and quiet today. So far, there's no crowd
here this early, making it perfect for fishing.

"Here, son." Dad hands me a cup of hot chocolate he
poured from the thermos before making two more for Logan
and his dad, Joel. It's our first fishing trip since the snow
melted, and I can tell Dad and Joel are excited. They've been
talking about this trip for weeks. Even Logan looks content as
he sips his drink, keeping an eye on his fishing pole.

I wish I could enjoy it as they do. I wish I could enjoy
anything at all.

"So let's hear the good news," Joel pipes up, his bearded face entering my peripheral as he leans forward in his camping chair to look at me with a grin. His eyes are wrinkled around the corners like he's spent many years genuinely laughing and smiling. Must be nice.

When I don't immediately speak because my brain is soup these days thanks to the new meds, my dad smacks a hand proudly against my shoulder.

"Tell him about the scholarship, Huck." I can see the worry in his eyes, but fuck if I can do anything to take it away other than pull my lips into what I hope is a convincing smile.

"I accepted a scholarship to UofU." There's no emotion in my tone, so I try to force it. "I'll be playing for the Utes in the fall."

Dad's smile falters, but Joel doesn't seem to notice. He nods, laughing and congratulating me before asking if I'll be playing with any of my high school teammates.

"Matthew Albrecht, I think."

Not everyone qualified for a scholarship, and not everyone on the team is attending college. Most of them will graduate and get jobs here in town. Settle down, marry, and have eight kids. Something I'm sure my dad wishes for me.

*Hate to disappoint you, pops.*

Dad and Joel begin conversing about college football brackets, and I try to stay present, but it's hard. Everything feels fuzzy most days. The doctor had said to give this shit time to work, for my body to acclimate, but I'm tired of feeling like I'm moving through mud.

Logan's eyes scan my face, watching me with that concerned look he's had since I broke down and begged him to drive me out to the city two months ago. I was desperate, hadn't slept in nearly a week, and on the verge of delirium. Since I currently have no car, I had no choice. I had to ask him to take me to my doctor because the anxiety and insomnia felt like they were killing me. And the guilt. So much fucking guilt. Two different failed medications later, and this is the result.

"You okay?" He asks quietly for the hundredth time this morning; all I can do is nod.

I'm not really, but I'm not *bad*, either. Not only does this stuff tamp down the anxiety, but everything else, too. I haven't decided if I like it. The last medication I tried didn't make me feel this numb, but the nightmares from it were brutal. Dreams of Taylor's body mutilated and twisted from the crash, his rotting corpse holding me under water...

Yeah, it's been a fucked up few months since he left.

"Got one!" Dad grabs his pole and yanks it back, reeling in the line. Logan and Joel are on the edge of their seats, waiting to see what he pulls out of the water. He struggles with it for a moment before a large brown trout breaks the surface, mouth impaled on his hook, and all three of them seem giddy with excitement.

Used to be something I got excited about, too. But now I don't even know anymore.

"You see, son?" Dad holds up the fish with a grin, and I can see behind his glasses that his eyes are searching for something, expecting a reaction from the Huck that would have been buzzing and offering to take a goofy picture for social media. But I feel like that guy drowned in a pool in December, so I nod and smile, flashing him a thumbs-up. If I could feel anything, the disappointment that flashes across his face would have gutted me more than the trout is about to become.

I can't be everything he wants me to be.

Even Royce has started noticing the difference in me. We started officially dating—albeit secretly because even though he finally came out to his family and his school, I never will. I haven't felt up to seeing him lately. Something he said back in February struck a chord with me, made me realize how fucked up everything really is.

*Some people have a hard time giving up control. It can be scary, letting someone have all that power over you.*

I never have control. Never have a choice. I'm trapped in this pit of expectations Dad holds for me, and it feels like I'll never escape. He's even over there talking like I'll be living at home while going to college, and I can't find it in me to tell him no. He's done so much for me already; all I do is disappoint him. Tack on the way Taylor used me for his own curiosity, made me feel like maybe something was there between us, and then took away my only form of freedom by crashing it into a tree...

I didn't even visit him in the fucking hospital. Because I couldn't bring myself to look at him after what he did.

Dad, Joel, and Logan continue to fish and bullshit for a few more hours. I interject when I can. Finally, Joel decides to call it a day, and we all load everything into both cars.

"Well," Dad says once everything is packed up, "Joel and I want to hit the range and shoot a couple of clay pigeons while the wives are busy doing their own thing. You boys want to come?"

I really don't. The thought of being around a gun in this state of mind makes me nervous, not for everyone else's safety but my own. Logan must sense it, too, because he tells our dads that he'll drop me off at home and meet them there.

"Thank you," I say to him as we're buckling ourselves into his dad's Range Rover, and his honey eyes glance at me sideways.

"I'm worried about you, Huck."

We pull away from the lake just as a line of cars pass to get in, likely for a day of BBQing and swimming if it warms up.

"I know."

"Look, I know that Taylor's accident was hard on you. But I just don't understand why. You haven't even talked to him."

I sigh because this isn't the first time we've had this conversation since he took me to see my doctor. I've shut him down the last two times he's tried talking with me about it.

Logan continues as we pull onto the main road. "I mean, he was always an asshole, right? He made school terrible for you. Stealing your car and wrecking it was honestly the most Taylor thing he could have done."

Of course, he knew about the car theft thing. I may have told Dad and the cops I gave permission, but Logan is my best friend.

"Just...help me understand, Huck. You can talk to me, man. I'm here for you."

*But for how long?*

It's on the tip of my tongue to ask, but I don't. It would just lead him to more questions I don't think he's ready for me to answer.

"I know, Loge. I know you are. I just..." Shaking my head, I try to sort through my muddled thoughts. "It got too much, you know? The wedding, living with him." *Kissing him.* "On top of the swim team and entrance exams and scholarship deadlines, preparing for graduation, it's all just a lot right now."

He looks at me like he doesn't believe me for a second but lets it go, much to my relief. We make the rest of the drive back to my house in silence, catchy pop music occupying my mind from the radio. When he pulls into the driveway and I see who's walking out of the garage...my heart starts to pound almost painfully in my chest.

Taylor slows to a stop at the same time we do, his bike by his side, the duffle bag he showed up with last year hanging from his arm. There's a frown on his face as he stares at us from where he stands, just as we stare back, and the way he shifts on his feet has my stomach doing flips, and holy shit, am I nervous right now? Am I actually feeling something?

"Do you want me to stay?" Logan murmurs, his brows furrowed, but I quickly shake my head.

"No. No, no. It's fine. Have fun at the range."

There's more emotion in my voice than I've heard in weeks, and Logan also realizes by the wide-eyed look he gives me. I wave him off, exiting the vehicle before heading up the driveway.

Taylor says nothing as he watches me approach, expression blank. I don't mean to get as close to him as I do, but when I'm within touching distance, it feels like I'm a satellite that's finally returned to orbit.

I was knocked out of his gravitational pull, but now I'm back in place.

He's wearing a Metal Mulisha beanie and a denim jacket with band patches sewn into it, dark hair longer than the last time I saw him. He looks gaunt, and his blue-green eyes are dull–

Holy shit.

My stomach bottoms out when I notice the fucking scar.

I can see the stitch marks running from the corner of his brow to just under his cheek. It's jagged and thick, giving his pretty features a more rugged look.

But Jesus. How bad had the injury been to create a scar like that?

"Hey," he says slowly, taking me in silently with cautious eyes as I internally freak out.

I've decided. I liked it better when I felt nothing.

"Hey," is all I respond because what else am I supposed to say to someone I've ignored for four months?

It's awkward momentarily, both of us studying the other before he looks away.

"I didn't think anyone would be home." He swallows, and I watch the strong column of his throat flex with the movement. "Needed to come by and grab the shit I left. I still remembered the garage code, so..."

My lungs squeeze as I try to calm my breathing, not realizing until now that I'd been holding onto the hope he'd come back if his stuff was still here.

Fucking hell, when did I go from dreading living with him to hating when he left? One handjob in a pool was enough to shift my entire focus?

*Because it wasn't just the handjob.*

It was the fact that it came from Taylor fucking Tottman.

I wrack my brain to respond, but it still feels like I'm running on Internet Explorer. My mouth opens, and I pray that something at least half intelligible comes out when the bag at his hip jerks. A loud cry comes from the duffle, and my eyes widen as Taylor rolls his lips.

"Are you–" I cough. "Are you kidnapping the cat?"

A brief flash of his sheepish smile appears before it's gone, taking my heart with it when a scowl takes its place.

Not gonna lie; this hurts. I've grown attached to Lasagna over the last few months. On the nights when things get bad inside my head, having her curled up at the end of my bed or in my closet brings comfort. Feeding her, caring for her, even cleaning her litter box gives me something to focus on. A presence to look forward to. Dad had never allowed a pet before until last year.

Jesus, it feels like we're getting divorced, and he's taking the baby.

Taylor searches my face before dropping his gaze. Scuffing the ground with a toe of his Docs, he looks up from beneath his lashes. "I mean, I guess we could...share custody or something. Switch off every weekend."

Hope has me perking up, but I tamp it down immediately.

The offer feels like an olive branch, but that would mean seeing him at least once a week, and I don't think I can handle that. Instead of spending the last four months trying to process the shit that's happened between us, I've been busy burying it. And having him here now in front of me, looking like some sexy punk-rock motocross god, is blurring the lines that we already crossed in December. The lines I redrew the moment he stole my car. Because he used me, and it's clear that he's not ready to handle what's been happening between us, either.

Nothing can change history.

"No, it's fine," I find myself saying, even though my tongue feels raw forming the words. "She's been crying at your door for months, anyway. You're her person."

He nods, licking his bottom lip. "You gonna be racing next week?"

Feeling lightheaded, I hum a confirmation as I soak up the sight of him, searching for anything else that might be new while he seems to do the same. The urge to step into him and reacquaint myself with his mouth comes on strong, forcing my fists to clench, and I have to fold my arms to hide how badly they're shaking.

Eventually, Lasagna screams from his bag, breaking whatever daze we'd found ourselves in.

"Good luck, Huck," he whispers before wheeling his bike away. His shoulder brushes mine, sending an involuntary shiver through me, and before I know what I'm doing, my hand is gripped around his arm, pulling him toward me. I don't care that we're in the middle of the driveway in broad daylight—I need to kiss him. At least just once, even if it's the last time.

Even if it's to say goodbye to whatever this is between us. Just one kiss, and then we can go back to the fucked up way we were before.

But right before our mouths collide, he's snarling in my face.

"Why the fuck did you tell the cops that I borrowed your car?"

# TAYLOR

Huck blinks rapidly at me for several seconds, his face inches from mine as the grip on my arm loosens in shock.

"What?"

I tried to hold it all in—I really did. Even went as far as scoping the place out before entering the house to ensure no one was home because *I did not want this to happen.*

But then Logan pulled up with Huckslee in the passenger seat, and the moment he stepped out of that car looking cute as fuck in his oversized coat, I only saw rage. And hurt.

I wanted us to part on somewhat stable ground, but I know Huckslee. The way his eyes hyper-focused on my lips told me everything. So the minute he grabbed me, I knew. I fucking knew he was going to try to kiss me, and if I let him? It would be all over for me.

After four months of radio silence, that shit ain't flying.

"Why," I spit through clenched teeth. "Did you. Tell the cops. That I borrowed your car?"

He rears back, baring his teeth. "Are you fucking kidding me right now?"

"Dead serious." Yanking my arm from his grasp, I step back to put some much-needed space between us. "Why the hell would you lie to the cops, dude? You know how much trouble you could have gotten into for that?"

"Me? I did it to save your ass, motherfucker!"

"I didn't ask you to do that."

Those dark, starry eyes widen as he scoffs. "You're an ungrateful piece of shit, you know that?"

His words lack the normal bite I'm used to, like he's holding back, and it only fuels my fire.

"At least I own it, Huckslee." My leg swings over the seat of my bike as I seethe at him. "I don't pretend to be something I'm not."

"What is that supposed to mean?" He goes still, pupils dilating in quiet rage.

A mirthless laugh pushes past my lips. "Mister football star, with his good grades and his charming smile. But it's all bullshit. I know what's really underneath. You're a fucking fake."

"And you're a fucking hypocrite," he growls, suddenly in my face, "because I'm not the one telling himself he's not gay despite kissing and jerking a guy off in a goddamn pool!"

I'm off my bike instantly, Huckslee's coat gripped in my fist as my other one clocks back. He flinches, eyes squeezing shut to brace himself, and in that moment, I pause.

My heart is racing, blood rushing to my ears as I fight every impulse inside of me to punch his gorgeous fucking face in. Old Taylor would have done it without hesitation.

But I don't want to hurt him. I don't. I've hurt him enough.

So I pause. Take a breath. Close my eyes. Slowly lower my fist.

And step back, and back, until I'm once again on the bike.

When I open my eyes, Huck studies me like we're strangers, and it hits me that we *are*. It's unreal how quickly two people can change in four months.

"You weren't there," I accuse softly, gripping the handlebars. He must not have heard me because he tilts his head and steps closer. "I don't know what we are, Huckslee. Maybe at one point, I did, but all of that changed. And I know I can't undo everything I've done, but I almost fucking died, and you weren't there."

I tried to play it off like it didn't bother me, but that court-ordered therapist is actually good at her job. She presses into my bruises until I have no choice but to bleed, and honestly, it's cathartic. I've seen her more than just the three times I was supposed to. It feels good to talk to someone about stuff when you're not worried about their bullshit.

"My dad tried..." Huck's voice trails off, and my bike roars to life as I nod grimly.

"Yeah, he did. But you didn't."

With a deep breath, I throttle forward and leave without looking back because if I do, I'll drown in those damn dark eyes and never escape.

# HUCKSLEE

The rumble of my bike against the dirt shakes me so hard it rattles my teeth.

Twenty-five other racers envelop me, each fighting for first place on the track. Even though it's an exceptionally mild late spring day, I'm sweating in my gear from the adrenaline as I lean into a bend. We're in the second moto now, and the competitive spirit is palpable.

In officially sanctioned races, two thirty-minute motos around the track plus two additional laps determine the winner. Points are earned by winning, obviously. In the first moto, I placed third and was awarded twenty points. Taylor placed second, with twenty-two points. First place had twenty-five.

The terrain shifts, propelling me into a jump, and I search for Taylor's ugly yellow bike when I'm in the air. I've fallen back to seventh place, but I see him up ahead, battling for first with the girl who won the last race. They're currently neck and neck, and we have one lap left. Even though she won last time, he'll win if he places first this round. It doesn't matter if they have the same number of points. And I want him to win. I really fucking do.

Someone loses control of their bike in front of me, the front wheel shaking before they tip sideways and go flying. Jerking to the side, I narrowly avoid being clipped by their rolling body, but the movement throws me off balance, and I come around a bend too close to the edge of the track. It slows me down, allowing two more riders to pull ahead.

Fuck.

Ninth place is not where I want to be.

So I lean forward, shut out all the noise inside my head, and focus. Forget about everyone else rushing by or all the spectators on the sidelines; it's just me, my bike, and the dirt. Eventually, I make my way up the line to the front, two places behind Taylor. I recognize Christian from his helmet in third. From what I've seen, Taylor hasn't attempted any fancy tricks on the jumps, which tells me how badly he wants to win.

Three more bends until the finish line.

It's fucking nerve-wracking, trying to split my attention between not crashing and watching Taylor race. He's one of the best riders I've seen. His skills with his bike are phenomenal despite the crash back in August. When it comes down to it, Taylor is a fucking beast on the track. His wheel pulls ahead, followed by his opponent, and they dance until I can see the finish line in the distance.

So fucking close...

Twenty meters to go, and Christian seems to lose control. He hits a divot in the track wrong, spiraling out and hitting the ground hard. My heart jumps into my throat. I can't breathe beneath my helmet. His bike slams into the girl, causing her to veer sideways and into Taylor. All three of them go flying.

"*No!*"

The sound of motorbikes revving up drowns out my scream. The rest of us part to avoid hitting them, and when I fly by, I see Taylor curled on his side, not moving. Christian is crawling over to him.

Fuck!

*Please be okay, please be okay.*

It's between me and one other rider as the finish line draws closer, and a fire ignites in my blood.

If Taylor can't win that scholarship, I'll do it for him.

It's a gift I can offer him if nothing else.

Leaning forward, I grit my teeth and throw everything I have into crossing that line. Praying to whatever shred of relationship is left between me and the big man upstairs that I'm good enough to pull this off. Out of my peripheral, I see the rider beside me surge ahead, his wheel gaining an inch.

I gun it, heart pounding, pushing my bike as far as possible.

Three meters.

Two meters.

One.

My wheel passes over the finish line just inches before his, solidifying my first-place victory.

*I won the fucking race.*

And Taylor's scholarship.

# TAYLOR

"**I**'m so fucking sorry, dude."

Christian is standing next to me as I sit in the back of the ambulance, getting checked out by the EMTs, but I don't see him.

I'm staring at Huck across the track, where he stands at the podium, lifting his trophy. The crowd erupts into cheers.

My chest is on fire, and vaguely, I wonder how many times you can break a rib before it just disintegrates, but I know that's not the source of the pain I'm feeling. Resentment burns in my gut, despair filling my lungs so deep it feels like I'm breathing flame.

"Taylor, I'm sorry," Christian repeats, his face in anguish, and I tell him it's okay. It wasn't his fault. There will be other races, we haven't lost our chance at the amateur championships, yadda, fucking yadda.

No, just the scholarship. The only shot I had at college because let's be real here. My parents make too much to qualify for grants but not enough to pay for me. Even if they did, I wouldn't ask them for shit. Haven't even seen my father since the night he nearly killed me. Or Maisie, for that matter.

Fuck, this hurts.

Huck stands next to the official, who holds up a giant check with the scholarship money written on it. Jealousy and rage make me clench my fists so hard that my palm bleeds. Everything I've been through over the last few years, all the shit with my dad I've gone through such lengths to hide, it was all for this moment. And it's gone. Stolen by golden boy Huckslee Davis, who always gets everything he fucking wants. He doesn't even need a damn scholarship! He has a full ride waiting for him, and Matty does too. Christian has grants because of his heritage, and Xed has already been taking college classes since junior year. Salem, too. They're graduating high school with fucking associates degrees.

And now I'll never escape this place.

"We need to get that rib looked at," the EMT states. "You need an x-ray."

"Nah, fuck that." Jumping down from the back of the ambulance with a wince, I make my way toward the remains of my bike. "I'm fine."

I'm not fucking fine. Not even close.

"You should really go to the hospital, Tay." Christian follows me, and a flash of green in the distance reveals Xed's mohawk working toward us from the crowd, Matty close behind.

"I'm done with hospitals."

Done with doctors, done with drug court. Just fucking done.

I don't even care at this point if the crash re-ruptured my spleen, and I bleed out internally.

It already feels like I'm dying inside.

The four of us gather up the wreckage of mine and Christian's bikes and load them into his Bronco. Skin prickles on my neck, and I can feel Huck's gaze, but I don't seek it out. The thought of looking at him right now makes me violent. I need to leave before he tries to talk to me because I know he will. Despite all the times he's told me to leave him alone, he can't fucking stay away. Neither can I.

But I'm done with that.

"We dropping your bike off at your dad's shop?" Christian asks as he hops into the driver's seat, Xed and Matthew taking up the back, and my world just...

Stops. Slams to a halt so hard that I feel myself reeling from it.

"No. Take it to the dump," I spit through clenched teeth.

Because I'd rather spend the rest of my life never setting foot on a dirt bike track again than be in my father's presence.

Apparently, I'm done with motocross, too. And it feels like the line on a heart monitor just went flat.

# HUCKSLEE

## MAY

I honestly never thought I'd be going to senior prom.

Actually, I've never been to a school dance in my life. Why would I? It's not like I was ever interested in asking a girl to be my date, and it's not like I could show up with a guy. Well, I mean, I'm here with Logan. But that's different.

The high school auditorium is packed to the brim, bright swatches of varying colors from dresses and ties making my head spin. Strobe lights flash in time to the second-rate DJ in the corner as he plays some shitty remix. Streamers billow from the rafters, a banner with the quote *'the best way to predict the future is to create it together'* from Joe Echevarria hangs above the doors. This year's prom theme is unity. What a crock of shit.

"I was going to get us a drink, but uh..." Logan rubs the back of his neck. "Someone apparently spiked the punch."

Three guesses who.

My eyes immediately find Taylor for the thousandth time, where he stands against the stage. He's wearing the tuxedo my dad bought him for the wedding, only the red tie has been replaced with a black and white checkered one that matches Salem's shoes. She's wearing a short white dress that makes her red hair stand out like liquid fire, and a black rose corsage on her wrist matches his boutonniere. He doesn't even go to school anymore, but Salem does, so he's her date. They look gorgeous together, like a celebrity couple, and I hate how it makes my stomach ache.

"Beautiful, huh," Logan mumbles beside me, and I turn in surprise to find his gaze on them. On Salem.

Well. That's new.

"Yeah," I agree. "Beautiful."

But I'm not talking about Salem.

Taylor's been avoiding me all week since the race. I've tried everything I can think of to get him to talk to me, to tell him what I did for him, but all my attempts are shot down. I even showed up at Christian's house, where he's been staying, when I found out he had changed his damn number, but according to his best friend, he wasn't home. And no, he didn't know where to find him. And, yes, he'll tell him to text me or call me.

But Taylor never did. And he hasn't even glanced my way all evening, which hurts more than it should.

I feel antsy. Skittish. It's a side effect from a different medication since the last one made me feel like fucking Eyore from Winnie the Pooh, and I can tell it's another one I'm not going to like. I hate them all, honestly, but what can you do?

Sleep is a human necessity, and without it, I'll die. So until I can finally get some shut-eye, the Russian roulette of anxiety pills continues. I just wish they didn't make me feel like pitching myself headfirst off a bridge. I'm barely holding on.

*You're a fucking fake.*

Taylor's words from a month ago echo in my ears, making me flinch. He's not wrong. And this pretense is killing me.

My phone alerts me to a new text, and my stomach flips, followed by disappointment when I see it isn't Taylor. Which makes me feel like a douchebag because it's my boyfriend.

> Royce: Just pulled up to the parking lot. Meet me outside? :)

Right. The reason I'm here. Even though Royce knows I'm not ready to come out, he still wants to go to prom together. My school dance is this week, and I'll be going with him to his own prom next week. And I feel guilty as hell because I haven't been as attentive to him as I should have been. He should be with someone who's not ashamed to be with him, so I plan on breaking it off before I start school in the fall. Because he deserves better than me. I can't give him what he needs, but I will for tonight. To give him something happy to hold onto when I break his heart.

"Hey, my friend Royce is here," I tell Logan, who's still watching Salem slow dance with Taylor. "I'm going to go meet him."

He nods without breaking his gaze, and I frown at him before turning away, making a mental note to ask him about his behavior later. When I'm halfway out of the building, my phone goes off again, and I get a text from an unknown number.

> Unknown: Tell your best friend to stop eye fucking my girl.

My hands start to shake as my chest constricts. It's Taylor, I know it. I can feel it. And I'm pissed off as hell at him for ignoring me.

> Me: Who's this?

Petty, I know. Sue me.

> Taylor: You know who the fuck this is. And I don't like how you and your buddy have been looking at us all night. It's creepy as fuck. So get back in here and tell him to stop.

My cheeks heat from embarrassment. How dare he?

> Me: Tell him yourself.

And with that, I pocket my phone, fucking fuming, as I exit into the parking lot. Another text comes through, but I don't bother to read it because fuck him. He'd be in goddamn prison if it weren't for me, but who cares, right? Just more shit Huck does for Taylor that goes unnoticed and un-fucking-appreciated. I've been such a pushover for the last four years; it's not even funny. But still, I'm a nice person, so I quickly pull my phone out again to send Taylor's new contact info to the business guy at the motorsports park before stepping over to find my boyfriend.

"I thought you forgot about me." His voice comes from my left, and I turn to see his small form striding toward me. He looks...so damn handsome, wearing a beige tux that makes his dark skin glow, the brown hair on his head shaved close in a fade. His hazel eyes lighten as he smiles at me, and my head throbs with guilt. I feel like an impostor.

"Never." I lean down to kiss him on the cheek, and he brings out a box from behind his back.

"Surprise," he laughs, a small smile forming on my lips at the matching boutonnieres in his hand. He's always so sweet like this. I don't deserve it.

He pins my boutonniere on my jacket, fingers lingering on the collar. "You look lovely, babe."

"You, too," I respond quickly, blushing and mentally kicking myself for not telling him sooner. He chuckles, always so full of laughter, before squeezing my hand.

"Ready for prom?"

At his wink, I'm pulling him toward school with a nod. We've only been dating for three months, and though we text constantly, it's been a few weeks since we've seen each other. Being at two different schools on two different schedules makes hanging out hard. I wish I was a decent boyfriend and could say that it bothered me, but really...it doesn't. Texting is fine—it's safe. Face-to-face, though, is always tough for me because of the effort it takes to maintain my mask. People exhaust me.

*Except for Taylor because he sees me as I am.*

That thought intrudes my brain, and I shake my head to shove it away.

As we near the gym doors, I let go of Royce's hand with an apologetic wince. "Sorry."

He shakes his head quickly. "Don't be sorry. I know what it feels like, babe. Whatever you're comfortable with."

Fuck, he's too nice.

"Thank you," I murmur, pushing open the double doors and pulling him inside. When I look around for Logan, I find him surrounded by a small group of people, and as we near them, a sweat breaks out on my palms.

Taylor and Logan are in each other's faces, clearly locked in a heated argument.

*Shit.*

I shout over the music once we're close enough for them to hear. "Hey, what's going on?"

They both turn in my direction and when Taylor's eyes take in Royce, he freezes. There's a moment where something like pain crosses his features before it morphs into pure, unadulterated rage.

"Who the fuck are you?" He snarls, suddenly in my boyfriend's space.

"Royce. And you are?"

"This is Taylor." My throat closes around his name, so I clear it. "My stepbrother."

Around us, I notice Matthew, Xed, and Christian warily taking in the scene.

"Ah." Recognition sparks in Royce's eyes, and he stares up at Taylor with disdain. "The stepbrother who bullied you and stole your car."

*Double shit.*

Taylor goes rigid before swinging his eyes to me, hissing. "You *told* him?"

Yes, I told him. Because he's my boyfriend, and I felt like shit for lying about it.

A familiar voice from behind causes us all to go still. "Is there a problem here?"

*Triple shit.* This night just keeps getting worse.

Stealing my spine, I plaster on a smile and face my dad, who's sternly eyeing us. He and a few other parents volunteered to chaperone tonight.

"No problem, Dad." I keep my voice as light as possible.

Royce straightens at that, spinning to face my dad with his arm outstretched. "Bishop Davis, hi, I'm Huckslee's friend, Royce."

They shake hands, and it would have been a sweet moment if not for the scoff that shoots from Taylor's mouth. He's still looking at Royce murderously while Logan smirks down at Salem in a way I've never seen him do before. Matt, Xed, and Christian are bouncing their eyes around in anticipation as if this is some sort of thriller, and they even have a bag of popcorn. Where the hell did they get popcorn? I feel like I've entered the fucking twilight zone.

"I'm getting a drink," I mutter, leaving the group behind to stalk toward a banquet table holding food. I don't care if the punch is spiked. Don't care if I've only ever had wine a few times in my life because my heart feels like a jackhammer, and this is too much.

As I'm ladling the red liquid into a plastic cup, my hair stands on end, and I turn to see Taylor glaring at me a few paces away, his arms folded across his chest.

"What's he doing here?" He jerks a thumb over to where Royce and Dad are still conversing. "He doesn't even go here."

"Neither do you." I sip my drink, keeping my eyes low.

His lips curl incredulously. "What, so he's your fucking boyfriend, now?"

"That's none of your business." Taking a giant gulp with a grimace, I turn away in time to see Salem stomping through the crowd toward the doors, Logan following close behind.

"What's going on with them?"

Taylor watches them go with disinterest, which I find really odd considering how pissed off he was at Logan for looking at Salem five minutes ago. His eyes find mine again, and he opens his mouth to speak, but someone blocks him from view before he can get a word out.

"That for me?" Royce grabs my cup with a grin and downs it, coughing harshly as he swallows. "Jesus. What's in this?"

"Everything, I'm pretty sure. It's nasty."

He chuckles, but the smile on his face quickly disappears when a hand slaps down on his shoulder from behind.

"Excuse you." Taylor steps in between us. "We were in the middle of a conversation."

Royce glances over at me before meeting Taylor's gaze. "I think your conversation is over. Remove your hand, please."

All I can do is gape as the two stare each other down. After several heated moments, Taylor huffs harshly, releasing Royce's shoulder with a shove.

He turns to me and sneers before sauntering away into the crowd. "Enjoy your prom."

My boyfriend leans in close to whisper in my ear as we both watch him go. "What is his deal? Is it because I'm Black?"

Gasping, I whip around with eyes like saucers. "What? N-no, Taylor isn't like that—"

"Relax, babe." His shoulders shake as he releases a full-bodied laugh. "I'm teasing."

"Oh." I chuckle in relief, running a hand through my curls. "You got me."

With a sigh, I gaze over all the dancing bodies, looking for signs of a dark head of hair. "Taylor doesn't really like anyone, honestly. Except his close friends."

"He likes you." Royce's eyes glitter and my heart kicks up as I frown down at him.

"Yeah, no. Pretty sure he hates me."

"Hmm," he hums as he grabs my arm, pulling me away toward the stage. "I saw the way he looked at you. Pretty sure your stepbrother is in love with you, babe."

He...*what?*

I stammer, completely flabbergasted, because that's just ridiculous. Taylor has done nothing but make my life hell for years. He's hurt me, not just emotionally but physically. His fist has connected with my face more times than I can count. I may not know much about love, but I know what it looked like for my parents, and you don't do those sorts of things to someone you love. Right?

Royce grins. "I can see how thrilled you are about that revelation."

No, actually, I feel like I'm going to be sick. Because there's no way in hell Taylor fucking Tottman could love anything else other than himself and his bike. That's just who he is.

"He's a narcissistic asshole who uses people," I mutter, wishing I had another drink. "I seriously doubt he can love anyone."

"We all feel it in our own ways." He tilts his head, studying me, and I drop my gaze because I'm worried about what he'll see. The room starts to feel too hot, too crowded, too many bodies pressed together. Suddenly, I feel adrift, like I've been capsized in a sea of strangers, and they're all watching me drown. I can't breathe.

"Hey, hey." Royce cups my face, his brows furrowed as he searches my eyes. After a long moment, his forehead smooths out, and he nods slowly. "Ah, I see. You love him, too."

"*No.*" I nearly shout the word, pulling back from his touch with a shaky breath. "I do not love Taylor. I hate him."

Because I do. I fucking hate him for all the shit he's done to me. For the near-constant state of panic I've been in, even if it was my mother's death that started it. His antics sure as hell didn't help. I hate his stupid fucking smirk, and his snarky comments, and the way I can't tell what color his eyes actually are. Hate his ridiculous shirts and angry music, that crooked incisor that only shows when he genuinely smiles, and the messy state of his hair. The way he made me crave him just to fuck with my head.

"I hate him," I repeat adamantly, even if it comes out weak.

Royce smiles sadly. "I believe that, too."

The music switches up, slowing to something rhythmically sweet, and it feels like the floor is shifting beneath me. My skin feels flushed, the wall of bodies beginning to close in. I need to escape.

"Do you want to dance?" I ask him suddenly, nodding at the curtain covering the stage, and he flashes me a warm smile.

"Love to."

We agree to part ways for a few, so that he can head up behind the curtain first and then I'd follow. When I meet him back there five minutes later, however, I find him with his shoulders slumped, rubbing the back of his head. Looking uncertain. He straightens when he sees me and smiles his usual big grin, but there's less light behind it. And it kills me that I did that to him.

As he holds out his hand, I feel a shift between us when I take it. See the understanding in his eyes. This is goodbye.

"Royce..."

"It's okay." His hands clasp behind my neck, tangling with my curls while my arms wrap around his waist. "Let's just have tonight. Everything else can wait until tomorrow."

*But why do I feel like there won't be one?*

We slowly dance without speaking, surrounded by dust and band equipment. 'Lost In Yesterday' by Tame Impala filters in through the speakers, low and melodic. It's dark back here, comfortable. My chin falls to the top of his head as I finally relax, feeling like I can breathe again.

"Do you want him?" He asks quietly, breaking our silence after a while, and I stiffen, knowing who he's asking about.

I want to say *hell no, I don't.* In fact, my lips part to say the words. But they don't come. Because the truth is that I've wanted Taylor since the eighth grade. Even after everything. There's something twisted about the way I yearned for his attention, even if the attention I got was all bruises and closed fists. How I avoided him, knowing he'd seek me out because I wanted the fucking chase. I just got good at lying to myself about it.

174

"I don't know." I feel myself shrug. "Maybe. Even if I did, it wouldn't matter. Nothing can come from it. There's too much...history. Too much toxicity."

Plus, there's the little fact that he can't stand being touched by me. So, how would that work?

"I think you two should talk it out."

A dry snort leaves my throat. "Yeah, right. Conversations with us usually end in bloodshed."

*Or with his lips against mine as we writhe against each other, followed by a fallout.*

There's no middle ground between us, even with my failed attempt at making the backyard track into some sort of neutral 'Delaware' like an idiot.

Royce's chest vibrates as he laughs. "What did you expect when you fell for your bully? Who also happens to be your stepbrother."

"I didn't—" I blow a curl out of my eyes, sighing. "I don't think I've 'fallen' for him. It's more like...infatuated." He pulls back to look up at me, unconvinced, and I smile crookedly. "Very *strongly* infatuated."

Royce shakes his head with a *tsk* before pulling my forehead down to his. "If you're this stubborn admitting your feelings, I think I'm dodging a bullet."

He says it lightly, like a joke, but I still feel the sting.

"I'm all messed up," I whisper, closing my eyes as our breaths mingle. His nose rubs against mine sweetly, causing my forehead to wrinkle, and he chuckles.

"We're still young, babe. You've got plenty of time to get your head on straight."

Except it feels like I don't. Something in the pit of my stomach is telling me that a storm is brewing on the horizon, and I don't know if it's my intuition or the anxiety. I can't trust myself anymore.

"How about a kiss goodbye?" Royce's arms tighten around me, and despite my earlier convictions, I want to kiss him. Give him a piece of me to cherish when I'm gone for being kind to me when I didn't deserve it.

So I pull him closer and press my mouth to his, savoring the feel of its softness. We breathe each other in, our lips moving together in a kiss that's not as sexual as it is comfortable, full of understanding and friendship. If I had the time, I would have wanted to keep him. Maybe not as a romantic partner, but as a companion who shared his deepest secrets with me, and I with him. A close confidant. I think he would have liked that.

We hold each other for several moments, still pressed together, when I feel my stomach unexpectedly drop. It's... quiet. Whatever music that had been playing through the gym speakers has stopped. And then comes that feeling skittering across my skin, hair rising in a way that tells you when eyes are watching. Or, in this case, hundreds.

Hundreds of eyes.

Royce and I part with a *smack*, turning in each other's arms to see the curtain wide open. The entire senior class gapes at us as we stand tangled together on the stage. The blood drains from my face when I realize what they just saw—not only my fellow students but teachers and parents as well.

*My* parent.

Frantically, my eyes dart around the crowd, praying and pleading that he isn't among them, that he left early or stepped out to use the bathroom or something.

But my prayers go unanswered because I catch him standing close to the stage, staring at me with a reddened, unsettled expression behind his glasses. He's uncomfortable.

My dad just saw me kissing another man, and he's embarrassed. Sickened.

Behind him stands Logan, who looks just as shocked, his eyes taking me in as if I'm a stranger instead of the best friend he's known for twelve fucking years.

*No, no, no.*

Bile rises in my throat, threatening to make this night worse than it already is by having me puke in front of everyone. Royce says my name, but I barely register him over the pounding in my ears as my heart tries to tear its way from my chest. There's movement in my peripheral, off to the right, and my lungs seize as my eyes snap to the figure standing next to the edge.

Taylor drops his arm from the rope he used to pull open the curtain and slowly backs away, a dead look in his eyes as they meet mine.

Blood fills my mouth as I bite my tongue, betrayal so raw and hot burning through me that I feel myself cleave in two.

And my entire being fucking shatters.

It doesn't take long for the silence to break, whispers from my peers battering my ears.

*"Bishop Davis, did you know?"*

*"The running back is a fucking faggot."*

*"I caught him checking me out once in the locker room!"*

Over and over, the fears I've been running from riddle my body in the form of words aimed at me like bullets from the mouths of a community I've been nothing but kind to.

Faggot.

Queer.

Disgusting.

I don't think. Don't speak. Ignoring Royce calling my name, I just turn around and run without looking back. Run from the judgment, the snickers, the looks. Luckily, Logan gave me his keys to hold earlier in the night, and I gun it out of the school parking lot in his car toward home.

I don't even remember the drive, don't even remember unlocking the front door or going to my room—all I know is I'm standing in the bathroom gazing at myself in the mirror. A bottle of pills in my hand. I've been through so fucking many over the last six months that I couldn't even tell you which medication it is, but I'm holding it in a death grip.

And I don't recognize the person in the mirror, the stranger gazing back at me with haunted eyes, tears staining his stricken face. Short, shallow gasps leave his throat, chest heaving as he grips his hair and just fucking screams. This isn't the Huckslee who stands up and sings every Sunday in church or the football player with a scholarship. Not even Huckslee the swimmer, or Huckslee the artist, or anything other than the real me underneath the mask that's finally splintered into tiny pieces.

This is the Huckslee whose mother left him, whose father will disown him, whose best friend will turn his back on him.

Whose stepbrother just broke his fucking heart.

And I hate this Huckslee. Hate the sight of this broken mess sobbing so hard that vessels in his eyes are blowing out. Hate the man cursing a God he no longer believes in for making him this way.

I can't change me. *I can't fucking change me.*

And I'm tired of trying.

My fist connects with my reflection, shattering the image staring back at me to match my soul, glass, and crimson raining down over the sink.

The distorted, authentic version of Huckslee gazes down at the bottle white-knuckled in his bleeding grip. He's unscrewing the lid, lifting the pill bottle to his mouth as one last sob leaves his throat.

He tips it back. Swallows.

And swallows.

Until there's nothing left of him to change at all.

# TAYLOR

I thought I fucked up the night I broke Huckslee's arm, but that was child's play compared to this.

Because *I fucked up*.

Tonight, I did something so despicable and unforgivable that I'll spend the rest of my life hating myself for it.

The minute I saw Huck's face when he realized I'd opened the curtain, I wanted to take it back. To change it. Rewind time to that night in the pool or when I kissed him on the track; rewrite our fucking stars because *we can't come back from this*.

I know I've lost him. With that one look, I felt whatever thread of fate that connected us obliterate, shredding my heart in its wake.

What the fuck is wrong with me?

I'd been so blinded by rage, by jealousy at his lips on someone else and the fucking scholarship, that I hurt him in the worst way possible. Worse than anything I've ever done.

I'm racing out into the crowd, hollering at Christian to give me his fucking keys before booking it toward the parking lot. There's a rising panic in my bones, warning bells blaring at me that something is really wrong, and I need to get to Huck quickly.

Pulling out my phone, I intend to call him to apologize, beg him for forgiveness, and plead with him not to hate me when a text from an unknown number catches my attention.

> Unknown: Hello Taylor, this is Bill Shulz with the Mo-torsports Park. I've been trying to reach you for a week regarding your scholarship. I would appreciate it if you could give me a call as soon as possible, as the details of your scholarship are time-sensitive. Thank you.

I'm almost to Christian's Bronco when I come to a halt, reading over the message two more times.

What the fuck?

Pressing the call button, I wait as it rings several times before someone picks up.

"Taylor Tottman, as I live and breathe," a gravelly voice answers on the other line, "you've been hard to get a hold of, son."

"Uh, hi. Bill Shulz?"

The man laughs. "The one and only. Look, Taylor, we have some paperwork down here at the track we need you to sign before we can submit your scholarship for the coming school year. Can you come in tomorrow?"

Fighting the icy dread clawing through my veins, I jump into the car and start it up. "Um, forgive me, Mr. Shulz, but I'm a little confused. I thought Huckslee Davis won the scholarship? He won the race."

There's a pause. "Did he not tell you?"

"Tell me what?" Frowning, I tap the speaker button and toss the phone onto the passenger seat to handle the shifter. Putting the Bronco into gear, I whip onto the street toward Huck's house. Something in the back of my skull is screaming at me to *hurry, hurry, hurry.*

"After winning the race, Mr. Huckslee informed us that he already had a scholarship and that he wished to transfer this one to someone else. That someone else, namely, being you."

*What the fuck?!*

My foot comes down on the break, tires smoking to a halt as my phone flies off the seat.

No, this can't be happening.

"So, will tomorrow work for you? I'll be out at the track, say, bout eleven?"

Guilt tears a hole inside of me so vast it's physically painful. I feel my throat swell, shame burning my stinging eyes.

*God, what have I done?*

"Taylor? You still there, son?"

"Yeah." My voice comes out in a ragged whisper, and I clear my throat, wiping away tears. "Yeah, eleven works fine."

"Super. See you in the morning, kiddo."

The line goes dead, and I grab my phone off the floor to call Huck. Putting the Bronco back into gear, I floor it toward his house as his phone rings and rings.

And goes to voicemail.

"Fuck." Hitting the call button again, I struggle to focus on the road as a wave of nausea barrels into me. "Come on, come on. Pick up the phone, goddammit."

But it only ever rings.

I don't even turn off the car when I pull into the driveway. I just pull the parking brake before flinging myself out, not even bothering to close the door as I bolt up the porch and into the house.

"HUCK!"

There's no response. It's quiet, almost eerily so, and that voice in my head is screaming at me louder as I run up the stairs.

Something isn't right. Something is off.

"Huckslee?!"

His bedroom is empty, and I notice the light on beneath the bathroom door.

"Hey, Huck, can we talk?" I knock, waiting for his usual biting response to greet me.

But it doesn't come.

"Open up, man." My fist pounds on the door. "Please. I'm so sorry."

Still, no response. Trying the handle, I find it locked.

An awareness prickles my scalp, like a sixth sense telling me that I need to get into the bathroom now *now NOW*.

"Huck, I'm coming in."

My shoulder rams into the door, but it doesn't budge. It's not some flimsy wooden slab like the ones in my father's trailer—this door is solidly thick. So I go again, over and over, until I feel my collarbone snap, burning pain shooting down my arm. But I don't stop. Not until the door is almost hanging off its hinges from being battered by my six-foot-two body.

Glancing through the cracks, all I see is blood. Adrenaline makes me dizzy, and when my arm is dead weight at my side, I kick until the door finally splinters off its hinges.

"Huckslee?"

No. No, this cannot be happening.

Please, no.

"...Huck?"

*I'm so sorry.*

Please forgive me.

*God, I'm so fucking sorry.*

# PART TWO

## FOUR YEARS LATER

# TAYLOR

## JANUARY

The crowd's roar is deafening, even louder than the monster trucks revving their engines around the arena.

Excitement and adrenaline are palpable in the air, as thick as the smell of sweat, gasoline, and beer. Every seat is packed wall to wall, as it always is during the week-long Big BIC Energy Monster Truck Rally that takes place every year in Salt Lake City.

Hollowed-out cars litter the dirt, crushed from monster truck wheels. Smoke still lingers from the bus they set on fire for Christian and me to perform tricks over. The crowd had gone fucking wild for that, but now our final stunt of the night is being set up. Just one of many to come over the next week, each performance ramping up until our final show Sunday night, when our biggest, most dangerous stunt will occur. We spent the entire year preparing for this.

The announcer's voice echoes around the arena. "Laaaaaadies and gentlemen, how are we doing tonight?"

Everyone screams so loud it vibrates my body, and I grin as I continue inspecting my bike beneath the stands. This is the shit I fucking live and breathe for.

"Why don't we give our trucks a bit of a break and switch it up, yeah?"

The two ramps we'd used earlier are pulled wider apart, and three monster trucks rev their engines as they line up between them, bumper to bumper. The crowd goes ballistic for it, stomping their feet to the beat of the music pounding from the sound system.

A hand slaps my shoulder. "You ready, *cariño?*"

"Fuck no." Grinning over at my best friend, I watch as Christian pulls his long brown hair back, and I follow suit. It's not as long as his, barely tickling the underside of my jaw. Pulling gloves over my inked knuckles, my heart kicks up in anticipation as I start my bike.

The announcer continues. "Please put your hands together once again for Utah's very own Twins Of Terror, Tottman and Totillo!"

Sliding on our helmets, we share a ceremonial fist bump before riding into the arena. Cheers from the crowd nearly erupt my eardrums, and cameras flashing from the stands almost blind me. Raising a hand, I amp up the crowd as I take my spot on one side, Christian at the ramp on the other. Hand-made signs rise up in the stands with *T.O.T.* emblazoned on them, our logo of a double-bladed scythe drawn beneath.

This is the second year we've been invited to perform at the rally. Ticket sales jumped massively this year, which is to be expected, thanks to Christian's no-handed double backflip going viral last summer. He landed it on actual dirt, not into a foam pit. Seriously, that stunt got him all kinds of deals and sponsorships, which makes me so fucking proud. Dumbass deserves all of it.

The trucks lined up between the ramps gun their engines again, signaling the act to begin. Inhaling deeply, I close my lids, stealing a moment to get into the zone. Images come to mind that help calm my nerves: summer rains, bunny rabbit feet, a pair of dark brown eyes, and the smell of chlorine.

And on the exhale, I'm gone. Whizzing up the ramp at breakneck speed as Christian does the same on the other side. We crest the top simultaneously, flying toward each other in the air over the monster trucks. He leaves his seat, hanging onto the handlebars while his legs straighten out behind him in a trick called the Superman.

Falling back in mid-air, I let go of mine and grip my seat in my hands, body going vertical in a Hart Attack before I'm back in place to stick my landing on the other side, teeth rattling and shoulder twinging from the impact. The crowd's roar tells me that Christian landed his as well, and I shout excitedly before rounding the arena to jump the ramp I started with once again. We do this several times, rotating through different tricks with each jump, and the blood sings in my veins at the thrill.

The announcer once again speaks up over the intercom as Christian and I circle each other in the dirt. "I don't know, boys, the crowd doesn't seem impressed."

A mixture of cheers and faux boos echo from the stands. Shaking my head dramatically, I throw up my hands with a wide grin while Christian gives the crowd two thumbs down. I fucking love this shit.

"Let's see if this will make 'em happy?"

Behind us, the ramps widen even further, two more trucks lining up with the other three, and I swear you could hear all of the noise in the arena from space.

We retake our spots, revving our bikes as nearly seventy-five feet and five monster trucks separate us. All of my senses are tuned in to the two-stroke vibrating beneath me, to the sound of my heart thumping in my ears, the way my lungs steadily expand. A small, tiny trickle of uncertainty niggles at the back of my mind, but I tamp that shit down. Because we've got this. We've practiced over and over for months just for this rally. We've been doing stunts since we were kids. We're fucking certified pros. *We've got this.*

My wheels hit the ramp, propelling me up, up, up until I'm flying. I see Christian in the distance, tipping his bike back at the same time as I do. The crowd goes mad, recognizing our signature move as we grip our bikes with our thighs and flip backwards. Raising my hands above me, I stick both middle fingers in the air, as does Christian, using our core strength to fling ourselves into a backflip before gripping the bars again to land on opposite ramps.

A breath gunshots from my lungs, hair sticking to my scalp with sweat. *Hell. Yes.*

"Ladies and gentlemen," the announcer booms over the noise, "the Twins Of Terror!"

We circle each other before hopping off our bikes, and I whip my helmet off to grin broadly at the crowd.

Christian throws an arm around my shoulder, hazel eyes glittering as he jostles me. "We fucking did it!"

A wild, ecstatic laugh leaves my throat as we bow to the crowd. "Did you doubt me?!"

"Never. Not one damn minute, brother."

My throat closes from emotion at the confidence in his voice, and my smile falters for a fraction of a second. But then I swallow and wave goodbye to the crowd before getting on my bike to head back into the tunnel under the stands. A tall, familiar feminine figure paces before a set of double doors, bright red hair pulled into French braids, a black hoodie with **STAFF** written on the front hugging her thin frame.

"Strike a pose for the socials!" Salem hands me my sponsored snapback before raising her camera to get a picture, whether for the arena's marketing page or my own; I'm not sure. Christian flexes his inked arms while I put my hat on backwards and stick my tongue between the V of my pointer and middle fingers in the universal sign for eating pussy, which causes Salem to snort as the flash goes off.

"Mature, Tay." She shoots me a look of annoyance over the lens. "Now, a family-friendly one, please."

I oblige, but only because our Quadruple Fuck You backflip move already gets us into trouble with the soccer moms in the crowd. We refuse to change it, though. That would go against everything the move represents, and the owners of the arena respect that, which is why they invited us back this year.

A group of attendants with matching hoodies to Salem's come to wheel our bikes away for storage until tomorrow night, and we enter through the double doors while the sounds of the monster trucks still causing mayhem up above rumble the walls. The show will continue for at least another twenty to thirty minutes, but our part is done for the night, which honestly disappoints me a little because I'm fucking buzzing. Once the adrenaline wears off, I know I'll crash, but I just want to ride this high for as long as I can.

"Did you get some kick-ass shots?" I ask as we head down a long hallway to the lounge. The noise from up above is lessened down here.

"I'd be a shitty marketing manager if I didn't." She rolls her gray eyes, the lights glinting off her septum piercing as she hits me with a gaze that shouts *duh* and I grin before pulling her in for a noogie.

Christian's boots slap the floor as he all but skips behind us. "Dude, I'm so amped up right now. That was fucking intense. I'm going to get so much *coño* tonight."

"You're gross!" Salem shoves him into the cinder block wall outside of the metal lounge door, and he grabs his chest dramatically.

"What? What I say?"

"You know I took Spanish in high school, right?"

A laugh bursts from my lips as I turn the handle. "I doubt old Senor Diaz back in school was teaching his students the Spanish word for–"

A small body hits my knees, causing me to trip into the door frame and wince when it presses against my collarbone.

"Uncle Tayto!"

Looking down into a set of big blue eyes and a toothy grin, my heart warms as I bend down to scoop up the little girl at my feet despite the pain.

"Hey, Hannah Banana." I smile as her little fingers curl into the collar of my moto jacket, a pair of earmuffs still covering her messy brown hair to protect her from the engine noise. "Did you like the show?"

She nods her head erratically. "Yeah! It was loud. I had nachos."

Christian steps up to pout at her. "What? Where's mine?"

"They're in my belly," she giggles, reaching out to him for a hug, and I hand her off with a chuckle.

Stepping into the lounge, warm air from the heater hits my skin. It's a cold winter day outside, but the exhilaration and my heavy gear keep the chill at bay.

Several large flat screens line the walls, and soft sectionals scatter about where members of the arena staff are sitting and chatting. There's an entire wall of snacks, which I head toward, plus an espresso machine and soda fountain. Xed is leaning against the counter, his arms crossed over a leather jacket, as he watches Christian pretend to cry while Hannah laughs in his arms. A small smile plays on his pierced lips.

"No Valerie again, I take it?" I ask with a raised brow, ripping open a small bag of Cheetos.

Xed shakes his head, a blue strip of hair lining his scalp where a Mohawk used to be. "Nope. She's, uh..." He glances at Hannah, who's now in earshot. "She's busy."

Giving him a look, I say nothing as I munch on my snack. His lips thin, but he forces them into a smile as the little girl who's stolen all our hearts begins to chatter his ear off. Salem's sad eyes meet mine, and we share a silent conversation.

It's fucked up, honestly, how Xed is pretty much a glorified babysitter since Valerie can't keep her fucking nose clean, and poor Matty spends half his time worried about being a single dad when he should be focusing on his career-

I gasp as that thought crosses my mind. "The game!"

Salem points an acrylic nail to a TV on the far wall. "Already turned it on for you, love. Figured you'd want to catch the end."

"You da bomb, Sally Mal."

Plopping a wet Cheeto-covered kiss on her cheek, which she wipes off with a gag, I make my way over to watch the season championships playing on the screen and look at the score.

**California Golden Bears 29**
**Utah Utes 17**

Fuuuck, we're getting slaughtered.

The camera zooms across the players in formation on the field, with five minutes left in the fourth quarter. A hollow feeling blooms in my stomach, dropping my mood. I've basically missed the whole game, and this one's special. It couldn't be helped, of course, because I wasn't going to pass up the chance to perform tonight just to watch a football game, but...

I missed my chance to watch *him*.

The Utes have the ball, breaking formation, and I catch sight of Matt's broad shoulders as he defends his wide receiver, but my eyes move across the players on the other team. Searching...searching...

*There.*

My breath hitches when the camera zooms in on the running back for the Golden Bears as he intercepts the ball, making a run for the end zone. His name appears across the bottom of the screen, along with his stats.

Huckslee Davis, jersey number twenty, currently in his fourth and final season playing for the California Golden Bears at CU Berkeley.

I hear the others close in around me as they sit on the surrounding couches to watch the game, but my focus is glued to the screen, my eyes greedily taking in Huck as he books it across the field. Strong legs pump him forward, and his thick bicep grips the ball. My mouth goes dry, as always, when I watch him play.

And I've watched every game over the last four years.

The camera zooms in on him again, cutting to the ball in his arms, and I stiffen when I see what looks like a scroll of black ink near his elbow. Leaning in, I try to read it, but the image changes and I'm left gritting my teeth.

Did he...did he get a tattoo? When? I didn't notice it during the last game. What does it say?

Fuck, I hate not knowing. It's been years, yet the knowledge that I know nothing about what's happening with Huck still hurts. It's an ache I doubt will ever go away.

"Hey, *tonto*," Christian shouts from behind, snapping me back to reality. "You make a better door than a window. Move, fucker."

Throwing a glare over my shoulder, I shift to the side, realizing that I had my forehead on the screen. Jesus.

And this is why I usually watch his games alone.

Huck nearly makes it ten yards before Matty tackles him, bringing him to the ground so hard the ball drops from his hands. Absently, I reach up and massage my sore shoulder.

"Look, there's your daddy." Salem points to Matt on the screen, eliciting a string of claps from Hannah, who sits on her lap.

Cheers erupt in the room, but it doesn't matter. The game is already lost, anyway. Matty stands and offers a hand down to Huck, who takes it and lets himself be pulled to his feet. They share a conversation for a moment before tapping the front of their helmets together, and I hate the way my throat burns with jealousy for Matthew right now.

Me and jealousy? We don't mix. I never once felt possessive of any girl I've dated over the last four years, but for some reason, it's all I feel when it comes to Huckslee. And it's fucking toxic.

The clock ticks down for several tense minutes, and the Utes let the time run out. The game is over. The Golden Bears have won. Poor Matty. But...

"Congrats, Huck," I whisper, low enough for only myself to hear.

And the moment that I spend every second of every game waiting for comes when the camera catches him pulling off his helmet. That mess of blond curls flops onto his brows, plastered with sweat, and he grins triumphantly as his teammates surround him in celebration. He looks...ecstatic. Elated. It's a look I never got to see with him, and I drink it down like the alcoholic I am, needing my fix.

His jawline is sharper, and his skin is a deep bronze shade from spending time in the California sun. Not for the first time,

I hope he's happy—genuinely, authentically happy. I hope life got better when he moved in with his grandparents out there, and I hope he's been able to find peace. Because he deserves it. After everything, he deserves good things.

"There's a party tonight at the Prospector if you want to go," Christian says, bumping his shoulder to mine. "Juanita promised me free drinks."

The Prospector is our favorite hangout in the 801, a small-ish dive bar squished between a bakery and a Polynesian market on State Street. The parties there are lively, the women lovely, and the pool tables are usually free, which is the main reason I went in the first place. Nothing sucks more for an alcoholic who can't drink than watching other people slurp liquor down like it's water, so keeping myself focused on a game of pool keeps my hands busy. But tonight, after watching the game...I'm just not in the mood.

"Nah, you go ahead," I shrug, running a hand through my hair and wincing when my fingers catch on a knot. "I'll have Salem or Xed drop me off at home."

"You sure? I don't have to. We can totally grab takeout and watch some shitty cartoon with Xed and Hannah or something."

But I can tell in his eyes that he wants to. He's still pretty lit from the show earlier, and I know my best friend enough to understand that he's going to have restless energy all night unless he either drinks it, fights it or fucks it off. Or all three. But I also know he's worried about me after watching the game; he just won't admit it.

Rolling my eyes, I lightly smack him on the cheek. "Go, Christian. I'm fine. I promise I'll hold Xed's hand if I need to cross the street."

He cracks a grin before pulling me in for a hug. "You fucking better, baby boy."

"Get the fuck out of here." Shoving him away with a chuckle, I approach Salem, standing near the door.

"I have to stay to get a few more shots in." She pulls out my wallet, phone and keys from her purse, handing them to me. "You can either wait or go with Xed and Hannah to Chuck E. Cheese."

"Hell no, that robot rat is creepy as shit." A little gasp reaches my ears, and I find Xed standing beside me with a gaping Hannah in his arms. Oops. "I mean, uh...heck no?"

"Uncle Tayto said a bad word," she whispers to Xed, who smirks as he passes us out the door.

"Yeah, he did. That's why he doesn't get any pizza."

"Bye, love you," I shout after them, grinning, before plopping my ass on a nearby couch to wait for Salem. The game highlights are on, and I engross myself with them for the twenty minutes or so it takes her to wrap things up. Then I throw my denim over the motocross gear and follow her outside to the snow-covered employee parking lot, where we climb into her jeep.

As I'm buckling my seatbelt, I reach into the glove box, pull out the pack of cigarettes that Salem keeps in there just for me since she doesn't smoke, and light one up.

I tried to quit—I really did. But when all of your other vices are taken away, what can you do?

After several quiet minutes of me puffing on my cigarette, Salem glances at me as she pulls onto the freeway. "You alright?"

"Yeah, why?"

"You're rubbing your shoulder again."

Blinking, I notice she's right. I didn't even realize.

"Tweaked my collarbone during landing. I'll ice it when I get home."

"Okay." She doesn't say anything for a second as she switches lanes. "What else is on your mind?"

"Nothing." I frown at her but stifle a smile when I catch her glaring sideways at me.

"Don't lie to me, Taytortot. You only smoke when you're upset."

Exhaling slowly, I let my head fall back against the headrest and gather my thoughts momentarily. Finally, after a beat of silence, I quietly admit, "I missed the game."

"Ah. You know they record that shit and put it on YouTube, right?"

I do know. And the time I've spent repeatedly watching his games over the years is embarrassing, but...

"It's not the same."

Because watching it live means that I know where he is and what he's doing for once. I'm living the moment with him in real-time. And I know that he's breathing.

Salem pauses. "I know. But you caught the end. You saw him, Taylor. He's fine."

"Yeah."

That's what it looks like on the outside, right? That he's okay. Happy. Winning damn near every game and undoubtedly getting all kinds of offers from the NFL. His social media pages all showcase the star athlete-who's openly gay by the way- surrounded by friends and teammates, surfing in the ocean, and having dinner with his grandparents or boyfriend. My jaw clenches.

It's precisely how it all seemed with him in high school, too. Picture perfect.

Until it wasn't.

A sharp pain shoots through my collarbone from a memory I've done my best to bury, threatening to bring up shit I don't want to face right now, so I connect my phone to the Bluetooth and put on my favorite album, The Emptiness by Alesana. Salem doesn't protest, knowing I need the music to keep my mind from wandering.

By the time she pulls into the driveway of the duplex I rent with Christian, the album is half over and my mood is worse. It's always like this after I catch one of Huck's games. But I must be a masochist because I keep watching.

"I can come in if you want?" Salem smiles with a shrug, "I won't be too entertaining since I've got all these photos to edit and a pile of homework, but I don't mind sitting with you. I brought my backpack and laptop."

"Nah, your man's waiting at home. I'll probably just shower and hit the sack anyway."

She gives me an uncertain look. "You sure? You know he won't mind."

"Yes, Salem, I'm sure."

I can't keep the irritation from my voice, and I bite my lip. I absolutely *hate* when she and Christian get this way. When I say I'm fine, I'm fine. If I say I'm sure, I'm sure. I'm not the one they need to worry about. It's not like *I'm* the one who attempted suicide, right?

*No, just caused someone else to do it.*

I hide my wince as Salem leans over to kiss my cheek. "Sorry, Tay. I just worry. Text me if you change your mind, yeah?"

"I will. Love you."

"Love you too."

Exiting the car, I wave to her before heading toward the building. My ancient yellow Chevy pickup sits in the driveway, and Christian's spot beside it is empty. We decided to carpool today to save on gas. I'll probably have to give him a ride to get his car in the morning; he'll likely take an Uber home.

Our two-bedroom, two-bath unit is on the right, and I step onto the small porch to unlock the door. It's pretty small, smaller than what we pay for it, but we're putting our money away to someday buy two houses next to each other and build a track in the backyard. It's an open floor plan, with an island separating the kitchen from the living room, where a large flat screen sits in front of the brand-new leather sofa we just bought. We were both pretty pumped about that because neither of us has ever owned furniture that wasn't used. We even threw a party to celebrate it, invited the neighbors, and had a cookout.

"Goddammit, Christian," I sigh in exasperation, taking in the food wrappers and dirty socks covering the couch and coffee table. I love my best friend, but the fucker is a slob.

Turning on some music, I get to work clearing up the mess in case he decides to bring home a chick—or two. He's done it multiple times before and tries to get me to hook up with them. Sometimes, I do. Most times, I don't. Usually, I just watch. Depends on my mood.

Tonight, I don't feel like company.

Putting the oven on preheat, I grab a few celery sticks from the fridge and enter my bedroom just off the kitchen. It's not as big as Christian's, but that's fine by me because mine gets far less action than his. Little excited oinks greet my ears from an enclosure in the corner, and I bend down to open a wire cage door.

"Snack time, BB," I tell my rabbit, Baby Bones, as I place the celery before her. She's the coolest bunny I've ever seen, all black except for the white parts of her face that look like a skull. A fellow motocross buddy gave her to Christian to feed to his very illegal python currently taking up space in his bedroom, and the minute I saw her, I fell in love. She's gorgeous. And then I threw a fit and made him swear that he'd only feed the fucking thing rats from then on. Still makes me sad, but lesser of two evils, I guess.

Her nose twitches as she munches on her celery, and I leave the cage door open for her before grabbing fresh clothes and heading to my adjoining bathroom. It consists of a toilet, a pedestal sink, and a tiny shower, but it's mine, and I don't have to share. Stripping out of my moto gear, I study myself in the round mirror, eyes dropping down to the outline tattooed on my muscled chest, over my heart. The empty feeling inside of me intensifies.

Stepping into the shower, my head fills with images of Huck from the game, the smile on his face, the damp curls stuck to his forehead, the way his uniform clung to his thighs and ass. My cock swells along with my shame, and I wrap my hand around it as I think about the fact that the last time I got to taste him was in a shower.

I'd been so drunk and coming down from shrooms that I hardly remember. But the taste of his lips, the way he felt against my palm when I jerked him, those memories are burned into my core so deep that I'll never forget. So are the sounds he made for me when I made him come inside the pool back in high school. I work myself hard to the memory, as I've done so many fucking times over the last four years that I've lost count. It's all I have left of him now. All I deserve, honestly.

And just like every time I do this, the self-hatred and guilt eat me alive as I spray my cum on the shower wall with his name on my tongue.

I hate it. It kills me.

But I can't seem to let Huckslee Davis go.

After my shower, I cook a frozen casserole, then sit on the floor in my room to eat it while Baby Bones hops around exploring.

I've always liked being on the floor. Something about it grounds me. Also makes my weak ribs and back feel better when they ache, so there's that.

Taking my phone, I tap social media and log into Salem's account. Her password has been the same since high school, and she doesn't seem to give a shit that I use it since I sure as hell don't use mine. Everything posted about me on social media is done by Salem, my 'marketing manager,' or so she calls herself. She's got a degree in the field and has been managing all of the ads for the arena since she interned for them after graduation, so I figure she's the expert.

After a solid minute of deliberation, I pull up Huck's profile. It's still public, like when I looked months ago and promised myself I'd never look again. His picture, which used to be of him and his boyfriend, was updated an hour ago to one of him encompassed by his team, holding the championship trophy.

Torturing myself further, I read the comments, hardly recognizing anyone from his life in Cali. He's a whole stranger to me now. And even though I'm surrounded by my friends, it makes me feel so damn lonely. Because even if they know me better than anyone...nobody knows me like Huck does. Well, did.

I type out a quick comment and post it before I can think better of it.

> Congratulations, bro! Amazing game.

I know it'll come from Salem's profile, but I don't care. I want him to know that at least someone from back home is proud of him.

A few seconds later, the notification tab lights up, and my heart pounds when I see that Huck liked the comment and replied.

> Thanks!

It suddenly feels hard to breathe.

He responded. *Actually* responded, which is the most I've interacted with him in almost four years. Clicking off his profile before I do something stupid, like send him a message, I update Salem's status with a shit-eating grin before putting down the phone.

> Burps turn me on.

A few minutes later, someone comments on it, and I snort.

> Logan: Haha, hilarious, Taylor.

So I log out of her account and into mine, ignoring the hundreds of unread messages and notifications as I go to her profile to reply:

> Me: No one wants to hear about your sex life, dude.

Yeah, Logan and Salem starting a relationship was a surprise to everyone else except me. He's pined after her since summer before senior year of high school, and she finally decided to give him a chance two years ago. According to her, he hasn't told Huckslee about it. Odd, but not my business. They still talk daily, which makes me glad he has someone in his corner.

Of course, it took almost a year for Logan to warm up to me after everything. But Salem's always made it clear to every guy she dates that we come as a package deal, and if they don't like it, then there's the door. She's not a cheater. If she's with someone monogamous, which Logan very much is, we keep our hands off each other. We respect boundaries. She's the most important person to me besides Christian, and I can't imagine my life without her.

My phone begins blaring in my hand, alerting me to an incoming call, and I smile when I see who it is.

Speak of the devil.

Or, well, *think* of the devil in this case.

"My bad, I'll delete it," I answer with a laugh, thinking Salem's calling to bitch me out about the social media status.

"Taylor, hey," she responds, and her serious tone has me stiffening.

"What's going on?"

She clears her throat. "Logan just got off a FaceTime call with Huckslee."

My stomach flips in a way that makes me dizzy. Pulling BB onto my lap, I bury my fingers into her soft fur. "Yeah? How'd it go?"

There's a pause, a low murmur from Logan speaking to her in the background before she breathes into the phone. "Have you heard from your mother recently?"

Now, that question throws me for a loop. "Not in almost a year." Not since she and Aaron invited me to lunch after not speaking for nearly two years. It was awkward, to say the least, and we did not part on good terms. "Why? What's up?"

"It's Aaron." She swallows audibly over the phone. "He's sick, Taylor. Huckslee's coming home."

# Huckslee

F uck, I hate it here.

Resting my elbows on my knees, my fingers curl into my hair as I lean on a bench outside SLC International Airport. It's cold as hell, which, of course, is because it's January in Utah. I didn't miss this shit. I left mid-sixty temperatures and shorts for lower twenties and ice. Blue skies for gray smog. I really, really hate it here.

My knee begins to bounce erratically, showcasing my nerves. I haven't stepped foot inside this state in almost four years. Didn't plan on ever coming back, either. I barely survived this place the last time I was here, so why would I? Things in Cali are good. Grandma and Grandpa Jones are amazing people. They offered to put me through college when I fucked up my scholarship, and I'll forever be grateful to them for saving me when I felt like I couldn't save myself. Berkeley's fantastic, I love my roomie, and I made some friends. Get to swim in the ocean every day. It finally feels like I have the space to breathe.

And then I got the call a week ago that threw my life back into turmoil.

No one tells you that every day feels like a waste when you get a second chance at life. Not as 'wasteful because I'm here,' but more like 'there are so many other things I can be doing right now, but instead, here I am doing Political-Science homework.'

There's an entire world out there and so many things I've yet to see with my own eyes.

For example, my grandparents took me on a cruise to the Bahamas last year, and I'd never seen such clear blue water. We visited Harbour Island, where the sand was pink, and I swam with sea turtles. *Actual* sea turtles, like Crush from Finding Nemo. And don't even get me started on the dolphins.

My team winning our championship was another big moment. No, I was never super passionate about football, but that feeling of accomplishing something I've spent years putting blood, sweat, and tears into? The most satisfying high on the planet.

The point is, I almost missed out on all that shit. And I never want to miss out on anything ever again. Which is why I'm freaking out right now.

A car horn draws my attention, and I spy a dark BMW pull up to the curb in the loading area. The passenger window glides down to reveal Logan's frowning face.

"Sorry, Huck. There were like two accidents on i80."

Heaving a sigh, I grab the handle of my luggage and push to my feet. Let's get this shit over with. "I see Utah drivers still suck in the snow."

The trunk pops open, and I heave my bag inside before slamming it shut.

"It's all you Californians moving here without any idea how to drive in the winter." He watches me open the passenger door to climb inside, coughing out a laugh. "Dang, dude, will you even fit in here? When did you get so much muscle?"

"Four years of college football will do that to you," I grin, giving him the best side hug I can in the car. He looks the same, for the most part. His brown hair is shorter, but he's still wearing a button-up polo and a pair of tan shorts like he's always done, even in the winter.

Some things never change.

An awkward silence settles over us as he exits the airport and pulls onto the freeway. Though we've talked to each other through text, phone calls, and FaceTime, this is the first time I've actually seen him in person since I left. And I won't lie; I'm a bit salty about it. I asked him numerous times during past summers to come see me, but he's always had an excuse. Yeah, I wasn't exactly traveling to visit him either, but I feel like I had a valid reason.

"Thanks for offering to pick me up." I clear my throat, adjusting the radio until I find a tolerable station. "I know it's out of the way for you."

He shrugs a shoulder. "It's no biggie. I've got some things I need to do in town, anyway."

"Really? What could you possibly have to do in Gville that you can't do in the city?"

"Just...things with my parents." He shoots me a sideways glance, and we fall quiet again as Post Malone's 'Hollywood's Bleeding' plays on the radio.

Logan's been hiding something from me for a while. I don't know what it is, but I can feel it. Another thing I'm salty about. I know I have no right to be because I hid the fact that I was gay from him for years, but it sucks when someone who was like a brother to you turns into a stranger.

"So, how's the boyfriend?" Logan asks, and I go rigid before forcing myself to relax. Even though he knows, it'll always be weird having my sexuality out in the open with him.

"Eh. I broke up with him on the plane."

His eyes widen in surprise. "What, why? Weren't you guys together for, like, a while?"

If you consider eight months a while.

Running a hand through my curls, I lift a shoulder. "We just wanted different things in life, I guess."

"Like what?"

*Everything*, honestly.

"I don't know. Marriage. Kids. A dog."

Logan's brows raise. "Like adoption?"

"Obviously," I laugh, and his neck reddens slightly in embarrassment.

"So you wanted to marry him?"

"No, the other way around. He wanted to marry me."

In all honesty, Greg was a sweet guy. He treated me well, all my friends loved him, and he wasn't selfish in bed. Kind to everyone. But that was just the problem. He was...*too* nice. How fucked up is that? I've broken it off with every guy I've ever dated because they aren't assholes, apparently. I won't even get into what my therapist thinks about that.

Logan gives me an unreadable look. "You don't want marriage and kids?"

"No." Feeling uncomfortable with the subject, I shift in my seat. "Not really. Is that bad?"

He's quiet for a long moment, and I wonder if it bothers him. Logan grew up religious like I did. Marriage and babies are pretty much pounded into our heads from the minute we're baptized at eight years old.

"So, is not agreeing on marriage a valid reason to break up with someone, do you think?" He asks it softly, genuinely, and it's my turn to gaze at him in surprise. His eyes are trained straight ahead, so I can't tell what he's thinking.

"I mean, I think so. The whole point of dating is to create a life together, right? At least, that's how I see it. Obviously, everyone sees relationships differently, but I'd rather he find someone who wants the same things as he does instead of wasting his time on me. Because I don't think I'll ever want marriage. You know?"

He nods but doesn't respond; it seems like he's lost in his thoughts for a while. I let him have his moment, turning up the radio as I watch snow-covered mountains pass by out the window. The Great Salt Lake looks even more dried up than it did four years ago.

"So, Berkeley's gonna let you finish the year with online classes?" He breaks the silence, and I nod in response.

"Yep. What about you? Balancing everything ok?"

Logan's taking business management courses and working at his dad's company, processing mortgage loans. Sounds boring to me, but he seems to like it well enough.

He gives me a non-committal reply, and then we're taking exit 99 toward home. The closer we draw toward Gville, the worse my anxiety gets. It always starts in the pit of my stomach, squeezing my muscles until it spreads into my chest, shoulders, and neck. I can feel my back stiffening against the seat when we pull into town. My fingers itch to pull my anxiety meds out of my pocket, but I don't. Not only because I don't want to freak Logan out, but...well, I don't want to freak him out.

It's not the same as it was before. Honestly, living in a place where I feel safe to be myself has done wonders for my mental health, but years of pretending and hiding growing up did their damage. 'General Anxiety Disorder' is what my psychiatrist calls it. Triggered by thoughts or feelings of helplessness. But I'm doing better. We found a great care plan and a fantastic therapist, and I've hardly had any anxiety attacks in the last year. Though, I also had the vastness of the ocean and a large city with plenty of space and freedom. Gville is small. Tiny. Claustrophobic.

When we're pulling into the driveway, it feels like ants are crawling under my skin.

Fuck.

*Just breathe, Huck. Breathe.*

But it's so fucking hard.

"You alright, man?"

Glancing sideways, I notice Logan turned fully in his seat toward me, a deep frown of concern pulling at his mouth.

"Yeah. It's just..." Breathe. Inhale. Exhale. "I haven't been back here since, well, you know."

Since I OD'd on my prescription meds that nobody knew about and apparently almost bled out from slicing my arm open on a shard of glass when I collapsed.

Crazy, right?

My fingers brush along the scar near the crook of my arm, now covered by a script of black ink. Coincidentally, it's the same arm that Taylor broke in high school—

*Nope.* Not thinking about anything to do with him or that.

Logan nods in understanding as he chews on his cheek. "Do you need me to come inside with you?"

*Yes.* "No, but thank you. I appreciate it. And thanks for the ride."

Getting out, I pull my luggage from his trunk and stop at the driver's side window to give him a fist bump. "Drive safe. Still want to do lunch in the city tomorrow?"

He grins, but it doesn't reach his eyes as he nods. "Yep. I'll text you the address." A pause. "Good luck, man. Give your dad my best."

"You know I will."

Standing on the front lawn, I watch him drive away, continuing to stare long after his car has faded from view. Only then do I pull out the bottle and swallow a pill. With the way my hands are shaking, I should take two, but I get nervous doing more than the prescribed dose for obvious reasons.

Taking several deep breaths, I let the cold air sting some clarity into my lungs before I pick up my bag and walk into the house that almost became my tomb.

Did this dining room always feel so small?

Sitting at the table across from Dad, listening to him speak, all I can think is how it feels like the room has shrunk since the last time I was here.

"I'm glad you're here, son, but you didn't have to come all this way just for me." He looks the same, only skinnier. Tired. More drained. The glasses keep sliding down his nose like they no longer fit his thin face. His shirt hangs off his shoulders.

I guess stage-two bladder cancer will do that to a person.

"Yes, I did." Swallowing hard, I glance away toward the fireplace where all the pictures of Mom still sit. "At least until you get better."

Because this isn't permanent. I'm not back in Utah forever, and Dad will beat this.

He smiles, but it seems weary.

Maisie reaches out across the table to take my hand. "Well, we're just glad to have you back for however long we get you."

I squeeze her fingers, nodding but can't look at her. Can't force myself to meet those blue-green eyes and dark hair that are like the ones that have been haunting my dreams for four years. So I sweep my gaze around the room, taking in all the photos of me hanging on the walls since I was in youth soccer. All of my sports accomplishments, school pictures, family photos. It's like a monument to my childhood, but all

I see behind those happy smiles is a kid being crushed by expectations. However, something's missing...

With a frown, I realize for the first time that there's only me in here. No pictures of another dark-haired boy anywhere to be found. And now that I think about it, I don't think there ever was.

"When is the surgery?" I ask, pulling at my collar. It suddenly feels too hot in here, the fireplace stifling.

Dad leans back in his seat, removing his glasses to clean them on his shirt. "Next month."

"What?" My eyes fly to him, slightly panicked, and I don't miss the way Maisie's lips thin. "Why so far away?!"

"That's the earliest they can get me in." His tone is calm and gentle, but there's an edge to his voice that you'd only notice if you've spent twenty-two years with the man. "It'll be alright, Huck. The doctors say it's a slow-moving cancer. We've got time."

*But it doesn't feel like we do.*

It feels like that night at prom when I felt like my world was about to come crashing down around me. A wave of dizziness makes my head spin, and I tune out Dad and Maisie's explanations of his treatments to focus on my breathing.

Inhale. Exhale. Inhale. Exhale.

*I am me. I have control.*

My fingers start to shake, so I fist my hands, nodding along to the conversation like I'm taking it all in, but I'm not here. I'm on a dark stage, spilling my heart out as the curtain opens, hundreds of eyes watching me bleed onto the floor. And just like that night, the walls feel like they're beginning to move in on me. I can't breathe. I need out *out OUT.*

"Is my old dirt bike still in the garage?" I cut Dad off mid-sentence, and he blinks at me with a frown.

"Yeah, it's still there. I've been keeping fresh gas in it and starting it occasionally, just in case, you know..." In case I ever came back. "Why, son?"

Inhale. Exhale.

"Think I might go for a ride on the track."

He raises a brow. "It's covered in snow."

"I'll throw the snow tires on."

Leaving my seat quickly, I head toward the garage as Maisie tells me she'll start lunch. Less than thirty minutes later, I'm sitting on the track, gazing over the white powder-covered field. It's been years since I've ridden a dirt bike. Even longer since I've ridden one in the snow.

I don't have moto gear anymore, and my fingers are frozen to the handlebars, but it feels good. Kicking on the bike, I start slow, re-adjusting to the feeling of my heavier body on the two-stroke. I'm almost jostled off when I hit a jump, but muscle memory takes over, and I correct myself.

A small chuckle leaves me at the sight I must make. I definitely won't be winning any races anytime soon, that's for sure.

Honestly, the conversation with Dad could have gone better, and I lasted longer than I thought I would inside that house. But, fuck...

I don't know if I can stay here.

I thought I could do it, thought it had been long enough that I'd be over it, and that Dad's surgery would be sooner. But if I can't even stand being in there for longer than an hour, how can I stay for possibly two or three months until he recovers and gets the all-clear? It's not like he needs me here. He's got Maisie to take care of him; I don't necessarily have to stay in the house...but there's no way I can afford a hotel, and I'm not asking Grandpa Jones for more money.

An odd sound starts to come from my bike's engine, so I slow to a halt and put a foot out, listening. It sounds like an engine revving, but I'm not doing it. Turning the bike off, I realize the sound is coming from behind me.

*What the fuck?*

It gets closer, and I twist slightly to look over my shoulder, only to have my heart drop into my stomach when I see who's riding toward me.

He's covered head to toe, but I know it's him. I can feel it.

I'm frozen as I watch Taylor approach until he stops beside me.

For a moment, we just look at each other. Take each other in.

He's wearing a helmet, a denim jacket, and leather gloves covering his hands. Dark hair dyed red at the tips peeks from the collar, curling around his nape. His bike is still that awful yellow color, but this one is shiny and new. A decal says *T.O.T* on the radiator shroud, whatever that means. A pair of black jeans cling to his thighs, combat boots on his feet.

Like I said, he's completely covered. But fuck, if my body doesn't light up at the nearness of his presence after four years. And it only serves to wring my nerves tighter than they already are.

How the hell did he know I'd be here?

Jerking his chin, Taylor kicks his bike into gear. "We racing or what?"

And then he's speeding ahead of me down the track.

*Motherfucker.*

So I start up mine and haul ass after him, spell broken, because how *dare* he show up here after the shit he did to me? Does he think four years was enough to clear the air between us, racing on this track like my life wasn't entirely altered by the stunt he pulled?

Like he didn't break me into pieces.

His bike is much newer and faster than mine, so I struggle to keep up. I'm sure he's also kept up racing over the years instead of giving it up like I did, so he has an advantage over me.

When I start to creep up on him, he fishtails his back wheel, spraying snow all over me, and I growl angrily as I wipe it from my visor.

Dirty, cheating son of a bitch.

It's clear I have no shot at winning, no matter how hard I try, so I give up and let him pull farther ahead of me as I idle my way through the track. I'm not going at a snail's pace, but definitely not as fast as I used to go, because I didn't fucking come out here to race. I just needed some goddamn air.

The end of the track comes into view, and my vision narrows on Taylor leaning against his bike, arms crossed like he's been waiting for me. My hands are nearly frozen solid, but I don't even feel it because I'm burning, boiling under my skin at the sight of him standing there nonchalantly like everything is cool.

I'll lose it if I talk to him or see his face, and I can't afford that right now with everything going on, so I pass him on my bike before bringing it to a stop. Swinging my leg off, I begin wheeling it through the snow toward the house without acknowledging him whatsoever, praying to whatever powers that be for him to stay where he is and let me go.

Don't do it. *Don't you fucking do it, Taylor.*

Snow crunches behind me as he starts to follow, and my body stiffens.

"Hey, Huck. Wait."

*Goddammit.*

I keep going, mentally pleading that he gets the hint and leaves me the fuck alone.

But apparently, not much has changed about him in four years because his hand wraps around my arm as he tugs me to a stop.

"Will you please hold up a minute–"

Letting go of my bike, I whirl on him, planting my hands on his shoulders to shove him back and away from me. "What the fuck do you want, Taylor?"

He slips on the ice, falling flat on his ass with an *oomph*, and when he looks up at me in surprise...

I forget to breathe. To think. For an instant, when his ocean eyes meet mine, it's like all the years between us are gone. I'm back in that pool, thrusting into his hand while he places kisses all over my lips and neck.

"Just wanted to say hi, man," he grumbles as he slowly pulls himself to his feet, and I gape at him, taken aback.

"You just wanted to say hi." It comes out slowly, my voice leaden with disbelief, because is he fucking serious? "You just wanted to say hi?!" I step into him, curling my lips over my teeth in a sneer. "That's really all you wanted to say to me after all this time?"

His jaw tightens as his eyes jump over my face, and I can't help but notice the scar on his brow is less prominent now. Still noticeable but faded. Still complimenting his features. The midday sun glints off an ear piercing, which catches my attention briefly. But he says nothing in all these seconds I've had to make these little observations. Of course. Did I expect anything less?

With a scoff, I glare in disgust before returning to grab my bike.

"You broke your rule," he shouts after me when I hit the backyard. "No fighting in Delaware, remember?"

I grind down on my molars as I force my legs to keep moving forward before I go back there to beat his ass. "Fuck you, Taylor."

Once in the garage, I pull out my phone to text Logan.

> Me: Did you tell Taylor I was gonna be here today?

I don't know why he would. That makes no sense. He responds within seconds.

> Logan: No?

Another angry growl works its way from my throat, and I shove open the door into the kitchen where Dad sits at the island, Maisie setting food on its surface.

"Did you invite Taylor over?" I ask sharply, trying to reign in my rage. They don't know that he was the one who opened the curtain at prom. At least, I've never told them. Doubtful Taylor did, either.

Maisie's eyes darken, and she frowns as she sits beside Dad. "He just showed up."

Something in her tone tells me that this isn't normal for him and that he's not welcome, which makes me pause. Despite how terrible of a person Taylor is...this is his mother. Pity is the last thing I want to feel for him, but I'm not heartless. As I'm looking at this house for the first time with adult eyes, it's eerie how there's no trace of Maisie's son to be found here. But then again, maybe I just don't know the whole story.

I sit across from them, and the backdoor opens as Maisie dishes some pasta salad onto my plate. All three of us look up as Taylor's eyes run over my dad before landing on me, completely bypassing his mother. A snapback rests backwards on his head, and he slowly pulls off his leather gloves before stuffing them into his jacket pocket.

My attention catches on the heavily tattooed skin at the backs of his hands and fingers.

*Hmm. I bet they look good wrapped around his cock—*

What. The. Hell.

No.

Shut up, brain. *Shut up, shut up, shut up.*

I am *not* going to think of Taylor fucking Tottman in that way. Not anymore.

I can feel his eyes on my face, but refuse to meet them, instead focusing on the food in front of me. Rather than sitting down, he leans back against the counter and folds his arms, watching us eat. A tense atmosphere thickens the air.

Eventually, breaking the silence, he clears his throat and moves his irritatingly heavy gaze from me to my dad. "How are you feeling?"

I resist the urge to scoff and roll my eyes.

"I've been better," Dad answers politely with a strained smile, and Taylor nods.

"I'm sorry to hear."

To his credit, he sounds genuine, at least. More awkwardness follows.

"How is the show coming, Taylor?" Dad asks almost haltingly like he's trying his best to make small talk, but it pains him. When Taylor shrugs, I glance between them with a frown.

"What show?"

Dad waves a hand through the air. "That monster truck show that happens every year in the city. What's it called again?"

Taylor pauses. "Big BIC Energy Monster Rally."

I choke on the water I'd just taken a sip of, wondering if I'd heard what I thought I did, and Dad slaps a hand across my back while I cough. Glancing up, I barely catch an amused grin stretching across Taylor's face before he covers it with a hand.

"It's sponsored by the lighter. Christian and I do a joint performance every night during the run of the rally," he says, clearing his throat before bringing his eyes back to mine. "You should come. Tonight and tomorrow are the final two shows until next year."

I don't engage, though my tongue is burning with questions as I look away. What kind of performance? It's a monster truck rally. Does that mean he drives those now? Is that what he does for a living?

*Why do you care?*

Good question. I don't.

"That's good to hear, son," Dad answers mechanically as if he's going through the motions and not really listening.

"How is Salem?" Maisie asks, speaking to her son for the first time since he walked in the door. "She seems like a nice girl."

My throat burns, and I take another sip of water to ease my resentment. Over the last four years, they've never asked about anyone I've dated. Not once. I'd mention a boyfriend over the phone or when they'd fly out to visit, but they'd usually either ignore it or change the subject. Ever since coming out, it's like they pretend it's not real. Not that I actually got to come out...more like I was *forced* out.

Taylor rolls his eyes at his mother, though only I notice because no one else is actually paying attention to him. "She's good."

"That's great to hear. You've both been together a long time. Do you have any plans for marriage soon?"

Jesus.

I really do not need to hear about his love life. Not a conversation I want to be a part of.

So I begin to rise from my seat, wanting to be anywhere else but here, when Taylor's following words make me pause.

"We aren't together anymore."

I glance up at him to find his gaze on me intently.

"We aren't together," he repeats firmly, and I sink back down with a soft scoff. Why do I care who he does or doesn't date? Not my business. Don't fucking care. I tell him all of this with my eyes, glaring at him.

It only seems to amuse him, though, and he raises his brows.

"That's too bad," Maisie responds. "You both were very cute together."

My scowl deepens at that, and the corners of Taylor's mouth twitch like he's fighting a smile. His teeth sink into his bottom lip, snagging my attention as I watch the way he pulls it in for a suck before releasing it, now red and plump. A memory plays in the back of my mind, my own teeth nibbling on that lip a lifetime ago, how soft it was.

Snapping my eyes back up to his, I find him looking at me with a knowing smirk, and I mentally kick myself.

*Get it together, Huck*. Damn.

"Actually," he says slowly, holding my gaze, "Salem has been dating Logan."

Wait...*what?*

My lungs go still like I've stopped breathing. Like the earth momentarily stopped spinning.

"That's a lie," I state flatly, blinking rapidly. Because it has to be. There's no way. Logan would have told me something like that.

Even Dad looks up with a frown. "His father didn't mention anything like that to me."

Taylor shrugs a shoulder. "Ask Logan yourself."

Fucking bet.

Pulling my phone from my pocket, I tap my messages and see Logan is still the last person I texted.

> Me: Are you dating Salem???

> Logan: ...where did you hear that?

> Why do I even ask. Taylor, right?

> Me: Is it true?

Logan: God, he's such an asshole.

Look, I was going to tell you at lunch tomorrow.

Was even planning on bringing her with me.

Maisie, Dad, and Taylor are conversing about something, but I don't pay attention. I'm fucking pissed. Betrayed. I've told him about every single relationship I've been in. Although I didn't go into details, he always knew what was happening in my life.

Me: And this isn't something you could have mentioned over the hundreds of calls and FaceTimes we've done? Really?

Logan: It's a conversation I wanted to have in person because I knew you'd freak out.

Me: Oh in person, when? All the times I asked you to visit me and you made excuses?

My skin prickles with a rising tension from whatever Dad and Taylor discuss, but I can't focus on that right now because I'm *livid*.

Logan: You weren't exactly coming out here to visit me either, Huck. Let's talk about this all tomorrow, yeah?

I won't even bring Salem, it can just be you and me. But keep this on the DL. My parents don't exactly approve of her, so that's why we've been hiding it.

> Me: Yeah, well so much for that. Taylor just dropped the bomb in front of my dad and Maisie during afternoon lunch. I'm sure your dad's gonna get a call soon.

> Logan: ...fucking hell.

Maisie's raised, irritated voice brings me back to the conversation. "Really, Taylor, that's just poor manners."

"Manners?" Taylor scoffs, and my head snaps up to re-familiarize myself with my surroundings. "I wasn't taught those, remember? You can take the boy out of the trailer, but you can't take the trailer out of the boy, right?"

He's leveling a glare at my dad, who drops his gaze, and Maisie looks beyond pissed.

Shit, what did I miss?

"What just happened?" I ask, frowning as I bounce my gaze between all three.

No one responds, and Taylor exhales sharply before reaching up to take off his hat and run a hand through his hair. The action causes his jacket to ride up, revealing a smooth patch of pale skin above the waistband of his jeans. I catch a muscled V and a dark trail of hair leading down before he lowers his arms again.

"I'm going to load up my bike," he mutters, turning toward the door. His hand closes around the handle before he glances back at me over his shoulder, meeting my baffled gaze. "It was nice seeing you, Huck. You look good."

And with that, he's gone.

What the hell?

*You look good?*

Turning to my dad with a frown, I see him staring at the table while Maisie gently rubs his shoulder. "Dad? What was that about?"

When his gaze rises to mine, I'm taken aback by the shame swimming in them.

"Let's go into the garage and talk, son." He sighs as he lifts from his seat, Maisie helping him stand. I follow him out but hesitate at the food still covering the table.

Maisie gives me a kind smile. "It's alright, I'll clean up. Go spend some time with your father."

When I step out into the garage, I find him staring down at the 1970 Chevy Nova we've been fixing up, looking sad. We started working on it together when I was ten.

My chest tightens, and I reach up to rub it. "We'll still finish it. Plenty of time left."

It feels like a lie because I don't plan on staying here any longer than I have to, but his expression right now is tying my stomach into knots. He throws me a small, knowing smile before turning toward the fridge in the corner. Opening it up, he pulls out two beers and offers me one.

I gape down at it for a moment, stunned. "I...since when do you drink, Dad?"

He chuckles as he pries off the cap with the edge of his wedding ring. "I've always drank, Huck. Just knew how to hide it."

Dazedly, I take the beer, studying him like I've never seen him before. My mind runs through all the times growing up I might have seen him with liquor in his hand or witnessed him drunk, but other than wine on New Year's Eve, I come up with a blank.

"I missed my chance at sharing a beer with you on your twenty-first, so we're making up for it." He plops down into a camping chair, taking a sip, and I sit opposite him.

"Does Maisie know?"

"She does...now. Not in the beginning, though."

My entire world has just been rocked, but I take a swig and rest my arms on my knees. "So what did you want to talk about, pops?"

He stares into his beer for a long moment as if gathering his thoughts. When he finally speaks, his voice sounds gritty. "Did I ever tell you why I left the Priesthood, son?"

My body locks up, and I shake my head as I look away. "No. I just always assumed it was because of...what happened that night. At prom."

Dad excommunicated himself a year after everything went down, and I carry so much guilt over it. He's never come outright and said it, but I guess it'd be hard to be a Bishop when you have a gay son who tried to commit suicide. Bad for the image, right?

"I'll be honest, that was part of it," he admits, and it feels like a punch to the gut. Tears sting the backs of my eyes. He quickly shakes his head when he glances up and sees me trying to blink them away. "Not for the reasons you think, Huckslee. I failed my sons. Both you and Taylor."

"What?" Curling my lip, I gaze at him incredulously. "How in the fu-" He throws me a look, and I correct myself. "How the heck did you fail Taylor?"

Taking a long pull off his beer, a sight I don't think I'll ever get used to, he leans forward in his seat. "Something happened, Huck. A year after you left for California. Something I never told you, and I suppose Taylor never did, either, because you never asked about it."

A sweat breaks out on my neck as he takes a deep breath and speaks.

And what he tells me has my blood boiling with rage.

# TAYLOR

The cameras do not do Huckslee Davis justice because, *holy shit.*

Cranking the strap that secures my bike to the bed of my truck, I take a deep puff off my cigarette. If it weren't for the end conversation with Maisie and Aaron, I wouldn't have even needed one right now; seeing him again felt that good. Like I've been half alive for four years, and his presence just breathed new life into me.

The California weather turned his skin a glowing golden brown, sun bleached his curls, and the years of football filled out his form to the point where his sweater stretched around his biceps and chest. He's fucking beautiful.

And still hates me.

Not that I blame him. I still hate myself for what I did, too. I guess I'd just hoped...well, it's ridiculous, but I'd hoped that he had lived such a good life out there that he'd moved past what had happened between us. But that's just the coward in me talking. Nothing in my life has ever been easy; why would it start now?

Giving the strap one last good tug, I pinch the smoke between my lips and check my phone, seeing one missed call and text from Salem.

> MySalGal: Fucking call me, asshole. NOW.

Oops. Time to face the music.

In hindsight, it really wasn't my place to out Salem and Logan like that, but, fuck, man. Two years is a long time to keep a relationship in the dark; honestly, Salem deserves better. Obviously, the friend group knows, but he refuses to tell his family and won't let her say anything to hers, either. It's bullshit if you ask me. Why be with someone you have to hide?

I'm about to hit the call button when the front door flies open.

"TAYLOR!"

My head whips up in time to see Huckslee approaching me from the house. And he's on a fucking warpath.

"You beat up my dad?!"

*Oh, shit.*

His hand is around my throat in an instant, banging my head off the truck window so hard my hat and phone go flying. I grab his wrist just as he starts to squeeze, and deja vu hits me from that night at the track after I broke his arm.

*Why do we always seem to end up here?*

"Don't you *ever* come near my dad again," he snarls, so close to my face that his saliva lands on my cheek, and all I can do is stare helplessly while he crushes my throat.

The last time he did this, I was barely eighteen and turned on.

This time? I don't recognize the Huck glaring down at me. His pupils are so dilated that his eyes are nearly black, the hatred in them searing my skin. And I know I deserve it.

Which is why I don't fight. I didn't last time, and I won't now. For everything I've ever done, I'd let Huck kill me right here if it brought him closure.

It doesn't matter that I hurt him time and again because I was a kid being abused, nor does it matter that I went after Aaron that night on the front lawn because I was shit-faced and my father had just died of an overdose.

It doesn't matter that I was also hurting or that I spent half a year in jail for violating probation afterward. It doesn't even matter that I'm two years sober because, in the process of dealing with my own pain, I brought it onto others. And it's taken me years in therapy to be able to come to terms with that.

Forgiving myself for it, though? Can't seem to do it.

Aaron's words echo in my mind from that as black spots fill my vision, my lungs spasming for air.

*"You're trailer trash, just like your father was. Stay away from my family."*

I hear Aaron's voice now, and I try to focus on the sight of him with his hand gripping Huck's shoulder. Panic in his eyes, he murmurs for his son to stop. *Please, let go, Huck, LET HIM GO.*

Tears freeze on my cheeks, eyes sliding shut, and despite the pressure crushing my windpipe, I find my thumb gently rubbing circles into Huck's wrist. Telling him that it's alright. It's okay, I understand. I've wanted to do this to myself, too.

But then the pressure is gone. Air shoots down my throat, burning from the chill, my knees hitting the frozen ground. A cough sputters out of me, and I look up through my wet lashes to see Aaron pulling Huckslee back toward the porch, both shocked as hell.

I remain kneeling well after they've disappeared into the house, catching my breath. I gather my phone and hat with shaking hands before slowly getting to my feet. Numbly climb into the truck and back out of the driveway. Try to focus on driving home.

But once I'm far enough away, I'm yanking the wheel to the side of the road, thumbing my now cracked screen to pull up my contacts. When I find the one I'm looking for, I press call while fresh, hot tears stream down my face.

She answers on the third ring.

"Taylor? What can I do for you?"

"I need to make an appointment, Doctor Hart. As soon as possible."

# HUCKSLEE

I t's crazy to think I've never been to a monster truck show before.

Gville, for as small as it is, has all kinds of crash derbies, rodeos, and ATV races. I don't know why I assumed watching the Big BIC–whatever would be like those events, but it's nowhere close. It's so much bigger. And louder.

And violent.

The crowd is feral for it, people going fucking crazy every time a pair of giant wheels crushes a car or a truck tips over. I don't get it.

The tricks are cool, don't get me wrong. Watching a vehicle that big drive in circles on only two of its wheels, plus doing jumps, takes a lot of skill, I'm sure. It's entertainment at its finest, which is why the show is completely sold out tonight for the final show. We were only able to get seats because Salem works for the arena and got us tickets.

But my eyes can't stay off Taylor.

Watching the way he and Christian are so perfectly synced in their performances is mesmerizing. But it's also downright terrifying because they spend more time out of their damn seats flinging their bikes around in the air than they do on them.

Seriously, at one point, Taylor hooked his ankles to his handlebars and threw his hands in the air while he back-flipped. The fans went insane for that, shaking their *T.O.T* signs around—which I snorted at—while they screamed at him to have their babies. Danger is sexy, apparently.

I'll admit, despite how much I fucking hate Taylor, even I spent half the show chewing on my nails, waiting for him or Christian to crash into a pile of dust and cease to exist. I don't want to compliment the asshole, but he's really skilled at what he does. It makes me wish I'd kept up on motocross instead of focusing on football when my heart isn't in it.

Logan shouts something at me, but it's too hard to hear with the engine and crowd noise, especially with my ear-muffs, so I lean closer. Yes, I'm wearing the earmuffs because I have sensitive ears that are also shaped weirdly and can't do earplugs. So fuckin' what.

"It's time for their final performance," he repeats, grinning excitedly, and I can't help but grin back despite how upset I still am with him. We talked things out at lunch, for the most part, but the fact that he hid a relationship from me for two years will always hurt.

His reason for not wanting to send me over the deep end about it stung, but I understand that's what happens when you're an attempt survivor. Those you love will fear losing you, and the trust has to be rebuilt. And that's the thing about trust.

It takes years to build, but only one minor lapse in judgment to blast it all to smithereens.

The lights in the entire arena suddenly cut out, followed by yelps of surprise from the crowd. Speakers crackle as the announcer comes on.

"Ladies and gentlemen, please put your hands together for the night's final act. Once again, let's hear it for the Twins Of Terror!"

Drums begin to beat as beams of flames shoot off, and when the lights come back on, a large mesh sphere has been placed in the middle of the pit. It's hollow and see-through, with a gate, like a...

Like a cage.

"They wouldn't." I gape in disbelief, watching Taylor and Christian ride onto the dirt, circling each other. Everyone in the stands has lost their damn minds, the screams are so loud.

Logan turns to me with his brows nearly in his hairline. "Is that...?"

"Yeah." Nodding grimly, I shout back, "That's a fucking Globe of Death."

I've seen this stunt once before when my parents took me to a circus in Las Vegas. I think I was seven then, and the Globe was bigger. Four motorcyclists were in that one, all crisscrossing each other as they raced around the Globe. Upside down, sideways, diagonal. And you know what happened? One of them fucking crashed. I don't know if he died or not, but I still remember the sounds the bike made as it bounced around the Globe while the other riders barely avoided being taken out, too.

My stomach feels like it's about to fall out of my ass when the two of them ride into the Globe while an attendant shuts the gate. They throw their hands out, amping up the crowd before giving each other a fist bump. And then the show starts.

More fire erupts as Taylor takes off first, sideways, circling his best friend in the middle. Then Christian rides in the opposite direction, looping around the top and bottom of the sphere while Taylor continues around the sides. They're narrowly missing each other, the timing so perfect that they're an inch away from slamming together. I feel my jaw fall open as I watch the spectacle, transfixed. Everyone else seems to be doing the same because the crowd has gone quiet as if we're all waiting on bated breath for something to go either very right or very wrong.

They swap directions, and I feel like I'm going to faint. Over and over, they pass each other for what feels like an eternity, changing up their path every few seconds until they're both on the sides of the Globe going in the same direction on opposite ends, and what do these motherfuckers do? As if tempting fate wasn't enough, they each release one hand from the handlebars and grab onto each other. Letting inertia take control, they hang on to the other's arm for dear life while spinning one-handed until I'm dizzy.

Finally, it ends. They right themselves on the bottom of the Globe, the crowd roaring when Christian pumps his fists and tackles Taylor to the ground. You can tell how excited they are at not dying, but the way Christian is lying on top of Taylor has my gut doing weird shit, so I turn away instead to look over at Logan.

And burst out laughing.

"You look like you're going to puke, dude," I shout at him, shoulders shaking at the greenish tint on his face.

He just shakes his head. "They're freaking crazy."

Yeah, I can agree with that.

The two exit the Globe on their bikes and ride to face the stands, where an attendant runs out with a microphone. They both take off their helmets, and as Taylor takes the microphone to speak, I find myself standing on my toes to get a better look at him.

Just to see if he's injured, of course. Not because I care but because I'm curious.

"Let me start by saying how much we love you guys." Taylor grins widely into the microphone, pushing dark hair out of his eyes. "I'm so sorry I was under the weather and couldn't be here last night, but let's give it to my fellow Twin of Terror, Totillo, for fucking killing it!"

The crowd erupts into cheers, but I feel a frown pull at my lips. He didn't seem sick when I saw him yesterday morning. Unless it was because...

Guilt has my chest tightening, but I shove it away. I have no reason to feel guilty. He deserved it.

Christian takes the mic and throws an arm over Taylor's shoulders, his long brown hair coming out of the tie to fall around his face. "We are so grateful to each and every one of you who's come out to support us over the last week. Y'all are why we get up every day and get on that bike, so thank you for real!"

More shouts and screams.

"Just as we did last year," Christian continues, "ten percent of the proceeds we've made this week are being donated to the American Foundation for Suicide Prevention, so from the bottom of our hearts, thank you."

My smile drops instantly, and a prickly feeling crawls under my skin as Christian hands Taylor the microphone.

"Just remember that you are loved, and you matter." Taylor presses two fingers to his lips before raising them up to the crowd. "Thank you, Utah! We can't wait to see you all next year!"

Hundreds of hands clap together, but my ears are ringing underneath the muffs. Everyone starts to move out of the stands, almost in slow motion. My feet are glued to the ground, stuck as waves of bodies push and shove by me. Pressing on me. Crushing me until I'm drowning.

*I'm drowning, I'm drowning, I'm drowning–*

"HUCKSLEE!"

Noise floods my senses as the earmuffs are lifted off, and I turn to blink rapidly at Logan. He stands beside me, gazing down into my eyes with a furrowed brow.

"Huh?"

His frown deepens. "I said we've got to get off the stands, man. People are waiting."

"Oh." Looking over his shoulder, I notice the line of angry eyes staring at me to move, and I mumble an apology as I make my way to the stairs. The dwindling crowd is still too much for my ears right now, so I yank my earmuffs out of Logan's hand and slide them back onto my head. Nausea slightly roils in my stomach.

"You alright?" Logan asks close enough to my face that I can hear, and I just nod as I continue toward the exit on legs that feel like jelly. Before I can get there, though, Logan pulls me toward a side door.

"Where are we going? Shows over, isn't it?"

"Yeah." He doesn't stop, just keeps tugging on me until we're inside a concrete stairwell. "But Salem said to find her once it ended."

Fucking great. That's the last thing I want to do right now, but because he's my ride, I follow him down two or three flights until we pop out into a long hallway. A few doors are lining it, but only one is thrown open with ample noise coming from within.

Logan leads me toward it, and we step into what looks like some sort of staff party. There are tables lined with liquor and food, couches spread out, and televisions mounted on the walls with various event photographs hanging between them. Some people are in black STAFF hoodies, some in dress suits, and some in racing gear, which I figure are the monster truck drivers.

Taylor's in here. I can feel it, but I force my eyes to stay ahead as Logan takes us over to where Salem is chatting with Christian and another driver. Her hoodie matches the other staff, red hair loose down her back. She turns as we approach, and I don't miss how her eyes narrow at me before she leans up to kiss Logan. Before I can decipher that look, though, Christian yanks me into a bear hug.

"Huckslee!" He smells like gasoline and sweat. My nose wrinkles as he pulls back with a crooked grin. "How you been, *hermano*?! Haven't seen you in a minute. You've been looking good out there on the field, my guy."

Awkwardly stepping out of his touch, I give him a perplexed look. "You watch my games?"

He jerks his chin, and I follow his gaze to see Taylor leaning against a far wall, engaged in conversation. "Baby boy never misses any. And if he does, he gets moody as fuck."

He...what?

*Baby boy?*

I don't really know how to respond to that because I'm pretty sure it's a lie, so instead, I turn to Salem, who's staring at me with that same narrowed gaze.

"We're having a staff party to celebrate the end of the rally run," she says, grabbing Logan's hand, "but you guys are free to stay as long as you want."

Logan leans down to kiss her on the forehead. "You sure? I don't want to get you into trouble."

"Perks of being my own boss, remember?" She winks at him with a grin, and I stay quiet as I watch them whisper in each other's ears. His hands are on her hips, and there's a softness to his expression that I haven't seen before.

Growing up, dating wasn't strictly allowed, so I've never seen Logan in a relationship before. His lips are curved into a coy smile, and Salem's gazing up at him with a twinkle in her gray eyes. They both look happily in love. It radiates off of them from the way they hold each other, as if magnetized.

Somewhere in the darkest pits of my mind, I wonder what the fuck Royce was talking about the night he told me that Taylor was in love with me. And mistakenly, that I was in love with him, too. We didn't look like that. No, more than half the time, we wanted to kill each other.

"Those are cute."

Speak of the devil.

Taylor somehow crept up on me, appearing at my side with a smirk on his lips, his moto jacket tied at the waist with a shirt depicting Barbie dressed as a flag girl covering his torso.

Still with the weird fucking shirts.

Scowling at him, I try to ignore studying the tattoos that cover his arms. "What's cute?"

"The earmuffs," he laughs, and my cheeks heat as I reach up to yank them off.

"Forgot they were on."

He smiles, biting his lip in the annoying way he does, and my gaze lowers to study the bruises covering his neck. A sick feeling settles in my gut, something between horror and satisfaction at my marks on him. His throat flexes as he swallows, and my eyes snap back to his.

Tucking a dark strand behind his ear, he clears his throat. "Did you enjoy the show?"

There's a waver in his voice, almost like he's...nervous?

I cock a brow with a shrug. "Suicide prevention, huh? Bit hypocritical."

The minute it's out of my mouth, I hear how petty it sounds, but I can't help it. After the shit he put me through, hearing him say those words felt like a slap to the face.

Taylor's smile immediately disappears, leaving an odd, empty feeling in me when a flash of pain crosses his features. It tugs at my heart, but I don't give a fuck because he doesn't deserve sympathy.

"I'm trying to move on and do better, Huck," he says quietly, sad eyes holding my gaze. "That's all I can do."

"Some of us don't have the luxury of moving on," I respond before returning to Logan. He's got an arm around Salem with a drink in his hand, laughing at something one of the truck drivers says.

Inwardly, I groan. Clearly, this means we're staying a while. And I'm not about to do it sober.

Making my way to the liquor table, I grab an empty solo cup and fix myself a drink, not even caring if it's for the staff only. There aren't many options, but I bartended for two summers in Cali and know what I like, so I make myself a Highball with whiskey and ginger ale before returning to my best friend, getting irritated when I spot Taylor leaning into Logan's other side, opposite Salem.

He's massaging his shoulder, staring at the ground with a frown, and something like possessiveness twists in my gut. Because Logan's *my* friend, not his. So why the fuck is he leaning against him like that?

Gulping down my drink, I glare as Salem reaches over Logan to grab Taylor's jaw, tilting it up. He gives her a smile, and she searches his face for several seconds before she turns those gray eyes toward me. I stiffen at the fire I see in them. Like she's pissed at me or something. So I jut my chin and stare her down because what the hell did I do?

Her lips tighten, but she returns to whatever conversation they're having with a man and woman in business suits. Taylor eventually joins in, resting his elbow on Logan's shoulder like they're pals. A pair of arms wrap around his waist from behind, and he looks down with a smile at a petite brunette wearing a lovely dress. He pulls her in for a hug and kisses the top of her head, all while his arm still touches Logan, and in this moment, I've never felt like more of an outsider.

Watching my best friend become a stranger.

Logan pre-Salem would have never cozied up to my enemy like that. But here he is, laughing at something Taylor says while they're practically hugging. When did they get so comfortable with each other? What is that about? Downing the rest of my first drink, I make myself another.

"Damn, man, what happened to your neck?" One of the monster truck drivers, a man looking to be in his forties with a grizzled beard, inspects the bruises on Taylor's throat, and I stiffen, waiting for him to throw me under the bus.

But Taylor just shrugs and flashes a coy smile. "Got a little too kinky in the bedroom, you know?"

The woman at his side laughs, eyeing him like a full meal, while the truck driver shakes his head.

"Well, throw out your safe word next time or something cuz that looks rough, buddy."

I feel eyes on me and slide my attention to Salem, who's watching me again. Awareness prickles my scalp, telling me she knows I'm the reason for Taylor's bruises, so I sip my drink while challenging her with my gaze to do something about it.

She just raises a hand to itch her eye with her middle finger, a clear *'fuck you,'* before grabbing Taylor by the shirt and hauling him away toward another group of people.

The minute they're gone, I pounce on Logan.

"This isn't weird to you, like at all?" I hiss in his ear, and he turns to me in surprise, looking for all the world like he forgot I was even here. Which pisses me off even more.

"What's weird?"

I throw a hand over in Taylor and Salem's general direction. "The fact that they used to fuck each other?"

His brows shoot up and he lifts a shoulder, sipping his drink. "Not really."

"Seriously?" Grabbing his shoulder, I spin him around, showing him how Taylor is now braiding Salem's hair. "He's all over her. He's all over you. That's not weird?"

Again, he shrugs, reaching up to rub the back of his neck. "Honestly, Taylor's pretty affectionate when you get to know him."

A scoff leaves my lips, and I drop my hand from his arm like it burns. "So you *know* him, now?"

"Look, Huck." Logan sighs deeply, facing me. "He's not the same guy he was in high school, ok?"

"Yeah, well." I gulp down the rest of my drink, turning back to make a third. "Neither are you."

"Come on, man, don't do this here."

He follows me to the liquor table, and I scowl as I take his empty cup and mix up two drinks. "Do what, Logan? You're speaking nonsense. He literally outed you and Salem to my dad, just like he outed me to the entire school. He's clearly the same person."

"What he did to you was messed up, Huckslee." Logan takes his drink from me before putting a hand on my shoulder. "But he had his reasons for spilling the beans on me and Salem. He talked to her about it."

"He had reasons. Right."

"I'm serious. I was being an idiot anyway, keeping everything under wraps. It was time."

I roll my eyes, swallowing down straight whiskey. "Whatever justifications you need to make, Loge."

He exhales out of his nose, raising his honeyed eyes toward the ceiling. "You should probably slow down on the drinking, Huck."

"You should probably mind your business."

"Ok, you know what?" He sets his drink on the table and turns away, heading back toward Salem. "You stand here and wallow. I'm going to have some fun."

So I do. I fucking stand here and seeth while I drain my drink and the rest of his, too, watching while he snuggles Salem from behind as Taylor constantly touches him.

Seriously, what's Taylor's issue? His arms seem to be always brushing Logan's, fingers grabbing my best friend's shoulder every once in a while. He's leaning in so close that his lips are practically on Logan's ear when he talks.

The more I drink, the angrier I get until he runs his fingers through Logan's hair, tugging it playfully, and I snap.

Seriously, I lose it.

Marching over there, I grab his arm and yank it away from Logan's head. "Keep your fucking hands to yourself, dude."

Everyone in the vicinity quiets down, and Taylor's eyes widen as he gapes at me.

"What the fuck is your problem?" He snaps, going to pull his arm from my grip, but I tighten my hold.

"My problem is you. Stop touching him!"

"Huckslee, stop," Logan warns as Taylor gets in my face with a sneer.

"What, I'm not allowed to touch Logan?"

"No, because he's not your friend."

I can tell how childish that sounds, but I'm far beyond tipsy now. Eyes are on us all over the room, and warning bells are going off in my brain, but when it comes to Taylor, I just can't stop.

"My best friend is dating your best friend," Taylor scoffs, rearing back. "Pretty sure that makes him my friend, too."

Somewhere nearby, Christian's head pops up over the crowd. "Logan, we're dating?"

Salem steps up, trying to put herself between us. "Huck, I think you need to leave. You're drunk."

"Me?!" Snarling, I pull Taylor closer and away from Logan." He's the one with his hands all over your boyfriend!"

"You don't own him, asshole." Taylor tries to escape my hold on his arm again, but I'm not letting go. So he grabs Logan's wrist and holds it up, shaking his hand around. "What, does this piss you off?"

"Let go," I growl, seeing red when he threads his fingers through Logan's, holding his hand.

"How 'bout this? This not ok?"

Salem whips around, glaring at him. "Taylor quit it."

But Taylor isn't done. I feel my grip tighten around him with bruising force as he reaches up to grab Logan's jaw.

"You know what I think will *really* make you mad, though? *This.*"

He yanks Logan's face down to his and plants a kiss square on my best friend's lips.

For a moment, I'm stunned. Shook.

There are multiple gasps throughout the room, and Salem is even gaping with her jaw on the floor. The two of them part with a smack that leaves Logan looking dazed, and Taylor smirks as he looks up at me from under his lashes, lips wet from Logan's spit.

Before I can even comprehend what I'm doing or think about the repercussions of my actions, my fist slams into Taylor's jaw, knocking him out cold.

An arm snakes around my throat, pulling me backwards, the smell of sweat and gasoline filling my nostrils as Christian puts me into a headlock.

"You crossed a line, motherfucker," he hisses in my ear before pressing a thumb into the pressure point beneath my chin. Pain erupts throughout my body, muscles spasming.

And then it all goes black.

# TAYLOR

## FEBRUARY

Smoke swirls around the ceiling, dancing in the light streaming through the blinds.

I'm lying on the floor in my room, a cigarette in my mouth with a fan blowing toward the open window since we aren't supposed to smoke inside the apartment, and I don't want to make Baby Bones sick. Usually, I'd just step outside for a quick drag, but it's cold as shit, and I needed to lay on my back to think. Process the last few weeks.

Christian's in his room bumping tunes, 'Killing You' by Asking Alexandria vibrating through the walls. He's the only person I know who cures a hangover with loud music. Before I got sober, any amount of noise after a night of heavy drinking was like nails on a chalkboard; unfathomable and to be avoided. But not Christian. Heavy breakdowns and excess amounts of coffee seem to get him going again.

He's been drinking a lot lately since we quit our jobs at the local Jiffy Lube. More than normal. I know it's boredom. Between the rally, my father's life insurance, and the content Salem posts of us on social media, we're doing fine financially, but it leaves us with too much time on our hands. Which leaves me lying here, poisoning the environment with my vices, overthinking.

And, of course, as always, my mind is on Huckslee.

Haven't seen or heard from him since the night he whooped my ass, which is to be expected. Can't really say I didn't deserve it. The moment Logan whispered to me that Huck was pissed off at me for touching his best friend, I may have laid it on a little thicker than I usually would have. Because I'm a dickhead, first and foremost, but I also wanted to see what he'd do. In hindsight, kissing Logan was not the best way to do that. I fucked around and found out.

And, unfortunately, there's a small scar on my chin from Huck's class ring to prove it. Honestly, I like it. Reminds me that maybe things aren't utterly hopeless between us. I'm not stupid; I know why he was mad that night. It had little to do with Logan and everything to do with the fact that I wasn't touching *him*. I could see it.

Maybe I'm a bit delulu, but I don't care. I'm holding on to that hope like it's a lifeline.

We got extremely lucky that the arena owners were cool with the whole thing and promised we'd still be invited back next year, so that's good, all things considered.

The sound of the front door slamming shut echoes over Christian's music, and I hear Salem call out from the front room.

"In here," I reply around my cigarette, glancing up when she appears in my doorway.

"I've got good news," she starts but pauses and makes a face when she sees where I'm lying. "Uh oh. Floortime, huh?"

Shrugging out of her winter coat and kicking off her boots, she bends down to give BB a pat before crawling over to lay next to me on the carpet, shoulder to shoulder.

After a minute, she speaks. "So. Tell me what's up."

"Huck still staying with you and Logan?" Apparently, he'd asked if he could sleep on their couch shortly after everything went down, stating that being in his dad's house again was what set him off.

"You know he is."

Sitting up, I put my smoke into the ashtray on my nightstand before stretching out on my back. "How's that going?"

She purses her lips under her septum piercing. "I stay out of his way and he stays out of mine."

"Don't do that." I turn my head to frown over at her. "Don't let what's going on between Huck and me ruin shit for you and Logan. I won't have that."

Her eyes meet mine as she lifts a brow. "And what is going on between you two, exactly?"

Ain't that the question.

"I don't know what the fuck I'm doing," I groan, covering my face with my hands, and Salem just hums. Waiting for me to continue.

Taking a deep breath, I speak into my palms. "I have to tell you something." Hard swallow. "Right before school ended in the eighth grade, I kissed Huckslee under the bleachers in PE. And he kissed me back. I was so fucking happy that I fucked up—I was babbling about him at home, about how fun I thought he was, and how I couldn't wait to spend every day over the summer racing with him. Of course, my dad had to go and say some shit."

She's silent for a moment. "What did he say?"

"I'm not going to repeat the word he called me." I huff a humorless laugh. "Basically, he made it really fucking clear he'd take away my bike and keep me from racing if he found out that I was gay."

"Ah. So that's why everything changed between you two."

Blinking up at the ceiling, I give her a nod, not ready to meet her gaze yet. "God, I was such a little asshole to him, Salem. Didn't respond to any of his texts all summer and ignored him at races. When he got too close, I'd lash out."

"I remember."

"Motocross was everything to me. *Is* everything. I couldn't let it get taken from me. And then our parents married, and we moved in together. And I really fucking liked him. Some things happened between us...but then he won that scholarship, and I was so pissed off. So confused. It felt like he'd ruined my life. And when I saw him kissing Royce behind that curtain, I lost it. I was jealous, ok? So I snapped and made the biggest mistake of my life." With a groan, I turn away from her and curl onto my side, burying my face in my arms. "Everything's so fucking complicated."

"Hey." She crawls over my body to my other side, prying my arms away from my face. "Tell me why you're freaking out. Is it because he's a dude?"

I shake my head, and she blinks in surprise before nodding.

"Ok. Is it because he's your stepbrother?"

That makes me hesitate because I've actually never processed that.

"Mm-hmm." Salem nods again. "What else?"

Swallowing, I drop my gaze to our connected hands. "I ruined his life."

"No, you didn't, Tay," she sighs heavily, rolling onto her back, and I follow until I'm half on top of her.

"Yes, I did. I almost killed him."

"We've been over this. Your therapist has been over this. What happened was not your fault."

"But I was the catalyst. And he blames me."

She tilts her head. "How do you know? Have you asked?"

"He's made it pretty fucking clear with his actions toward me."

"Look, Tay, I think you're focusing on all the wrong shit here. You were jealous, so you opened a curtain. He was jealous, so he hit you. Those things are kind of far apart on the fucked up scale."

"It was more than that, and you know it." I squint down at her, frowning. "I outed him to the entire town and his dad before he was ready. Took that choice from him."

"Yeah." She reaches up to touch the scar on my chin. "Yeah, you did. But you didn't hit him."

My jaw tightens as I look away. "I've hit him before. Used to do it just to blame the bullshit from my father on him."

"You should talk to him. Really talk to him about it all. Everything, including the parts with your dad. I think he'd understand."

Shaking my head, I flop back over onto my back. "It doesn't excuse what I did."

"No. But we can't change the past. Only move on from it. And you can't do that without bridging the gaps between you two."

I'm silent momentarily, listening to Baby Bones scuffle around the room. "What if I'm scared?"

Her hair brushes my shoulder as she turns her head to look at me. "Of what? That he doesn't feel the same way you do?"

"No. I honestly don't expect him to. I'm just...scared of how he'll make me feel when he rejects me. Which is really fucking hypocritical because of what I did to him in the eighth grade. And senior year."

"You have to face the music, Tay," she sighs again, and I nod.

"I know."

We're both quiet for a long moment, sorting through everything in our heads. After a while, she turns to me again with a pout.

"What?" I ask, grinning.

"So you're telling me I wasn't your first kiss?"

"Nope. Sorry."

"It's ok," she hums, looking pleased. "I took your V card and popped your ass cherry, so I win."

"Fucking Christ, Salem."

Cackling, she sits up to lightly punch me in the gut. "Ok, enough with this sad shit. Let's get down to business. I brought good news."

"Hit me with it."

"First, we need Christian."

Heaving a heavy sigh, I get to my feet and offer her my hand. "I'll get the coffee started. You can be the one to drag him out of bed. He's hungover and moody as shit."

Ten minutes and three mugs of coffee later, Christian and I are curled on the sofa with Baby Bones between us while Salem paces the length of the living room.

"So after that stunt at the monster truck rally," she starts, "your TikTok accounts have started blowing up, which is really working for us. I also posted updates on Twitter."

"It's called X now," Christian grumbles into his coffee, looking like hell with bags under his eyes.

"Well, whatever. Point is, you guys are making an impression. Which leads me to the good news." She pauses, glancing between us excitedly.

When nothing more comes out of her mouth, I roll my eyes and throw a leg over Christian's lap. "What's the good news, Salem?"

"Why, thank you for asking, Taylor." Her hands clap together as she smirks. "You both received messages on your IG accounts from a representative of the...wait for it...Nitro Fuel Games."

Christian spits out his coffee as my lips part in surprise. "You fucking serious? What did they say?"

Nitro Fuel Games is one of the biggest action sports competitions of the year. The best athletes from around the country come to compete, doing their best tricks in freestyle motocross, bicycle motocross, skateboarding, and scooters.

"What do you think they said? You've both been invited to compete in their qualifier this April!"

"No way." I jump to my feet, accidentally scaring my rabbit, as Christian sets his cup down hard on the coffee table.

"Are you sure it's legit? It's not like a scam or anything?"

"Oh, it's legit." Salem pulls up her phone. "I have all the info being sent to your emails as we speak."

My fingers curl into my hair as I gaze at her, awestruck. "How did this happen?"

"I tagged them in the videos I posted of your stunts at the rally, and they apparently liked what they saw. You guys and twenty-three others will compete to win a spot in their FMX and Best Trick competitions in August."

Christian and I blink at her. "Only one spot?"

She nods, smiling. "Yep. Only one. They're picking someone from every state."

A slow, wicked grin spreads on my lips. When I glance at Christian, I see a matching one staring back at me.

"May the best rider win, motherfucker." He raises his fist to bump it against mine, and I feel absolutely ecstatic. On cloud fucking nine.

This is the shit we've been dreaming about since we started doing jumps in Christian's backyard when we were seven.

Plopping back down on the couch, I grab my coffee for a sip. "Where's the qualifier at?"

"It changes yearly, but lucky for us, it's at the motorsport's park near Gville."

Christian looks over and flicks my nose. "The same place you ate shit and lost your scholarship to your douchebag stepbrother, *cariño*."

"Thanks for the reminder, asshole," I mutter, chest tightening. He doesn't know about Huck transferring the scholarship to me. Nor does he know that violating my probation and getting thrown into jail lost me the scholarship, but I don't plan on telling him. It's tender, still.

"Alright, now that all that's out of the way." Salem picks up her mug and finally takes a sip because she's a psycho who likes room-temperature coffee. "On to the next point, I came over here to make. Your brand."

"*T.O.T*?"

"Yeah. Videos of stunts will only get us so far, I want to start expanding outwards."

Christian rubs his temples. "You our manager now or something?"

"No, I'm your *marketing* manager." A pensive look crosses her face. "I was actually thinking of making Logan your manager."

"What, why?"

"Because he's graduating this year with a degree in business management," she deadpans, and Christian just nods.

"Shit, yeah. That checks."

Shaking my head, I set BB down on the floor before she destroys the leather couch. "What did you mean about expanding the brand?"

"I don't know, like branching out beyond just your rally performances." She takes up a spot in between us. "Any ideas?"

Christian snaps his fingers. "I got one. OnlyFans."

Salem bursts out laughing while I scoff.

"Uh, no. I'm a grower, not a shower."

"That's not even what that means," he grins. "And you show off more than anyone I know."

"Yeah, with my bike. Not my dick."

"Ok, no OnlyFans," Salem says in between chuckles. "Any other ideas that don't involve getting naked?"

"Fuck, I'm out." Christian throws up his hands while I reach over to give him a shove.

"We could start filming YouTube videos."

"Of us doing stunts?"

"Yeah. Like, really cool ones."

Salem shakes her head. "I already post on YouTube for you guys."

"Damn." Christian lets out a low whistle, "give this chica a raise."

"You don't even pay me."

"What about clothing?" I suggest, watching them from the corner of my eye. Salem sits up straighter, looking like a light bulb just went off above her head, and Christian raises his brows.

"Clothes?"

Shrugging, I look down into my mug. "Yeah. Like t-shirts and shit. We can find an artist and make some sick stuff. Maybe even sell them at the rally next year."

Salem gasps, turning to grip my arm. "We can open an Etsy shop!"

"Yeah, sure. Whatever that is."

"I'm in." Christian punches me on the shoulder. "Only one problem. Who do we know that can draw?"

"I mean, I know someone." Inhaling deeply, I rub the heels of my palms into my eyes. "But you guys aren't gonna like who it is."

# HUCKSLEE

The hospital PA system crackles to life, causing me to stiffen and hold my breath.

Logically, I know they wouldn't announce anything about my dad's surgery over their intercom. Still, it doesn't stop the pulse from quickening in my veins whenever some disembodied voice ripples through the speakers.

When all I hear is a call for some doctor to dial line three, I relax where I'm sitting in the waiting room. Dad's already been in surgery for three hours now, but they're removing his entire bladder, so I suppose that takes time. Even though the longer I wait, the more nervous I get. Maisie is across from me, nose buried in one of her magazines, while Joel and Logan are out grabbing us some food.

My body aches from the last three hours spent hunched over my sketchbook and the couch at Logan and Salem's. It's the most uncomfortable couch I've ever slept on, adding to the insomnia rearing its ugly head.

Arching my back into a stretch, I scowl at my drawing of Dad standing next to the Nova in the garage. It's still good, but nowhere near the level it should have been. I've hardly drawn so much as a stick figure in four years.

It's crazy how I fled to California for the freedom to be myself, yet I left so much of who I was behind—drawing, motocross, swimming. Don't get me wrong; I still swam in the ocean every chance I got, but pools were strictly a no-go.

As my pencil glides across the paper, I can't help but wonder if I left all of those things back here on purpose. Like parts of myself that no longer fit who I needed to become, which is wild because I fell back into football the minute I got into Berkeley. The one part of my life here that I never really had a passion for, yet I made it my whole world out there. Why?

*Because it's easy*, a voice inside my head states, one that sounds strangely like my therapist. And it's absolutely right.

Football is easy. It's the ruse around myself I'd created in high school, and even though I've been openly gay in college, making my life all about football meant that I didn't have to confront these other parts of myself that I never really gave space for. And where has that gotten me? Nearly a college graduate in a field I'm not really interested in, and a whole steaming pile of missed calls from my coach at Berkeley about the NFL draft in April. Which I'm also not looking forward to.

Yeah, that feeling of every day being a waste? After seeing how passionate Taylor and Christian are about what they choose to do for a living, I can't help but feel like I've wasted the last four years of my life.

Taking another glance at my sketchbook, I toss it onto the seat next to me in disgust just as Logan and Joel appear in the doorway with bags of fast food. There's a noticeable tension between them, from Joel's expression and how Logan's shoulders are hunched. Likely arguing about Salem again.

"Any news?" Joel sits beside Maisie, fishing a sandwich out of the bag to hand to her, while Logan picks up my sketchbook and sits beside me.

"None yet," I shake my head, taking a burger from Logan before devouring it. Dad's surgery was scheduled at the butt-crack of dawn this morning, so we barely had a chance to grab pop-tarts before we were out the door.

"No news is good news." Maisie gives me a small smile, but I can see the strain in her features. The battle won't end for her and Dad today. If all goes well, recovery from a radical cystectomy takes a while–

Not *if*. When. *When* it all goes well.

"This is really good," Logan says softly. For a minute, I think he's talking about the food until I catch him gazing down at my sketch.

Reaching out to take it from him, I shrug self-consciously. "Used to be better. But I haven't practiced in four years, and my proportions are all cartoonish."

"Let's see." Joel leans forward, gesturing for the book, which I reluctantly pass over.

He and Maisie study it quietly.

"Wow." Joel glances up at me with twinkling eyes. "Impressive, son."

Maisie nods, "I didn't know you drew, Huckslee. This is very beautiful. He's going to love it."

My throat closes as they hand it back to me. "Thank you."

I should have kept up on it. Should have kept up on a lot of things.

Rubbing my eyes, I stuff the sketchbook into my backpack before pulling out the homework I've neglected. My body is too big to really 'curl up' in a chair, so I use the backpack as a makeshift desk, losing myself in the nuances of American Government to take my mind off everything. Logan seems to have the same idea, pulling out his laptop while Joel and Maisie chitchat.

This is the worst part of it all. The waiting, the not knowing, the hoping and praying that everything goes well and life returns to normal. Even though I know there will never be a 'normal' anymore. At least, not an old one. But a new normal. He'll be alive, though, and that's all that matters. Because I can't lose another parent.

Eventually, when the thoughts get too loud, I give up on homework and scroll through my phone, answering texts from friends back in Cali and browsing socials. Somehow, I end up on Taylor's Instagram with my body turned away from Logan, and his newest post catches my eye. It's a photo of him in the middle of a backflip on his bike, his feet on the seat, and his knees pulled up to his chest. Must be an older picture because there's no snow in the background, and the caption reads:

> Guess who's going to the qualifier for Nitro Fuel Games in April?! This motherfucker, baby! Life is good.

Hashtag blessed, blah fucking blah. Thousands of likes. Resentment coils in my chest.

As usual, Taylor's living his best life while mine slowly unravels. It's not fair. But just to mock him, I pull up a photo my roommate Shawn took of me sitting on a surfboard shirtless and post it to my own IG with the caption:

Who's ready for the NFL draft in April?! This mother-fucker, baby! Life is good.

My pettiness knows no bounds, apparently. And not even three seconds later, Taylor hearts my post and comments on it with the hands raised emoji.

It doesn't feel good being this way. I know I should be the bigger person, but he drives me fucking crazy. Seriously, he brings out the absolute worst in me.

Footfalls against the tile draw my attention, and my heart jumps into my throat when I glance up to see a nurse coming forward. We all straighten in our seats as she stops before us, and the smile on her face has relief coursing through me.

"Mr. Davis is out of surgery and doing well," the nurse says, looking tired, "he's still under anesthesia right now, but the immediate family may see him. Would you like me to take you?"

"Yes, please." Maisie stands, tears in her eyes, as Joel hugs her and Logan claps me on the back.

"Give him our best," he says, smiling, "text me when you're ready, and I'll come get you."

"It's fine, I'll just call an Uber. Go do what you gotta do, Loge."

He and Salem are spending the weekend in the mountains at his dad's cabin, so I get the apartment to myself for a few days.

Taking Maisie's arm, I squeze it as we're led through a hallway to Dad's room, but I freeze just beyond the doorway at the sight of him in his hospital bed. He looks so...small. Frail.

A memory replays in my head of my mother dying of cancer, lying in a similar bed with all kinds of tubes hooked to her body. My last image of her. It's too similar.

Maisie steps up to his side, running a hand through his hair, and I just stand there with my throat working like a lunatic because I can't. I can't go in there. My legs won't move. I'm sure the nurse begins to speak, saying something about his condition, but the blood rushing to my ears drowns it out.

*Shit, shit, shit.*

"I..."

Maisie looks over at me, her brows pulling together in concern, and I flounder for something to say. The room pitches, a tremble in my fingers warning me of the oncoming anxiety attack, chest heaving.

"I'm sorry, Maisie." Backing out of the room, I spin to make a break for it. "I can't. I can't."

She calls after me, but I'm already speed-walking away down the hall, pressing my phone to my ear while bile rises in my throat.

Logan answers immediately. "Huck? What's wrong?"

"Have you left yet?" My voice breaks, the tears that were welling finally spilling onto my lashes.

He pauses. "I'm still in the parking lot. Why? Did something happen?"

"D-don't leave yet." Nausea churns my stomach as I make my way to the stairs, unable to stand the thought of the elevator. "I'm coming out. I can't...Logan, I think I'm dying."

"Hey, hey, it'll be alright. I'll meet you at the front entrance, ok? Just hold on, Huck. Breathe."

The stairs spin as I race down them, my hand clutching my chest as if to keep the organ inside from thundering to a stop. Shame and guilt war with the panic gripping my lungs.

*Just hold on, Huck.* Just hold on.

Breathe. Hold on. Breathe.

*Breathe, breathe, breathe, breathe—*

# TAYLOR

"**A**re you sure this is a good idea?"

My truck bumps and rattles along an icy, snow-covered path as we snake our way up the mountain, 'Bad Blood' by Bastille filtering through the speakers. The main road ended a few miles ago, giving way to nothing but trees as far as the eye can see. If it weren't for Salem telling me where to go, I would have driven off a fucking cliff. Thank fuck for the four-wheel drive.

Opening her mouth, Salem pauses. "No."

She's in the passenger seat, feet resting on my dash. Christian's snowmobiles are in the bed of my truck, shifting and creaking with every divot and bump we hit.

"But you wanted a chance to talk to him, right?" She looks over at me, waggling her brows as she sinks into her fur-capped winter coat. "Bridge those gaps?"

"Yeah, but I was thinking somewhere more...public." My gaze sweeps out over the mountainous terrain. "Not an isolated cabin in the fucking woods. Do you want us to kill each other?"

Her lips smack as she scoffs. "Nonsense. Logan and I will be there the entire time."

Right, because it's Logan's family cabin we're driving to for what was supposed to be a romantic Valentine's weekend for the two of them. But at the last minute, Logan declared that Huckslee was having a hard time with his dad's surgery, even though it went well, and that he'd be coming, too. So, naturally, Salem invited me as well. Without telling anyone. Because I desperately want to talk things out with Huck, and what better place to do that than in the middle of nowhere, apparently?

"Speaking of Logan." The truck bounces off a chunk of ice, making me wince. "He still mad at me for kissing him?"

"He was never mad. More confused than anything."

A laugh leaves my shivering lips. "Confused? About what? He *liked* it?"

"No, dumbass." She hits me on the shoulder. "About Huckslee. He doesn't know the full story about you two. Seeing his best friend act that way made him worry."

"Ah." An uncomfortable feeling that I'm unwilling to process settles in my stomach, so I shoot her a devilish smirk. "I don't hear you saying he *didn't* like it."

"Shut up and watch the road before you hurt the snowmobiles or kill us."

"Priorities," I snort, but close my mouth when another deep dip has us nearly hitting the roof. Light snowfall has started, but luckily, it isn't long before we're curving a bend, and the cabin rises up in the distance at the mountain's base.

It's your typical A-shaped log structure, with a covered front porch and a cute circular window above it. The entire front wall is glass, and fat puffs of smoke rise up from the chimney. Aspens and pine trees surround it, giving it a picturesque look, complete with an irate Logan standing on the porch with his arms crossed over his red winter coat.

He watches us rumble up to a stop, and he's already speaking before Salem opens her door to jump out.

"...said you were borrowing Taylor's truck, not the whole Taylor."

She lifts her chin up at him. "You brought your best friend, so I brought mine."

I wince as they glare at each other, rolling down my window so that I can open the driver's side door because the inside handle doesn't work. "Look, if it's too much trouble, I'll-"

"You shut the fuck up," Salem points at me, reaching in to grab her backpack off the floor, "if Huck can be here, so can you."

Logan pinches the bridge of his nose. "His dad just had surgery, Salem. He needed some space to deal with it."

Suddenly, I feel like a piece of shit. What the fuck am I doing here? Logan's right; Huck is dealing with some heavy stuff, and I want to bombard him with our problems? I really am a selfish bastard.

"Look, it's fine," I start, jumping out of the cab. "Let's just unload the snowmobiles for you guys, and then I'll go. Pick them up on Monday."

Salem shakes her head, pausing to protest when the screen door creaks. Huckslee exits onto the porch wearing a light blue beanie that matches his hoodie, his hair curling over his ears.

"What's going on?" His gaze finds mine, those dark eyes looking so miserable that it hits me in the chest. Fuck, even sad, he's adorable. Makes me want to make him hot chocolate and shit. Tuck a blanket around him. Sit on his face.

"Just dropping off the snowmobiles," I mumble, feeling around my denim jacket for a pack of smokes before cursing myself for running out.

The truck door slams as Salem comes around to my side. "Taylor, you don't even know the way back. You'll end up at the bottom of a river or something. Just stay."

"Nah, I can swim," I grin, hoping it's convincing. She's absolutely right, though. I don't know how I'd make it back if I had to leave, especially with the snow getting heavier now, covering up our tire tracks. But I'd figure it out if need be.

"This is ridiculous," she continues angrily, and I cringe because I can sense one of her meltdowns coming on, "it's not fair that Huck's allowed, but you're not. If I'd have known-"

Huckslee cuts her off with a sigh of resignation. "Shut up and get inside before you both freeze to death, fucking hell."

He spins back into the cabin, Logan gazing after him with a frown as Salem hums triumphantly. She marches up the cabin steps to follow Huck without even looking at her boyfriend, the tension between them palpable.

*Great.* More shit I'm probably ruining.

Getting my own bag from the truck, I climb the steps but pause when Logan's hand touches my arm.

"It's nothing personal, okay?" His golden brown eyes hold mine with sincerity. "He's just having a tough time. I don't want him to...you know."

Involuntarily, I take a step back as if he slapped me. My chest tightens painfully, and I drop my gaze to the floor, fingers in my free hand curling. He doesn't want Huck to spiral again. And he's worried my presence will set him off.

I am such a piece of fucking shit.

"I'm sorry," he says softly, studying my face, "it's not that I'm blaming you or anything. It's just when the two of you are together..."

Nodding stiffly, I step away from him. "Yeah. I get it. No worries. I'll try not to be a problem."

He tries to say something else, but I ignore him and open the screen door instead. Because what else is there to say? I get it. Huckslee and I are fucking toxic together. Which is precisely why I'm addicted to him.

The heat from inside hits me instantly, warming my bones, and I stomp my snow-packed boots on the rug before sweeping my gaze around. The ceilings are vaulted, with a brick hearth in the living room and a loft above where the bedroom is located. A small kitchen sits in the back, complete with a two-burner stove, a small sink, and a fridge. The round wooden table near the bathroom is big enough to play a card game or two. It's cozy, inviting, and also hella small.

"So where is everyone sleeping, Salem?" Logan asks with barely contained irritation. "There's only one bed and one couch."

Eyeing the soft-looking plaid sofa, I shrug as I set my bag down. "I'm fine on the floor."

"We can switch off between the couch," Huck offers, sitting at the table without looking at me, and Logan rubs the back of his neck.

"Or we can switch off between the bed?"

Salem huffs. "Or we can all four just sleep in the bed together."

That earns her a look from all of us, causing her to roll her eyes. "What? It's a King. Not like we wouldn't all fit."

Yeah, right.

Masking a snort, I cough as I head to the fireplace to warm my hands. "I'm fine on the floor, really. You know that, Salem. No worries."

It's the second time I've repeated that phrase, but in all honesty, there's a fuck-ton of worries because this cabin is smaller than my apartment, and Huckslee is so close I can smell the aftershave he uses. It's spicy and intoxicating.

Salem grabs her backpack and stomps angrily up the stairs, grumbling while awkward silence settles over us.

Shifting my shoulders uncomfortably, I stuff my fists into my pockets. "So what now?"

Logan only responds with a sigh.

"What were your plans gonna be before we interrupted," Huck asks, sounding slightly off, but I force myself not to look at his face.

"Make dinner, have wine, and play a game."

"Sweet." Unbuttoning my jacket, I pull it off my shoulders. "No point in changing up plans now. What are we cooking?"

About an hour or so later, after an awkward dinner full of cringe-worthy small talk, Salem and I stand at the sink doing dishes while the other two search for a game to play.

"There's the usual stuff in here," Logan calls from the closet next to the bathroom. "Monopoly, clue, picture book. What do we want?"

Honestly, all of that sounds boring as fuck, and I can tell Salem agrees by the breath of annoyance shooting from her nostrils.

"Strip poker?" I toss out, earning a '*haha*' from the closet. Glancing over my shoulder, a grimace pulls at my mouth when I see Logan about to grab Monopoly, but then Huck grabs something off the shelf and holds it up.

"What's this?"

Logan takes it, squinting down at some sort of card game. "Never Have I Ever?"

My fingers snap together twice. "That's the one, we're playing it. Bring it out."

"We can turn it into a drinking game," Salem gasps, and I smirk down at her as I dry my hands on a towel.

"You sure about that, Sally Mal? Because you and I will lose."

"It won't matter if you lose or not," she waves me off with a flick of her wrist. "I'm the one in danger."

"Okay, true."

The skin on the back of my neck prickles, and I turn to see Huck standing close behind me, bouncing his gaze between us with a frown.

"What's that supposed to mean?"

Salem raises a brow but busies herself with pouring the wine, leaving me to answer.

My tongue darts out to lick my bottom lip. "I'm two years sober."

Surprise flickers in his starry eyes, followed by something I don't have time to decipher before he locks his emotions down tight. "How are you going to play a drinking game if you're sober?"

"With hot chocolate." Lifting the box of Swiss Miss with a crooked grin, I give him a wink as I get my mug ready.

When we settle down into a circle in front of the fireplace, Logan's rubbing the back of his neck again like he's uncomfortable, shooting Salem little glances under his lashes. I feel slightly bad for the guy, ruining his romantic monopoly plans, but come on. What's so sexy about corporate greed and tax evasion? Nothing, that's what.

Salem pushes the box of cards towards me, curling her legs beneath herself. "You start."

"K." Flipping open the box, I pull out the first card and stare blankly at it for a long moment, blinking.

What the fuck?

"What?" Huck raises a brow at me. "What does it say?"

"Uh," clearing my throat, I read the card aloud. "Never have I ever kissed someone of the same gender?"

"Shut up, it does not say that." Salem snatches the card from me, a wild laugh bursting from her lips when she reads it. "It sure as shit does."

Huckslee's gaze meets mine before sliding away as we raise our cups to take a drink. Salem doesn't drink, and we all stare at Logan momentarily, waiting. He looks around at us, confused before the realization hits, and he lifts his cup with a scowl.

"Screw you, Taylor," he mutters, sipping, and a snicker leaves my throat.

"Aw, was I your first?"

From the corner of my eye, Huck's jaw tightens.

Logan takes the next card, frowning down at it. "Never have I ever had sex in a car? What kind of game is this? I don't even remember ever seeing this here."

He raises the box to check the back of it as the rest of us drink, a giggle shaking Salem's shoulders.

"Who stayed here last?"

"My parents," he grumbles, and she snorts.

"Your parents are freaks, babe." Reaching over, she grabs the next card from the box. "Never have I ever done oral. Hmm."

"Like, giving or receiving?" Huck asks absently, and I try to shrug nonchalantly.

"Both?"

Again, Huck, Salem, and I all drink because it doesn't specify, but what gets my attention is Logan sitting there with his lips pressed together. Huck notices, too, because he does a double take, and I see Salem gazing at him with narrowed eyes.

"Wait," I choke out, shaking my head. "What? You've never given or received oral?"

His cheeks turn red, but Salem aggressively shoves the box toward Huck. "I'm establishing a no-elaborating rule. Next question."

Huckslee picks up the next card, his eyes widening to the size of saucers as he reads it. His lips sort of part, like he can't believe what he's reading.

"N-never have I ever done anal," he stammers, not taking his attention off the card, and Salem laughs.

"Okay, but same as the oral question. Given or received? I feel like that's more of an important distinction here."

"Fine, we'll do one at a time." Huck sets the card down. "Never have I ever, uh...given anal?"

Huck, Salem, and I all drink, and the way Logan gapes at Salem has me cracking up.

Huck asks the next question. "Never have I ever received anal."

Raising my hot chocolate to my lips, it takes me a minute to notice I'm the only one drinking. Salem's smirking, of course, but Huck looks at me perplexed.

"Oh, come on," I gaze back at him in disbelief. "*Never?*"

I already know anal isn't Salem's thing, but Huckslee? He's never really...?

His lips curl into a sneer. "What, because I'm gay means I automatically like dick in my ass?"

Logan coughs as I drop my gaze, mumbling unintelligible words into my cup as he pushes the box back to me.

With heated cheeks, I read off the next question. "Never have I ever touched a member of the same gender on the genitals."

Salem snorts, and I stare at Huck over my cup as we drink, remembering a deep pool and steamy shower. He meets my gaze, eyes darkening.

Logan turns to me in surprise. "That's unexpected. Taylor, are you...?"

My attention snaps over to him, and I freeze, realizing what he's asking. Huckslee does, too, because he's suddenly searching my face intently, waiting for an answer. My pulse quickens.

"We said no elaborating." Salem gestures at him to take the next card, glancing at me sideways, and if Huck wasn't still staring a hole in my head, I'd mouth her a thank you.

"Never have I ever had male genitalia in my mouth." Logan grimaces. "Why did they word it like this?"

Both Salem and Huck drink, and I raise my hand to Logan with a grin. "Yeah, up top. We win."

"I'm not high-fiving you over my girlfriend having your dick in her mouth," he deadpans, shocking the fuck out of me while Salem chokes on her wine.

Blinking at him, my lips twitch. "Yeah, like, years ago."

Literally, before she got with Logan, Salem was with a guy for almost a year who wasn't interested in sharing. We haven't done anything together other than kiss on the cheek in like three years. And honestly, even if they didn't work out, I don't think I'd be interested in her like that again. Mainly because my head is full of someone with dark brown eyes and soft, blond curls...

Salem gives Logan a curious look, her cheeks flushed from the alcohol as she picks up the next card. "Never have I ever made love."

Her gray eyes grow sad at that, making my heart clench. We both raise our cups to drink because we did at one point love each other in the romantic sense, but as Logan's cup remains in his hands, it hits me why she seems upset.

"Wait, wait." I glance between them, vaguely realizing that Huck didn't raise his cup either. "Logan, what are you trying to say?"

"Drop it, Taylor." Salem gazes down at her cup forlornly. "No elaborating, remember?"

"No, I want to know." The broken look on her face is setting me off, and I round on her boyfriend. "You don't love her?"

The blood drains from Logan's face as he gazes up at me, terrified. "Of course I do!"

"I don't understand." I shake my head, but Huck is suddenly in my face.

"How come he's the only one who has to explain his answer?" His breath is hot on my face as he glares down at me. "If he has to explain, then so do you."

"Fine." I throw up a hand to Logan with gritted teeth. "Which question do you want me to elaborate on?"

Huckslee whips around to his best friend. "The one you were going to ask him earlier. Ask it."

His tone is harsh, and Logan glances between us, clearly uncomfortable, but I already know what he's going to ask before he opens his mouth.

"Taylor, are you bi?"

# TAYLOR

My mouth opens, but I close it, feeling like I swallowed sandpaper.

Everyone's attention is on me, but Huckslee's dark eyes are the only ones I see, boring down into mine with such force that I find myself moving closer.

This answer should be easy. I've thought about it constantly over the last four years, a subject I've broached with Doctor Hart numerous times. Being out of small-town Utah and free from my father's bullshit helped.

But I've never...put it into words before. Like, out loud. Given my feelings a name.

"Answer the question, Taylor," Huckslee snaps, causing Salem to glare at him with red-rimmed eyes.

"Leave him alone!"

*Why does he want to know so bad?*

"No, he needs to answer." My stepbrother's gaze is like a black hole, swallowing me in. "I didn't get a choice in coming out, so why should he?"

*Ah.* So that's it. Revenge.

Sitting back on my heels, my shoulders slump as I stare at the floor. "I don't...I don't know."

He turns away, his scoff like a knife to the chest.

"I don't have a lot of experience, okay? I've only ever been with one guy, and he's the only one I've ever...felt like that with. The only guy I've ever thought about in that way, so I don't know if bi is the right word for it?" Breaking off with a frown, I bite my lip. "Either way, I don't think I need to put a name to it. I just am."

Huck is watching me, but I can't look at him. Instead, I turn to Logan, who's looking at Salem with a mixture of longing and sorrow.

"Your turn."

Logan swallows, pausing a moment before hanging his head. "Look, I do love her, okay? It's just that we've never... I've never had sex, much less made love."

My shocked gaze bounces between them, and Huckslee does the same. Like, I'm really not one to judge because other people's relationships aren't my business, but I can't fathom it. The fact that they've been together for two years, even live together, and haven't even fucked?

"Why?" Huck finally asks, just as flabbergasted as I am.

Salem downs the rest of her wine before climbing to her feet. "Because I don't want to get married!"

Next thing I know, she's stomping up the stairs with tears on her cheeks, and Logan is brokenly watching her go. The urge to console her is strong, but that's not my place right now, so I duck my head until Logan's watery gaze meets mine. "You better go after her."

And he does. He's up in the loft within minutes, playing music, so we can't hear their conversation. Huck and I kneel there for a moment, avoiding each other's gazes, and he slowly starts to collect the cards with his head bent.

"You wanna keep playing?" He asks.

We could. It would be an excellent way to 'bridge the gap' as Salem puts it, and open up some form of communication. But I really don't want to know about his sex life, and I doubt he wants to hear about mine.

"I'm out of hot chocolate," I find myself saying, scooping up everyone's cups. "And it's getting late. We should probably clean up."

He only nods, silently putting the cards back into the box. One of them catches his eye, though, and he pauses momentarily as he stares at it.

I quickly wash the cups at the sink before drying them and placing them on the rack. When I turn around, Huckslee is still kneeling, bent over that one card.

"One more question," he says slowly, turning it over in his hand, "then we can put the game away."

Rising from a crouch, he thoughtfully brings the card over to the sink, grabbing two glasses before filling them with water. After setting them in front of us, he lifts the card to read it.

"Never have I ever been in love."

His eyes meet mine, a starry night against snow-capped mountains. He doesn't make a move toward his drink.

But I do.

Holding his gaze, I pick up my glass and drain its contents before placing it in the sink.

Neither of us looks away from the other. I don't think he's breathing. For all he knows, I could be drinking for Salem or any other girl I've dated over the years, but I know I'm not.

And I make sure that he knows it, too, by how I look at him.

Realizing I was in love with Huckslee wasn't as earth-shattering as the books and movies make it out to be. I kind of always knew in the back of my mind. That's why I couldn't seem to stay away from him. I just never thought he felt the same, especially after the way I treated him. At least, until he punched me out for kissing Logan, and then hope pulsed to life inside this cold, dead heart.

His eyes zero in on my lip, where it's caught between my teeth, and he leans in slightly. My breath is trapped inside my lungs, little flutters of emotion flipping around in my stomach. Just when I think he's going to press those soft, full lips against mine...he spins around, grabs his bag, and enters the bathroom before shutting the door tightly. Sliding the lock into place.

Dazedly, I blink at his full glass, feeling my heart race. A numbness spreads over me, moving my limbs mechanically as I wash out the glasses before grabbing my own bag to change into sweats. Huckslee doesn't emerge until I've settled on the floor before the fire, a blanket beneath me while one covers my body. I also laid a few for him on the sofa with a pillow from the closet.

"Thank you," he murmurs, lying down, but I don't respond. Instead, I'm listening to the music still playing softly from upstairs, staring into the flames, reliving all my worst moments.

Like all of the times my dad laid hands on me, and I was so desperate to replace the memories of his fists with someone else's. Anyone else's. And then Huck saw my bruises for the first time in the locker room after ninth-grade football practice.

*"Hey, are you okay?"*

*Crap. I already know who it is before I turn around, his voice being the first sound I listen for in the halls. Should have checked better, but I thought everyone had left ready.*

*Bunching up my face, I glance over my shoulder at him and glare. "What do you want, Fuckslee?"*

*His big brown eyes are wide as he takes in my bare back. "What happened to you? Are those fingerprints?"*

*Shit. No, no, no.*

*He's gonna tell. I just know it. And then Dad and my bike will be gone. I'll get sent somewhere far away, and I'll never see Christian again.*

*No, no, no no*

*I can't let him. So I spout off the first thing that comes to my head.*

*"Are you checking me out, dude?! In the locker room?"*

*His face goes white, and his lips part as he stammers. "N-no, I wasn't! I j-just thought-"*

*Something twists in my stomach at seeing him out of sorts. It makes me feel icky, like I want to stop his stuttering and take it back, but I can't. And it makes me angry.*

*So I throw out my fist, connecting it with his stomach, causing him to double over and groan. But the sick feeling doesn't go away. It just worsens.*

*"Don't let me catch you ever looking at me in the locker room again," I snarl close to his head, but before I know what's happening, he's knocked me onto my back. Pain erupts as he hits me once, twice, right in the sides. And then he's glaring down at me, calling me an asshole before storming off. I decide to lay here for a while, breathing through the aches on my body and in my chest. I feel bad.*

*But at least if Huck goes to a teacher and tells them what he saw, I can blame the bruises on him.*

*Even if I kind of hate myself for hurting him.*

A deep sigh from the couch draws me out of my head.

"I can tell you're awake," Huck grumbles, "and it's keeping *me* awake. Go to sleep, Taylor."

With a hum, I draw my blanket tighter around me. "How can you tell?"

He's silent for a moment. "Your thoughts are basically screaming."

"What are they saying?" I whisper, stomach quivering.

For a moment, I don't think he hears me.

"I don't know what they're saying," he mutters, blankets rustling. "I never know what's going on inside your head."

Yeah, Old Taylor was a mess at explaining his feelings. But slightly jaded, sober Taylor, who's been in therapy for years, has formed healthier habits—well, healthy-ish.

So I flip around to find Huck's eyes wide open, on his side facing me. "I can tell you if you like?"

He blinks. "Not interested."

Yeah, I bet.

"Well, I need to say it," I swallow, keeping my gaze on him. "Huckslee, I'm sorry."

"I said I'm not interested." His face hardens, lips curling into a snarl. "I don't want to hear it, Taylor."

"Maybe you need to."

He growls angrily, rolling over. "I don't need to do shit. Leave me alone."

For a second, I just stare at him, feeling hollow.

I've offered him an olive branch, not for the first time, and it feels like he keeps shutting me down. You'd think I'd take the hint. Move on, let him go, realize he can't feel anything for me after our past. But hope still burns inside me, and I refuse to let it die. I *can't*. Not when there are so many things unknown and unspoken between us. Because not only does he deserve closure, but so do I, dammit.

I fucking deserve closure.

"*No.*" I'm up off the floor instantly, standing above the sofa. "No, you don't get to shut me out."

He turns over onto his back and yelps in surprise when I climb on top of him, straddling my legs on either side of his hard stomach. Pinning his arms to his sides, I glare at his shell-shocked expression.

"You're going to listen to me, Huckslee, whether you like it or not."

"Get the fuck off!" He tries to squirm beneath me but freezes when he realizes the movement puts his dick right at my ass. It has my cock twitching, but I ignore it because that's not the head I want to think with right now. He has no choice but to sit still, and he knows it, so he presses his face into the pillow as his lids squeeze shut.

"Close your eyes all you want, baby, but you can't close your ears, so just fucking listen," I breathe fiercely, reveling in the way those dark starry eyes pop wide open. "The things I did to you in high school were wrong, and I'm so fucking sorry. I know saying it won't make a difference, it won't change anything that happened, but–"

He cuts me off with a snarl. "Then why say it at all?"

"Because your feelings fucking mattered, Huckslee, and I played with them like they didn't."

"Is that supposed to make me feel better?"

"No," I shake my head, licking my lips. "It's supposed to make you feel however you feel. And whatever that is, it matters, and I'm sorry I ever made you feel like it didn't. I hurt you in ways I'll never be able to mend. And I need you to know I acknowledge what I did to you."

"Got it, thanks." He tries to shift under me again, but it only worsens his position. "Now get off."

"I'm not done."

He scoffs, eyes as black as night. "What is this? Some kind of forced therapy type shit? If you're waiting for forgiveness, Taylor, you'll be six feet under before that ever happens–"

Dropping his gaze, his breath hitches, and I follow his attention to where it rests on my hard dick poking into his solid six-pack through my sweats.

Oops.

Okay, maybe sitting on him wasn't the best idea for this conversation. Especially when he's shirtless and my hands are wrapped around his thick biceps, dusky pink nipples teasing me for a bite. He's so much broader than he was before, and fuck, he feels good under me. But this isn't what I crawled on top of him for.

"My eyes are up here," I smirk, biting my lip when his gaze shoots up to mine, pulse pounding on the side of his throat. I can feel his heartbeat through my thighs. Taking a deep breath, I lean forward to get closer to his face. "Huck, I never hated you. In fact, I really fucking liked you, okay? Like a lot. Remember when I explained all of this at the track?"

He nods slowly. "Yeah. You fucked with me because you didn't want to lose your bike."

"There's more to it, though." I wince, contemplating how much I'm willing to tell him. "My home life was...shitty. I've told you my dad was an asshole. He wasn't good to me, smacked me around sometimes. That morning in your bed, after the pool, remember when I couldn't—"

"Please stop," he rasps, and I peek up at him from under my lashes to find his face contorted in pain. "I don't want to think about that."

His cock swelling against my ass tells a different story, but I also know that sometimes the mind and body don't always agree.

"I wanted you to touch me, Huck," I whisper, fighting every urge right now to grind against him. "But all I could hear was his voice in my head, spouting his bullshit. It fucked me up."

He twitches beneath me, battling urges of his own. "And that day in the shower?"

"Same thing." I pause, pursing my lips. "I was also on shrooms, though, so I was tripping balls."

His abs clench with a small, husky laugh, and Jesus, it's the most beautiful sound I've ever heard. The thick column of his throat flexes as he swallows, eyes bouncing between mine.

"What do you hear in your head now?"

Tilting my head to listen, dark hair falls into my eyes as I give in and roll my hips over his stiff length. "Just you, Huckslee."

A hushed gasp leaves his lips, followed by that low moan I've heard in my dreams as he bucks off the couch, pressing his stiff cock into the crease of my ass.

God, I want to feel him. To taste his lips again and feel his cock pulse in my hands, explore his body properly with my tongue. But I can't start down that road without talking to him about prom. I just can't. It doesn't feel right. Because I want him, and I know he can't give himself fully without coming to terms with what happened. Forgiveness or not.

So I lift off him, biting my lip to stifle a smile at his whine. "I still have more to say."

"Fucking hell, Tay." He draws a ragged breath, hips moving yearningly against the couch in a way that kills me. "Can't it wait until later?"

I fucking wish.

"No. Because if I go any further without saying this to you, I'd be such a selfish asshole, and I'm trying not to be that person anymore."

Keyword: *trying*.

Huck goes still, eyes growing cautious as his brows pinch together.

"Okay," he says slowly, waiting.

Licking my lips nervously, I brace myself. "We need to talk about prom."

He goes rigid beneath me, face immediately hardening, and I almost physically feel the wall he slams up between us. "No. Hard fucking no, I'm not talking about that."

"We need to get it out, Huck."

"Get it out?" He curls his lip incredulously. "What the fuck is that supposed to mean? Get *what* out?"

"This shit between us!" I almost shout, starting to feel frustrated. "It's fucking toxic, man. Poison. It's like a cancer that'll only get worse unless we talk about it—"

I realize I fucked up as soon as that word leaves my mouth.

"Shit." Releasing one of his arms, I run trembling fingers through my hair. "I'm sorry, Huck, I shouldn't have put it that way. I didn't think."

"You never do." His dark eyes burn like coals as he glares up at me. "You don't care about anyone or anything else other than yourself and your bike, Taylor."

"Maybe at one time, yeah. I admit that I was a prick, but I'm trying to make up for that now."

"Bull-fucking-shit." He starts to buck again, trying to free himself from under me. "You'll always be the same, and you can go fuck yourself with your half-assed apologies."

I know he's upset because I brought up prom and cancer, but his words still sting. My legs tighten as I try to maintain my hold on him, but he uses his free arm to shove me over onto the floor, and I hit it *hard*. Right on my shoulder, the collar bone popping as an ache shoots down my arm.

"Goddammit," I hiss, lifting to my feet with a wince. "You know what, I'm not doing this with you. Not anymore. When you can have a conversation without getting violent, come find me."

Grabbing my blanket off the floor and wrapping it around myself like a fucking toddler, I climb the steps up to the loft where Logan and Salem are currently snuggled up.

"Scoot over. Huckslee's pissing me off."

"Seriously, Taylor," Logan grumbles groggily but shifts himself and Salem closer to the middle so I can slide in behind him.

Loud stomps come from the stairs, and suddenly, Huckslee is rounding the bed to the other side. "Nuh-uh, no way. If you three get to sleep in the bed, then so do I."

He pulls back the covers but hesitates when he realizes he'll basically be spooning Salem.

"Either get in or leave," she snaps, shivering. "It's fucking freezing."

Making a decision, he crawls in behind her, as close to the edge of the bed as he can, before pulling the blanket up. His glare meets mine over both of their heads, making me even more irritated, so I decide to make everyone uncomfortable because now I'm in a bad mood.

"If we all had a foursome, who would go where?"

"Jesus Christ." Logan burrows his face into Salem's neck while Huck curls his lip at me.

"Are you kidding me, Taylor?"

"Hypothetically, of course."

Everyone's quiet for a long moment, and I settle into my pillow, smirking when I think I've accomplished my goal. Then Salem's sleepy voice breaks the silence.

"I'd be in the back with a strap on," she mumbles, "obviously."

That gets a snort out of me.

Logan huffs in annoyance. "But who would you be fucking?"

"Huckslee."

All three of us raise our heads off the bed in unison.

"What?"

"M-me?"

"Why the hell would you be fucking Huckslee?" I squint over at where she lays with her eyes still closed, lips pursed as she tries to fight a smile.

"Because he's the only one in this bed I haven't dated. Can I sleep now?"

I guess that's fair.

"Well, Huckslee's not fucking *me*," Logan grumbles, laying his head back down, and Huck groans as he runs a hand over his red face.

"Oh my God, stop this."

Snickering, I snuggle into Logan. "I'll fuck you, princess."

"That would mean that Huckslee has to fuck *you*," Salem grunts.

My eyes snap to Huck as everything goes still. When our gazes lock, it feels like the breath is knocked out of my lungs at the heat that flashes across his features before he schools his expression. Warmth pools in my lower stomach, tingling up my spine at the thought of Huckslee above me, inside me, pounding into me, owning me...

"This scenario is fucking stupid." I flip over onto my sore shoulder, deciding I'd rather deal with the pain than the embarrassment of my hard cock touching Logan's back.

"You started it, dumbass."

Yeah, I did.

And now it'll be near impossible for me to get it out of my head.

# Huckslee

Sleeping in a bed with three other people isn't as unpleasant as I initially thought.

Even when I wake up to Salem's hot morning breath on the side of my neck and Logan's leg tossed over us, it feels oddly...nice. Safe, I guess. Despite all the shit that happened last night, it was the best night's sleep I've had in a long time. Even the sight of Taylor on his back with his hand resting on Logan's hip doesn't piss me off. It feels like we were all going through our own things last night and just needed comfort or something. Knowledge that we aren't alone. I'll be honest; it's a weird bubble I don't want to leave, but it pops the minute Taylor's chest moves as he wakes and turns toward me. Like he sensed my alertness.

Fixing my face into a scowl, I watch as he flashes me a sleepy grin and stretches, the hem of his shirt—Tweety Bird flipping two middle fingers—riding up to showcase his completely lickable abs. He moans into the stretch, the sound bolting through my cock, and I have to shove Logan's leg off before he feels it jerk against him.

And now everyone's awake.

*Nice going, Taylor.*

I glare at him as Salem pulls away from me, rubbing her eyes. "Sorry. You're like a space heater. So warm."

"I know, it's okay."

Logan tightens his hold on her, grumbling and unwilling to get up. He's never been a morning person.

On the other hand, Taylor springs to his feet with a chuckle, his dark hair adorably sticking up in the back where it flattened against the pillow. "Mornin'!"

Those bright blue-green eyes slide over to me, and I can't help but remember the way they looked last night when they darkened after Salem joked about me fucking him. How they glazed with interest as if he actually imagined it. Just like I did. The way he'd look, bent over for me, the sounds he'd make...

And now I'm hard. Great.

"What's for breakfast?" Salem extricates herself from Logan's hold, kissing his forehead before reaching up to tighten the messy bun on her head.

"Bacon in the fridge," Logan mumbles, pressing his face further into the pillow. "Eggs. OJ."

"Please tell me you brought coffee." I roll out of bed, wrapping a blanket around myself not only because it's freezing but to hide my boner.

Salem crawls to the edge of the bed, pulling on a thick robe before stuffing her feet into a pair of fuzzy red slippers. "I brought some. Logan doesn't like it."

"Cuz he's an absolute menace." Taylor raises his arms above his head in a move that has his back and ass muscles flexing before following her downstairs, and I curse him silently. I wasn't this aware of him until last night when he climbed on top of me. It's going to be a problem.

Hanging back, I take a moment to stand there and cool off. Get my bearings. Try to process everything that took place over the last twenty-four hours.

"You alright?" Logan's voice comes from the bed, gazing up at me with one eye open.

"Yep." I nod, for once feeling like it's the truth. "All good."

Because I am. Really. Yeah, the whole thing with Taylor is irritating, but I don't feel like I'm spiraling. I feel...lighter this morning. Rested. Settled.

"Good." He closes his eyes, pulling the blanket over his head to block out the sun from the wall of glass downstairs. "Bring me breakfast."

I did not, in fact, bring him breakfast.

Salem went up there to jump on the bed until he came downstairs, grumbling the entire time. After everyone had eaten and showered an hour and a half later, we were out in the freezing cold, dressed in snowsuits, getting the snowmobiles ready. There are only two of them, and for some reason, I thought I'd ride with Logan until he climbs on behind Salem, which leaves...

"So, who's gonna be the backpack?" Taylor asks, adjusting the goggles under his helmet. I just scowl at the snowmobile like it personally offended my grandma, and after a moment, he laughs.

"You've never been on one of these, have you?"

Fuck, how does he read me so easily?

Shaking my head, the scowl deepens when I catch his grin before he climbs onto the machine.

"Hold on tight, spider monkey," he drawls, patting the seat behind him.

"Really? You're quoting Twilight?"

He shrugs as I take my place against his back. "It's Salem's favorite movie."

"Actually," she shouts next to us, voice muffled by her helmet, "he's lying. He's seen it a hundred times—"

Taylor cuts her off by starting the snowmobile, and my arms barely have time to wrap around him before he lurches forward. He takes the lead, guiding us through trees and over the frozen terrain with hand signals, and holy shit, I didn't expect snowmobiles to be this fast. Nearly as fast as a dirt bike, except with gears instead of wheels. And just like a dirt bike, Taylor handles it with expertise, navigating us over bumps and dips like it's second nature to him.

I'll admit, the scenery we pass is breathtaking. As much as I miss the warmth and forests of California, nothing compares to Utah's winter. The sun reflects off icicles dripping through frozen birch branches, creating kaleidoscopes of color against powdered snow. A sea of white falls over pine trees like icing, flakes sparkling in the air.

As Taylor accelerates, we pull into a clearing, weaving the snowmobile in a zigzag that has me tightening my hold on his middle. His shoulders shake with laughter before he whips us into spins, snow spraying around us in wide arcs. Salem and Logan follow suit, doing doughnuts in the fresh powder, whoops of joy ringing out over the engines.

My lungs empty as a shout bursts from me, one arm up in the air while the other clings to Taylor for dear life. I feel lighter than air. For once, every thought and worry leaves my brain other than this very moment. Despite the adrenaline shooting through my veins, the noise inside me is calm.

Eventually, Taylor brings the snowmobile to a halt and motions with his hand for me to get off. When I do, I watch curiously as he guns it toward a tall hill, riding up the side of it and clearing air before coming back down. Like the slope is a half-pipe or something. He does this several times, and a soft laugh to my left has me looking down at Salem, who's shaking her head affectionately as she films him.

"I call those the Taylor zoomies," she grins.

Honestly, it's fitting. The way he's jumping up and sliding down the hill repeatedly reminds me of a golden retriever who's been let off his leash. It's oddly endearing.

Once he's gotten it out of his system, we're back on the trail again, and by mid-day, we stop at a vast lake after an hour or two. The early afternoon sun glints off the lake, beams of light dancing through the trees. It's so bright without the helmet that I pull out my Oakleys, shoving them on to shade my eyes as I gaze out at the frozen water from a wooden dock.

It's beautiful and quiet, all sound cushioned by the surrounding snowfall like we've stepped into a snow globe. If I could, I'd paint the scene before me. But I've never been good with paints, much less landscapes. Pencils are my strong skill, and even then, I feel my sketches lack a sort of realism to them. Proportions are usually too big, dramatized, or wonky. It's why I gave up the comic I was working on in high school; I'll never compare to the late greats like Steve Ditko or Jack Kirby.

Despite the sun, a chill hits me from being out in the cold all day, which has me crossing my arms with a shiver. The snowsuit I borrowed from Logan is warm, but the air hitting my neck bites. A thermos appears in my vision, and I look over to see Taylor standing next to me, lines on his red cheeks from the ski goggles on his forehead, pushing his hair back. Nose pink. He looks so fucking cute that I automatically scowl.

"Here." He shakes the thermos. "It'll warm ya."

I don't know why I'm expecting something like rum or whiskey when I take a swig, especially when he told me yesterday that he's two years sober, but what I'm not expecting is the thick, hot sweetness that rolls over my tongue.

"Hot chocolate?"

He grins, flashing his crooked incisor when he nods in encouragement, and I find myself staring at his bright eyes as I take a few more gulps before handing it back to him. The color in his irises seems more green today against the sea of white surrounding us.

After he screws the lid shut, we gaze out at the frozen lake in silence. Logan's laugh comes from behind us, followed by Salem's voice, but I don't feel like joining their conversation right now. I like the calm I've found near the water.

But, of course, Taylor has to disturb it because the guy doesn't know how to shut up.

"Want to ice skate with me?" He throws an offering hand out to the lake, and I raise my brows over my sunglasses.

"Are you kidding?"

That damn grin taunts me again.

"Uh, negatory." My eyes sweep over the lake. "Who knows how thin or thick that ice is?"

His lips smack in protest. "Where's your sense of whimsy, Huck?"

"My sense of self-preservation outweighs it," I choke out, and I feel him freeze next to me. The look on his face clearly indicates he's been taken off guard, but he recovers quickly, and I stare at him perplexed until the words I said dawn on me.

*Sense of self-preservation.*

What, the knowledge that I want to live threw him for a loop?

My chest tightens painfully as I turn away. I guess I get it. The whole trust thing, remember? Between the looks of worry I get from my grandparents and Logan, I should be used to it by now. And I am. Even if it still stings a little when it happens, I understand. But coming from Taylor? Something about it hurts more, and I can't understand why.

Things get awkward after that. I wish he'd join Logan and Salem and leave me be. The peace I felt earlier, that comfortable buzz inside of me, is fading fast with his presence so close, different from when I was pressed against him on the snowmobile. Against the cushioned hush of the lake, his nearness feels almost intimate, making my skin itch.

"Have you ever ice-fished?" He blurts suddenly, startling me, and I shake my head.

"Nope."

"Me either." He's quiet for a moment. "I'd go ice fishing. With you."

Brows pulling down, I turn to find him gazing at me cautiously. My lips twitch, and as hard as I try to keep it in, a laugh bursts out of me because that was just...such a weird thing to say. And the way he said it. Haltingly, like he was unsure how to speak.

"I'd go ice fishing with you, too," I chuckle, grinning widely, but then it falls off my face when I remember who I'm talking to.

This is Taylor fucking Tottman, and I'm supposed to hate him. Because he's an asshole. And selfish. And the cute, charming act he's got on right now is just that; an act.

As if sensing my sudden shift in mood, his face tightens, shoulders tensing like he's bracing for something. We gaze at each other momentarily before I pull away, turning toward where Logan and Salem are sunbathing on a nearby picnic table.

"We should probably head back to the cabin soon."

"Yeah. Right."

As he follows, the dejected tone in his voice makes my jaw clench, but I say nothing while we all pile back onto our snow-mobiles and head out. I catch Salem's helmet turning toward Taylor occasionally as if she sees something she doesn't like, but whatever. Not my problem. Taylor's feelings are not my problem.

We must have gone far because it takes us over an hour to get back to the cabin. The hearth is freezing because *someone* (Taylor) was so excited to go snowmobiling that he forgot it was his turn to load the fireplace before we left. As he begins piling in the wood, I let off a string of grumbled curses that have Salem narrowing her eyes at me before locking myself in the bathroom to shower.

Good mood gone. Peace bubble popped.

*Fuck you, Taylor.*

My mood improves slightly later that night.

Salem and I are on opposite ends of the sofa, sharing a blanket while she does homework, and I attempt to draw in my sketchbook. Logan and Taylor are sitting on the floor playing Monopoly, and I'll admit that Taylor's hatred for the game is pretty funny. He's been bitching and moaning about it since they started playing.

"All right, I give up." He throws his hands in the air, face bunched up as he shoves his properties toward Logan. "Take all my shit. I'm done."

"You're such a sore loser." Logan gathers his winnings with a satisfied smirk, and Taylor scrubs at his face.

"I do not understand this fucking game. Who enjoys escaping from the reality of paying rent and taxes by playing a game about paying rent and taxes?!"

I raise my hand with a pencil, eyes still focused on my sketch. "Me."

Taylor scoffs. "Says the Poli-Sci major."

Blinking, I force myself to keep my gaze down instead of glancing up at him. How does he know I'm going for a Political Science degree? Logan may have mentioned something.

Christian's voice from that night at the rally replays in my head.

*"Baby boy never misses any. And if he does, he gets moody as fuck."*

I honestly thought it was an exaggeration, but if it wasn't? An uncomfortable feeling settles in my gut, and I shift around on the couch to displace it.

As Logan cleans up the game, Taylor rises with a huff before unceremoniously plopping down between us, sending her textbook on media ethics sliding to the floor.

"You fucker," she grunts, and he smiles as he picks it up for her before turning his attention to me. To the sketchbook on my lap.

He watches quietly until Salem kicks him in the thigh.

"You still draw?" He clears his throat as I shoot him a look. "Obviously."

Taylor says nothing, only studies the sketch I'm trying to do of the lake.

"I didn't, for a long time," I admit with a shrug, "but I'm trying to get back into it."

"Yeah?" Another kick from Salem. "Um, so I might have an idea for you if you're interested."

With a raised brow, I turn to look at him, waiting. His eyes nervously bounce from mine to the sketch, and I grit my teeth impatiently.

"So, Christian and I had this idea–" A third kick to his thigh. "*Salem*, Christian, and I had this idea of expanding our T.O.T brand into things like merchandise. Shirts and hats and stuff. Maybe stickers. We would need an artist to help with the designs, and I figured since you're an artist and all..." His fingers pick at a loose thread on his sleeve. "If you wanted to, you know, collaborate. Help with ideas."

I stare at him wordlessly because I don't know how to respond.

"You'd get compensated, of course," Salem pipes in. "We'd pay you for the work, and you'd get a cut of the sales. You're not expected to work for free. Unlike me."

She snickers at Taylor, who rolls his eyes before placing them on me expectantly.

My lips pull down while I blink a few times. "I'm...not very good."

He holds a hand out for the sketchbook. "I highly doubt that, but let's see."

That self-conscious feeling churns in my stomach again like it did when Logan's dad and Maisie were looking, but I hand the book over to him and focus on the fire as he slowly flips through it. Salem leans in, making little *'oohs'* and *'ahs.'* It's a new sketchbook, so there isn't a lot in it yet, but a slight sound comes out of Taylor's throat that has me whipping my head toward him. I go very still when I see what he's studying with wide eyes.

*Shit.* I forgot that was in there.

Motherfuck.

"This is my bike?" Taylor taps the page with a finger, lips parted as he brings it closer to his face. He's almost enraptured, completely awed, and sweat starts to bead on my neck. The wheels are bigger than they should be, and big puffs of cartoonish smoke billow out of the tailpipe.

Faking an easy shrug, I swallow the lump forming in my throat. "I was trying something new, is all."

"Your attention to detail is amazing, man," he laughs, pointing at a spot near the rear fender. "I scraped it right there when

I overcorrected a landing at a buddy's house and laid the bike down. And look at all of my decals!"

Yeah, the amount of time I spent studying his IG posts to get everything right is embarrassing. I was going to add him in, too, eventually, but thank fuck that I didn't. I don't think I'd ever come back from that embarrassment.

Handing the book back, his eyes shine as he smiles brightly at me. "You're a real artist, Huck. I'm serious. Those are so good."

Damn, the pride in his eyes. It makes me feel...

I hate the way it makes me feel.

"I agree," Salem nods. "You've got talent, Huckslee. Think about our offer. If you're interested, let us know, and we'll sort out the logistics."

I huff an anxious laugh as I shove the book into my bag. "Logistics. What, are you their manager or something?"

"Marketing manager." She rolls her eyes before glancing over her shoulder at where Logan is fixing dinner. "I'm trying to make my boyfriend their business manager, but he's being a little bitch."

"I don't know the first thing about managing a business, Salem," he grumbles, chopping onions, and that gets a laugh out of me.

"Isn't that, like, the whole purpose of your college degree? To learn how?"

"Doing something in theory and practice are two totally different things."

"How will you learn if you don't try, babe?" She squints at him. "Why do you think I do all this shit for Taylor and

Christian without getting paid? The experience. Knowledge. Duh. Well, and plus, they're both broke as a joke."

Dinner is spent with the two of them poking fun at each other while Taylor chimes in, and that peaceful feeling starts to settle over me again. It's kind of...easy spending time with them. Despite all the heavy stuff between Taylor and me, the vibe that all three of them put off is warm and inviting, like family.

After moving to Cali, I spent a lot of time alone. Sure, I had my grandparents over the summer, who were amazing and took me on trips whenever possible. I had my roomie Shawn, who's pretty chill and taught me to surf. A few friends from classes. I had my teammates, but they were just that; teammates. Coworkers. I never really hung out with any of them off the field. And then there were the boyfriends. One boyfriend after another, no relationship lasting longer than a year at most, because despite how hard I tried to make things work, I always felt...lonely. And fake.

But I loved the ocean. A painful, almost homesickness chokes me up when I think about how much I miss that wide-open, churning vastness. Sitting on a surfboard, tossed about by something alive and free and more significant than any of my problems. But still. The sea never made me feel this way, even on its calmest days. And I don't know how to handle it because I ran away from Utah in the first place to feel like this. So why is it hitting me now, here, of all places?

Once dinner is cleaned up, Logan and Salem head upstairs while Taylor follows like a lost puppy. I stay on the couch, listening to their conversations while working on homework. I planned on sleeping down here; I really did. But when their chattering starts to fade, I find myself heading up, throat closing with emotion at how they all make room for me in the bed like it's an unspoken invitation.

Taylor's eyes meet mine briefly before they sink closed, and I can't help but think:

After all these years, why does it feel like I'm finally coming home?

# TAYLOR

It's our final day at the cabin, and Logan left for the day with Salem.

They borrowed my truck because Logan had some surprise or something for her, which means I'm stuck here alone. With Huckslee. On Valentine's Day. Until they return later tonight.

He's currently downstairs on the couch, doing homework or whatever, while I'm up here on the floor in the loft staring at the ceiling. Trying to get my feelings in order, wishing I could go down there and climb on his lap again, but that's a big ol' negative because he's been in a piss poor mood all morning. All weekend, really, despite the few smiles I've dragged out of him like the sun playing peek-a-boo during a storm.

Fuck, he's such a grump.

*Probably needs to get laid.*

Yeah, well, he can get in line because I'm the only one who's touched my dick in like two months. Not really a record, seeing as how I spent six months in jail at one point, but it's been many a year since I've gone this long without at least a blowjob, and it's making me cranky as fuck.

Not for lack of trying. Really, every time Christian brings a chick back from the Prospector, he tries to share, but I'm just not into it. Seems my shit only stands at attention lately when it involves the sulky fucker downstairs who hates me, so that's just great.

Hasn't even touched me, and he owns this dick.

How unfair is that?

Thumping comes from the stairs, and I lift onto my elbows in time to see Huckslee pause on the top step, frowning.

"Why are you on the floor?"

He's wearing a Calvin Klein sweater, sleeves rolled up to showcase his veiny forearms and jeans that hug his thighs. His curls are still damp from a shower.

"Uh." Swallowing, I follow the way his gaze tracks down my torso, taking in my exposed belly button. "Just thinkin'."

*With my dick.*

"Okay," he says slowly, eyeing me curiously. "Well, do you want to take a break from that and go for a hike, maybe? I'm feeling cooped up."

Hope spikes in my chest, and I sit up quickly. "Do we have snow shoes?"

He wants to hike with me? Like, *actually* spend time with me?

"Let's find out."

Ten minutes later, after searching the closet top to bottom, it's clear that we do not, in fact, have snow shoes. Trying to hide my disappointment, I stand at the wall of windows, watching the snow lightly fall. Wherever Logan and Salem went, I hope they're okay. I'm sure they are—Logan knows these woods inside out. But still. Worry niggles at the back of my mind. It's not snowing hard, but it could pick up later.

"What now?" Huck asks, standing next to me, and an idea pops into my head.

"Wanna build a snowman?" Turning to him with a grin, I waggle my brows. "Doesn't have to be a snowman."

He blinks at me for several seconds, a gesture I'm beginning to understand means he's confused or caught off guard.

"You're quoting Frozen now? Are you five?"

With a snort, I turn toward the closet to grab my snowsuit off the hook. "If only you knew how often I had to watch that movie with Hannah. I can quote the whole thing in my sleep, I shit you not."

"Who's Hannah?"

He follows me in, leaning against the doorway as I pull the suit over my clothes. "Matty's three-year-old daughter."

"Oh." A pause. "I didn't know he had a daughter."

"Yeah. He kinda messed up one night, got drunk, and fucked Valerie after he'd finally gotten rid of her. Well, I guess not 'messed up' because Hannah is the sweetest, coolest kid ever, but it sucks he has to share her with Val." I start buttoning up the suit. "She's not what you call motherly material, constantly on and off drugs, in and out of rehab. Sometimes even goes missing for a while. Matty has full custody, and Xed has pretty much helped raise Hannah for the last three years."

I'm about to pull on my boots when Huckslee holds up a hand to stop me.

"I'm not building a snowman with you, Taylor."

My shoulders slump as I deflate, and I push out my bottom lip while I peek at him from under my lashes.

*Aw.*

He blinks at me again, a myriad of emotions crossing his face before he mutters a curse and grabs his snowsuit.

*Yay!*

It's freezing outside, but not as bad as yesterday, and I pull on my leather gloves before gathering a pile of snow. It's fresh due to the current snowfall and doesn't stick together at all. Huckslee stands on the porch, watching me struggle for several minutes with his lips twitching before he takes mercy on me and comes to help.

Eventually, we erect the saddest looking snowman you'll ever see. Seriously, it looks half-melted already, and one of the rocks I used for eyes kind of droops. We stare at it for half a second before the fucker's head just lolls to the side and falls clean off with a *plop.*

Huckslee bursts out laughing, startling me enough that I jump, and he doubles over while holding his midsection in the most full-bodied guffaw I've ever heard. It's beautiful.

"Your...fucking face," he says in between breaths, eyes actually watering while his cheeks puff up from grinning. "God, that was the...funniest shit."

I'm also chuckling, bending to scoop up a handful of snow that I toss at him. "Don't be a dick. I worked hard on that thing."

"Seriously, don't you know making a snowman with fresh snow is impossible? You have to wait until it hardens."

"No, actually." I grin crookedly, gazing down at the severed snowman head. "First one I've ever tried."

"What?!" His lips part as he studies me. "You've lived in Utah your whole life, and you've never built a snowman?"

Coughing nervously, I lick my lips and tug my beanie down over my ears. "Yeah, weird, huh? Just never thought about it until now."

Let's be honest, my childhood was shit. And building snowmen when you're a teenager sounds lame as fuck, but now I kind of want to do stuff with Huck that I've never done before. Like building snowmen and going ice fishing, apparently.

"Well, now I feel bad." He squints with pursed lips at the monstrosity we made, and it's so fucking cute that an overwhelming urge to press against those lips with my own hits me like a steamroller. His gaze swings to mine as he goes still, eyes darkening from whatever he sees on my features. We're standing so close that I can see the flakes of snow gathering on his lashes, but it's still too far. I want to feel his breath on my skin, feel its warmth soak into my bones.

Before I know what I'm doing, I'm leaning in closer, gaze bouncing between his eyes and mouth as his nostrils flare. His chest hitches, gloved fingers clenching at his sides, and a small gasp leaves his lips when I get close enough for our noses to touch. I mean to capture it, to open my mouth against his and taste what I've been craving since he ordered me out of the shower four years ago. Before we can connect, though, he jerks back so hard that he nearly slips on the ice.

On reflex, my hand shoots out to steady him, but he smacks it away. His cheeks are red, pupils dilated. Not in desire, no...

In anger. Wrath.

Pure, unadulterated rage.

*Shit.* I fucked up.

"Huckslee, wait!" I shout as he spins around and runs toward the cabin. It's more of a fast shuffle, really, because of the ice, but I can see the tension in his back even through the snowsuit, chords taut in his neck. He gets inside before I do, and when I enter the cabin, I find him in the kitchen with his hands in his hair and shoulders heaving.

"Hey, look, I'm sorry–"

He whirls around, cutting me off with the wild look in his eyes. "What the fuck, Taylor? What was that?"

I raise my hands up, palms out, as I take a cautious step toward him. "It-it was an accident, okay? I just got caught up in the moment. I won't do it again."

I'll try. Lord, I'll try because how he's looking at me right now makes me terrified that I've chased him away again.

"What makes you think that you have the right to touch me?" His voice rises steadily, basically shouting. "What makes you think you can kiss me, Taylor? After everything?"

I flinch hard enough to clack my teeth together, and the blood rushes to my ears. "I know. I know, Huck, I'm sorry. Please. It was a mistake."

*Please don't pull away from me again.*

He's across the kitchen in two strides, in my face, with his lips curled back. "What do you want from me, huh? Why the fuck won't you leave me alone?!"

I could point out that he was the one who invited me outside, but I don't. Instead, I stand there while he screams at me, my heart squeezing like it's in a vice, memories from my worst nightmares flashing in my vision. Everything but Huck's furious voice fades around me, and I shut my eyes to try and block out the visions that want to pull me under. Ones that I've spent years in therapy trying to cope with.

My father's fists on my body.

Broken bones.

*Blood, blood everywhere, soaking into the bathroom tile.*

*"Don't you fucking leave me here alone, Huck! Don't you fucking dare."*

*Breathe. Please, baby, breathe.*

*Don't bleed out, don't bleed out, don't bleed out.*

"Answer me!" Hands wrap around my throat, slamming me into the kitchen counter, and my eyes fly open to meet Huckslee's, black with venom. "What. Do. You. Want. Taylor?"

He's not cutting off my air, but nothing comes out when I open my mouth. I'm frozen in place while pain shoots down my arm like it did the night I snapped my collarbone trying to save him.

I'm sorry. *I'm sorry.*

"What is it, huh?" Huck presses into me, grinding our hips together, and with a shock, I realize that he's hard as steel. "You wanna be my sissy bottom bitch, is that it?"

*Will that make you forgive me?*

His lips find my jaw, licking and nipping his way up to my ear as my cock starts to swell from the pressure he's placing on it. "You want me to own you, Taylor? Take away your choices while I fucking use you? Like you did to me?"

*Will that make you love me?*

His teeth sink into the sensitive skin beneath my lobe, causing a moan to escape my lips.

"Take off the snowsuit," he barks harshly, backing up.

In a daze, I comply, reaching up to tug at the buttons. When I take too long due to shaking fingers, he hisses and practically rips at the suit until it puddles at my feet. Kicking it aside, I peer up at him from under my lashes, awaiting instruction. Because I'm not the one in control right now.

He takes me in, gaze tracking down my body until it lands on the bulge in my jeans. "Kneel."

"W-what," I stammer, and he growls angrily.

"You want my forgiveness?" His eyes are two black holes, utterly void of light. "Beg for it on your fucking knees, Taylor."

My bones crack as I hit the ground. A sweat breaks out on my palms, anticipation mixed with fear zipping through my spine. Huck stands above me, arms crossed over his chest as his lips curl back.

"Shirt off."

The command sends my fingers to the hem of my t-shirt, but I hesitate, pulse pounding in my ears. His brow quirks, curls falling over his forehead, and I don't think I've ever seen Huckslee look more dangerous.

There's a warning in his voice that sends goosebumps over my skin. "Don't make me ask again."

Fuck, my cock has never been harder.

The shirt goes flying as I fight the urge to cross my arms. Not because I'm self-conscious about my body; I think I'm fucking sexy as hell. But I don't think I'm ready for him to see the outline I have tattooed on me, right over my heart.

His gaze slides down my chest, pausing at my nipples which have hardened against the cold, before continuing over my abs and down to my dick that's pressing against my zipper.

Desire sparks in his eyes. He doesn't seem to notice the tattoo, and I can't tell if relief or disappointment makes me dizzy.

"Are you ready to beg?" Reaching down, he unsnaps the few buttons over the crotch of his snowsuit before undoing his pants. Moving closer, he stands inches from my face, yanking my head back by my hair. "Open those pretty lips for me."

Heat floods my body, burning me up from the inside as my mouth falls open, fingers clenching on my thighs. He slowly pulls out his hard cock, and I can't help the whimper that leaves my throat when I see it.

God, it's exactly like I remember. Long and thick, with a vein running up the shaft, a bead of precum already pooling in the slit. Stroking it slowly, he watches me, my mouth open and ready.

"Fuck, Taylor," he breathes, voice deep and husky, eyes shuttering. "I like the sight of you like this. Kneeling and waiting for my cock."

Pulling me forward, he touches his tip to my lips, swirling it around until my tongue darts out to flick it. He hisses, salty pleasure exploding on my taste buds, the pressure in my jeans beyond excruciating. One hand flies to my belt while the other reaches up to wrap around his length, but Huck is having none of that.

"Oh, I don't think so." Grabbing both my arms, he wrenches them above my head, pinning them against the counter with one hand. "You don't get to touch me with anything other than your mouth, and you don't get to touch yourself. If you need to tap out, flip me the middle finger."

Goddamn, he's turned me into a mess because a whine actually comes out of me, my hips bucking, the friction of my pants not enough. He smiles, dark and cruel, before shoving his cock between my lips without warning. It fills my mouth, my jaw widening painfully to accommodate his size, and when he hits the back of my throat, I gag.

"*Fuuuck.*" He groans as he keeps my face pressed against the rough material of his snowsuit, and I tug at my wrists, struggling to breathe. Another gag works its way out of me, saliva pooling at the corners of my mouth, my dick weeping.

Shit, how do women do this?

It's not uncomfortable, at least not the feeling of him on my tongue, but he's so far down my throat that I can't even inhale through my nose. Dark spots fill my vision, his hand at the back of my head keeping me in place. Just when I think he's going to let me pass out, he pulls back suddenly, a string of spit connecting my mouth to his cock as I suck in a wet gasp.

Growling in pleasure, Huck barely gives me a second to breathe before he pushes back in so deep and hard that tears spill onto my cheeks. He doesn't hold me there for long, sliding out only to slam back in again and again, making me wince. His hand leaves the back of my head to grip the counter, pulverizing my tonsils as he fucks my face with savage force.

It's vicious and brutal, the slick sounds of my mouth and our panting breaths filling the cabin. My shoulder screams from the angle he has it twisted in, his grip on my wrists so tight that my bones begin to protest. The skin on my lips feels raw from how it rubs against the snowsuit repeatedly. And I fucking love it.

I'm so turned on right now that I'm nearly spilling in my jeans at the small noises coming out of Huck. He's gone completely feral, his self-control torn asunder, the real man beneath the mask coming out to play. It's a version of him that's only for me, and no matter how messed up this situation is right now, I crave it. Even if my collarbone threatens to break again, like my heart.

"Is this what you wanted, Taylor?" He grits out, voice like gravel. "To be violated while someone takes away your choice to breathe?"

His cock slides to the back of my tongue as he goes still, a moan that I've obsessed over for years leaving his mouth. Hot cum pours down my throat. "Now you know what it's like to drown."

I groan around him, sticky wetness splashing against my leg as my own dick spills its release, the taste of Huck filling my mouth, leaking out of my lips as he milks every last drop from his cock.

"Swallow," he snaps, and I drink him down, the texture foreign but not unpleasant.

When he's completely drained, he pulls out and lets me go, stepping back as I collapse onto the ground. My arms have gone numb, not strong enough to catch my fall when I crumple into a ball. The fireplace has long grown cold, and I'm shaking, shivering so fucking hard that I can see my breath as my teeth chatter. There's a dampness running down my chin, on my chest, and a wet spot on my crotch from my own cum.

"Look at you," Huckslee muses, that cruel smile on his lips, "a fucking mess. Now you know what I felt like that night at prom, lying on the bathroom floor, broken and alone."

*I already knew* I want to say, but my throat is so damn raw; each breath is like a shard of glass.

Like the shard of glass I pulled out of his arm that night, putting pressure on the wound as I begged him not to bleed out.

After tucking himself away, he grabs his bag off the floor and swipes Logan's keys from where they hang near the door. Yanking it open, he pauses in the doorway, his head turned as if he wants to look back but can't bring himself to do it.

*Wait, don't leave me here.*

My stomach churns with nausea, threatening to make me puke. Just like when I made him vomit that night, pushing my fingers down his throat to get the pills to come back up.

Huck's shoulders lift with a deep breath, and then he steps out onto the porch without a backward glance. The door snicks softly shut, leaving me curled up on the floor, half-naked and freezing. Heart bleeding.

Broken and alone.

# Huckslee

## March

S hades of green flash before my eyes, different hues ranging from dark to neon.

Twinkling string lights in the shape of little shamrocks
are draped over the bar's low ceilings, and green and gold
streamers are hanging down low enough that I have to dodge
them. An Irish band stands on a small stage in the corner,
stomping their feet to the fiddles they play while people dance
and swing about. I've never been to this place before, but the
owners of the Prospector sure know how to throw a St. Patty's
Day party.

"What can I get you, love?" asks the bartender, a tag on her
green dress displaying the name 'Juanita' and salt-and-pepper
curls falling over her shoulders.

"Is there a special?" Giving her a relaxed smile, I follow
her finger when she points to a chalkboard above the mirror
behind her.

"Midori Sour," she says with a wink, green eyeshadow glittering. "It's got Midori liqueur, vodka, lemon juice, lime juice, and seltzer."

I already know what's in it, but I grin in response. "Sounds delicious, I'll take two."

Chuckling, she goes about making the drinks while I watch the Jazz game on a flatscreen hanging from the wall. March Madness is in full swing. Basketball was never my thing, but I know enough to get by, thanks to Dad making me watch every game as a teen.

"Never seen you in here before." Juanita pushes two drinks over to me in green plastic cups, 'I'm *Feeling Lucky*' emblazoned on them.

I take a sip as I hand her some cash. "I'm meeting a friend."

And I'm nervous as hell. I don't know why; I have no reason to be. Though I haven't seen him since I left, we've kept in touch. It's not like he's a stranger. Far from it. So why am I sweating?

*Probably because he thinks this is a booty call.*

Well, it's not. At least, I'm pretty sure it's not. Just because this last month has been the loneliest, most depressing month of my life doesn't mean I have to fuck him. I won't.

Honestly, Logan's desolate mood has started worsening my own. Even the fact that I now have my own room is overshadowed by the knowledge that it used to be Salem's darkroom for her photography. Seriously, I've never seen my best friend cry harder than when he was helping me move my stuff in, and I felt so bad for him.

As upset as I am at Salem for breaking his heart, I can't help but also feel like he deserved it. The idiot proposed to

317

her on Valentine's Day. If that's not cliche enough, he also did it knowing her views on marriage fully well, and I mean...what else was he expecting? Still, though. Harsh deal, man.

"Who is it?" The bartender's voice drags me out of my thoughts, and I blink at her in confusion.

"Who's who?"

She laughs softly. "This friend you're meeting. We get a lot of regulars here, maybe I know them."

Doubtful because he said he's never been here before, but I open my mouth to say his name right as I catch him walking through the door.

"Royce!" Waving a hand, I call him over to the bar with a grin that I hope comes off as laid back. Honestly, I feel like I'm grimacing. Smiling is hard these days, just like sleeping.

Royce makes his way through the crowd, ducking around streamers, his eyes brightening the closer he gets. His dark brown hair is longer than the last time I saw him, pulled back in locs that tumble down his back. A gold sweater hugs his frame, matching the gold blush on his cheeks that sets his dark skin a shimmer. Green Air Jordans are on his feet.

"Huckslee, it's so good to see you." He tugs me in for a tight hug before pulling back to gaze over me. "Look at you, dressed like a snack!"

*Look at me. A fucking mess.*

Royce chuckles deeply. "It's a good thing you're wearing green, or I'd have to pinch you."

Swallowing hard through the pain in my chest, I force a smile as I glance down at my dark green flannel and black jeans. "Same."

Handing him the other drink I ordered, we make our way over to one of the only empty tables in the back next to the pool hall, where it's quieter and less crowded.

"This place is a bit of a dive, but my sister's boyfriend swears on their smothered burritos." He slips into the seat across from me, taking in the exposed ceiling beams and black-painted walls covered in graffiti art. "So far, I like the vibe though."

"The bartender is nice," I shrug as the band switches up the music to something slower.

"So, how's your dad? Last we talked, he was getting his surgery last month." Royce takes a swig from his cup and grimaces, sniffing the concoction before gulping at it again.

"He's doing much better. Out of the hospital now, thank-fully, because I had a hard time visiting him when he was there. He's recovering well."

It's been an adjustment for him and Maisie, but they're getting through it. According to the doctors, it's not a definite fix. Time will only tell if the cancer comes back even after removing his bladder, but for now, we're holding out hope. Once he's back to his full health, I can start arranging to return to Cali. Or wherever the NFL might send me next month if my name comes up in the Draft. According to my coach, it likely will.

"Good, good, that's great news," he smiles warmly before his eyes tighten. "Seen that asshole stepbrother of yours yet?"

Of course, Royce knows about what happened at prom. He was there. He saw Taylor step away from the curtain, and when I basically went dark afterward while in the ICU—on suicide watch—he reached out to Logan and discovered it all.

"Uh, not...not in a while." It's not a lie. I really haven't seen him in weeks.

And I fucking hate it...

A wary flicker crosses his features. "I'm glad you asked to meet, Huck, though I'll be honest, I am surprised. We haven't met up in...how long has it been? Four years now?"

Running a hand through my curls, I blow out a breath as I nod. "Yeah, 'bout that long. I, uh... haven't been back since I left. So I figured while I was in town, why not see an old friend?"

Plus, Logan's moping was causing me to spiral, and I desperately needed to get out of the apartment. I'm sympathetic to the guy, I really am, but there are only so many nights I can spend patting his shoulder while he sobs into a beer. It makes me feel like a shitty friend, but my own mental health has already been on the fritz after...what happened at the cabin. I just needed to breathe. And the only other person I want to talk to probably hates my guts now, so it was a toss-up between texting Royce or visiting my parents. Royce won.

"Cheers to that!" He clicks our cups together before taking another sip with a pinched frown that gets a chuckle out of me.

"It's called a Midori Sour. Not your thing?"

Shaking his head, he licks the liquor off his lips. "I'm more of a wine person, myself. All these fancy cocktails have way too much sugar."

"Good to know. How's the business running?"

"Like a dream. Growing every day."

Royce owns a small shop that prints decals on things like tumblers and coffee cups. It's on the tip of my tongue to ask him if he can print on material like t-shirts, but the question gets stuck and dies in my throat. Not like the offer Salem made me last month would still be on the table, anyway. After thinking about it daily since then, I realized that it's something I really want to do.

But I fucked that all up.

We chat for a long while, catching up on life. We've texted occasionally, but there's still so much you miss when you don't see someone for years. We talk about football—he hates it—and he mentions seeing someone and how he's only caught one of my games over the years, which I try not to feel too stung about. Things have been good for him, and it makes me happy because Royce is the kind of guy who just puts great energy into the universe. He deserves to have it come back for him.

Eventually the band finishes their set, a DJ taking their place on stage, and Royce is on his second glass of wine. I'm on my third drink (or fourth?) and starting to feel pretty relaxed, busting up at the story he's telling me about a wardrobe malfunction while sledding.

"Yeah, yeah, laugh it up." He presses his lips together, clearly trying to keep from laughing himself. "I hope it happens to you the next time you're on a sled. I still have ice burns on my ass cheeks."

A cold wind blows in as the front door opens, but I focus on Royce as I chuckle. "Don't you put that evil on me, Ricky Bobby. Seriously, who decides it's a good idea to wear latex pants while sledding–"

An odd electric current crackles the air, causing the hairs on my arms to stand on end. I go rigid in my seat, back stiffening, and I can already feel his gaze on me before I look toward the group of people that just walked in.

My gaze clashes with a pair of familiar ocean eyes.

Eyes that are narrowed, bouncing between me and Royce as he stands near the bar, arms crossed. Christian and Matt are beside him, along with someone who looks like his high school friend Xed but minus the mohawk. Of course, they're all clad in black except for Matt, who's wearing a tan hoodie. Christian leans over to kiss the bartender on the cheek, and as they all give their orders to her, Taylor's attention never leaves me. A frown pulls at his lips.

There's something different about him...

When he reaches up to adjust the snapback on his head, dark hair shifts around his jawline, and I realize with a bit of a jolt that the red-dyed tips are now pink. Bright fucking neon pink. Jesus.

Royce doesn't seem to notice I'm distracted, instead laughing about another story involving torn clothes. I try to listen attentively, but every fiber and molecule is pulled toward my stepbrother across the room.

The stepbrother I haven't seen in a month after I violently throat fucked him and left him curled on the floor.

My entire body flinches at the memory, turning the vodka in my stomach leaden.

Why is he here, in a bar? Isn't he two years sober?

After they'd gotten home that night on Valentine's, I'd asked Logan how Taylor had been, but he'd shrugged through his tears and had said that the drive back had been awkward as hell. I'd taken his dad's Range Rover when I'd left, and the three had to squeeze into Taylor's truck.

I felt horrible about that, but how was I supposed to know they'd break up? When Salem moved her things out, Taylor helped, but I'd been visiting my dad, so I hadn't been there. Thankfully. Because honestly, after what I did, I didn't think I could ever face him again. Didn't plan on it.

And now here he is, marching over with his eyes trained on the back of Royce's head, and—

*Wait, what?!*

He's doing what?!

My eyes nearly bug out of my skull as he approaches. I shake my head at him, but he's not looking at me.

*Don't you do it, Taylor. Don't.*

Royce has noticed my face by now, and he's gazing at me with furrowed brows, asking if I'm alright, when my stepbrother stops at our table. He looks like shit, with dark circles under his eyes and lines beside his mouth, yet still so heartbreakingly beautiful that I want to scream.

"Hey, Royce," he chirps almost cheerfully, smirking.

*Oh, you motherfucker.*

Royce looks up at him in surprise before his expression morphs into fury.

"You," he points, nostrils flaring, and Taylor's eyes flutter.

"Me."

Royce launches out of his seat, hand fisted into Taylor's denim jacket while his other arm clocks back to throw a punch. I'm beside him instantly, holding his arm to prevent the hit while Taylor grins.

"Royce, stop." Trying to tug him back, I lose my balance slightly. "It's not worth it. He's not worth it."

Something flashes in Taylor's eyes, but he keeps them on Royce as his friends hurry over, followed by the bouncer who's got muscles in places I never even knew muscles could grow. Christian's fists are already raised and ready to jump in while Matt and Xed crowd around us.

"Is there a problem here, Tay?" The bouncer puffs his chest, apparently on a first-name basis, but Taylor shakes his head quickly.

"Nah, Robbie, we're all good. Just saying hi to my bro and his friend. Right, guys?"

I bite my cheek so hard I taste blood, I swear.

He and Royce stare each other down, a tense moment passing before Juanita swoops in and sets two shots down on our table.

"*No pelees*," she says firmly, lips pressed into a harsh line as she meets everyone's gaze before heading back to the bar. I know enough Spanish to understand the gist of what she said.

Don't fight.

"B-but we didn't order anything," I frown.

Taylor wraps a hand around Royce's wrist. "They're from me. A peace offering on my open tab. Order whatever you want."

A minute passes before Royce releases Taylor with a shove, pushing him back into Christian's chest, who's eyeing us like he's more than prepared to hide two bodies.

Taylor straightens, smooths down his jacket, and then throws an arm out toward the shots with a bow. "Bone-apple-teeth. Enjoy your date."

He grabs his best friend by the shirt and drags him into the pool hall, Xed following after giving me a death glare. Matthew stands there momentarily, looking awkward, but he throws us an apologetic smile as he leaves with his friends.

Royce scoffs, gazing after them until they take up a pool table on the other side of the bar. "Fucking douche. I just got deja vu."

"From prom?" Huffing a dry, empty laugh, I look toward the DJ as 'Something Real' by Post Malone starts up. "There's even a stage and everything."

Just minus Logan and Salem. I'm surprised she's not here with Taylor, honestly. Logan seems to think they're probably dating again, and I hate how much that possibility makes me feel nauseous.

Royce picks up the shots and hands me one. "Well, we aren't having a repeat of that night. Here, bottoms up."

Clinking the shots together, we drink them down, Royce grimacing while I smack my lips at the taste of sweet Southern Comfort whiskey. He stares into the empty glass before his hazel eyes flick up to mine, a spark of mischief in them.

"Did he say order whatever we want?"

"Uh, maybe we shouldn't, Royce." Running a hand through my hair, a hint of unease skitters across my skin, but he's already grinning broadly.

Clapping me on the shoulder, he tells me he'll be back before going to the bar. So I slide back into my seat and pull out my phone, genuinely trying not to look over at Taylor, but as always, he's like a gravitational constant pulling me in, and I can't help it. The minute my eyes find him, I feel my mouth go dry.

His denim jacket is gone, and a loose black tank top hangs from his shoulders. There are holes cut into the fabric on the sides, the tattooed skin of his ribs playing peek-a-boo as he racks up the pool balls, his inked biceps flexing, and the pink tips of his hair fall across his face.

Fuck, he's hot.

And I'm not the only one who notices. A group of women surround the pool table, introducing themselves to him and his friends. Or maybe *re*-introducing with the way Christian throws his arms around some of them like they've met before. A blonde chick with a low neckline and ample cleavage puts her hand on Taylor's arm while he chalks the tip of his pool stick, and he looks down at her with a sultry smile that makes my stomach clench. He hasn't even glanced my way when I *know* he can feel my eyes on him.

A loud thunk draws my attention to where Royce is sliding back onto his stool with a pitcher of beer, two glasses, and six shots on a tray before us.

"Jesus, Royce. What happened to wine?"

He laughs as he starts pouring up the beer. "If it's free, I'll drink anything. We're getting wasted tonight, Huck."

"Is it even legal for the bartender to give us this much at once?" Taking the glass from him, I take a sip of whatever dark Guinness he gave me while he shrugs. It's bitter and not my usual, I'm more of an ale drinker, but Royce has a point. It's free, so I won't complain.

"Maybe we should just go to a different bar," I mumble, but he's already shaking his head before I finish.

"No, no way, babe. We aren't gonna let them ruin our night. I don't care how close they are to the bouncer, bartender, or whoever. We were here first."

Yeah, true, but Taylor's currently got Blondie bent over, pressed between him and the pool table while he shows her how to break from behind, and I don't want to see that shit.

*Oldest trick in the book, asshole.* Very original.

He whispers something in her ear that causes her to giggle, a high-pitched noise that carries over the music. My grip tightens on the glass so hard I'm surprised it doesn't break. As she pulls the stick back to hit the cue ball, his hand flutters to her side, sliding down to her hip in a caressing touch, and I feel like I'm on fire, painfully melting to ash.

Why do I feel like this? Isn't this what I wanted? For him to leave me alone?

*No, I wanted revenge.* And I got it. But it feels like the cost for it was my goddamn soul.

"Holy shit!"

My gaze swings back over to Royce, who's currently gaping at me with his eyes bugging out, a hand over his mouth.

My brows slam together. "What?"

"Still?" His hand drops to his chest, clutching it like a string of pearls. "Even after everything?"

"Still what? What are you talking about?"

He slides two shots over to me, shaking his head in disbelief. "Here, sweetie, you need these more than I do."

"What, why?" Sighing, I raise my gaze to the ceiling. "Just spit it out, Royce."

His eyes narrow as he jerks his head in Taylor's direction. "You're still in love with him."

Not a question. A statement.

I open my mouth to refute that statement, but nothing comes out. Because I can't.

"He used to beat the shit out of you, call you names, totaled your car, and then outed you to your dad and everyone after you gave him your scholarship." Royce sips his beer slowly, studying me. "I'm not one to judge, Huckslee, but that's...wow."

"It's fucking toxic," I growl as I scrub my face, hanging my head. "Everything about this shit with him is toxic. And I fucked up. I fucked up so bad."

Royce blinks in surprise. "You? What did you do?"

"I...I hurt him."

So much more than that, I took something from him. Something that didn't belong to me.

God, Taylor's first time with a man, and that's the experience I left him with? Shame coils inside my chest like a venomous snake. I wouldn't blame him if he never wanted another dick in his mouth ever again.

"Huckslee, he hurts you too. What else is new?"

"No, it's—" I lick my lips, resting my forehead on my arm. "He hasn't even laid a hand on me since that night in high school when he broke my arm. And he was so torn up about it, I remember." He nearly threw up in the hospital room when he apologized to me. And then later, when he'd taken me by the hand and pulled me onto the track to explain himself...when he'd kissed me...

Memories flood my brain, everything I've shoved deep down over the last four years boiling to the surface. All the times Taylor tried to make things right, to communicate like a fucking adult, and I just pushed him away. Literally. Onto his ass in the snow when I saw him for the first time since I left.

Royce's voice pulls me back to reality. "So, because he hasn't hit you in a long time, does it mean he gets a free pass for what he did at prom? I'm not trying to get into your business, Huck, but the guy is clearly not good for you."

"I'm not good for him," I find myself answering, raising my head to stare at him in despair. "He's been trying, and I've been the one with the problem."

*My dad used to smack me around sometimes.*

Taylor's words from the cabin hit me then, straight to the fucking lungs, stealing the oxygen right out of my body. An image flashes before my eyes of his back in the ninth-grade locker room, covered in bruised fingerprints. How he freaked out when I noticed them, and when I told the school counselor, I got detention for hitting him first. I was so blinded by anger from his lying about who started the fight that I completely forgot about what started it in the first place. *The fucking bruises!*

All those times he told me his dad was an asshole, how he always came home from visits seeming stiff and withdrawn, the story he told me about his bike getting taken away. This whole fucking time, I was hung up on the bike, but it wasn't about the bike at all. It was always about getting away from his father, who was hurting him.

And I've been doing the exact same goddamn thing.

He tried so hard to tell me, but I was so focused on the past that I wouldn't listen.

*Oh, God.*

"Royce, I think–" Nausea roils in my gut as I hop off the stool quickly, bumping the table and upturning a few shots. "I think I'm gonna be sick."

I make a beeline for the bathroom, keeping my head down and not hearing whatever he hollers after me. A short hallway leads to the men's room, but the door is locked when I get there. Banging my fist on it, I yell at whoever is inside to hurry up before leaning back against the concrete wall.

The floor spins beneath me, threatening to lay me out flat. Bile is working its way up my throat, but I swallow it down, breathing through my nose while I pound on the bathroom door again. I didn't even feel the panic attack coming, but now it's hitting me with full force, and I know I'm about to lose it.

A muffled voice shouts from the other side of the door. "Fuck off!"

"Dude, hurry the hell up, I'm gonna puke!"

There's a string of muted curses and some shuffling before the door swings open. I launch toward the door, the hallway starting to close in, but I come to an almost violent halt when I see who's standing in the doorway. The chaos in me stills.

"T-Taylor," I stammer, my eyes meeting the surprise in his before they harden into a glare.

"What do *you* want?" Taylor snaps coldly, looking for all the world like he's just seen a roach, and I shrink back from the vitriol in his expression.

Licking my lips nervously, I raise my palms. "I just...can we chat?"

*Chat? Seriously, Huckslee?*

"I'm sorry," I rush out before I can stop myself, the liquor loosening my lips. "I'm sorry for all of it, Taylor. I've been treating you like fucking shit when all you were trying to do was make me see, and I get it now. It all makes sense, and I'm so fucking sorry it took me so long."

His eyes widen as his pouty lips part, but his expression quickly shutters again. "What the fuck are you talking about, Huck? Are you drunk?"

"No! I mean, a little, but not as much as I wish I was. I'm just–" Cutting myself off, I fall back against the wall, feeling out of breath, not quite knowing what I'm trying to say. "C-can we start over? Go somewhere and talk, please?"

Taylor studies me cautiously for a moment before opening his mouth to answer, but a giggle behind him interrupts whatever he'd been about to say. A very feminine, high-pitched giggle. He freezes, and I notice for the first time that his hat is gone, and his dark hair is messy as if someone's fingers have been running through it. He looks flushed, lips a bit swollen, and as my gaze tracks down his body, I find his belt buckle undone. When my eyes meet his again, a spark of guilt swims in them.

Finally, glancing over his shoulder, I see Blondie near the sink, adjusting her shirt and grinning at me. Red lipstick smeared.

Coincidentally, lipstick that matches the red smear on Taylor's green boxer briefs peeking out from his unbuttoned jeans.

Right over his crotch.

# Huckslee

F uck, this hurts.

The floor pitches again, concrete walls like a vice, and I turn away before I embarrass myself further by puking all over his Docs.

"Sorry to interrupt," I mutter, dashing up the hallway toward a door that reads *'Employees Only.'* Taylor calls after me, but I will make a mess in this hallway if I don't get out now.

The door opens to some sort of back alley between buildings, and I barely have time to catch Matthew leap away from Xed before bending over and throwing up all over the ground. Everything I've had to eat and drink tonight comes back up, barely missing my shoes. It burns so bad my eyes well up, stomach muscles working painfully against the force of it.

There's a low curse and a hushed conversation behind me before the door slams shut. And then there's a tentative hand on my back.

"Damn, man." Matt stands above me, brows wrinkled in concern. "Looks like someone took 'order whatever you want' too far. You okay?"

I don't respond because I physically can't; all effort is focused on not getting the contents of my insides on anything important, like my clothes. When my body has finally expelled everything, I stay bent over for a few minutes, eyes squeezed shut as I just try to fucking breathe.

The hand on my back sweeps around in wide, soothing circles, and it feels nice. Grounding. So, I let Matthew do that for a bit longer than I should as I try to piece my thoughts together.

Eventually, when I don't feel like passing out, I wipe my mouth on my sleeve and straighten, wincing as I clear my throat. "Thank you."

"Of course, man." Matt smiles crookedly as he backs up a step, giving me space. There's something in his eyes, though, an anxiousness that has me doing a double take as I study him curiously. His mouth is tight despite the smile, his brows pulled in, and he looks like a kid who got caught with his hand in the cookie jar.

"Xed and I were just talking," he explains quickly, biting his lip.

"Okay."

His big eyes fly to mine, a hint of fear flashing. "It's the truth. Just a heated conversation. I mean, not heated like *that*, but we-we were just–"

"I get panic attacks," I cut him off, not only because it's painful watching him try to save face but also because it's none of my business what I just saw the two of them doing.

He blinks, clearly not expecting me to say that. "Oh..."

"Yeah..." Curling my fingers into my hair, I tug on the strands as I glare at the ground. "Sometimes I can kind of feel when one is coming. Like a tingling in my fingers or muscle spasms. Hard to explain. Other times, though, they kind of hit out of nowhere."

"Is that why you threw up?"

"Uh." I grimace as my stomach churns again when I think about Taylor and Blondie. "Partly. When I'm like that, though, I sometimes get tunnel vision and don't really notice what's happening around me until it's over."

It's pretty much the truth, especially if it's bad. When I first got to California, I came to once in the middle of a grocery aisle surrounded by concerned shoppers and had no clue how long I'd been freaking out. It took a long while, constant therapy sessions, and the right meds to finally make the anxiety and panic attacks less debilitating.

A frown pulls at my lips. Speaking of therapy, I haven't had a session in months. Maybe my therapist back in Cali can do a FaceTime or a Zoom call...

"So what set you off?" Relief softens Matthew's features as my words register, even though it's a lie. I did, in fact, see something, but I'm not about to say anything.

I'm not Taylor.

The thought brings a fresh batch of knife wounds to my gut.

Taylor...was in that bathroom with Blondie. Probably getting his dick sucked by the looks of it.

Why does the thought of him with someone else tear me up like this? He's my stepbrother, for fucks sake. We're not...we're not anything to each other.

*Just each other's first kiss and first love.*

*First and only person to ever break your heart.*

And just like that, the anger is back, pulling me into its poison, eating away at whatever feelings I may have had toward Taylor ten minutes ago before I saw him banging some stranger in a dive bar bathroom.

*Fuck you, asshole.*

Spinning away from Matt, I head back through the door, seething and aching with rage. "I need another drink."

He follows behind, those big feet of his clunking along the floor. "Look, I don't want to be a downer, but maybe you should slow down, Huckslee."

No. Hell no.

"And why would I do that when Taylor so generously offered me all the alcohol I can drink?"

He curses as we step into the bar area again and peels away, muttering something along the lines of *'gonna tell that stupid idiot to close the damn tab.'*

Royce looks up from his phone when I appear beside him, looking relieved and shaken. "Hey, I just texted you. Are you okay? Your stepbrother was over here like two seconds ago asking where you went–"

"I'm fine, but he's about to close his tab. Let's go order as much shit as we can."

And we do. Seriously, I should feel bad at the table in front of me lined with a shot of every bottle they have in the bar, but I don't. (Which, according to Google, is very much illegal, but Juanita seems to march to the beat of her own drum, and I think she's my new best friend.)

Mixing liquor is never a good idea. The more Royce and I drink and dance, though, the less I give a shit. Whatever booze I threw up is quickly replaced, and I feel Taylor's eyes on me the entire time. Blondie is nowhere to be seen, but he's watching me with an expression I can't read whenever I glance over at the pool table.

I fucking hate it.

I fucking hate him.

For making me feel this way. For never getting out of my head. For hurting me.

But mostly, I hate myself for hurting him back.

The longer the night goes on, the drunker I get. I don't even think we finish all the shots, vaguely remembering Royce handing them out like candy. I think he quit drinking a while ago, but I can't seem to stop.

The longer Taylor stares, the more I want to forget him. Forget his bright eyes that can't seem to pick a fucking color, forget the way he kisses even though it's never left my mind in over four years, forget the joy on his face from building a fucking snowman. Even the feel of his mouth on my cock, which is so sick and twisted that I'm even thinking about that.

Sick and twisted.

Toxic.

*He's no good for you*, Royce said.

I'm no good for him.

We're no good for each other, and yet

I

Can't

Let

Him

Go.

Juanita announces last call, which means it's somewhere around one in the morning. I don't even remember the hours passing—where did the night go?

Royce wipes his eyes as he laughs after we finish a terrible karaoke rendition of Cher's 'Believe,' pushing outside into the chilly night air.

"I've got my man coming to pick me up," he says as we lean against the outside of the bar, sharing a cigarette. "Want a ride?"

Wait, why am I smoking? I don't even smoke. This stuff tastes like shit.

Huffing a cough, I hand him the cigarette and shake my head. "I'll call an Uber."

"You sure, babe? He won't mind."

"Yeah," I grin at him, having difficulty focusing on his face. "S'all good, man. Thanks for hangin'."

"You're fun as hell, Huck. Let's do this again."

I think I agree, even though I don't ever want to drink like this again in my life. Can't seem to think straight. Eyes hurt.

Royce's ride pulls up, and after a tight hug, I'm alone, leaning against the building. So I slide to the ground, squinting down at my phone as I pull up the Uber app and try to get my hand to stop moving for five seconds so I can fucking see. When the Uber is ordered, I lean back while waiting. The wall is cold against me, cooling my heated skin, and a breeze dries the sweat on my neck. It feels so damn good that my eyes sink closed, only for a minute.

Just for one minute.

I'm so exhausted that I'll just close them until my ride shows up.

Just a minute...

"Wake the fuck up, Huckslee!"

Next thing I know, I'm being shaken violently, and I peel my lids open to glare up into two blue-green eyes.

"Ah, what the hell?" My head is pounding so hard I can feel it in my ears. "Stop shakin' me!"

Taylor stands above me with his hands on my shoulders, brows pinched. His teeth are sunk into his bottom lip, gaze bouncing around my face in a panic-stricken way, and hell, if that doesn't sober me right up.

"Why are you sleeping out here?!" His voice is shrill, loud enough against the quiet night that I flinch. "Where the fuck did Royce go?"

"Wasn't s-sleeping." Frowning up at him, I lift my phone to his face. "W-was waiting for my Uber."

He looks at it for a few seconds, reading the screen, before his expression hardens.

"Jesus Christ, Huck." Grabbing my phone out of my hand, he turns it around so that I can see. "Your driver called and texted twenty minutes ago looking for you. Pretty sure they're gone by now."

"What?!" *Shit.* Does that mean... I've been sleeping against this building for almost half an hour, looking like a homeless person? In the cold? "Fuck, dude."

Now that I notice it, my teeth chatter as my body shivers violently.

Taylor stares at me briefly before releasing my shoulders, scrubbing a hand down his face. "Check your pockets. Make sure no one robbed you while you were out."

Ah, hell.

I pat myself down, pulling out my wallet with frozen fingers to ensure nothing is amiss. When everything is accounted for, I sigh in relief and try to stand. The minute I do, the earth tilts on its axis, and I fall with a groan, head swimming. Clearly, I'm still fucked up.

"Goddammit." Taylor tries to catch me, looping his arms under my own, and I notice his wince as he pulls me to my feet. The warmth from his body floods me as he presses me into the wall for stability, and my arms tighten around him involuntarily.

He stiffens, trying to back away. "Let me go, Huck."

"S-sorry," I chatter, willing my frozen hands to unhook themselves from around his shoulders. "C-c-cold."

My arms fall from him, and I brace for the frosty air to hit me when he steps away.

But he doesn't. He hesitates, keeping our bodies flush, his face tilted down so I can't read his eyes.

"Did Royce leave you like this?" There's a catch in his voice, almost like anger, and I shake my head quickly.

"No, I was-s awake when h-he left. T-told him I'd be f-fi-iiiine." That last word turns like a whine as the cold wind hits me, and I find myself burying my frozen nose into the crook of Taylor's neck. He jolts but doesn't move, thank fuck, because I feel like a damn icicle right now. Seriously, I wouldn't be surprised if my lips are blue.

We stay like that for a moment, pressed against each other outside of the bar, and eventually, Taylor's warm cheek falls against the side of my head.

"You scared the shit of me," he whispers, hot breath against my ear, and I murmur a *'how so?'* into his skin. "When I walked out here and saw you slumped over like that... you're ice cold, Huckslee. I tried to wake you twice. I thought..."

He trails off, and the reality of what he's saying hits me like a ton of bricks.

Dead. He thought I was dead.

Fuck.

Guilt flattens me like a steamroller, causing my arms to come up and crush him to my chest. His grip tightens on me as well, and for a moment all the bullshit falls away while we just hold each other.

"I'm s-so sorry, Taylor." My voice breaks, fingers curling into the hair at his nape. "So goddamn sorry."

"You could have frozen to death, man. What were you thinking?"

I shake my head, trying to burrow further into him even though I'm as far as I can go. "Wasn't thinking. Was t-tired. Drunk."

"I shouldn't have let you use my tab," he mutters, and I feel his swallow against my lips. "You have a drinking problem, Huck."

"I know. I know."

I do. Had one for a while, but it's only gotten worse since coming back. Which is hilarious if you think about how strict Utah's liquor laws are compared to California's. How the hell does that make sense?

The door of the bar flings open, bursting whatever bubble Taylor and I had found ourselves in because he pulls away from me quickly. It's almost painful, like a bandaid being ripped away, taking a piece of myself with him. Matthew and Xed step out onto the sidewalk, eyeing us curiously, and my heart sinks when Christian steps out after them with Blondie tucked under his arm.

Reality is a cold, hard, big-tittied bitch.

"What's going on, Tay?" Christian asks slowly, glancing between us, and I turn away to pull up the Uber app again, not interested in hearing this conversation. My insides feel hollow, like they've been scooped out with a spoon. I get about ten feet away when Taylor calls my name, and my plan is to ignore him until his hand wraps around my arm, yanking me back.

"Where do you think you're going?" His nose is scrunched, adorably irritated. If it weren't for the empty feeling in my bones, the look on his face would make me smile.

"I'm calling another Uber."

He spins around and tugs me back toward the bar. "Yeah, I don't think so. I'm driving you home."

Driving? So he's still sober?

"Taylor, no." I try to dig in my heels, but he's strong, and I'm still freezing. And drunk. "You don't have to do that. It's fine."

"It's not fucking fine, Huckslee. Something bad could have happened to you. And if I ever see Royce again, I'll kick his ass for not making sure you got home safely."

He pulls us into the parking lot, where his yellow truck sits next to a black Subaru. Christian is near the passenger door, glaring daggers at me. There's no Blondie to be found, and I can't say I'm sad about that.

"It's not Royce's fault, I told him I was fine. Really, Taylor, let me call an Uber."

He says nothing, depositing me next to Christian before rounding to the driver's side. Matthew and Xed exchange their goodbyes before climbing into the Subaru together, and Christian opens the passenger door as he motions for me to get in. His nostrils are flared.

"I'm not going with you guys."

He growls before grabbing my shoulder and manhandling me into the cab. "Get the fuck in, you cock blocking asshole."

"Get your hands off me, dude." I crawl into the middle seat beside Taylor, seething as Christian jumps in next to me. "I didn't cock block shit."

"You're doing it right now, fucker." He slams the door with a huff, crossing his arms. "I'd rather have Kelsie's sweet ass sitting next to me instead of yours, but *someone*," he glares over at Taylor, "had to go all Superman and swoop into the rescue. Again."

I only catch on to one part of what he just said. "You think my ass is sweet?"

Can't help it. Still drunk.

A snort comes from Taylor as he pulls out of the parking lot while Christian mutters something in Spanish that's too fast for my ears to hear.

"What the fuck ever," Taylor laughs, and I find myself studying his face, trying to commit the smile to memory. "You get laid almost every day at this point. Pretty sure you're a sex addict, dude."

"And you're a fucking monk," Christian fires back. "Seriously, *cariño*, what's up with you? It's been like three months since you've gotten some pussy."

"Whooa." My mouth speaks before I can stop it, Taylor going rigid against my side. I hadn't realized I'd leaned into him.

"My sex life isn't your business, asshole," he mutters, staring straight ahead as a flush spreads on his cheek. I try not to stare; I really do, but he makes it so hard when he's this close to me. That hollow feeling inside me is slowly starting to fade.

*Three months?!*

"Kinda hard not to make it my business when we live together. I notice things. You went from fucking just as much as I do to *nada*. And I'd know if you were getting any because the walls are thin as fuck. You come loudly."

Oh my god. How does he know that?

I don't even know that.

Fuck, I wish I knew that.

"Christian, for the love of all that is holy, please shut up," Taylor hollers, face getting redder, but his best friend is having none of it.

"What didn't you like about Kelsie? She was sexy as hell. Was the blowie in the bathroom bad or something?"

And the hollow feeling slams back, enveloping me tenfold.

I should have known better. Just because Christian said he wasn't getting any didn't mean he wasn't getting *head*.

Turning away, I blink rapidly out the windshield, trying to get my breathing under control. Taylor's fingers tighten on the steering wheel, but he doesn't respond.

Christian continues. "She was down to let us share her, man. You know how much I like it when they do that. I bet she'd even let you—"

Taylor reaches out to crank up the radio, drowning out whatever Christian was about to say, and I've never felt more relieved. For fucks sake, I didn't want to hear any of that.

Straightening away from him, I focus on the passing buildings to occupy my mind for the rest of the drive. At one point, Taylor bumps my knee with his, but I scoot away, leaning into Christian instead. His jaw feathers at the corners, but he doesn't look my way.

Eventually, after grabbing some late-night tacos and water to soak up the liquor, we round a corner, pulling into a driveway where Christian's old Bronco sits near the front porch of what looks like a duplex.

My eyes fly to the side of Taylor's face as he puts the truck in park. "I thought you were taking me home?"

"Logan's apartment is on the other side of the valley." He gets out, still not meeting my gaze. "My place was closer. I can take you home in the morning."

Christian grumbles something in Spanish but gets out, leaving the door open for me. He doesn't even wait for us as he stomps up the steps and unlocks the front door, slamming it shut behind him. A lighter sparks, and I see Taylor leaning against the front of the truck with a smoke in his mouth, staring after his best friend.

"He's such a pissy drunk," he mumbles around the cigarette, inhaling deep as he leans his head back. I watch his throat flex with a swallow.

"I'm sure getting laid would have helped. Sorry to ruin your night."

He shrugs, not responding as he blows out smoke, and for some reason it pisses me off.

"Look, I can just call an Uber from here. No need to stay. Thanks for the ride." Even though I'm now further from Logan's apartment than I was at the bar, but whatever. It's fine.

"Get the fuck inside, Huckslee." Taylor leans down to put the cigarette out on the driveway before heading up the steps. When he gets to the front door, he pauses, waiting. So I reluctantly follow, feeling a little unwelcome.

The inside of his apartment is nice, though clearly a bachelor pad. It's a bit messy but not disgusting. It's just 'lived in by two single men,' if that makes sense. There are a few dishes in the sink, and the trash needs to be taken out, but honestly, it feels pretty homey. The walls are plastered with band and motocross posters.

Taylor leads me to a door just off the kitchen, and I freeze when I realize I'm about to walk into his bedroom. A place I've never entered, a boundary I never crossed. Even when we lived together.

The room is decently sized, with a desk in the corner holding a laptop and a lava lamp. There's a queen-sized bed against a wall completely covered in photos, so many that I find myself floating over to look. Most of them are of him, Salem, and Christian, posing with silly faces or in front of cool shit. Doing cool things, like climbing a rock wall or snowboarding. Some of Matt and Xed with a little girl who must be Matt's daughter. There are a few with people I've never seen before, but one picture in particular catches my eye. It's closest to the bed, near enough to be in his direct line of sight if he turns onto his side. Squinting, I lean over to study it and feel my heart skip when I recognize where it's from.

It's him and me, seventeen years old at our parents' wedding, dressed in tuxedos and bruised all to hell. I have a black eye and his nose is two sizes too big.

"It's the only picture we have together, so..." He clears his throat behind me, voice uneven, and I turn to watch him unlatch a wire cage in the corner, where a rabbit is making noise. "Bathroom is through that door, fresh pack of toothbrushes in the cabinet. Feel free to use one. And by feel free, I mean please do. No offense, Huck, but your breath is rank."

An embarrassed laugh leaves my throat as I head into the bathroom, shutting the door behind me. It's small but not claustrophobic and smells like Taylor's body wash. I do my business, taking a piss and finding a toothbrush, but my mind keeps circling back to that photo. Why would he have a picture of me on his wall? And right where he'd see it first thing in the morning? A feeling blooms inside me, warmth and softness I can't place spreading throughout my chest.

When I finish up, I enter the bedroom again to find him sitting on the side of his bed in his tank top, smiling down at the rabbit on his lap.

"This is Baby Bones," he says, holding the animal up for me to see. "BB or Beebs for short. Saved her from Christian's python."

Dropping to my knees before him, I try to focus on the bunny instead of panicking about a giant snake nearby. "Hi, Baby Bones. Nice to meet you." Reaching out to pet her black ears, I take in the white pattern of a skull on her face. "That's natural?"

"Yep. Cool, huh?"

My throat closes at the adoration on his face, reminding me of how he used to look at our cat in high school. "Whatever happened to Lasagna?"

His eyes darken as he sighs deeply, turning toward a photo of an orange ball of fur on his nightstand. "Ah, pasta cat. May she rest in peace."

I don't know why, but the sadness in those blue-green irises fucking guts me, so I lean over his knees and wrap my arms around his waist, pressing my face into his stomach. "I'm sorry, Taylor."

His breath hitches as he sets BB on the bed before lightly touching my shoulder. "Thanks. It's okay. She was old. I gave her a good life."

Still, my hold on him tightens, silently cursing the animal gods for blessing us with pets that live for far too short a time. I'm definitely more sober now than I was before, but the effects of the alcohol are still swimming in my system, and I'm a sad sap when I drink.

"Not just for Lasagna," I mumble against his shirt, breathing him in, "for everything. All of it. I'm sorry for hurting you."

He's quiet for a long time, so long that I don't think he'll respond, but his arms slowly come around me as his fingers gently entwine with my curls. "I hurt you, too."

Pressing a kiss to his sternum, I shake my head. "What I did was so much worse."

"Huckslee, I broke your arm," he scoffs, "nearly drowned you, crashed your car, embarrassed you in front of our entire senior class, and beat up your dad. Not to mention all the other fucked up shit I did in high school. What you did to me was pretty mild in comparison."

"Don't do that." Leaning back, I frown at him, finding his gaze above my head. "Don't downplay it like you deserved it. You didn't deserve to be treated like that, and I'll never forgive myself."

"We both did things we can't take back."

His eyes are still everywhere except where I want them, and it makes me crazy, so I reach up to lightly cup his cheek. "Taylor. Look at me."

Those pupils expand, his attention bouncing around for a moment before landing on me, and the weight of his gaze hits me like a crashing wave. I lose myself in the emotion passing between us like a torrent threatening to chew me up and spit me out. Anger, fear, regret, longing. It's all there, written in plain language on the strands of his eyes, and I'm powerless to turn away from it. His lips part, tongue darting out to lick at the skin, reminding me of what it felt like when he did that to the tip of my cock, and I inhale sharply.

My other hand comes up, thumb running along the dark circles beneath his lower lids. "Did I do this?"

He says nothing, only searches my face with a hint of caution that has me pulling away, dropping my arms from him before getting to my feet. Everything feels shaky and unstable, but I manage to remain steady as I back up a step. Putting space between us.

"Do you want me to sleep on the couch?" I ask unevenly, running my hands through my hair where I can still feel his touch.

Taylor studies me while I watch his rabbit play with some toy under the desk, and then he reaches down to untie his Docs. Kicking them off, he scoots onto the bed until he's against the headboard near the wall and then pats the empty spot beside him. It looks like an invitation, but something in his eyes tells me it's not. No, I know what this is, and it fucking breaks me.

But I take off my own sneakers and lie down, feeling the warmth of his body as he leans over me to click off the lamp. When he settles in, we turn to face each other, light from the bathroom enough to make out his glittering gaze as he looks at me. Every part of my being aches to touch him, but I don't. I'll never touch him again without permission. Even if it never comes.

"Huckslee," he whispers, but I shake my head.

"Please don't."

*Don't ruin this moment. Don't make it hurt more than it already does.*

He sighs, swallowing audibly. "But I have to. I need to. As of right now, this bed is Delaware, so just listen. Please."

There's a desperate urgency in his tone that makes my skin crawl, a dread yawning in the pit of my stomach. But I take a deep breath and close my eyes to shield myself.

"Okay."

And I just listen. Like I should have been doing from the very start.

# TAYLOR

Huckslee's entire body is stiff as a board, muscles so tense that it looks painful. His hands fist the sheets, bracing for a blow he feels I'm about to deliver.

And in a way, I guess I am.

My heart is beating rapidly in my chest, the terror in my veins still present from when I found him sitting on the ground outside the Prospector, looking gray as a ghost. Not breathing.

Fuck, I thought I killed him. *Again.*

Taking a shaky breath, I moisten my lips and close my eyes, needing to block out the sight of him if I'm going to get through this. Because he's here, and he's finally willing to listen to me. I'm going to tell him all of it. Even the hard parts.

"Huckslee, I've been in love with you since the eighth grade." My skin prickles under his gaze, but I keep my eyes closed. "I didn't realize it until after I crashed your car, though. But before I get to that, there's something else I need to say." Another breath. "I used to...I used to start fights with you so

350

that I could hide the bruises from my dad. Blame it on you. In case anyone came asking, you know? Like that time freshman year. I know you think it was only my bike I cared about, but if he got caught, I knew I'd get taken away. And Maisie proved she didn't want me, so I figured they'd send me here to the city where I'd never see Christian or the guys again.

And if he found out there was even an inkling of me being interested in guys, the same thing would happen. No more motocross, no more Christian, no more anything that made life at least a little better. Looking back, it's kind of dumb because other kids had it worse. Like, all he did was break my hand once, maybe a rib a few times, but—"

"Stop that," Huckslee cuts me off fiercely. "You're downplaying. He hurt you, Taylor. It doesn't matter if it wasn't as bad as you think it could have been, it was bad enough. And it happened to you, so it matters, dammit."

A hoarse laugh leaves my dry throat. "You sound like my therapist."

"So listen to them. None of this 'others had it worse' bullshit. Your experiences are valid. Say it."

I crack open an eye to catch him staring at me with his lips pressed into a hard line. He looks so serious. Fucking cute. I can't help it; my mouth twitches into a crooked grin.

"It's not a joke," he growls, glaring at me. "Say it right now."

"Ok, Jesus. My experiences are valid. Happy?"

"No. Continue."

God, he's so grumpy.

Huffing a laugh, I scoot closer to him, unable to stop myself from seeking comfort in his touch. His chest hitches when it collides with mine, and I close my eyes again, pressing my face into his shoulder. "Remember New Year's Eve?"

His arms tentatively come up around me, warm breath caressing my cheek. "Yes."

"I still don't remember much about what happened. Some things are blank, either from the drinking or the head injury." I frown, trying to sort through the fog in my brain as his fingers slip between the holes of my tank top, tracing my skin. "I can recall the fight with Maisie and your dad, getting kicked out. I...I stole your car because I knew it would piss you off, and you'd have to talk to me. You were kind of giving me the cold shoulder, remember?"

"Seems to be my thing," he mumbles into my hair, and shit, if that ain't the truth.

"I thought you were done with me. It drove me crazy. At the risk of sounding like a total creep, you've been my obsession since that first kiss under the bleachers, Huck. I just... couldn't have you. Couldn't even have a friendship with you because I knew I couldn't keep it that way for long, and my dad would suspect something. He noticed, man, how infatuated I was with you. But I couldn't ignore you, either. So in my fucked up brain, becoming your enemy seemed like the next best idea."

"You were such a little asshole, dude."

Groaning, I cover my face with my hands. "I know. There's really no excuse for any of it. All I can say is I joined every sport you did because I wanted to be close to you."

He pauses, and I'm glad I'm not looking at him because I can only imagine what's on his face right now. "That's...actually really sweet, in a fucked kind of way."

"Yeah..."

"But you quit the swim team?"

"Uh," I clear my throat. "I couldn't always hide the marks. Kind of hard to do that, being shirtless all the time."

"Oh." Another pause. "Right."

"Anyway, I got off track." The soft touch of his fingertips on my ribs causes me to shiver, sending sparks down my groin. *Focus.* "Things had started to shift between us, and I wanted you so fucking bad. But years of mental abuse are hard to overcome, you know? We already talked about this at the...the cabin." I falter at the memory but rush forward quickly. "You weren't talking to me, so I took your car and left. Went to my dad's. I was so angry at him for fucking up my head, I started a fight, and it did not end well."

"What did he do?"

So, I tell him. As much as I can remember, anyway. His eyes watch as I touch my scar, still feeling the phantom pains of skin splitting when my face hit the bathroom sink. Lifting my shirt, I show him the mark from where they fixed the ruptured spleen. And then I tell him about the car. How I sent it careening down an incline to cover for my piece of shit father, who should be in jail right now instead of six feet under. He doesn't speak or even breathe; he just lets my words simmer between us.

"Honestly, I think it happened in the hospital," I whisper, pressing my lips to his throat, feeling raw from so much speaking and soul searching, "when you never visited. I had nothing but time on my hands while I recovered, and every thought was on my stepbrother, who thought I hated him, but the truth is that I've never hated you, Huck. I wanted you from the moment I saw you that first day in eighth grade. And it was torture, each day that passed with you not walking through the hospital room door, and I just...knew. That I loved you. But then four months passed with no contact, you started dating Royce, and it felt like my heart had ripped in two."

The featherlight circles on my skin pause as he speaks; his voice is so low I have to strain to hear. "We were...we barely even..."

"I know, we'd hardly touched at that point. Had only kissed like three times, but it was enough for me. It's fucking stupid and embarrassing, but that was all it took." A bitter laugh leaves my throat. "It doesn't take much for me, apparently. The slightest crumb of affection, and I'm a goner."

He swallows audibly. "Taylor..."

"According to Doctor Hart, it makes sense because I wasn't given a lot of it as a kid, blah blah blah, you know? She's my therapist, by the way. Nice lady. Anyway, it's not like I'm out here falling in love left and right with every person I meet. I've dated plenty of women over the last four years that I didn't love. And, of course, I love Salem in a platonic way, but...it's only you, Huckslee. It's only ever been you."

"*Taylor.*" His hand cups my jaw as he pulls back, head lowering, eyes trained on my mouth.

Like he's going to kiss me.

And fuck, as much as my entire being craves to taste his tongue again, I throw a hand up between us at the last minute. Firstly, because I'm not done. And secondly, because the last time I tried to kiss him, I ended up on my knees, so it's really not fair.

"I have to talk about prom."

Huck goes still, his gaze burning like fire, but he slowly lowers himself back down. "Alright."

I can feel his body vibrating through mine.

Blowing out a breath, I bury my face into his neck once again. "Not gonna lie, losing that race for the scholarship sucked pretty bad. And after the shit that happened with my dad, and you ignoring me, plus being on probation and not allowed to drink or smoke, I was kind of in a dark place. Which sounds so fucking selfish compared to where your head was at, Huck." He tries to interrupt again, but I shake my head. "It is, though. You were struggling, and you didn't even have a support system like I did. Luckily, I had Christian, Matty, Xed, and Salem to fall back on."

"I had Logan."

Lifting my head, I throw him a pointed glance. "No one knew what was going on with you, Huckslee. But I did. I knew you were pretending to be something you weren't. I called you a fucking *fake*, man."

"Yeah, we aren't doing that." His hand gently cups my throat. "We aren't playing the blame game. Do you know how many times I've had to hear this from Logan and our parents? My grandparents? Taylor, it wasn't anyone's fault. *No one* is to blame here."

"But what I did to you is," I say softly, meeting his gaze. "My actions drove you over that ledge."

He growls softly, flopping onto his back to squint at the ceiling, fists clenching. I give him a moment to gather his thoughts while I watch Baby Bones try to dig into the blankets piled at our feet.

"I think," Huck starts slowly, pausing a moment before continuing, "I think I was going to do it that night anyway, Taylor."

My attention flies to his face, breath catching at the way his eyes glitter when they connect with mine. I can't even respond, the gears spinning in my head as I try to process what he just said. In my silence, he speaks.

"I had this feeling while dancing behind that curtain with Royce...it's hard to explain, but I felt like my time had run out. Like I was at the end of the road. I'd been feeling it coming for a while, like a passenger in a speeding vehicle heading toward the barricade." He turns away from me, flattening his other cheek against the pillow. "Royce told me that night that you were in love with me. Said he could see it in your eyes, and when he looked in mine...he saw that I was in love with you, too."

The earth stops turning for a fraction of a second, my pulse slowing, everything coming to a halt as his revelation rearranges my entire existence.

"I was diagnosed with an anxiety disorder after everything happened. According to my therapist, the way I was feeling at prom was my brain's way of warning me about an oncoming episode. When Royce said those words, making me realize what I felt for you, it triggered the anxiety. And when the curtain opened..."

He finally turns back toward me with a heavy gaze. "'Panic-induced psychosis' is what the doctors said, brought on by high stress. I'd been playing Russian roulette with different meds for over six months at that point, and everything just hit me all at once. But I was already in free fall, Tay. I fully believe it would have happened that night regardless."

Everything he's saying begins to register, the weight of it all crashing over me. My mouth opens but quickly shuts, any response sounding shallow.

Anxiety disorder. Panic attacks. And I put a tarantula in his locker because I thought it would be fucking funny?

I nearly drowned him because I thought it would be hot.

The shame that's always present grows, sprouting tentacles that wrap around my heart and squeeze.

"Taylor, look at me." Huck's voice is closer than it was a moment ago, and I glance up to find him inches from my face, brows pinched together. "I told you all this to take away the guilt, not make it worse."

"Did I cause it?" I ask hoarsely, feeling dizzy. "The anxiety disorder? Was that me?"

He exhales, running a hand through his hair. "Well, you certainly didn't help, but no. It started after my mom died."

That should come as a relief, but it doesn't. I feel like the worst scum on the planet.

Fuck, he just admitted that he's in love with me-well, *was*-and all I can focus on is how I'm not worthy of it and don't deserve it.

Is love supposed to be like this? How can you claim you love someone when all you do is hurt them repeatedly?

"Hey." He covers his hand over mine where I've been massaging my shoulder. "What's up with that? I've seen you wince a few times, and you rub it a lot."

"Snapped the collarbone trying to get to you after prom," I answer absently, still working through my guilt. If I wasn't so

357

wrapped up in my own head, I would have noticed the way he goes entirely still. I would have listened to the feeling in my gut telling me something is wrong, but instead, I focus on myself and my own misery. "I know you say I'm not to blame, but how do we know that? How do we know that the shit I put you through didn't ultimately lead to that moment?" Life is full of what-ifs. I know my regret isn't Huckslee's problem, but it's eating me alive. "Huck, how do we know—"

"What do you mean, *'trying to get to me'*?"

He cuts me off with a biting tone, and I finally look at him, *really* look at him. His pupils are blown out, lips parted as his gaze frantically bounces around my face, breathing erratic. Sirens begin blaring in my brain, loud and confusing.

*Danger, danger, danger.*

*Where, where, where?*

"That night when you swallowed those pills." I frown up at him, noticing the pulse point jumping on the side of his neck. "I followed you home and had a bad feeling." *Like right now.* "You weren't answering the door, and I-I had to break into the bathroom. With my shoulder..."

"What? No," he shakes his head dazedly, reaching up to tug at his curls. "My dad, he's the one that found me?"

Oh.

*Oh, fuck.*

Licking my lips nervously, I touch his cheek, not liking the sallow color of his skin. "He got home shortly after I did. Found me in there with you, trying to..." *Keep the fucking blood inside your body.* "Trying to stabilize you. He's the one that called the ambulance."

Huck's freaking out. I can see it in how his fingers tighten in his hair, knuckles white, and I reach up to disentangle them before threading them with my own. There's a glazed, sort of far-off look in his eyes. Gripping his jaw, I turn his face toward me.

"Hey, you're alright. It's alright. I've got you."

A choked sound leaves his throat like he's trying to say something, but it gets trapped inside. Just like he's trapped inside his own head right now.

"Huckslee? Baby, stay with me." I shake his shoulder, but he still doesn't acknowledge me, clearly on the verge of a major freakout.

So I do the only thing I can think of to bring him back to me.

Sliding a palm around the back of his neck, I draw us together and bring his lips to mine.

At first, it doesn't work.

His mouth is firmly shut, lips pressed together, but I keep kissing and swiping with my tongue until his jaw softens. That dazed look in his eyes fades, a slow building heat taking its place when his lips finally ease open, granting me access. And as our tongues touch for the first time in years, pulling a moan out of him, a flame inside of me flares to life.

He relaxes onto me, fingers running through my hair as he deepens the kiss, tongues tangling desperately. His teeth sink into my bottom lip as my hands slip beneath the hem of his shirt, smoothing over the stiff muscles of his back. Our hips grind together, his cock already hard and pressing into mine with a friction that sends sparks of pleasure up my spine.

When his lips leave mine to trail a line of kisses down my jaw, I gasp, melting under the flame of his touch.

It's not enough. Need more.

"Taylor," he groans against my throat, nipping at my skin. "I want to feel you. Please."

*Great minds think alike.*

My shaking fingers fly to the buttons on his flannel between us, frantically trying to undo them. They're small, slippery, and I have no fucking patience right now, so I grip the shirt and yank it apart with a growl. Buttons go flying as it parts down the middle, and a grin cracks across Huckslee's face when my hands slide up his bare chest and down his shoulders, pushing the shirt away. His own fingers press into the holes along the side of my tank top before he rips it off my body, too, and I can't help but roll my eyes at him.

"Really? I destroy your shirt, so you destroy mine?"

"Give and take, baby." He's back against my body in an instant, our bare chests now flush as our mouths find each other again, and my stomach somersaults at the word he just called me.

*Baby.* I'm baby.

A giddiness envelopes me as I suck on his lips, running my nails over his skin, earning a hiss and a bite in reward. Huck's eyes are bright and present with lust, but there's still a haze in them that has me pulling back from him, unsure.

He goes still, brows wrinkling as he stares down at me, breathing heavily. "What's wrong?"

Swallowing hard, I bite my lip. "You're still drunk, Huckslee."

A smile slowly pulls at his lips as he leans down to run his tongue along my nipple, the sensation shooting straight to my already aching cock. "Worried about taking advantage of me, Tay?"

"Uh, I mean, kinda." *Not really.*

He laughs, rolling the sensitive skin in between his teeth, and I moan as I rock my hips, needing to feel him everywhere. His palms run up and down my abs, forcing a yelp out of me, followed by a chuckle as I bat his hands away.

"Ticklish."

Groaning, he drags his mouth back up to mine. "I forgot about that. You know how hard it's gonna be not to touch your stomach? Your abs are sexy as fuck."

I kiss him greedily, savoring the taste like it's the last time I'll get to have it. With Huckslee, you never know when that'll be the case. He's made a habit of disappearing, and that fact alone should stop me in my tracks, but it only fuels the inferno blazing under my skin. Burning up for the man on top of me who I've denied myself for so long.

And I'm sick of fighting it. Fighting him.

So damn sick and tired that I wrap my arms around his neck and thrust up into him desperately.

"Can I..." He presses a line of soft kisses along my throat. "Can I touch you, baby?"

There's a waver in his voice that makes my heart clench, the uncertainty in it, so I take his hand and push it down to the painfully hard bulge in my jeans. "Please, Huck. I need it."

His fingers work the button expertly, popping it open to lower my zipper, releasing the pressure on my cock. He palms it over my briefs, rubbing me as he slides down to take my nipple in between his teeth again, and I buck against him, moaning, pleading for more. He grins wickedly, so fucking gorgeous with his curls tousled from my hands. As he sits up and hooks a finger into my waistband, though, the smile fades from his face when he stares down at me. Blinking.

*Uh oh.*

"Blondie," he whispers, lips pursing, and I follow his line of vision to my briefs, where a smear of lipstick is smudged smack in the middle of my crotch.

"We didn't—" My eyes fly to his face. "Nothing happened, Huck. I couldn't get it up. She tried, but...all I could think about was you."

And I'd been so mad about it, too.

The sight of a woman on her knees with her tits out used to get me going, but all I wanted was a pair of strong arms and sinfully dark brown eyes.

He studies me momentarily, almost pouting, before brushing his lips over my jaw. "I wasn't on a date with Royce. He's taken, we're just friends." Leaning his forehead against mine, we breathe each other in, noses touching. "I can't get you out of my head, Taylor. I haven't been able to for four years."

My tongue darts out to wet my lips, flicking his in the process. "Are we doing this, then?"

"Doing what?"

I pause. "Us."

My pulse quickens, the blood in my veins near boiling from the heat in his gaze as he looks at me. I know he wants this. I can feel it in the possessive way his fingers tighten on my hips, see it in the desire and need crossing his features. He likes the idea of it, of having me. Owning me. Even though I've been his from the start. And I want him, too. God, I want him. More than I've ever wanted anything, even motocross.

His eyes shutter, head dropping to hide himself. "Ask me again in the morning."

And then he's lowering himself down my body, placing kisses on my neck, all over my chest, running his tongue over both nipples until I'm a moaning mess beneath him, fingers in his hair. He even lightly kisses my abs, laughing when I twitch and squirm. His teeth sink into my hip, biting and sucking as he rubs my length over the material of my briefs until I can't stand it.

Hooking my thumbs into the waistband, I lift off the bed enough to push my jeans down past my ass. When my hard cock springs free, slapping against my lower stomach, his eyes go nearly black.

"Jesus fucking Christ," he mutters, voice thick, and I grin up at him as I take my length in my hands.

"Can't say I see the resemblance."

He watches me stroke myself for a moment, adjusting himself while his eyes run all over my body. "Fuck, Taylor. The pink hair, the tats, that cock...you're such a fucking dream."

His mouth practically waters at the sight of me, and it spurs me on. Sure, I've been called hot before by plenty of women. I know I'm attractive; I use it to my advantage any chance I get, but the sound of praise coming from Huck's lips is unlike anything else.

"Yeah? You like my cock?" I glance at him from under my lashes, biting my lip while I work myself, melting under his gaze.

A deep, desperate groan rumbles from his chest, watching me as he rubs himself over his pants. "I've been dying for it."

Fucking hell.

"Come get it, then." My lips curve into a challenging smirk.

Flames blaze in his eyes, burning bright, and when his fingers wrap around my length, I feel like I'll spontaneously combust. He jerks me from base to tip, swiping his thumb over the bead of precum on my slit before rubbing it into that sensitive spot beneath my crown, and I swear I see stars. His gaze holds mine as he slowly lowers, curls falling over his brow, stealing my breath when the flat of his tongue drags along the underside of my shaft, swirling around the tip. As his lips close around it, sucking me into his mouth, something between a whimper and a moan leaves me at the sight of him, at the warmth and softness as he takes me all the way to the back of his throat.

"Goddamn, Huck." I tangle my fingers into his curls, teeth working my lip to keep myself from getting too loud. "You look fucking gorgeous with my cock in your mouth."

It's everything I ever imagined, all those nights I pictured this scene playing out. He's making me feel so fucking good with his tongue that I'm thrusting my hips, abs clenching when he smiles and hollows his cheeks, deep-throating me again before popping off with a groan.

"You taste so good." His arm slips down as he palms himself, and I know the constraints of his jeans must be painful.

"Hey." Pulling him up to me, I steal a kiss. "Take it out, Huck. I want you to feel good, too."

Shaking his head, he nibbles on my lower lip while he continues to work me with his hand. "This isn't about me, Tay. I...I took it all last time. I just want to touch you."

I rear back with a frown. "We aren't doing that anymore. It's give *and* take, not give *or* take."

Huck still looks uncertain, shuttering his eyes to watch himself jerk my cock, so I grip his chin between two fingers and force his face back up to mine. "I'm not gonna make you if you don't want to, but...I need you to feel this with me, baby. Please."

His gaze searches mine for a moment, bouncing between my eyes and mouth before he nods. "Okay. Then I have an idea."

While his hand still works me into a frenzy, he kisses me senselessly for a bit, exploring every inch of my mouth with his tongue. Biting, sucking, robbing me of breath until I'm a trembling puddle beneath him, and then he leans back to undo his belt buckle and jeans. In the absence of his hand, I grip myself, stroking up and around the crown as I watch him pull down his Calvin Klein's and free his cock.

"Fuck, you're beautiful," I moan, mouth watering at the sight of his hard length standing at attention for me, abs clenching. I remember the taste of it on my tongue, down my throat, and I want it again. But before I can get my mouth on him, Huckslee bats my hand away from my dick before lining it up with his own. He spits into his palm and then wraps his strong fingers around the both of us, stroking our cocks from root to tip in firm languid tugs that have me short-circuiting as I nearly come from the sensation.

God, it's unlike anything I've ever experienced. The feeling of us pressed together, the sight of precum dripping from his tip onto my own as he works us, the scent of his aftershave, and the moans coming out of his mouth as he leans down to bite onto my shoulder. It's too much, too many senses overloaded, every nerve in my body firing off at once as I thrust my hips to meet his pace. It feels like I'm levitating, vibrating so hard that if it weren't for Huckslee holding me in place, I'd lift through the fucking ceiling and disappear.

My fingers dig into his arms so hard that I'm probably leaving bruises, but it wouldn't be the first time I've left my marks on him. When he takes my lobe in between his teeth at the same time his free hand comes up to pinch my nipple, I'm fucking gone.

Obliterated.

Imploding as my warm cum shoots onto my chest and neck, coming so hard I have to stuff my knuckles into my mouth and bite down, strangled whines clawing up my throat.

"Holy fucking shit." Huckslee's release follows, his own cum spilling over my cock and dripping onto my abs in the sexiest waterfall I've ever seen. It coats his fingers, and he spreads the sticky mess over both of us, stroking us through our orgasms until we're wrung completely dry.

Releasing our dicks, he places a long kiss on my lips before falling over, collapsing next to me in a heap of groans. We both lie still for a second, trying to catch our breaths. A sated sigh leaves me, eyes falling closed.

I feel lighter than air and yet anchored at the same time by Huck's body pressed into my side. Warmth blooms in my chest, spreading down into my ribs, like a sense of rightness settling over my bones. When I open my eyes and turn to look at Huck, I find his lidded gaze already on me, a lopsided grin pulling at his mouth.

"What's that look for?" I smile back, moving closer for a kiss, needing to share his air.

He chuckles as he shakes his head, rubbing our lips together. "Christian was definitely right. You come loudly."

"Fuck off." A laugh bursts out of me as I study myself with raised brows. "I've never come that hard in my life."

Following my line of vision, his eyes darken as he takes in our mess of cum covering my body. The mattress shifts when he lifts to his knees, leg coming over my hips to straddle me, and I watch curiously as he leans down toward me.

His glittering gaze meets mine before his tongue darts out, running a line in the mess from my abs up to my chest. The tickling sensation doesn't even register as he brings his dripping tongue to my lips, which are already parted, and fills my mouth with our mixed tastes. The action is so unexpectedly filthy coming from Huckslee that a moan wrenches out of me, my cock nearly standing at full attention again as I suck on his tongue, swallowing every last salty drop like it's capable of sustaining me.

He breaks away to dip his head again, and then he fucking *licks me clean.* Every ounce of cum on my neck, chest and stomach. Laps it up like it's fucking delicious, and by the time he's done, my cock is jutting toward my belly button again, loud and proud. His wicked grin flashes before he's sucking me into his mouth once more.

"Mhmfuuck." I huff a surprised moan, running my fingers through his hair, and I'm so keyed up that it doesn't take long before I'm spilling my load a second time, only down his throat. He smacks his lips when he's done, taking in my wide, astonished expression with a bashful smile.

"I like cum," he shrugs, crawling up the bed to flop down beside me. "So what?"

"That was the hottest thing that has ever happened to me." Grabbing the back of his neck, I pull him in for a sloppy kiss. "Like, ever. Jesus fuck, Huckslee."

A chuckle vibrates his chest before he throws an arm over me and settles in, face buried into the side of my neck. My fingers trail down his bicep, tracing the hard muscles, and I tap the tattoo covering the scar on his arm that says '*Break The Glass*.'

"I've been wondering about this."

"I got it when I first got to California," he answers after a quiet moment. "It's a quote from a Jelly Roll song, but I liked the meaning behind it. Essentially, the mirror is a barrier between our past and future. You can let it stop you from moving forward or break the glass."

Hmm. I like that.

For a long while, we just lay in each other's silence. Baby Bones is somewhere in the room making noise, chewing on something, or playing with one of her toys. Combined with Huck's breath, the sound has my heavy lids sliding shut.

Fuck, I'm tired. It's gotta be close to five or six in the morning at this point. Sleep is on the horizon, but Huck's lips move against my throat just before I doze off.

"What does this mean?" He murmurs, tracing a finger over the outline inked on my left peck.

"Uh," I cough a nervous laugh, suddenly wide awake. "You really need to study geography, Huck."

He goes still, eyelashes fluttering against my neck as he blinks. Rising up on an elbow, he squints down at me. "Did you seriously get the shape of Delaware tattooed on you?"

"Yep." My teeth sink into my lip as I fight a sheepish grin. "Right over my heart."

Those dark eyes widen as he slightly rears back, breath catching, and my stomach drops.

Shit. He hates it. It's so stupid. I should have lied and told him it was just a blank spot I was saving for something, like Lasagna's name or a tattoo for BB. Why did I say anything-

A crushing kiss drowns out every negative thought, his mouth on mine shredding every doubt. Our tongues intertwine, dancing as he gently palms my throat. It's not a kiss filled with heat or lust, but one of passion, tinged with desperation, filled with regret, and all the words we never got to say.

When we finally part, exhausted and out of breath, he places a quick kiss on my peck before pushing me onto my side. "Turn over. I want to hold you."

Strong limbs encage me, pressing my back to his chest and enveloping me in a safety that feels foreign yet familiar. His lips rest against the back of my neck, breaths stirring my hair until they even out, and that's how we fall asleep.

In each other's arms, Huckslee's hand resting over my heart.

The first thing I notice when the sun wakes me is that the bed has grown cold.

There's a vacancy inside me that wasn't there last night, a gaping void in my being where something vital should have been. When I roll over with a groan and pat the sheets next to me, I find them empty. No warmth, like I've been here alone for a while. If it weren't for the button stuck to the side of my face from ripping Huck's shirt, I would have believed that last night was a fever dream. The words he'd said when I asked him if we were doing this thing between us pop into my head.

*Ask me again in the morning.*

I knew he'd run. He always does. I expected it.

So why does it feel like I'm falling apart?

BB starts snorting angrily under the bed, asking for breakfast now that she knows I'm awake, and I rub my eyes with the back of my palms before sitting up. Pain shoots down my arm, collarbone popping, matching the ache that's in my chest as I swing my feet to the ground and busy myself with feeding her.

He knew. The whole time he was kissing me and giving me the best pleasure of my life, he knew he'd be gone when I woke up.

The reality burns bitterly on my tongue, still heavy with his taste.

Once again, Huckslee Davis breaks my fucking heart. And I can't even blame him because I was the idiot who gave it to him when I should have known better.

After taking a piss and grabbing a quick shower to wash the scent of him off my skin, I pad out into the kitchen.

And come to a dead halt when I see Christian sitting on the couch in silence, a cup of coffee raised halfway to his lips, sociology homework spread out next to him, an accusing glint in his eye.

He looks at me.

I look at him.

And that's about when I realize I heard no music coming from his room last night, but I was too caught up in Huck to notice.

*Ah, fuck.*

"How much did you hear?" I grit through my teeth, scrubbing my face.

His gaze narrows as he takes a loud sip. "Caught the whole show plus the after-credit scene." He pauses. "Unwillingly, I might add."

"Fucking great."

Turning my back to hide my red cheeks, I grab a mug from the cupboard and pop a pod in the coffee maker before searching for some breakfast. He stays silent while I busy myself, the constant slurping from his cup grating on my nerves. Only when I have a plate of toaster strudels and some caffeine do I turn around.

"So tell me," he starts slowly, scooting over to make room on the couch as I flop down, "how long have you been fucking your stepbrother?"

*Oh, my god.*

# HUCKSLEE

## APRIL

L aughter fills the house, little feet pitter-pattering off the tile as my baby cousins ricochet off the walls.

The dining room is packed full, aunts and uncles filling every chair as Dad sits at the head of the table, looking happier than I've seen him in a while, enjoying everyone's company.

We even had to set up a few tables in the foyer to accommodate all the extra people. There's enough food to feed an entire army since Maisie and Logan's mom spent days cooking for this. It's Dad's first holiday out of recovery, so they wanted to go big and celebrate.

A full house, overflowing with so much family that it's bursting.

And yet, it feels empty to me because one person is missing.

*Where the fuck is he?*

Scowling down at my plate, I check my phone for what has to be the millionth time today, billions in the last week. Plenty of texts, just not from him. It's been two weeks since we exchanged numbers on Instagram, but I've been too cowardly to reach out first.

Just like I was too big of a coward to face him that morning a month ago after St. Patrick's Day.

A month. Four weeks. Nearly thirty days since I've seen Taylor, or touched him, or felt his lips on mine. I'm going fucking crazy.

"What's with you today?" Logan asks next to me, looking about as bad as I feel. "You've been in a bad mood since we left the apartment."

"So have you," I counter dryly, and he just lifts the corner of his mouth in response.

Yeah, we haven't been fun to be around the last few weeks. A moping Logan was bad enough, but add in my surly ass, and now being cooped up in that damn apartment is becoming unbearable. It's been nothing but studying for finals, piles of homework, and being alone with my thoughts. I started dragging Logan to the gym for something to do, but that still gave me too much time to think.

Like thoughts about the fact that Taylor saved my fucking life, and I assaulted him after disappearing for four years. And then I made out with him, sucked the soul out of his dick after he admitted he was in love with me, then disappeared *again*. Cue the self-loathing. Between Logan and I, there's plenty to go around.

"Hey, Huckslee," one of my uncles calls from across the room. "Any news on that draft pick yet?"

*Ugh, don't remind me.*

"Not yet. Pick's not until next weekend. It's anyone's guess."

The top players know which NFL team they're getting picked for ahead of time, but seeing as I'm just reasonably decent, it could be anywhere.

Dad takes a sip of his drink. "Who you hoping for, son?"

Honestly, I'm hoping I don't get picked at all. It's an odd thing to say for someone who spent four years playing football, but I just don't think I want to make it my career. Free agency would be ideal.

"Somewhere close," I shrug, pushing my food around. "Or at least on the West Coast."

My cousin Angela gags. "Really, like the Seahawks? Booo!"

That starts a whole discussion about NFL teams that I'm just not in the mood for, so I finally pull out my phone again and text Taylor.

> Me: Where are you?

He doesn't respond immediately, and I listen to the conversation around me for a minute until the screen lights up.

> Taylor: Who dis?

Seriously, asshole?

> Me: Huckslee.

Another minute passes.

> Taylor: How did you get my number?

> Me: You gave it to me on IG, remember?

He did. Right? I pull up my Instagram account to read over the message again, making sure I'm not crazy. Another text comes through.

> Taylor: Salem runs my social media accounts. I'm never on those haha.

> What's up?

What's up? *What's up is that I haven't stopped thinking about the way your lips feel or the way your cock tastes, motherfucker.*

> Me: Where are you?

> Taylor: Uh in my room?

My brows pinch together.

> Me: No you're not

> Taylor: Yes huh

A picture comes through, his hand flipping the middle finger with his room at his apartment in the background.

Ah, that room. I don't know why I thought he meant his room here, at this house.

> Me: Why aren't you here?

Taylor: Where's here?

Me: Our parents house. Easter Sunday dinner.

Taylor: Wasn't invited.

He...what?

Glancing up, I look around at all the members of Maisie's side of the family. *His* side of the family. Why the fuck didn't his own mother invite him? Why didn't my dad? He should be here.

"Is Taylor coming today?" I ask Maisie, and she blinks as the room goes quiet.

"I don't think so, dear," she replies vaguely, slicing into the ham in the middle of the table, not meeting my gaze.

A frown pulls at my mouth. "Why not?"

She exchanges a look with Dad before shrugging, a tight smile on her face. "Oh, we figured he'd be busy with his biking thing. No big deal."

*Bullshit.*

Seriously, it sounds like the biggest crock of shit I've ever heard, and the words nearly spill from my mouth until I grind my molars to keep them in. I can feel Dad's eyes on me, so I meet them, not bothering to hide the disappointment in him that I'm feeling for the first time in my life.

Logan bumps my shoulder. "What's going on?"

"Taylor should be here," I mutter, looking away from my dad. "This is his family too."

He sweeps his gaze around the room before slowly nodding. "I agree."

Turning back to my phone, I send Taylor another message.

> Me: You shouldn't have to be invited. It's family.

> Taylor: Oh? You missing me, big bro? ;P

I cringe so hard at that, it's not even funny, but I ignore his Taylorisms and ask what he's up to because I'd rather talk to him than anyone else.

> Taylor: Puzzles

> Me: Haha, funny

> Taylor: You?

> Me: Trying to get through this awkward dinner without discussing football or my life plans.

> Taylor: Yeah, good luck with that.

> Being the family pariah has its benefits. Nobody asks me shit.

Well, that's sad as hell.

> Me: What are your life plans Taylor?

A moment passes before I see the bubbles appear while he types.

Taylor: Become a muthafuckin freestyle legend.

Buy a house next to Christian and build a track in our backyard.

Maybe get a goat.

Me: A goat?

That makes me snort. Logan gives me a funny look, but I wave him off.

Taylor: Yeah one of those fainting ones.

Me: Most people want the house with the wife, kids and a dog.

Taylor: Dogs are cool. I'd rather have a ferret or something. I'm too lazy for walks.

Me: And the wife and kids?

I don't even know why I'm asking or what possessed me to bring it up, but my palms are damp, and my heart is beating a little hard. He reads the text but doesn't respond. Not for a while. I try to interject myself into the surrounding conversations, to focus on whatever my little cousins try to show me, but I can't concentrate.

Finally, the phone buzzes, and I feel slightly dizzy.

Taylor: I'm with Salem on the whole marriage thing. Don't really see the point in it, to be honest.

And I think I'd make a shitty dad, so kids are definitely not on the list.

Me: I don't think so. You doted on Lasagna, and I could tell your rabbit is happy.

Taylor: Don't know if you know this, Huckslee, but children and animals are entirely different.

Me: No shit, Sherlock. I'm just saying you have like, fatherly instincts.

Taylor: Fatherly, huh?

Me: Fuck off. I'm trying to compliment you.

Taylor: Why bother?

Sighing heavily, I rub my eyes before sending a gif of a cat waving a white flag.

Me: Let's not fight, okay? That's not why I texted. Truce?

He leaves me on read for ten minutes. Twenty. I help clear the table, chat with Logan and his dad, and even play tag in the backyard with my cousins. Two hours later, still no response, so I pull up my phone and create a group chat titled *'Delaware'* before adding Taylor's number to it. Not even a minute passes before he sends a message in the thread.

Taylor: Really, a group chat with just the two of us?

Me: This chat is Delaware. Fighting is off-limits.

Taylor: What do you want, Huck? I'm busy.

Me: With your puzzles?

Taylor: No, I'm about to get on my bike.

Been practicing for the qualifier this weekend.

Me: Shit, that's this weekend?

No response. I type out a quick *'good luck, I hope you win'* because it's clear he doesn't want to talk to me, and I don't blame him. Yeah, I tried reaching out via Instagram, but I didn't know he doesn't even read his social media messages. And I shouldn't have left him in the first place, but I was just...confused.

Ashamed, not because of what we did together but because of how I treated him. His dad almost killed him and hurt him so bad he was in the hospital for a month, but I just ignored him. It was easier to believe he was the villain than to try and understand him, just like how our parents are acting now.

I've noticed in my short twenty-two years of life that people are comfortable taking things at face value. No one hardly ever digs beneath the surface, too afraid they might delve too deep and find something that makes them uncomfortable. I should know; I put on a show for years that nobody noticed. Nobody except Taylor.

But just like everyone else, I saw his asshole kid exterior and automatically decided he was a bad egg, even when he showed me his true self in eighth grade. When he changed into a dick, I never questioned the switch. I should have known something was up.

I should have fucking known.

Eventually, the evening ends. Logan and I make the long drive back to his apartment in the city, and I'm tempted to ask him to drop me off at Taylor's, but I don't. Instead, when we walk into his two-bedroom, one-bathroom on the top floor of a high rise, I throw my jacket onto a chair and close myself in my nearly empty room.

There's an air mattress, my suitcase, which I've been living out of, and a desk I purchased from IKEA with college money, which I'm steadily running out of. Seriously, I owe Logan so much money when all of this is over for letting me stay here and for eating his food. He says not to worry about it, but as soon as I figure out what the fuck I want to do with my life, I'll pay him back with interest.

Walking over to the desk, I plop down and let out a breath. My laptop sits to the left, and my sketchbook to the right. Finals are in a week and a half, so I should probably study.

And yet...

My hands reach for the sketchbook of their own volition, and I find myself flipping through the new pieces I've been working on. Drawings for Taylor and Christian's brand, even though it was never brought up again after February. It's given me something to do, though. Keeps my mind occupied. Flipping open the book, I lief through my latest sketches, feeling heartsick.

That night, after Taylor fell asleep, I studied every piece of ink on his skin, mapping them to memory. After a heavy Face-Time with my therapist, I started drawing them—renditions of them anyway, in designs I think Taylor would like based on his t-shirt choices. I learned a lot of things that night when I studied his body, just from his tattoos and the things I noticed around his room.

He seems to like old movies, like Young Frankenstein and Little Shop of Horrors. Judging from the few books on his shelf and the cosmos inked onto his arm, he loves sci-fi and space. There are constellations down his spine and a UFO abducting a cow on his ribcage that made me chuckle. His other arm has trees and mountains on it. I could tell there was more on his legs, but since we were both clothed from the waist down, I couldn't see those. The ones on his right knuckles are a mystery, Japanese letters I know nothing about. His left hand has a skull tattooed on the back of it.

The memory of those inked fingers wrapped around his cock sends a heated wave through me, and I reach down to adjust myself. Fuck, he looked perfect. Lips all swollen from biting kisses, his neck red from my stubble, the tip of his dick engorged and weeping for me. I want to taste him again. Make a mess all over him and clean it up. Fucking hell.

I'm about to take out my dick and pull up his Instagram for the umpteenth time when a new message comes through in the chat, his reply to my good luck text.

> Taylor: Thanks. I think I have a good shot at making it.

> Christian does, too, but there's only one spot, so it could be either of us.

> Me: Oh, damn. Is it causing issues?

> Taylor: With me and Christian?

> Nah. He's worked just as hard as me for this. I'm proud of him.

> We're solid.

Resentment festers in my gut as I read his words. Typing out a message, I hit send before I can stop myself.

> Me: So different from the scholarship, then?

I'm such a petty fucking bitch. Swiping on the screen, I'm about to apologize when his reply comes through.

> Taylor: I'm not a little punk-ass crybaby anymore, so no.

Right. Shit.
New leaf, Huck. Start fresh.

> Me: You're right. Sorry for assuming.

> Taylor: Well, you know what they say about those who assume...you make an ASS out of U and ME.

> Me: Yeah, yeah. I know lol

> Taylor: Speaking of asses...

My stomach flips, and I move from the desk to the air mattress, waiting for his response.

> Taylor: I miss yours.

> And you are one for leaving me.

Goddammit.

Pulling up his number, I hit the call button, holding my breath as it rings. When he picks up on the fifth round, he sounds flustered.

"Hey?"

His deep, husky voice sends a current to my dick, and I chuckle. "Hey. Why do you sound so confused?"

"Uh," he coughs a dry laugh, "besides the occasional call with Salem, I don't think I talk to anyone on the phone. Like ever. I'm strictly a texter."

That makes me smile. "Is it weird?"

"Little bit." There's a pause, some rustling in the background. "Not bad, though."

I wish I could see his face. An odd sound comes over the line, like a swallow, prompting me to ask him what he's up to.

"Eating a HotPocket," he mumbles, clearly with his mouth full.

I snort. "Do you ever eat real food?"

"Yeah, on Wednesdays when Salem takes pity on us and comes over to cook."

Sounds about right. "How is she doing?"

"Eh. Been better."

Sighing, I flop back onto my pillow. "Yeah. Logan, too."

He grunts, and we're both quiet while he eats. Usually, the sound of someone chewing in my ear sets me off, but with Taylor, it's different. Like it's proof he's still there, even after all I've done to drive him away.

"So what had to be said over the phone that you couldn't text?" He asks finally, presumably done with his food.

"Well, first, I-I kind of missed your voice," I stammer, feeling a little stupid for admitting it out loud. "And second, I wanted to explain why I left."

"Guess you can try."

He sounds upset, and I don't fucking blame him one bit. I wish I could get over my shit.

Taking a deep breath, my fingers tangle in my curls. "I feel like I'm always apologizing to you, so I'll skip that part and jump right in. Look, Tay, hearing that you found me on prom night really freaked me out."

"I know," he whispers. "I could tell."

And that's why he kissed me. Because I was on the verge of an episode, and his lips dragged me back to reality.

"This whole time, I thought my dad was the one who found me and that the EMTs had stabilized me. I didn't...I didn't know that you saved my life. Literally, Taylor, because I looked at the hospital report. I'd be dead if you'd been just a few seconds later."

There's silence on the other line, but I hear his breath, so I continue.

"You gave me a second chance, and I'll never be able to repay that. Look at what I've done to you since I've been back. I hurt you."

He sighs heavily. "I thought we got past this?"

"Not just the times I choked you and punched your face, but the cabin, Taylor. I...I violated you."

"You *what?!*" His sudden shout causes me to pull the phone away from my ear with a flinch. "Huckslee, hold the fuck up, what are you even talking about?"

Swallowing hard, I cover my eyes. "I forced you to get on your knees and take my dick down your throat."

He pauses, my heart pounding in my chest, and then he groans in disbelief. "Huck, I *wanted* to get on my knees for you. I wanted your dick in my mouth."

"But not like that," I whisper, feeling ashamed at the way I restrained him and pinned him against the counter, "not for your first time. I let this anger inside of me poison something that should have been good for you. I'll never forgive myself."

"Huckslee, listen to me very carefully. I *wanted* it. I liked it. Was it rougher than I expected, and could I have used some aftercare? Fuck yeah. But it...it wasn't what you're making it out to be, okay? So stop that line of thinking."

Not likely, but I mumble a weak '*ok*' and blink away the tears of shame. He might not feel the way I do, but I still twisted an experience for him into something ugly. It shouldn't have happened that way.

"Hey," he breathes softly in my ear, "I can hear the doubts in your head over the phone. I'm telling you, baby, it's alright. Listen to the words I'm saying."

My breath catches, warmth flooding my chest. "Okay. I am, I'm listening."

"We need to break this cycle, Huck. The running and hiding and keeping shit inside. It's not healthy. Next time you feel this way, you need to talk to me about it."

"I will," I promise earnestly, hope lighting up the darkness in my head now that he sounds less mad at me. "I swear."

"Good. And I know how I can make you feel better."

"Yeah? How?"

He laughs low, a sultry sound that sends a tingle to my balls. "We're going to rewrite the scene. Change it."

"Change it?"

"Yeah." Fabric rustles in the background as he swallows. "Like, hypothetically speaking, if we could go back and redo that night, what would you do?"

"Hmm." Heart thumping, I close my eyes as I think about it. "Well, first, I'd let you kiss me after your snowman fell apart."

"Still pissed about that," he whines. "The snowman and the kiss part. You looked cute."

"And then I'd take you upstairs, peel off your clothes, and kiss every inch of your body."

He hums, "mm-hmm, that's a good start."

"I'd have you suck on my fingers, get your mouth all wet and dripping for me. And then I'd slowly feed you my cock."

A breathy moan comes from his side. "I want to taste you again so bad, Huck."

*Goddamn.*

"Yeah?" I'm fully hard now, undoing my jeans to pull myself out and give my shaft a long, slow tug.

"Yeah. I liked the way it felt when your cum slid down my throat."

"Fuck, baby, I wish you were sucking on me right now."

He whimpers like he did when I first wrapped my hands around him, and God, it's the sexiest sound I've ever heard. Jerking myself from base to tip, I ask, "are you playing with your cock, Tay?"

"Just a little. Can't help it. You make me fucking horny."

Groaning and regretting my choice of not having Logan take me to Taylor's apartment, I spit into my palm, getting it nice and wet. "You know what I can't stop thinking about?"

"Hmm?"

"Remember that night in the cabin when we shared a bed?"

There's a pause. "You want to have a foursome with Salem and Logan?"

The seriousness of his tone makes a laugh burst out of me. "*No*. Salem is not my type, and Logan is like my brother. That'd be weird."

"Good to know," he chuckles, "cuz I don't want to share you."

My heart wrenches at that. "What I can't stop thinking about is when Salem mentioned in that hypothetically fucked up scenario that I'd be fucking you."

His breath catches and then quickens. "I've been thinking about that, too."

Oh, fuck. My cock is heavy in my hand as I pump myself, imagining Taylor bent over for me. "Does it turn you on?"

"Fuck, yes," he moans. "God, it makes me so fucking hard."

"Can I ask you something? When you did anal before...did you like it?"

A soft laugh reaches me through the phone. "Yeah. From what I remember, anyway. It was one time with Salem, and we were drunk."

Damn, so it's been over two years since he's done it? And only once?

"I'd make you feel good, baby." I let go of my cock to massage my aching balls. "I'd go slow. Play with you until you're ready."

He doesn't answer, but I can tell from his noises that he likes the idea very much. Stroking myself right along with him, I continue.

"Mm, I'd get your tight ass nice and stretched for me, then I'd fill you with my cock. Fuck you so good that you make a mess all over yourself, clenching around me. And after I've pumped you full of cum, I'll lick you clean."

"Shit, Huck," he inhales shakily. "I'm gonna...c-come..."

"Show me," I command, jerking myself harder. "Record it, Taylor. I need to see it."

"H-hang on." He moves the phone closer to his cock, and the slick sounds of him rubbing himself grace my ears. There's a muffled, choked cry as he orgasms, bringing me close to tumbling over that edge myself. When he comes back on the line, he's breathless. "Check the chat."

Pressing play on the video, I watch his tattooed hand stroke that big cock until he's shooting cum all over his abs, and I moan as my own release spills from me, running down my shaft and over my fingers.

"Mmm, damn, Tay." Working myself through it, I feel lighter than I have in weeks. "You're so fucking perfect."

He hums contentedly, and when I'm finished wringing myself dry, I stick my fingers in my mouth one by one.

"Did you–" Taylor groans into the phone. "Did you just suck your own cum from your fingers just now?"

"Well, I'm not wasting it."

"*Fuuck*, Huckslee. Next time film that shit, it's not fair that you got a video and I didn't."

Grinning, I huff a laugh. "Or next time, you can just suck my fingers for me?"

"Deal."

We fall into a comfortable silence, cleaning ourselves up from the mess we just made, the sounds of Warhammer from Logan's room playing in the background. Lately, that's all he does. Goes to work, goes to school, then comes home and sits in front of his computer for hours. He doesn't even eat half the time unless I suggest making something or ordering takeout.

Rolling over onto my side, I exhale sharply. "I've got to get Logan out of the apartment more. He's been moody since February."

"Salem isn't much better. She's starting to piss me off, honestly. I took her to a rage room last weekend to try and help, but I think it only made things worse."

"At least you don't have to live with her." I blow a curl out of my face. "We should do something because I think they're both being stupid."

He grunts in agreement, "like what?"

"I don't know. Like, parent trap them, or something. Lindsay Lohan style."

"I have no clue what the hell that means."

"What? You've never seen The Parent Trap?"

"Negative, Ghost Rider."

"Of course, you've seen Top Gun, though," I scoff, shaking my head. "It's a movie about two twins who try to get their divorced parents back together by tricking them into being at the same place at the same time."

"Ah." He pauses and then gasps. "Wait. Huckslee, you're a fucking genius. I have the perfect idea."

"Yeah?"

"Yep. This weekend, at the Nitro Fuel Games qualifier. We're gonna get mom and dad back together, baby."

Scrunching up my nose, I snort. "Weird way to put it, seeing as how our parents are literally married to each other. But I'm picking up what you're putting down."

"Yeah, and calling Salem mom is probably super weird, right? Since I've fucked her?"

"Jesus Christ, Taylor." Burying my face into the pillow, I choke out a laugh. "You say the most out-of-pocket shit."

"But you love it, though."

I can hear the smile in his voice, which has my heart doing flips.

"Yeah. I do."

I really fucking do.

# TAYLOR

S pring has officially sprung in Utah, and it's a hot one.

Hotter than Satan's fucking nutsack. I'm dying in my motocross gear as I wait my turn while the other riders compete with their best tricks off a twenty-foot-tall ramp. Christian's next to me, bouncing on the balls of his feet with excitement. Whenever a rider lands something good, like a Hart Attack or an Up-nac, he's pumping his fists and cheering them on. It's honestly kind of adorable.

There's a crowd gathered, albeit not very big, as the qualifier isn't open to the public. Each rider is allowed to bring their people to support them, and as I glance toward the stands, I can already see Salem's blazing red hair shining under the morning sun. She's got a pink streak in it now, matching my tips, and she's also sitting as far away from Huckslee and Logan as she can get.

Yeah, she's a little pissed at me for inviting them. But she can get over it because I'm doing this for her moody ass.

Xed, Matty, and Hannah are here too, the three-year-old already talking Huck's ear off. He's trying to be polite and pay attention to her, but his eyes keep flicking back up to me, and I grin. I'm dying to see him. Haven't seen him in person since that night in my room after the Prospector, and the pictures we've been sending each other all week aren't enough. We FaceTimed last night because he loves to watch me come, and even though it was sexy as hell, I'm more of the physical type. I need to touch and taste. Breathe people in. Feel them close to me.

"Dude, did you see that shit!" Christian grabs my shoulder, shaking me as he hollers toward the ramp at whatever trick I missed. "A double Superman seat grab, man! These guys are good, Tay."

"Well, guys and gals," I correct, eyeing the woman next to me who's currently leading the scoreboard with the best Oxecutioner I've ever seen. She winks up at me, pale purple hair freeing from her braid.

Karlee Kaliente, as she goes by, is one of the best up-and-coming motocross athletes in the country—besides Christian and me, of course. She's also the girl who almost beat me during the scholarship race in high school when we both got taken out by Christian, securing Huckslee the win.

"You're up next, big guy." She reaches around me to slap Christian on the arm. "Knock 'em dead, kid."

He scoffs, pulling his hair back with a grin. "You're like a whole year younger than me, *bebita*." Putting on his helmet and mounting his two-stroke, we share our fist bump before his engine roars to life, and he rides out onto the tarmac to warm up.

Karlee's shoulder bumps mine. "You got anyone watching today?"

"Yep. Christian's mom is here, plus our friends and my..." Shit. What do I call him? "My...Huckslee," I finish lamely. We haven't exactly discussed what we are to each other, and calling him my stepbrother after everything we've done over the last week feels wrong. Even if it is technically accurate.

"Your 'Huckslee,' huh?" Karlee smiles, pointing to the stands. "My girlfriend is here, too. And my parents."

Following her gaze, my chest tightens a little. "That's awesome that your parents are here to support you."

For the most part, the fact that Maisie and Aaron don't acknowledge my existence doesn't bother me. Hasn't for a long time. But there are still those moments where I'll watch other people with their parents and wonder, *what must that be like?*

"They're the best, honestly." Her face shines with so much love that I have to turn away and watch Christian take his spot.

I already know what trick he's about to do; we've been practicing since February. Still, watching him race toward the ramp and lift twenty feet into the air has my heart jumping into my throat. He extends his legs flat over the handlebars as he backflips, a move called a Dead Body, before extending them up toward the sky in a Rigamortis. Letting go of the handlebars, he lets the bike float away from him for a moment while he flips and then grabs the bars again to pull it back to his body. My breath catches as he comes back down toward earth, and he's back in his seat just in time to stick the landing down the ramp.

"Fuck yeah!" I shout as I throw out my hands, jumping up and down. "That's my best friend, motherfucker!"

People in the stands clap, and I see his mom doing the same as me, hopping around while she cheers on her son. He's back beside me soon after, hazel eyes bright with excitement as we wait for the judges to score him. Freestyle Big Air scores are given on a zero to one hundred scale based on style, trick, difficulty, and originality, among other things. I loop my arm through his while we wait in anticipation, Karlee hanging on to him from the other side. The judges release the final score, and my heart drops.

Eighty-six.

Two points below Karlee, giving him second place.

"Damn." Leaning my head on his shoulder, I pat his back. "I'm sorry, man. You did really well."

Karlee gives him a punch on the arm. "I agree. I thought you did better than me, Totillo. That Holy Grab was amazing!"

"It's all good," he shrugs, smiling broadly even though I can see the disappointment in his eyes, "I'm just happy to be here. And I bet Salem got some hella sick shots, so that's a win."

"For sure, buddy."

A few more riders go after him because the selection is randomized. All of them are skilled but don't score any higher. And as luck would have it, I'm the last contestant to go.

The sweat is pooling on my neck as I pull up half of my dark strands to keep them out of my face. Christian and Karlee give me nudges and thumbs up, and when I look to the stands, I immediately lock eyes with Huck. He's too far away for me to see what he's feeling, but his grin of encouragement reaches me all the way over here, and I grin back. I'm tempted to do some dumb shit like blow him a kiss or make a heart with my fingers at him, but I don't. Mainly because Xed, Matty, and Logan still don't know what's been going on between us, but also because I don't think Huckslee would appreciate the sentiment on Salem's livestream.

Sliding on my helmet as I climb onto my bike, I ride over the tarmac and do a few circles of warm-ups. Despite the nervous energy vibrating my body, I feel good. Strong. Capable. Especially knowing that Huck is here watching and sending positive vibes my way. It's like the night of the monster truck rally when Christian and I performed in the Globe of Death. I knew he was watching me, and it just...calmed me. Kept me focused.

I used to picture his eyes before a performance, but now, just seeing him there in the stands is enough to rev me up. My senses are heightened ten-fold, and as I line myself up with the ramp and take off, I can feel his presence keeping me steady. My feet come off the pegs, planting onto the seat in a crouch before my wheels hit the incline. Pulling back, I stand on the seat when I'm upside down and lift a leg onto the handlebars, placing my fists on my hips in what I hope is the first Captain Morgan backflip ever.

The world falls away as I spin, and I hold my breath in freefall for a moment. My stomach flutters up into my chest before I drop back down onto the seat just in time for the impact of the landing to rattle my bones. That ever-present ache shoots down my shoulder, but it's duller today, and my form is fucking solid.

Air shotguns out of my lungs, arms like jelly, but I did it! *I fucking did it!*

As I ride back over to Christian, I can see him punching the sky while Karlee stands with her hands on her cheeks, mouth agape. Christian jumps on me when my helmet comes off, hollering as he bumps his forehead into mine. "You *loco hijo de puta*, that shit was insane! And your feet on the seat starting out?!"

"Dude, I just came up with that on the spot," I laugh, elated as I swing him around in a circle.

Karlee shakes her head, grinning widely as we approach the scoreboard to await the judges. "You two are fuckin' cute."

"I know, right." Christian reaches over to ruffle my hair. "He doesn't have eyes for me, though." Leaning close enough that only I can hear, he whispers, "fucker likes to keep it in the family."

Hissing harshly, I shove him hard enough that he loses balance. "You sick fuck, cut it out."

Ever since finding out about Huck and I, he's been giving me non-stop shit for it. The jokes would bother me if they came from anyone else, but I've known my best friend all my life. There's no malicious intent behind his jabs. He's not one hundred percent on board with the idea, though, only because of Huck punching me out in January. Even after I explained our convoluted history, Christian still isn't sure he's over that. The fact that I'm into a guy doesn't even factor into the equation.

"He's looking at you right now, *cariño*." My best friend twiddles his fingers toward the stands, waggling his brows, and I pull him down into a headlock.

"Stop making it weird!"

"I'm not calling him dad." Christian struggles against me, quoting the movie Step Brothers for the thousandth time. "Even if there's a fire!"

"You're such a fucking jackass."

"Uh, guys." Karlee's voice has us glancing up from where I've got his arm twisted around his back. She's pointing at the board, mouth parted. When I take in the score, my knees nearly give out.

Ninety-two.

Ninety-fucking-two.

A near-perfect score.

And the fucking qualifying winner.

"Holy shit!" Christian shakes my shoulders as I gaze at the board, completely awestruck. "That's what I'm talking about, baby boy!"

"I won?" Oh, my God. "Dude, I won! *Hell fuckin' yeaaaah!*"

I damn near scream to the heavens as Karlee chuckles, pulling me into a congratulatory hug. Cheers and claps come from the stands, and I swear I can see the pride on Huckslee's face when I catch his gaze on me. It fills me up so much that I'm flying, and when Salem slams into me, wrapping herself around my body like a koala, I'm over the fucking moon.

I can't believe it. I *actually* won.

Come August, I'll be competing with some of the best action sports athletes in the entire country.

Jesus Christ, how did I get here?

Is this real life?

The next hour goes by in a blur as Salem drags me through the motions of talking to officials about August and doing an interview with a representative of Nitro Fuel. I can't even remember what I said, in all honesty, because the adrenaline was still cruising through my veins while I chilled on cloud nine. When the rush of everything finally calms, Christian, Salem, and I wheel our bikes out to my truck in the emptying parking lot where everyone's waiting.

Of course, the first thing I notice is that Huckslee looks fine as fuck. He's got on a gray Henley that hugs his chest, dark jeans, and curls falling over his forehead under a beanie. His eyes heat when they meet mine, but something else simmers there, too. Something I can't decipher. There's a smile on his lips, but it's...well, it looks tight. My brows pinch together as I open my mouth to ask him what's wrong, but before I get a chance, there's a tiny body in a sparkly tutu clinging onto my leg.

"Uncle Tayto!" Hannah sits on my foot, curling around my calf with a giggle, and I walk toward the truck's bed, pretending to shake her off.

"How's my favorite niece?"

"It's hot. Can I get ice cream?"

"Hmm." Leaving my bike for Christian, I scoop her up, wincing against the pain in my collarbone. "What did your dad say?"

She purses her lips. "He said, um." Her eyes dart to Matt lifting my bike onto the truck before widening them at Xed. He smiles affectionately, leaning down to whisper something in her ear, and she lights up as she grins at me. "He said winner buys."

"Of course he did," I snicker, feeling Huck's eyes on me as I set Hannah down. Matty immediately grabs me around the middle and lifts me into a bear hug.

"Knew you'd do it, Tay." He squeezes the air out of my lungs. "You and Christian both!"

"Down now. Need air," I wheeze, tapping his side.

Xed pries me from Matty's arms. "You're gonna kill him before he even gets to compete, Sasquatch, Jesus." Once I'm safely on the ground again, he flicks my nose. "Congrats, man. Proud of you."

"Thanks for saving my life."

He rolls his eyes and turns to help strap the bikes down, finally allowing me to face Logan and Huck.

Logan speaks first, his eyes darting from me to Salem, who has her back to us. "That trick you did was pretty cool, Taylor. Never seen anything like that before."

"No one has." Huck steps closer to me, dark eyes on my face. "Very first Captain Morgan backflip, right?"

"Pretty sure," I grin, watching him lick his lips and wishing I could do it for him. "You like that? Been working on it for a while."

He nods, eyeing the new tattoo of a dragonfly across my throat like he did over FaceTime last night. "You looked good. Really good."

A wave of heat different from the temperature tingles up my spine. "You think so?"

"Yeah." His burning gaze meets mine again, and it takes everything in me not to lean forward to claim his mouth.

"Party at our place tonight," Matty announces, grinning down at Xed, who looks like he was not informed of this plan, "to celebrate. Been too long since we had one."

Christian lets out a whoop and jumps from the truck as Hannah squeaks in Matt's arms. "Me too, Daddy?"

"Sorry, bean." He kisses the top of her head. "Your momma wants to see you tonight, remember?"

The way her little face falls has me breaking apart.

"But I don't want to," she whispers, burrowing into his chest, and he tightens his arms around her.

"You haven't seen her in so long, though. Don't you want to spend time with her?"

She shakes her head and reaches for Xed, tears glistening in her eyes, and I have to look away before I overstep and tell her she can have whatever the hell her little heart desires. It's not my place; I'm not her parent. But fuck, seeing her so miserable like this breaks my damn heart.

My eyes catch on Salem, standing there with her arms crossed, looking at Logan like he just showed her a bug. He smiles tentatively, and her glare deepens, not breaking eye contact, while she obliterates him with her scowl.

If looks could kill.

Inwardly, I cringe, having been on the receiving end of that glare myself.

Huck leans in close, his breath on my ear giving me goosebumps. "Looks like our plan failed."

He smiles sadly, stepping back toward Logan like he's preparing for them to leave, and my fists clench. Because *no*. I want to spend time with him, dammit. And I know him well enough to know that he'd never leave Logan in a time of need.

"Can Huck and Logan come, too?" I ask Matt, earning a death ray from Salem's eyes in response when he says yes.

"If he's coming, I won't be there," she hisses, and I scrub my face with a groan.

"Don't be like that, Sally Mal."

"No, fuck off, you meddling bitch." Her voice is low enough that Hannah doesn't hear, but when she stomps off toward her jeep with a growl, Logan and I step toward her simultaneously. He raises his palms when he sees the look in my eyes because, trust me, him going after her would only make shit ten times worse right now.

Trudging after her, I catch her right as she yanks open the driver's side door. "Salem, please don't be like this."

"Be like what?" She whips around and hits me with a black look. "Oh, you mean pissed at you for inviting my ex behind my back?"

"In his defense, he didn't know you'd be here either. Huckslee didn't tell him."

She blinks before pointing an acrylic at me, lips curled back. "You parent trapped us?!"

"I really need to see that movie," I mutter, running a hand through my sweaty hair. "Look, Salem, please just come to the party. Because if you don't come, I'm afraid Logan won't either, which means Huckslee won't be there, and I really, *really* want him to be there."

"Why?" Her gray eyes narrow at me. "I thought we were mad at him?"

My head bounces from side to side, a shoulder lifting into a shrug. "We're...working through shit."

"So take him to your own place!"

"I can't," I pout. "Logan doesn't know about us, and plus, I want to spend time with Matty and Xed, too."

She says nothing, only purses her lips as she gazes at me, so I cup her face and squish her cheeks.

"Please, Salem? Please? *Please, please, please, please, please, please—*"

"Alright!" She shoves me away by my chest. "Fine! But I'm bringing Arya and Owen."

*Ugh.* Whatever. It'll be alright. I've met Owen maybe twice, and he was cool, but Arya...

As long as I get to hang with Huck, nothing else matters.

"Deal." I extend my hand to her, which she slaps away before getting into the jeep. She throws it in reverse and then flips me off out the open window as she backs out of her spot, prompting me to holler after her.

"Love you, too, grump ass!"

When I return to the truck, Christian is mimicking monkey noises for Hannah as Logan steps forward, his attention on Salem's retreating jeep.

"Is she coming?" He asks anxiously, and I flash two thumbs up with a grin.

"Yep." Swinging my eyes to Huck, I find him watching me with that peculiar look, half heat, half sadness. "Text you the address?"

"See you there," he murmurs, and as he passes by toward Logan's car, his fingers brush against mine. Turning to study his back, my gaze drops to where the strong muscles of his bubble ass flex in his jeans. I bite my lip, fingers twitching to reach out and squeeze, but I refrain. He glances over his shoulder suddenly, brow quirked, and I turn away quickly, covering my mouth to hide the grin on my lips at being caught checking him out.

And notice Xed staring right at me.

"Uh..." Yeah, just gonna pretend that didn't happen. "Christian and I need to run the bikes home, grab a quick shower, and then we'll be over."

"Your shower or mine?" Christian snickers, climbing into the passenger seat, and I roll my eyes as Xed nods with a small smile.

"Okay. Grab beer."

Quoting that one Hollywood Undead song everyone knows, I say my goodbyes to Hannah before hopping into the truck. Christian turns on some tunes, jamming his hands on the dash, and I feel for the first time in years that everything is going right.

Like maybe I deserve to be happy, after all.

# TAYLOR

X ed and Matt's townhouse sits in the Avenues, a neighborhood northeast of downtown Salt Lake City.

The building is old, historic, and made of brick with vines
running up the front. Matty's parents own it, but they let him
and Xed rent it out since the University of Utah is only five
minutes from the place. There are no driveways, however, and
parking on the street is limited, so we had to park the truck
around the corner and walk the rest of the way.

By the time we arrive, everyone's already there. I can hear
the music bumping when we push open the door, 'Too Much'
by Pepper blasting from Xed's speakers. It's two stories, with
old carpeted stairs leading up to the second level from the
entryway and creaky hardwood under my feet. I'm about to
enter the living room behind the stairs when a high-pitched
scream makes me cringe.

"Taaaaaylor-uh!"

*God. Here we go.*

Arya's body hits me as she jumps into my arms, wrapping her legs around my waist. Pressing big fake tits into my chest, she leans in to try and kiss me, like usual, but I turn my head so that she catches my cheek. And that's when I notice Huck in the kitchen, gazing at me with narrowed eyes while he leans against the counter next to Owen, Salem's very attractive, very *gay* friend.

I narrow my own eyes as I extract myself from Arya, prying her off of me before setting her down on the ground.

She tosses her bleach blonde hair over a shoulder and pouts up at me, blinking big green eyes. "I was happy to hear about your win today, but I can't believe you didn't invite me, Tay."

"Yeah, it was close friends only." I brush by her, following Christian into the kitchen, noticing how he eyes her tight mini-skirt. They'll probably be fucking before the night is over. It wouldn't be the first time.

Huck watches me approach, and even though he smiles widely, there's something under the surface that I can't figure out.

"Hi," he says, dropping his gaze to take in my Rings of Saturn tank top, which shows a green alien chilling on a doughnut.

"Taylor, hey." Owen reaches out a hand to shake mine, light brown hair waving over his ears. "Good to see you again. Do you know Huckslee?"

Glancing between them, I can't help but notice how good they look together. Owen's not exceptionally muscled, not as much as me, but still toned. Soft in all the right places. He's shorter than us and would definitely be easier for Huck to lift. His whiskey-colored eyes, dimpled chin, tanned skin, and loose button-up hit a spot of familiarity in the back of my head, and not because I've met him twice. I just realized he looks similar to almost every guy Huck has dated—exactly his type.

My stomach drops.

"Yeah, I know him." Licking my lips, I run my gaze over Huck with a dark grin. "Know him pretty well."

Owen's face falls slightly as Huck's eyes heat, but before we can say anything, a slight body shoves herself in front of me.

"Oh gosh, hi." Arya smiles up at Huck. "We arrived only a few seconds before Taytay, so I don't think we've met. You must be his stepbrother I've heard so much about."

*Goddammit.*

Owen's face brightens, and I want to cover my hand over Arya's mouth to shut her up.

Huck's brows rise in amusement as he takes her in. "Oh? And what exactly have you heard?"

She giggles, making me want to jab knives into my ears. "Just how amazing you are at football. It was pretty annoying how obsessed he was with your games."

"Arya, shut the fuck up," I mutter, placing my hands on her shoulders to move her aside. Christian snickers, throwing the beer in the fridge after grabbing one and popping off the cap.

"Well, I don't know about amazing," Huckslee says somewhat bitterly before meeting my gaze. "And how do you know *Taytay?*"

He says it playfully, but I scowl as Arya rolls her eyes, brushing my arm.

"We used to date a few years ago."

"*Date* is a strong word." Shoving my hands in my pockets, I glance up at Huck from under my lashes, wanting to press my chest to his and feel him against me. Something is off about him today, but I can't figure out what it is. I need to get him alone to ask what the hell is going on under those soft curls. "Where is everyone?"

He jerks his head toward the staircase. "Matt is giving Logan a tour of his game collection upstairs, and Xed's in the living room with Salem setting up the pong table."

"Huckslee and I were just talking about his life in Cali," Owen smiles, flashing perfectly straight teeth that I kinda wanna punch. "He offered to make me a drink with his bartending skills."

*Huh?*

"You were a bartender?" I frown, not liking that this stranger knows more about Huck than I do.

"For a few summers, yeah," he shrugs, lifting a red cup to his lips while he avoids my gaze and my jaw tightens.

Well, this is different from how I expected the night to go. Did I say something? Do something to upset him? Or...is it because Owen is here looking at him like he's a grand prize?

"Come on, *cariño*," Christian grabs the back of my tank top, pulling me to the living room, "you're my pong partner. If you choose someone else, I'll scream."

Huck's eyes flash to mine briefly as I'm being hauled away, but then he turns back to face Owen while they continue their little chat, and jealousy burns deep, unfamiliar inside my gut.

I've never been the possessive type. Hell, all of my relationships have been open, which is why Christian has pretty much slept with every girl I've ever dated and vice versa. I *enjoy* sharing. But when it comes to Huckslee? He's mine. Always has been, always will be, and I'll be damned if he thinks he's going to run away again now that I finally have him.

I'll tie the fucker up if I have to.

Taking out my phone in the entryway, I pull up our Delaware group chat.

> Me: What's up with you?

He responds within seconds.

> Sucksme: Nothing? Also, when did you change my contact name?

Like, five seconds ago. Gritting my teeth, I thumb out my reply.

> Me: Lie to me again.

He changes my name in the chat to *'Taytay'* before sending a gif of some white dude slow blinking at the camera, so I send him one back of Bugs Bunny grabbing Daffy Duck by the throat and caption it **us rn**.

> Sucksme: Okay, but I'm Bugs.

> Me: Not even close.

> Sucksme: Jesus, what's got your undies in a bunch?

Me: You, motherfucker.

Something's up with you, and if you think you're gonna leave me for Owen, then I've got news for you.

Ain't happening.

Sucksme: Wtf? Taylor, what the hell are you talking about?

Me: Just saying. You're mine, Huck.

Sucksme: Meet me on the front porch right now.

Me: Can't.

Got a pong game to win, but enjoy your conversation with Owen.

Sucksme: Goddammit, Taylor. I need to talk to you.

*Too late.* Putting my phone away, I step into the living room, feeling a little like shit. Whatever he has to say isn't something I'll like; I just know it. I'll have to hear it eventually, but right now, I'll avoid it for as long as possible.

Xed and Matty's living room is significantly bigger than mine and Christian's, spacious enough to fit a sizeable U-shaped sectional and two recliners. Matt's parents haven't updated the place, so there's still some awful green wallpaper covering the walls, but the two of them made it look homey by hanging up all the road signs they used to steal in high school.

Salem and Xed have the recliners pushed to the side, making room for a pong table in the middle.

"We're up first," Christian calls, bouncing on his feet just as Matt and Logan make their way back downstairs. Salem casts them a vicious glare, Arya saddling up to her with a smirk. Even Xed is gazing at Matt in some way that has my stomach in knots, and when Huck enters the room with Owen, the vibe in the air is far from what it should be at a friendly get-together. Apprehension and animosity abound.

As usual, my best friend is oblivious as he takes his stance and shoots, shouting triumphantly when he sinks his ball into one of Xed's cups.

"Lucky shot." Xed picks it up and drinks, eyes still flicking over to Matty, who's currently trying to talk Logan into streaming games with him online.

The way Matt's back shifts speaks volumes, like he knows his best friend is looking at him, but he's ignoring it.

*What the fuck is going on right now?*

Speaking of ignoring. I can feel Huck's attention on me when I step up to take my turn, and though it kept me focused during the qualifier earlier, it only serves to set me off right now. I miss my shot, the ping-pong ball bouncing off the table and rolling under a bookshelf. Matty picks it up before taking his turn with a clean one.

Our game goes on like this for a bit, each of us throwing the ball and me sipping on soda when I lose while the others look on in some weird suspension of awkwardness. The only two who don't notice are Christian and Owen, the latter talking Huck's ear off about shit in California that I don't really care to pay attention to. Logan tries to get closer to Salem, but she puts Arya in between them, keeping her eyes on her phone while he looks at her with the most enormous puppy dog eyes. Finally, I can't handle it anymore.

"Stop, hold the fuck up," I snap, cutting Owen off mid-sentence. Everyone looks over at me in surprise. "What the fuck is happening right now?!"

Xed's brows pinch together. "What do you mean?"

"You know damn well what I mean!" Pointing between him and Matt, I squint accusingly. "Something is going on between you two. I know it." Matty's eyes bug out of his skull, jaw dropping while Xed's shoulder tense. He swings his gaze to Huck for some reason, but I move my finger over to Salem and Logan. "And you two! I'm fucking sick of this shit. It's been three months. Get your shit together!"

Salem glares at me with a hiss. "Mind your business, Taylor."

"No. Something's broken in this friend group right now, and we're going to fucking fix it."

Arya gapes at me as I grab Xed and Matty, shoving them onto the couch. Then I go after Salem, who already has her ass halfway to the stairs. Wrapping my arms around her from behind, I drag her snarling and screaming to the sectional, where I flop down with her on my lap.

"Come here," I grind out, crooking a finger at Logan while she fights tooth and nail to get free. He looks utterly shaken but obeys, shuffling over to take a tentative seat next to me, where I squish her down in between us.

Christian simply chuckles, leaning against the wall as he pulls Arya into his side, and Xed curses at me under his breath.

"You're a nosy bitch, Taylor," he growls, "you know that?"

"Well, if everyone in my life would talk shit out instead of pretending like it isn't happening, I wouldn't have to be," I shoot back, sliding my gaze to Huckslee as I say it. His eyes flash, but he stays silent while he lifts his drink to his lips. "As of right now, this is a friendship intervention. Christian, you want in on this?"

"All you, baby boy." He nestles his face into Arya's neck, earning a grimace from me when she giggles.

Salem goes fucking feral, kicking me while elbowing Logan, and just as she's about to sink her teeth into my arm, Matty's booming voice cuts through the music.

"ALRIGHT, THAT'S ENOUGH!"

The entire room goes silent. Seriously, if it weren't for the heavy bass blasting over the speakers, I've no doubt you could hear a pin drop.

Even Salem stops struggling as she whispers, "oh shit, he used his dad voice."

Jumping to his feet, Matt turns to me with a stern look. "Taylor, let Salem go. *Now.*"

Xed gazes up at him with begrudging admiration as my hands release Salem's arms. She gets one good kick in my ribs when she slides off the couch, plopping down onto the opposite end with a flushed face and flared nostrils. I smirk as she glares. Logan rubs the back of his neck awkwardly, Huck shakes his head while muttering under his breath, and Owen seems to want to look away but can't.

"Apologize," Matty demands.

I push my bottom lip out when I swing my eyes his way. "Sorry, Daddy. I'll behave."

A choking noise comes from Huck, and I laugh when I catch him coughing up the sip he just took.

"You're fucking unhinged," he sputters, slapping at his chest.

Xed sighs heavily as he gazes up at the ceiling, arms folded. "He's actually a lot tamer than he used to be now that he's sober. Consider yourself lucky."

"Are you saying all of your parties end up like this?" Owen asks, completely mystified.

There's a cacophony of answers from everyone, consisting of *'usually,' 'pretty much,'* and *'this isn't even the worst of it.'*

"Look, I do actually have a reason for inviting everyone over," Matt starts, running a hand over his short strands. "We got some news this morning that I wanted to share with everyone."

The anxiousness in his tone makes all of us wait uneasily.

"The results for the draft were made official this morning. I've been picked as a defensive lineman for the Cardinals."

I feel my heart drop all the way to the floor.

"Arizona?"

"Yeah." He places his hands on his hips, glancing at Xed sideways, whose jaw is feathering at the corners. "Come July, Hannah, Valerie, and I will be moving."

There's a moment when the air just leaves the room like a vacuum sucked out of our communal lung.

Christian steps forward, Arya momentarily forgotten as he stares at Matty incredulously. "Fucking *Val?!*"

"She's doing better," Matt sighs heavily, "she's been going to rehab. I think she's ready this time to be the mother Hannah needs."

"But…" I bounce my gaze between him and his best friend. "What about Xed?"

They've been friends for almost as long as Christian and I have.

And that's when the realization hits me.

My head whips to Huck, who's watching me warily. "Did *you* get drafted?"

His lips thin until they turn white before he utters words that throw me for a loop. "Yeah. Baltimore Ravens."

I stare at him momentarily, my brain lagging as it processes what he just said. Owen walks over to Arya and whispers something in her ear before pulling her toward the kitchen, even though she protests against it. But I don't hear her. I don't hear or see anything other than a pair of sad, dark eyes gazing back at me.

"Baltimore?" My voice sounds foreign, like it doesn't belong to me. "As in Maryland?"

*As in the other side of the fucking country?*

Matty continues. "My parents will let Xed stay here, so it's not like he's getting kicked out. Though he'll probably need to find a roommate."

"I can move in," Salem murmurs with watery eyes, all her anger gone. I feel Logan's shoulders slump from where he sits against me.

Xed swallows, still looking at the ceiling. "I don't want to put you out, Salem."

"You're not. I'm tired of being back at my parents anyway."

I'm still reeling. It feels like the floor has been ripped out from under me, careening my body through space. The room falls silent for a moment while we all just process this.

"Congratulations," I rasp, clearing my throat, "to both of you. This is supposed to be a good thing, yeah? You guys worked hard for this."

And yet, it feels like the farthest thing from it.

Matty smiles broadly, his eyes lighting up as he thanks me. It's obvious how excited he is to play for the NFL, even if it looks like Xed's heart is breaking.

As Huckslee continues to search my face silently, I feel like mine is, too.

Christian pulls Matt in for a hug, and Salem joins in as well, though her attention is on Xed and me.

After pulling away, Christian picks up a ball from the pong table. "Come on, you sad fucks, let's get this party started. We're supposed to be celebrating."

"Yeah. Celebrating." Xed rubs his eyes as he stands, muttering under his breath. "I need another drink."

*Amen to that.* Except I fucking can't.

He moves toward the kitchen while Matty launches into his plans for Arizona excitedly, not even giving his best friend a passing glance. Huck follows, pulling Xed aside in the entryway to whisper something in his ear, whatever that's about, so I mumble to Christian that I need to take a piss before hurriedly climbing the steps to the upstairs bathroom.

Once locked inside, I pull a pack of smokes out of my pocket and light one, standing in front of the mirror as I puff on it, staring at myself.

Fuck. Three months. That's all I have until Matty and Hannah leave. And Huckslee...

My chest feels like it's been kicked in.

I just got him back. After four years of pining from a distance, longer if you include high school, I finally get a chance to have him, and yet it's ending before it can truly begin.

Today was supposed to be a good day. A day of victory. And yet, I feel so lost.

A soft knock at the door pulls me out of my reverie, followed by a deep, familiar voice on the other side. "Taylor."

Hearing him say my name sends a pleasurable shiver down my spine. Opening the door, I pull Huck inside before closing it again, pressing him gently into the wood before backing up to the sink, afraid to touch him any more than that. He gazes at me with low brows, expression guarded.

"Why didn't you tell me?" I ask quietly around the cigarette, crossing my arms to shield myself from impact.

"I didn't find out until this morning, and I didn't want to distract you from the qualifier. I was going to tell you tonight. On the porch."

Smoke swirls around my face as I exhale, blowing it away from him toward the cracked window. There's a question on my tongue that I know I need to ask, but the answer terrifies me. Still. It needs to be asked.

"Is this it, then?"

He blinks. "It?"

Nodding, I pinch the cigarette between my fingers and gesture between our bodies. "Yeah, it. Us. Is this the end of the line for Taylor and Huckslee?"

"Do you want it to be?" His throat flexes as he swallows, a pained expression morphing his features, and I pause for a minute.

"You tell me."

He closes the distance between us slowly, coming close enough for me to feel the heat of his skin. "Did you mean what you texted earlier? Saying I'm yours?"

Studying his face, my gaze bounces between those beautiful, starry eyes and full, pink lips. "Yes. That doesn't change anything."

"It changes everything."

He dips his head as if to kiss me, but I bring my hand up between our mouths, earning a flash of hurt to bolt across his features.

"You've been drinking, Huck. Alcoholic, remember?"

A slow smile pulls at his cheeks, amusement dancing in his pupils. "I've only been drinking Diet Coke."

And then his mouth is on mine, a surprised gasp leaving my throat.

My hands come up to fist his shirt, pulling him against me as his fingers tangle in my hair. Our tongues glide and sweep together, the taste of the soda on his lips secondary to his own sweet, addicting flavor. A desperate moan vibrates his chest, and I drown in it, letting it drag me under where I'd gladly be crushed by the weight of it. His palms cup my face as the kiss turns slow and lazy, our mouths molding together while I run my fingers over his chest, ribs, and back.

When we part for air, Huck leans his forehead against mine, taking a shaky breath. "I've been dying to kiss you for weeks."

"Who's fault is that?" Swallowing hard, I nuzzle our noses together. The hardness of his chest feels so good against mine, our bodies aligning perfectly. He pulls back slightly, still in my arms, and opens his mouth to speak but pauses as his nostrils flare.

"Do you," he coughs, frowning around the bathroom, "do you smell something?"

"Huh?"

Chancing a sniff, I grimace as a burning smell assaults my senses before it dawns on me that the cigarette is no longer in my hands.

"Oh, fuck!" Smoke billows around a small burn hole in the rug at our feet, and I jump away from Huck to stomp on the butt I must have dropped when he kissed me, tugging on my hair as I gaze down at the ruined bath mat.

He doubles over in laughter at the sight. "Your fuckin' face right now."

"It's your fault, asshole," I pout, pulling him back into my arms, "you distracted me. Don't tell Xed."

"You drive me crazy when you do that," he groans, nipping at my bottom lip. "Your secrets are safe with me, baby."

*Ugh. My damn heart.*

Tracing a line of kisses down his throat, I pause when my mouth rests against the junction between his neck and shoulder. "Maryland?"

He's silent for a moment. "Yeah. Four-year contract, minimum. I declared in January, so it's too late to back out."

"That's very far away."

"I know." His fingers find my chin as he tips my face up, dark eyes searching mine. "You said you meant it, calling me yours. And you're mine, too. But whatever this is between us, I understand that it's new. I can't ask you to wait for me or enter into something long-distance–"

I cut him off, holding up a hand. "Whoa, whoa, wait, back up. Why does it sound like you're..." What the hell am I supposed to say? *Breaking up with me?* "Why does it sound like you're ending this?"

"We don't even know what *this* is, Taylor," he sighs, dropping his forehead to mine again, "or if *this* will even work. If we'll be good together. So far, our track record sucks."

"So you are ending it," I state flatly, feeling like my heart just split open.

Huck pauses, pressing his warm cheek to mine, blood pulsing so hard I can feel it through his body. There's such a long, heavy silence that I don't think he'll speak, but then:

"I don't want to." A desperate whisper across the shell of my ear, sending goosebumps over my flesh.

"Then *don't.*" I drag his mouth to mine, stealing a slow kiss. "Don't let this end before it even starts."

"Maybe it's better if we do," he murmurs against my lips. "Maybe it'll hurt less this way."

Deep down, I worry he's probably right. The longer you hold onto hope, the worse it is when it shatters. But I spent all our high school years hating myself for wanting Huckslee and the last four hating myself for losing him. I can't live like that anymore.

"No." Pulling back, I meet his gaze. "No, I don't believe that. Huck, we went through hell to get where we are, and I'm not letting it slip away again."

A sad smile crosses his face. "We only just stopped fighting a week ago, Tay. Five days into a relationship is not long enough to ask someone to wait four years for you."

"Relationship?" I grin crookedly up at him, stomach flipping, and he rolls his eyes.

"Of course, that's the only part you catch on to."

"Baby, I've already waited four years for you." My palm slides against his as I run my tongue along his throat. "And we've got three months until you leave for training camp. If you're worried about us 'being good' together, consider this the start of our ninety-day trial period."

He groans, vocal cords vibrating against my lips. "No fair. How long until that tattoo heals so I can lick it?"

"Bout another week," I chuckle, sucking on his Adam's apple. "Look, I'm not gonna force you into anything you don't want. If, when July ends, you decide that we don't work, the n...I'll let you go. Even if it hurts me."

Even if it kills me.

Huckslee's arms tighten around me as his teeth nip at my earlobe, quickening my breath. "You make it hard to think straight when you're touching me like that."

"Yeah, my thoughts are far from straight," I snort, slipping my palms under his shirt to run them over his abs.

"Shut up." Laughing into my hair, his fingers grip my hips, rubbing our steadily hardening cocks together. A breathy moan pushes past my lips, and he captures it with his mouth, stubble burning in the best way.

"Say yes," I murmur in between kisses, swiping a thumb over his pebbled nipple. "Say yes, Huckslee."

The bathroom fills with the sounds of our soft grunts and heavy pants as we move together, hands petting each other, tongues entangling. He cups me over my jeans, squeezing my length, and I thrust against him, chasing the friction.

When I reach down to grab his ass for better leverage, he growls deeply, sucking my bottom lip in between his teeth. "Okay, okay. You win, baby. Just don't stop grinding on me like that. You're so fucking sexy."

Biting down hard on his shoulder, I lick away the sting. "Yeah? Sexier than Owen?"

"*What?*" Fingers grip my hair as Huck yanks my head back by the strands, forcing my gaze to his. "Seriously, Taylor?"

Swallowing hard, my brain short-circuits at his sudden roughness, the sharp prickle on my scalp making my cock jerk with pleasure. "H-he's nice looking. Smaller than me, easier to throw around."

That gets his brows rising high. "Do you *want* me to throw you around?"

"Maybe," I shrug, chewing my lip while I drop my gaze. "Sometimes."

His hands slide down the backs of my legs before he lifts me up, whipping around abruptly to slam my back against the door. The new position lines our cocks up perfectly, my ankles hooking together behind his waist as I roll my hips against him like a needy bastard.

"I can handle you just fine," he whispers, running his tongue against my cheek. "Don't be jealous, baby. I like how strong you are. You've never had a problem fighting back."

"I was usually the one starting all the fights," I chuckle, pulling off his beanie to run my fingers through his curls. "These drive me wild, you know."

He hums, lips twisting. "Yeah, I noticed you have a thing for blondes."

"If you're talking about Arya, I never *actually* dated her." With a scowl, my head falls back against the door. "Salem wanted to watch me bang another chick. Obviously, I wasn't gonna say no, but Arya's annoying as hell."

"So why did you fuck her?"

A sheepish grin pulls at my cheeks. "If I say because she was willing, does that make me sound like your typical man-whore douchebag?"

"You're unbelievable." He shakes his head before planting a string of kisses on my lips, jaw, and face.

"Can't help it, I'm a horny fuck." To emphasize my point, I grind my aching cock against him again, impressed by the fact that he still has me pinned between his body and the door.

Lifting a brow, he smirks. "And yet, according to Christian, you haven't gotten laid since January."

"So fuck me."

The words tumble out before I can stop them, lust and need clouding my mind, but god, I want it. I've thought of nothing else since that night when we had phone sex. Which is crazy, by the way, because who even does that any more?

Huck goes still for a moment, throat flexing around a swallow. He sets me down before bracing an arm against the door beside my head. "I'm not fucking you for the first time in a bathroom, Taylor."

"Please? I'll be quiet." Hooking a finger beneath the waistband of his jeans, I rub his shaft softly. "I promise."

Groaning, his mouth captures mine. "I've heard you come, remember? Quiet for you is impossible. I'd have to gag you with something."

That idea has me grinning wide, but Huckslee grabs my jaw firmly, holding my gaze with dark intensity. "I am *not* fucking you in here."

"You're no fun."

"No?" Lifting a brow again, he pops open the button on my jeans in one swift move, hand plunging under the hem of my briefs to wrap around my length. "How about now?"

"Mm, yeah," I moan, thrusting into his hand. "Way more fun."

"That's what I thought."

Dropping to his knees, Huck shoves my pants down just past my ass, setting my cock free. It almost slaps him against the cheek, heavy and weeping, his tongue darting out to swirl around the swollen crown. My fingers twine in his curls as he teases me, licking from the base up to my tip and back down. When he gently sucks on my sac as he strokes me, my eyes nearly roll into the back of my head.

And then those gorgeous lips wrap around me as he takes it all the way to the back of his throat, gaze never leaving mine. It's the most erotic thing I've ever experienced, having Huckslee kneeling at my feet, taking me so good that I have to bite the hem of my tank top to keep silent.

"You suck my cock so good." I cradle his face, watching my length slide in and out of his soft mouth, dripping with spit. "It's like your throat was made for it."

I'm not small by any means, and the fact that he can fit my entire dick in his mouth without gagging is such a fucking turn-on. I've never had that before. He was molded just for me.

*Mine.*

He smiles around me, dark eyes glittering, so beautiful that I have to pull out and bend down to kiss him. As I'm about to dive in again, there's a quick knock on the bathroom door, and we both freeze.

"Taylor? It's Logan. Have you seen Huck? I can't find him anywhere."

Panic flickers in Huck's eyes, but I put a finger to my lips, silently telling him to stay quiet while I grab the back of his head and slowly push my cock back into his mouth.

"Uh." My voice cracks when I hit his throat, his nose flush with my stomach. "H-have you checked the bathroom?"

I hold him there, watching as the panic in his eyes changes to burning heat.

Logan sighs on the other side of the door. "Yeah, he's not in the downstairs bathroom. I hope he didn't leave."

Huck's face starts to redden as he chokes on my dick, and I answer his best friend thickly. "Do you think he needs some air?"

"I've checked outside already, but I guess I'll check again."

Tears well in the corners of Huck's eyes from lack of oxygen, making his irises sparkle like a starry night sky, too fucking sexy for his own good. His hands come up to play with my balls, gently squeezing, nearly making me come on the spot.

"Christian's wondering if you're okay, by the way," Logan continues, oblivious to what's happening inches from him. "Pizza's here, and everyone's waiting on you two to play a party game."

"J-just having a smoke," I grunt, starting to shake from how fucking good Huck's throat feels as he swallows. "I'm...about t-to...finish."

*Holy shit. I'm coming.*

I cry out as I spill into Huck's mouth, and he slaps a hand over my lips. His tongue swirls around my cock, lapping up every last drop, sucking me through the orgasm as I bite my cheek hard enough to bleed.

"Okay, if you see Huck before I do, tell him I'm looking for him." Logan pauses. "Also, I wanted to thank you for trying. You know, with Salem. I really appreciate it."

"Yeah," I breathe as Huck rises off the floor, lips pressed tightly together, holding in a mouthful of my cum. "Welcome."

I know what he's going to do just by the look in his eyes, and as he grabs my jaw, I open for him, stifling a moan when he spits my release onto my tongue. It's salty and slightly bitter, but fuck if I don't swallow it down greedily while Huckslee kisses me stupid. There's no answer from the hall, only fading footsteps, and I whimper as I suck on his tongue, desperate for more.

He hums approvingly against my lips, tucking me back into my briefs as he pulls up my jeans. "I love how much of a cumslut you're turning out to be."

"*Fuck*, you've got a filthy mouth." My fingers fly to his button, wanting to return the favor. "Keep talking like that. It gets me off."

He stops me when I try to pull out his hard dick, and my eyes fly to his face as I push out my bottom lip.

"Don't do that," he laughs, nipping at it. "We've been gone so long that it's sus. You can get your hands on me later."

It's on the tip of my tongue to tell him that I give two flying fucks if it's suspicious or not, but I know that he's not ready for Logan to know about us yet. We talked about this over the phone a few days ago. And even though I disapprove of all the hiding that he and Logan seem to do from each other, it's not my friendship. Not my business. Though let's be honest, I'm sure I'll make it my business eventually, one way or another.

I'm not entirely sure I'm ready for Xed and Matty to know, either. Me being into a guy is one thing, but my stepbrother, that I constantly bullied in high school? Yeah...that conversation with Christian was already awkward enough.

Sighing heavily, I fix my jeans. "Fine. But I'll go first. Wait like five minutes and then follow."

"Kay." He pulls me in for another slow kiss, wrapping me in his arms to hold me tight. When he pulls away, his eyes search mine deeply. "Taylor, I...you know I care about you. Right?"

My throat closes as my heart swells. "Yeah. I care about you, too."

That three-letter phrase pops into my head, but I can't bring myself to say it. I want to. Hell, I already told him I was in love with him, and he did the same. Those words, though. They mean something. Something permanent. I've only ever said them to four people in my life, all of whom are in this house currently waiting for us to come downstairs.

And Huckslee...he isn't even sure that we'll work out. Me? I already decided the moment Salem called to say he was coming home; Huck is endgame for me. He's all I want. I don't care that we've only started this thing a week ago; he could ask me to wait forever, and I would. But one-sided feelings does not a relationship make.

So I kiss his throat. Run my fingers through his hair. Open the door with a deviant grin and leave him in the bathroom as I enter the hall.

Wishing, hoping, *pleading* for his heart to feel for me like mine does for him.

# Huckslee

C limbing out of a second-story bathroom window isn't the proudest moment in my life, but the look on Taylor's face when I walk through the front door ten minutes later is priceless.

I'm obsessed with the way his lips part, head tilted to the side while his eyes glaze over when he's shocked. Like a puppy who's been bamboozled, and it's the cutest fucking thing.

"Where have you been, man?" Logan grabs my arm, pulling me into the living room where everyone sits crowded on the sectional. "I tried calling like five times."

"Sorry. Went for a walk around the block."

I really did. Needed to lose my boner.

Taylor is pressed between Salem and Arya, so I take the only available spot next to Owen, not missing the way Taylor's face twitches when Owen's shoulder bumps mine. Considering his past relationships, that possessiveness is a surprise, but I'd be lying if I said it isn't hot as hell.

He has his phone out, thumbing away at the screen, and then he looks up at me from under his lashes when my own phone buzzes with a new message.

> Taytay: Are you a fuckin magician?

> How'd you get outside?

> Me: Abracadabra, bitch.

I follow it up with a wand emoji and some sparkles for flare before hitting send, hiding a smile when he snorts loudly after reading it.

"So, what party game are we playing?" I ask, pulling two slices of extra cheesy goodness onto my plate, noticing the four currently stacked on Taylor's. Jesus Christ, how does he eat like that and still manage to look so good?

Matt chews slowly, swallowing before he answers. "How do you feel about Never Have I Ever?"

Simultaneously, Taylor, Salem, Logan, and I groan.

"No. Never again," Salem says harshly, and I agree. One game of that was enough for a lifetime.

"Ooh, let's play sexy Truth or Dare," Arya squeals, looping her arm through Taylor's. "I have the app on my phone. We can go around in a circle, asking the person next to us. If you refuse to answer or do the dare, you drink."

He shakes her off, but she's persistent, his grimace when she places a hand on his thigh making me snicker.

Logan rubs the back of his neck, looking slightly uncomfortable. "Maybe we shouldn't."

"Why not?" Matt replies with a grin. "I've played it before. Could be fun."

Xed mutters under his breath. "Or a disaster."

"I'm game." Owen glances at me with a grin, and I smile back politely. He's been staying close ever since I walked in the door, especially after Logan let it slip that I was also gay. I'm sure my best friend was just trying to be a good wingman, and even though Owen is friendly, it's kind of grating on my nerves.

Christian throws an arm behind Arya and Taylor. "I'm in, too. Let's get sexy."

"Let's not," Taylor groans around his food. Christian's fingers rest on his neck, but he doesn't seem to mind, and my gut churns slightly. I've noticed how much the two like to touch. But, then again, Taylor seems to enjoy touching everyone. Not in a pervy way but more in...a comfort-seeking way. Physical touch is definitely his love language. Still, the fact that he and his best friend have shared women and have seen each other naked...kind of bothers me.

"Raise of hands, who wants to play?" Matt asks, raising his hand high in the air. Owen and Arya raise theirs, followed by Christian. Logan notices Salem looking less than pleased, so his hand shoots up, too. I follow suit if only to see the flash of annoyance in Taylor's eyes that has me grinning broadly.

"Six against three, boom." Christian reaches over to punch Xed on the shoulder, who looks like he's ready to murder someone, before turning to Taylor. "What's up with you, *cariño*? This type of shit is usually your jam."

*Cariño?*

My Spanish is rusty, and I can't recall what that means for the life of me.

Taylor's eyes briefly glance between Owen and me before falling away as he shrugs, playing it off like he's tired, but it dawns on me that he's still jealous even after all that loving I gave him upstairs. The thought makes me wish I could trade places with Arya and be the one with my hands on him.

"Start the fucking game, I guess." Salem crosses her arms with a huff and leans back onto the couch between Taylor and Matt. I don't remember ever seeing her look so pissed off.

"Yaaay!" Arya looks around with a grin. "Everyone has their drinks? Good, okay, I'll start." She brings up the app on her phone and taps the screen. "Taylor, truth or dare?"

"Truth."

She purses her glossed lips in disappointment but reads him the question anyway. "Have you ever cried during sex?"

"No." He answers at the same time that Christian and Salem both give a resounding *yes.*

"Fuck off, nuh-uh!"

"Yes, huh." Salem studies her acrylic nails, glancing up at him slyly. "When you first got out of the hospital in high school, remember? In my parents' basement? Christian was there, he remembers."

Taylor scowls, eyes finding mine before he looks away. "I'd just recovered from surgery. I was in pain."

"Yeah, okay."

Fresh guilt forces me to swallow, recalling how I never went to see him. He'd been nearly beaten to death by his father, and yet I'd ignored him for four months. Anger quickly steals my breath when I think about what his father did to him for years, and no one noticed. Not even his best friend, from what I can tell. He'd been so good at hiding it.

"Fine, whatever, Salem's turn." He takes the phone from Arya. "Truth or dare?"

"Truth. Obviously."

Tapping the phone, he reads the question before grinning. "Have you ever been caught masturbating?"

Her eyes narrow into slits as she leans forward to pour a shot of vodka into her glass, prepared to drink instead of answer, but Logan pipes up next to me.

"Yes."

Taylor and I whip our heads toward him quickly, followed by Salem, who bares her teeth at him and hisses. Actually, *hisses* like a cat. Jesus.

She snatches the phone and turns angrily to Matt. "Truth or dare, Matty. Let me guess, dare. Right?"

He laughs, nodding enthusiastically despite the way Xed is watching him intently. "You know it."

"Read the last text message you received out loud."

The smile drops from his face, something peculiar crossing his features when he shifts his eyes to Xed before pulling out his cell. He stares at it for a long moment before clearing his throat and reading the text. "Hannah is so happy, babe. I'm so glad you let me take her for a whole night. She's having so much fun watching Peppa Pig."

"Bull-fucking-shit," Xed snaps suddenly, scoffing. "She doesn't even like Peppa Pig."

Matt responds quickly, face going red. "Yes, she does. Sometimes."

"No, she does not, Matthew. That pig gives her the willies. She's told me several times."

"Moving on." Matt shoots Xed a pleading look before tapping on the screen for Owen. "Truth or dare?"

"Dare," Owen smiles, sliding his gaze to me coyly.

Big surprise.

"Let's see...do a round of 'fuck, marry, kill' between the three people to your left?" Everyone turns to look at me, Logan, and Xed on the opposite side.

"Hmm." Squinting, he looks between the three of us. "Well, I haven't really known any of you that long, so...I guess I'll fuck Huckslee, marry Xed and kill Logan? No offense," he adds, smiling at Logan, who looks both offended and unamused. Glancing toward Taylor, I find him staring at Owen angrily, Salem wearing an almost identical expression next to him. Matt doesn't look too pleased, either.

"Alright, Huck, truth or dare?"

Taylor's ocean eyes slide to me, curiosity softening them, and I can't help the grin that crosses my face.

"Dare."

Maybe he's rubbing off on me, but I want to rile Taylor up tonight.

*Ninety-day trial period*, he'd said. Like a fucking subscription. But if he's down to try this out and see if we can make it, then I want to see how far I can push him. Just a little bit.

"Pick a woman in the room and have them pour a shot into your mouth from between their breasts," Owen reads, seeming a bit put out, and everyone looks toward the only two women in the room.

Salem smirks at me darkly. "Unfortunately, I'm part of the itty bitty titty committee, so you'll have to choose Miss Double D's over there."

Taylor coughs, hiding his laugh as Arya shouts and jumps from the couch excitedly.

"Yasss, this is so fun." She pours vodka into a shot glass before shoving it in between her cleavage, and I almost drink my soda to pass on the dare. I wasn't planning on drinking tonight. The way that Taylor's eyes sparkle wickedly, though, has me holding his gaze as I slide to the floor and kneel at Arya's feet.

Christian rubs his hands together. "Damn, you lucky boy."

Rolling my eyes, I let her place her hands on my shoulders as I open my mouth. Leaning forward, she brings her tits close to my face until the shot pours onto my bottom lip, mostly my chin, and when she straightens with a squeal of joy, I grimace as I wipe my face.

"I am so gay. That literally did nothing for me."

Taylor chuckles, flashing his teeth, but the smile vanishes when Owen laughs behind me.

"Oh my god, same."

*Right*. Okay...

Taking the phone from him, I turn to Logan, already knowing what he'll pick. "Here's your truth, Loge. What are, um..." Reading the question, I blink, lips twitching. "What are your secret fetishes?"

As he starts turning beat red, my cell buzzes with a new message.

> Taytay: Not the first time tonight you've gotten on your knees and taken it in the mouth ;)

Fucking hell.

I can feel his eyes on me as I thumb my reply.

> Me: Won't be the last, either.

His brows shoot to his hairline right as Logan takes a gulp of his beer, choosing not to answer the question. Salem shakes her head, looking away. Not for the first time, I wonder what someone so wild had ever seen in a guy as shy as Logan. Don't get me wrong, I love my best friend. But when it comes to women, he's as hopeless as me.

"Truth or dare, Xed?"

A heavy sigh falls from Xed's lips. "If I'm forced to play this shit, I guess I'll choose dare."

"That's what I'm talking about!" Christian jostles his shoulder as Logan reads off the screen.

"Make out with the prettiest boy in the room."

Everyone goes silent.

We all glance at each other, Matt's eye almost bugging out of his skull. He and Xed stare each other down, something passing briefly between them that has Matt shaking his head. After a moment, Xed lifts his beer to his lips and swigs, causing Matt's shoulders to relax imperceptibly.

Taylor lets out a playful scoff. "Rude, Xed. Everyone knows I'm the prettiest boy."

That makes me laugh, and heads nod in agreement because he's absolutely right. Even with that scar.

Pulling up our chat thread, I send him a quick message, testing the waters.

> Me: My pretty boy.

His eyes widen when he reads it.

> Taytay: Don't send me shit like that unless you're prepared for another round in the bathroom.

> Me: Why?

> Do you like it when I call you pretty?

> Taytay: I'll let you call me anything you want if you fuck me.

*Goddamn.* The broad smile on my lips freezes when I hear Xed read Christian his dare.

"Pick the person you've known the longest in the room and give them a hickey."

Christian turns to Taylor and grins maniacally, pointing a finger. "That's you, baby boy. Get over here."

I go rigid, and Taylor notices immediately. His gaze bounces uneasily between his best friend and me as my stomach clenches, grinding my molars against a surge of possessiveness.

"Where do you want it?" Christian laughs. "Side of your neck? Back?"

*Not a chance.*

My brain screams at me to intervene as Taylor switches places with Arya, biting his lip nervously. "Arm, maybe?"

"No, that won't work," Arya giggles, looking over Taylor's body. "You're covered in tattoos, and we want to see it. How about the stomach?"

Lifting up his shirt, she makes a move to touch his abs before he grabs her wrist. "No touchy."

"How about this spot?" Christian points to the blank space over Taylor's peck, where the shape of Delaware rests, and I can't keep silent anymore.

"Absolutely *not*," I grind out, earning a look from everyone in the room.

Salem smirks knowingly while Christian rolls his eyes.

"Fine, back of the shoulder it is."

He leans Taylor forward, moving aside the strap of his tank top before pressing his lips to his best friend's skin.

My fists tighten on my lap, both watching me with amusement. Christian meets my gaze challengingly as if staking a claim, the look in his eyes saying one thing: *mine.*

I don't think so, motherfucker.

He sits back when finished, grinning in satisfaction as Salem snaps her fingers.

"Well, get up," she commands with a sideways glance in my direction. "Show the class."

Taylor's lips twitch as he stands, doing a twirl to reveal the deepening purple mark on his shoulder before curtsying like a fucking brat. He plops back down on the other side of Arya, pushing hair out of his face, and I lean against the cushions while the game continues, seething.

Most everyone chooses truth after that, having learned their lessons. Until it gets to Owen again, at least.

Matthew reads off his dare. "Pick someone in the room, touch tongues for five minutes."

As soon as his drunken gaze swings to mine, I know I'm in trouble.

"Huckslee," he slurs, a sloppy smile on his face, and a low snarl echoes from Taylor's throat.

"No." He launches out of his seat, glaring down at Owen murderously. "Choose someone else."

"What, why?" Owen's eyes take on a dark glint. "It's my dare, I can pick who I want."

Taylor curls his lips. "Fine, but the other person has to be willing. You can't force someone to kiss you."

"It's not a kiss, Tay." Salem's lashes flutter. "Just touching tongues. But if it's an issue, you can always take over the dare and do it with Huckslee yourself."

Narrowing my gaze, I meet her impish grin with a glare. *Who's meddling now?*

Logan laughs beside me, thinking that her suggestion is the funniest thing he's ever heard. "That's weird, Salem. They're stepbrothers."

He raises his brows at me, silently seeking agreement, but I can only blink at him while my stomach sinks. If Logan thinks simply kissing Taylor for a dare is weird...I can only imagine what he'd feel if I told him what we're *actually* doing. A sickening feeling inside tells me that he wouldn't like it. Not one bit.

Owen's finger taps my shoulder. "What do you say, Huck? You down to do this with me?"

I can feel Taylor's eyes burning the side of my face, but nothing comes out when I open my mouth to answer. Everyone's attention is on me, watching and waiting, and I feel sweat on the back of my neck.

*Say no. Say no.*

I want to refuse. But a small tendril of fear is licking up my spine at the thought of Logan rejecting me if he knew about the things Taylor and I do in the dark, of him telling his dad, who would then tell *my* dad. The whole family would judge me. Deep down, I know it's an illogical worry because Logan would never do something like that...right? He kept his relationship with Salem a secret for two years; he'd keep my relationship to himself. I think. I hope.

Fuck, I really don't know.

But my deliberation at refusing Owen's dare sets Taylor off.

"Whatever. Do what the fuck you want, Huckslee. I need a smoke."

The front door slams behind him, causing me to wince, and I turn to see Christian and Salem glaring at me accusingly. Xed is staring after Taylor thoughtfully, and Matt just shakes his head.

"What the hell crawled up his ass?"

*Me, I wish.* Ugh.

Exhaling slowly, I rub the bridge of my nose before turning to Owen. "Sorry, man, but I'm gonna have to pass."

His face falls but quickly brightens when Xed pipes up. "I'll do it."

"Way to take one for the team, my guy." Christian slaps him on the shoulder, and it seems I'm the only one who's noticed how still Matthew just went. As much as I'd like to stick around and witness the show...

I've got some shit to smooth over.

"Think I also need some air," I murmur to Logan, avoiding eye contact. "I'll go see what's up with Taylor."

There's a heavy pause where he studies me, but he nods without an answer, so I get up to go outside. The second I step onto the porch and shut the door, a hand grabs mine, yanking me down the front steps. Taylor tugs me around the house, pulling us into a small space between our building and the next before shoving me against the wall, eyes blazing.

And then his mouth crashes into mine.

Our lips clash, his tongue forcing its way inside to sweep around my mouth viciously as if to wipe away any other taste than his own. Vaguely, in the back of my head, I hope that all the soda I drank was enough to cover the shot of vodka from earlier as I kiss him back with just as much fervor. My hands cup the back of his neck, holding him in place while I suck his lip, resisting the urge to bite down until I taste blood as his arms come around me, crushing us together.

He feels so perfect against me, so right. Like every mole-cule and atom in my body was formed specifically to combine with his, drawing us together magnetically in an explosion of gasps and moans when our hips grind together. For a moment, I'm ready to drag him back inside and kiss him proudly in front of everyone, consequences be damned.

When he rips himself away, I grunt in protest, immediately cold from the absence of his warmth. My arms reach out to pull him back, but he steps quickly out of range, leaning against the opposite wall to cross his arms and scowl at me.

"You know, you're actually really sexy when you're pissed off," I smile, tracing my jaw with a finger while I check him out, which only pisses him off.

"What the hell was that, Huck?" His tone is livid.

With a sigh, my head falls back against the wall. "I didn't do it, okay? I didn't kiss him."

"No, but you wanted to. I saw it in the way you hesitated."

"I hesitated because of Logan's comment. It got me all up in my head, and I'm sorry."

His jaw ticks at the corners. "About us being stepbrothers?"

"Yeah."

There's a moment of silence where he watches me closely. "Does that...does it bother you?"

The anger in his voice is gone, replaced by a vulnerability that has me closing the gap between us to place kisses along the side of his face.

"No, I'm not bothered by that, Tay," I breathe into his skin. "It's not like we were raised that way. But I'd be lying if I said I wasn't worried about how Logan will react."

"I don't give a fuck what he thinks." Taylor's fists bunch in my shirt, lips pressed to my throat. "Or what anyone thinks."

"I know. But I do." Closing my eyes briefly, I pull back to look down into his wide eyes. "I worry what he'll do if he finds out. If my dad finds out."

He goes still. "If? Not when?"

"Maybe when. Three months, remember?"

A flash of hurt in his eyes guts me, but it's gone in an instant as he leans in for a sweltering kiss. "Right. Trial by fire. So far, I think we're doing great."

"Great?" Snorting against his lips, I slip my fingers under his tank top to caress his lower back. "Storming off and slamming doors is far from great."

"You caught me in a weak moment," he says, burying his face in my chest. "The thought of you kissing someone else makes me angry. I... I'll try to work on it."

He would, too, if I asked him.

Grabbing his chin to lift his face, I give him a frown. "What do you mean, you'll 'work on it'?"

"Like, if you..." He swallows, throat flexing while his eyes bounce between mine. "If you wanted to...be with Owen, too. I'd try to accept it. I don't know if I could, but I'd try. For you."

His brows are pinched, creases forming at the corners of his mouth as if saying those words physically pains him, and my frown deepens.

"Why the hell would I want to do that? I'm yours, remember?"

"Fuck, I don't know, Huckslee. I've never–" Cutting himself off, he licks his lips nervously. "I've never been in a relationship like this before."

"With a man," I admit for him, which earns me an eye roll in response.

"Yes, obviously, with a man. But, also, like...*monogamy*."

"You've never been in a monogamous relationship?"

"Nope," he smiles weakly. "I've never been the settling down type. But with you, it's different. I don't want anyone but you. I don't want anyone else touching you, but if that's what you want–"

I silence his worries with my mouth, breathing in the small gasp that leaves his lips when my tongue lazily dances with his. "I don't want anyone but you, either, Tay. And I'm purely monogamous, so you won't get that same speech from me. I'm yours, and you're mine. Anything else is a deal breaker for me. Okay?"

"Okay," he sighs, relieved as he sags against me, "but I still don't care what anyone thinks about us. I love y-love being with you, so fuck 'em."

He licks up the side of my neck as if to distract me from the fact that he tripped over his words, but I noticed. I fucking noticed, and now my heart is doing somersaults.

My arms close around him tightly. "I just need some time."

"I know." He nuzzles into me like a cat, and it's so fucking cute that it makes me ache. Literally, because my cock's been hard since the moment he kissed me. I rub it against him, feeling his own hard length brush mine as I groan into his hair.

"I wish I could take you back to the apartment and lay you down. Take my time, make you feel good."

"We could go back to mine," he suggests quickly, an eager look in his eyes, and I just know what he's thinking about.

"Yeah? You want that?" Sliding my hands down to his ass, I cup his cheeks and squeeze hard. "Does my horny stepbro need to get fucked?"

"*God*, yes." He thrusts against me, teeth sinking into his lip as his breath quickens. "Need it so bad, baby."

A dark laugh rumbles out of me as I step back from him. "Hmm. Too bad."

His jaw practically drops to the floor. "W-what?"

"I'm not fucking you with another man's mark on you, Taylor. You'll just have to wait until it's gone."

Flames ignite in his eyes, sending a sickly pleasurable spark to my groin.

"You're a cruel asshole, you know that?" He shakes his head slowly.

"Noted."

"So, are blowjobs out of the question, too?" His bottom lip juts out. "Because I might just die if I don't get to taste your cum tonight."

Holy hell.

I'm about to whip my cock out when I hear our names being shouted from the porch.

"Huckslee?"

"Taylor!"

Christian and Logan.

Cursing under my breath, I pull away from Taylor as he tugs his tank top down over his crotch, and I do the same with my shirt. With a furtive glance toward the house, I place a chaste kiss on his lips just as Christian's voice gets closer.

"Put your dicks away, fools, we gotta go!"

"Fucking Christ, Christian," Taylor mutters, stalking around the corner with me close behind, and we catch sight of them standing on the sidewalk with Arya tucked under Christian's arms.

"What's going on?"

Logan's glassy eyes shift between us. "I don't really know. Xed and Owen started making out, Matthew got pissed, they started fighting, and so now we're leaving."

*Oh, shit.* I missed it.

"They're fighting?!" Taylor steps toward the porch quickly, but Christian puts a hand up to stop him.

"Salem's got it, *cariño*. She's cooling them both down. Let's bounce."

That word again. *Cariño.* I'll have to Google it.

Taylor looks back at me anxiously, his eyes darkening with so much longing that my heart skips a beat. For a brief moment, we share a silent conversation; neither of us wants the night to end. But he's Christian's designated driver, and since I'm also sober, that makes me Logan's, too.

"Come on, Huck." My best friend bumps my shoulder, skin slightly green. "I don't feel so good anyway."

Fuck.

"Uh," Taylor clears his throat, shaking off Arya when she tries to hold his hand. "I guess I'll see you guys later."

"Yeah...later."

Christian smirks at me when I give a half-assed wave as I turn around, walking in the opposite direction toward Logan's car. When I get to the driver's side, I glance up the street to see their backs nearing the corner, but Taylor turns around to meet my gaze and blows a kiss, making me chuckle. I really, *really* don't want to leave him tonight. So why should I? Who says the night must end because our friends want to go home?

While Logan is distracted trying to put on his seatbelt with drunk fingers, I pull up our Delaware chat to send him a message.

> Me: After you drop them off, come get me? We can drive around in your truck and hang out. If you want.

I don't know why I was nervous that he'd turn me down because his reply is instant, making my damn breath catch.

> Taytay: I want. See you in about thirty, baby.

# HUCKSLEE

The drive back to Logan's apartment is quietly awkward. His head keeps swiveling in my direction, mouth opening like he wants to ask something, but then he chickens out and turns back to the window. I'm not about to encourage him to ask whatever's on his mind because I'm honestly not ready to answer.

Anticipation buzzes through me, so much so that I swear my body is vibrating by the time we pull into the apartment complex. Sending Logan inside with his keys, I tell him I'm going to hang out with Royce and that I'll be out late, the lie getting caught in my throat. He seems to believe it, though, nodding as he tells me to be safe before disappearing into the building while I stand outside and wait for a yellow truck to pull up.

It's ridiculous how excited I am to see Taylor since we just parted ways twenty minutes ago. I feel like I'm addicted to him, intoxicated by his presence. I just want to breathe him in, hold him inside my lungs and never exhale, as if his very existence could give me life.

A thought occurs to me, and I hurriedly run up to the apartment to grab my sketchbook. Luckily, Logan is already in the shower, so he doesn't notice. By the time I come back down, Taylor is waiting on the curb in his truck with a big, crooked grin, snapback on backward.

"I'm here to pick up my date," he calls from the open window. "Have you seen him? Super tall, sexy curls, plays football?"

"Haven't seen him, but I'm happy to take his place." Hopping into the passenger seat, I lean over for a kiss. "I charge by the hour, though. Hundred bucks."

"Damn, that's cheap. I can swing that," he chuckles as he pulls out of the parking lot, and my chest swells. It feels...odd to be flirting with him like this. Not in a bad way, but freeing. It should have been this way between us from the start.

"So you survived Arya, I see."

"Barely." Shifting gears, he maneuvers the truck into traffic. "She practically grabbed my dick, trying to get me into a threesome with her and Christian. They started fucking right there on your seat."

"*Gross*, what the fuck!" I jump into the middle, pressing into Taylor's side as he bursts into laughter. His hand leaves the gearshift to rest on my knee, and I watch him drive for a minute. He looks completely at ease, his inked arm extended to grasp the wheel, strands of dark hair brushing his face, and his lips curled into a smile. Beautiful.

"Does that happen often?" I ask, tearing my gaze away when he tosses his phone and tells me to pick some music. "With you and Christian?"

"What, threesomes?" At my nod, his head bounces from side to side. "I wouldn't say they happen *often*, but frequently, yeah. Don't know if you remember, but Christian and I had issues in high school with stealing each other's girlfriends."

"He punched you for messing around with one, I remember." Settling on a playlist titled *'Songs I Miss Getting High To,'* I lean against him as 'Like This' by Breathe Carolina filters through the speakers. "The night you broke my arm, right?"

He squirms uncomfortably. "Yeah. We eventually decided that it made more sense for us to date *together*. Can't steal someone's girlfriend if she's already your girl, too."

My brows jump as I turn to gape at him. "Seriously? Like, at the same time?"

"Yep. It was practical, honestly, because we spend most of our time together anyway. So, it was like...killing two birds with one stone? Is that the right phrase?"

His hand leaves my leg to downshift before returning, and I stare at it thoughtfully.

"But you and Christian... you've never...?" I let the question hang in the air, feeling his eyes on my face.

"No," he answers softly, squeezing my thigh. "I said in the cabin that I've only had experience with one guy, remember? I don't feel that way about Christian. Only you, Huck."

We're stopped at a red light, his gaze is so intense that I have to turn away. Clearing my throat, I try to lighten the mood.

"Well, I'm not dating him, too, so don't ask."

That gets a snort out of him. "No offense, but you're not really his type. If that fucker could live in pussy twenty-four-seven, he would."

"I'm surprised he has no crotch goblins running around everywhere."

"You kidding? He got snipped the minute we turned eighteen." Taylor huffs a laugh, shaking his head. "I went with him when he did it. Not as scary as it sounds, honestly. He said he felt no pain."

"But you didn't do it?"

"Hell, no." He gives me an odd look, shifting again as he accelerates, and I narrow my gaze.

"Why not?"

Without responding, his teeth sink into his bottom lip as a blush creeps onto his neck. His eyes bounce around the road, fingers tightening on the wheel, throat flexing as he swallows hard. And that's when I realize he's *flustered.* Taylor fucking Tottman is embarrassed.

Turning my body into his, I lean close to brush my lips over his ear as I place my hand on his upper thigh. "Tell me, baby."

He grumbles something under his breath, and even though I caught every word, he looks too damn cute not to mess with him a little more.

"A little louder, I didn't hear you."

"I *like* having swimmers, ok?" He glares at me, his face entirely red as we turn down a quiet street. "Happy?"

Snorting louder than intended, I nip at his shoulder with a chuckle. "You just like cum."

Scoffing, he says nothing else, but I catch a hint of a smile as he turns away.

"So, that word Christian calls you, *cariño?* What does it mean?"

"It's a term of endearment," his expression softens, "like honey or darling. His mom has always called me that, and he started doing it when I moved in with them in high school. Started as a joke, mostly, but then it stuck."

My chest pinches at his words. "You're super close with his family."

"Yep. Pretty sure I spent more time at his house than mine growing up."

That makes sense. As tumultuous as his home life was, I'm sure Taylor used Christian's place as an escape. A sanctuary. For what it's worth, I'm glad he had somewhere to go that made him feel safe.

"Where are we going, anyway?" I ask, ready to change the subject.

"Up the canyon. Ever been to Silver Lake?"

"Nope."

His teeth flash as he grins, giving me a peek of that crooked incisor. "We'll be there soon. Bit of a drive, but I want to show you the view."

We fall into a comfortable silence other than the music, Taylor switching off from handling the gear shift and teasing my thigh. When we reach the mouth of the canyon, he speeds up, swerving around bends in the road expertly one-handed. It's fuckhot, honestly, watching him drift like a drag racer.

"I didn't know you could drive stick," I comment, tangling my fingers in his hair.

"Well, yeah. Gotta know how to operate a clutch before you get on a bike."

"No wonder you're so good at what you do."

He throws me a sideways glance. "Don't tell me you've never learned to drive a manual?"

I blink at him for a second, and his eyes widen.

"*Really?* Aaron never taught you?"

"My mom was the one who taught me to drive, and she only knew automatic, so...no."

"Damn." He grabs my hand and puts it on the shifter, "here, I'll show you."

Over the next twenty minutes or so, he tries to teach me about the different gears and how they tie into the clutch, and I try to pay attention. He's so confident, patiently answering my questions even though I'm not retaining much. I just like hearing him speak.

"Fifth gear is only for sixty-five miles per hour or above. But I'm not taking this corner that fast with you in the truck. I *have* done it before, though." Using our hands to downshift into second, he pulls onto a dirt path, taking us through the trees. It's too dark to see anything other than shadows beyond the beam of his headlights, but it doesn't seem to phase him.

"Who taught you to drive?" I ask, and his body slightly stiffens.

"My dad started teaching me when I was five." The truck slows, turning as he whips us around to back into a spot in the brush. "Couldn't even reach the pedals yet. He'd beat my ass every time I stalled on the clutch, but I sure learned fast."

My stomach twists at that, anger blooming for the little boy he'd been.

"I'm sorry. You deserved better parents."

It's true. Even though Maisie has always been kind to me, it doesn't excuse how she treats her flesh and blood. A part of me wonders if my dad has ever questioned it or saw anything wrong with it. Yes, Taylor fucked up. He did a lot of bad things growing up, but would he have still been that way if he'd grown up in a loving environment?

I guess I don't really know. I grew up with two caring, supportive parents, and what had that gotten me?

*Anxiety,* that's what.

Maybe instead of being 'nature versus nurture,' it's a bit of both.

Taylor shrugs tightly. "I had Salem and the guys. I was lucky."

"This the place?" Not wanting to make him uncomfortable by discussing his childhood, I steer us away from the conversation.

"Yeah." Reaching behind the seat, he grabs a wadded-up blanket and a plastic bag before rolling down the window to open his door. "Come on."

The chilly canyon air hits me when I leave the truck, making me shiver as I follow him to the back. Water sloshes in the distance, backed by a cacophony of crickets and croaking frogs. Taylor unlatches the tailgate, hopping onto the truck bed with a pat for me to join him, and as I settle in, the view before us catches my breath.

Silver Lake glitters under the waxing moon, the dark sky above so clear that I swear I can see our own galaxy flickering among the stars. Far away from the bright city lights, it's almost ethereal, watching the sky's reflection ripple in the water, surrounded by nothing but aspens and spruce.

"Unreal, huh?" Taylor's eyes are on my face, and I turn to give him an appreciative nod.

"It's beautiful. I can only imagine what it looks like in the daytime."

"During the day, it's just your typical lake. Still beautiful, sure, but at night?" He tips his head back, sweeping his gaze above with a small smile. "Everything goes quiet and still. There's nothing but you and space out here, stretching for miles."

Quiet is definitely right. Even the frogs have stopped their bellowing like our presence scared them off. The silence is almost deafening, unlike the water lapping on the shoreline. With the darkness of the trees around us, it's a bit eerie, if I'm being honest.

"You don't find it unnerving?"

"Nah." Leaning on his palms, he swings his legs back and forth. "It's the calm that settles me. Sometimes, after a big show or practice on my bike, I have a hard time coming down from the adrenaline. Weed used to help, but...yeah. Once I stopped smoking and drinking, I'd be antsy as fuck for hours. Couldn't sleep. So, my therapist suggested 'peaceful' activities to get my brain to shut off. Coming here is soothing."

I hum, keeping my eyes on the shadows in case something decides to jump out. "The first time I went to a doctor at eighteen with sleeping problems, they just threw pills at me."

He's silent for a bit, gazing at me sadly, but his eyes slip away when I turn to look at him.

"They tried that, too, at first," he admits softly, "but after...everything that happened, and with my newfound sobriety, I wanted to stay off meds. Took a while and some experimentation, but I found what worked for me. Everyone's brain is different."

"So coming here helps you sleep?" A slight breeze kicks up, rustling the leaves and sending chills through me.

Taylor unravels the blanket he brought from the truck to wrap around our shoulders, crowding into me so that our sides and thighs are pressed together. "Sometimes. It's easier in the summer when it's warm, and I can just fall asleep in the bed of my truck. Winter is a little harder, but I make do with shit like puzzles. And masturbation."

He winks at me, and I choke out a laugh. The warmth from his body floods my own. "I thought you were joking when I asked what you were doing, and you said puzzles."

"One hundred percent not a joke. I like the jigsaw ones with over a thousand pieces."

"Like a little old man." I bump his shoulder, grinning as he snorts. "Who knew the adrenaline junkie from high school would turn into such a grandpa."

"Hey," he gasps in mock offense. "*Still* a certified badass over here. My nervous system needs a break once in a while."

"Yeah, yeah, you're still cool." Smirking, I glance up again at the stars twinkling above. "So, which constellations up there are tattooed on your back?"

There's a startled flicker on his face before he follows my gaze to the sky. "Well, the first one is Libra, but you can't see it from the Northern Hemisphere just yet. It's my zodiac sign. Second one is Aries, for Christian, and the third is Taurus, for Salem. I think they're both there," he points, "and there. If I had a telescope, I could show you."

My throat closes with emotion. "You have your best friend's star signs tattooed on you? That's...actually really sweet."

"Shut up, no, it's not," he scoffs, shoving me playfully beneath the blanket. "You wanna know a secret? Most of my tats cover up scars from crashing my bike."

"Yeah?"

"Yep. I've broken both wrists, a femur, and my ribs more times than I can remember. Punctured a lung once. Got a few metal rods in my bones. Check this out." He jumps down to unbutton his pants while I gape, and when he shoves them down to his ankles, I'm graced with the sight of his toned thighs.

"This tat here," he touches a colorful dragon winding its way up from shin to just above his knee, "shattered my tibia, had to get staples. The scar was gnarly, and I wasn't supposed to ride for six months, but I got back on my bike after nine weeks."

"*Jesus Christ,* Taylor." Throwing him an incredulous glance, I try to ignore the imprint of his dick in the crotch of his briefs. "I've had my fair share of injuries on the field, but that's...damn."

He tugs his pants back up, much to my disappointment, but leaves them undone as he hops up next to me. "I know. Tore a ligament in your foot during your second season, right?"

"You remember that?"

"Well...yeah," he shrugs, pulling the blanket tight around him. "I was paying attention."

My brows furrow, an odd flutter mixed with shame blooming in my stomach at the knowledge that he'd been keeping an eye on me from afar for four years. Whereas I, on the other hand, spent those years pretending he didn't exist.

That familiar feeling creeps into my veins, quickening my pulse and making me lightheaded. But I fight it, telling Taylor I'll be right back as I slide off the tailgate and make my way to the cab. Reaching in to grab my sketchbook, I stand there momentarily and just breathe.

*Inhale. Exhale.*

*One. Two. Three.*

My fingers shake when I round the truck again, finding him studying me with wide, worried eyes. Swallowing, I gingerly place the sketchbook in his lap. "I don't know if that offer is still on the table, the one you and Salem brought up about helping design some of your merch, but... it's something that's kept me busy these last few months, and I wanted to show you what I've drawn."

The words come out in a rush, my breathing a bit ragged. He gives me a perplexed look before flipping open the book to the first sketch. A grin immediately lights up his eyes, easing the tension in my neck.

"Hey, Fizzgig," he laughs, pointing at the creature from The Dark Crystal movie. "I have a tattoo of the Crystal of Truth on my arm."

*I know.* Never seen the movie in my life, but he has a poster in his room, and a Google search told me what I needed to know.

"No fucking way!" He stares at the next drawing, a pinup girl dressed as the Audrey II from Little Shop of Horrors. Her mouth is open, tongue obscenely out, with a text bubble that says *'feed me, Seymour!'* "Holy shit, Huck, this is amazing! I want this on a shirt right fucking now. I want this *on* me. I already have a tattoo of the plant, but I probably-"

He cuts himself off when he turns to the next page, taking in yet another concept of the art he already has on his body. And then another. And another. It slowly dawns on him, his eyes flicking up to mine from under his lashes. Stepping closer, my legs bump his as I tap the sketchbook in his hands.

"I may be four years too late, Tay. But I've been paying attention, too. I'm just sorry it took me so long." Pausing, I run my hands through my hair with a nervous chuckle. "It's all mostly your ink, though. I'm not sure what Christian would like, but he's not as interesting to look at as you. No offense."

He gently, almost lovingly, closes the book and sets it aside before grabbing my shirt to pull me closer. Our lips meet halfway, opening for one another, an electric jolt zipping through me when our tongues touch like it's the first time all over again. His legs wrap around my waist, trapping me against him while his hands roam my back. Heating my blood, sending my heart into overdrive.

Out of all the guys I've kissed, none of them make me feel the way Taylor does, like his arms are the only place I belong. As if I could build a home inside his embrace and live in it forever. Ever since that night when he kissed me on the track behind my house, it's a feeling I searched for in every relationship I've ever had, and they always come up short.

"Get up here," he rasps between kisses on my throat. "Need you."

Practically dragging me onto the bed of the truck, he guides us to the back, where he pushes me against the cab beneath the window. Straddling my legs, he sits on my thighs to tangle his hands in my hair while he makes love to my mouth with his own. It's not long before we're both rock hard, grinding our cocks against each other with breathless moans. His jeans are still undone, and when I glance down, I can see his crown peeking out of the waistband of his briefs, already glistening with a bead of precum. He shivers when I swipe my thumb over it and bring it to my lips, sucking off the taste.

Reaching for my buckle, he undoes it before popping open the button on my pants, pulling down my underwear so that he can wrap his fingers around my cock.

"Fuck, baby," I groan, thrusting up into his fist. "One of these days, I'm gonna get you fully naked."

"It's too cold out here for that." He pulls out his own length and lines us up. "We could always move into the truck?"

"After what you told me happened on those seats, hard pass."

Huffing a throaty laugh, he lifts my shirt, exposing my nipples to the cold air as he leans down to take one between his teeth. He continues to work our shafts, pumping them together while he moves to give my other nipple attention, the chill on the one he left behind making me hiss with pleasure.

"A-am I doing ok?" He stammers, glancing up at me as he licks my sternum, a hint of uncertainty in his beautiful eyes. All I can do is blink at him dazedly, trying to think through the fog of desire.

Then, it hits me. The last time he actually *played* with me was in the shower, over four years ago, and that was only the second time he'd ever done it. The first was in the pool.

"You're making me feel so good, Tay." Pulling him up for a kiss, I buck my hips to fuck his fist. "So fucking good."

He hums against my mouth, tongue tangling with mine lazily before he leans back and sinks his teeth into his bottom lip. "Can I...can I suck on you?"

*Goddamn.* That's it. I'm wholly gone for this boy. And it terrifies me.

"Do you want to?" Cupping his face between my palms, I search his anxious gaze with a knot in my chest. "I know the last time wasn't what it should have been. I'd understand if you needed time. I don't want you to give me head just because you think it's what *I* want."

"No, no, I want to. Trust me," he chuckles, shaking his head quickly. "Other than you fucking me, it's been my number one fantasy for weeks. I'm just..."

"Just what?"

A sheepish smile pulls at his cheeks. "What if I'm bad at it?"

I can't help but laugh. "As long as you don't bite it, I'm sure you'll be fine."

"Shut up, fucker." He squeezes our cocks hard, causing my laugh to cut off into a groan. "You know what I mean. God, I feel like such a chick right now."

"You're adorable." I kiss his scowling lips until they soften for me before gently pushing him off. "I have an idea. Lay down on your side."

Interest and curiosity brighten his features as he obliges, spreading out on the blanket beneath him. I settle down with my head in the opposite direction so that our crotches are lined up directly in each other's faces, sixty-nining on our sides.

"Just mimic what I do," I say, dragging my tongue along his shaft, earning me a whimper in response. "Eventually, you'll learn what feels good in your mouth. Oral doesn't just have to be for the other person."

Following my lead, Taylor licks up my length slowly, making me moan against him when his tongue pauses to flick tentatively over the ridge at the bottom of my crown.

"Mm, just like that, baby. Explore all you want. It feels amazing."

Spurred on by my praise, he does just that, taking me at different tempos, finding what's comfortable for him while I take him to the back of my throat and swallow the way I know he likes. Eventually, he sighs contentedly and stills, suckling on my cock like a damn lollipop, and it's the hottest thing I've ever felt, almost spilling my load right there.

But I'm not finished with him yet.

Sliding his jeans down to mid-thigh, I tease my fingers along his crease. He jolts against me, vibrating my shaft with a moan, and I press between his ass cheeks to run my finger over his puckered hole.

"Huck," he groans around my cock, thrusting into my mouth, and I grin as I begin to circle him, feeling his muscles clench.

Bringing my finger to my mouth, I get it wet before putting it back, probing him slowly before popping off his cock. "You want me inside, Tay?"

He nods emphatically, whining while still sucking on me peacefully, and I probe him gently, the tip of my finger slipping past that tight ring of muscle. In and out, I work into him, shaking from the effort of staying still, fighting the urge to shove myself down his throat until he chokes. He thrusts into my mouth, fucking himself back and forth on my finger until

I'm seated up to the knuckle, so fucking tight, and I find that spot inside him that I know will make him see stars.

"Fuck, fuck, *fuck.*" It only takes three or four prods against his prostate before he's coming down my throat, the tickle of his cries on my balls sending me there as well. He echoes through the quiet night, drinking me down as he milks his orgasm on my tongue, clenching around my finger.

And when it's over, he laughs softly, nuzzling his lips against my hip, hugging my waist tightly like he's afraid to let go. As I slip out of him, resting my forehead against his thighs to catch my breath, I can't help but feel the same.

When the cold starts to nip at us, we right ourselves and snuggle beneath the blanket, my head on his chest while he flips through the rest of my sketchbook, and I cling to him, not wanting morning to come. Because even though he's mine for now, at least until July, there's a nagging voice in the back of my skull telling me to make the most of our moments together because they're limited. This can't last forever, no matter how much we want it to.

As he murmurs into my curls under the twinkling stars, I can only think one thing:

Our story has just begun, yet we're already running out of time.

# PART THREE

# TAYLOR

## MAY

"**Y**ou fuckers have exactly ten minutes to piss and grab your shit, then we're back on the road!"

Wiping the sweat off my forehead, I stick the gas pump into the tank of Salem's jeep while I watch Matty, Huck, and Logan disappear into the convenience store. We're somewhere just outside of Steamboat Springs, Colorado, so there's also a weed dispensary that Christian, Arya, and Xed just waltzed into. I've already been cooped up inside the jeep for six hours, and I'm going fucking crazy. The fact that I've also been stuck with Salem giving me the cold shoulder and a sulking Logan hasn't helped one bit.

Just four more hours. Four long hours until we get to Greeley, and then we can get this camping trip started. Then I'll get a tent alone with Huck. The anticipation is literally killing me, I swear. The last three and a half weeks since he showed me his sketchbook in my truck—which was the most romantic thing anyone's ever done for me, by the way—have been pure torture, having only been able to see him a handful of times do to his college schedule and finals coming up. Christian and I also started bussing tables at the Prospector during week-nights for some extra cash, so that's been throwing us off, too. He's leaving for Cali next weekend for his college graduation, and I'm dying to spend some time with him before then.

Shaking out the rest of the gas, I put the pump back and finish paying with my card before making my way over to where Salem stands with her back to me, snapping away at the Rockies in the distance with her camera. The sun is beating down on us, hot as hell, so I'm shirtless in a pair of sweats.

Sliding my arms around her waist from behind, I rest my chin on her head. "You still mad at me?"

Her camera snaps more shots. "Mm-hmm." *Snap, snap.*

"Come on, Sally Mal, don't do this to me. You know how much I hate the silent treatment."

I fucking hate it so much. She's barely spoken to me since the party at Xed and Matty's, but this morning, when I sprung it on her that Logan and Huckslee were coming with us on this trip...yeah, needless to say, she hasn't been in the best mood.

"I just don't get it." *Snap.* "Really, Taylor, I don't." *Snap, snap, snap.* "Because you've never bothered with any of my relationships before, so why do you care so much about this one?"

*Snap, snap, snap, SNAP, SNAP.*

Wrenching her camera away before she breaks it, I spin her around and stare down into her livid face. "I care because you were really happy, and I don't want to see you throw away something good because of a misunderstanding."

She rears back, smacking her lips as her gray eyes flash. "A misunderstanding? Really, Tay? He disrespected my wishes and proposed, knowing full well I'm against marriage."

"And you said no, so what's the big deal?"

"The big deal is that he won't fuck me unless we're married," she shouts, grabbing her camera back. "So what future does the relationship have, really?"

"You were perfectly fine without sex for two whole years, though? Would you have still been with him if he hadn't proposed?"

Her nostrils flare as she huffs, brushing by me to march toward her jeep. "This really isn't any of your business."

"Well, we all know how good I am at minding my own business." I follow close behind, not willing to let this go because I'm sick of her shit lately.

When we get to the car, she whirls around and points. "You're only trying to get us back together because you're fucking his best friend."

"Uh, first and second off, not true. We haven't even fucked yet, so..."

"What, why?" Her delicate brows shoot up, anger forgotten. "You're definitely a 'fuck on the first date' type."

I shake my head, adjusting my snapback before stuffing my hands in my pockets. "Nope. We aren't talking about my sex life if we can't talk about yours."

Growling in frustration, she yanks open the driver's side door and plops down into the seat, crossing her arms. "He only proposed because his parents made him, okay? They freaked on him once they found out we were living together unmarried. His dad threatened to–"

"SALEM, CHECK THIS SHIT OUT!"

Christian's loud as fuck voice cuts her off when he practically skips out of the dispensary with a shit-eating grin, as shirtless as I am. Arya and Xed follow behind, both looking blitzed as hell. Two more issues to add to my ever-overflowing plate.

Ever since that night of the party, Xed's been spending all of his time more stoned than sober, and Arya won't leave the fucking apartment now that she and Christian are apparently dating. Seriously, if I have to watch her walk around in nothing but a towel any longer because she's hoping I'll initiate something or some shit, I'm gonna lose it.

"I got us some grade-A kush, my dude." Christian flashes his bag of weed to Salem, waggling his brows, and I punch him on the shoulder.

"You interrupted something, asshole. And you better not be smoking in my truck."

Arya giggles, rolling her eyes while she tugs up the hem of her dress. "Don't be such a downer, Tay Bae."

Kill me now, fucking hell.

"Yeah, Tay Bae, lighten up," Christian mocks, smooshing my face between his fingers while Xed chuckles, looking like he has no idea where he even is.

Pulling a Zippo and a pipe out of his leather jacket, he reaches into the bag to pack a bowl. At first, I think nothing of it, bullshitting with Christian and Salem, until he flicks the flame right there next to the pump. I react instinctually, smacking the Zippo out of his hand and accidentally hitting the pipe, which shatters when it hits the ground.

"What the fuck?!"

Everyone stares down at the broken bits of glass in shock while I jab a finger into Xed's chest. "You're near a fucking gas pump, dumbass. You really think lighting up right here is a smart move?"

"God, my bad." He holds up his palms, clearly trying to stay focused while he sways. I can smell the whiskey on his breath.

"What's going on with you lately? I know Matty and Hannah leaving is gonna be hard on you, but come on, man—"

His palms connect with my chest as he shoves me against the jeep hard, spit landing on my cheek when he snarls in my face. "You don't know fucking *shit*, Taylor. What, is your own life so miserable that you have to mess with everyone else's?"

"*Pinche cabrón.*" Christian jolts forward, reaching for Xed to pull him back, but I throw out an arm to stop him.

"Xed, take your hands off of me," I warn slowly, balling up my fists as I fight the urge to swing at him, reminding myself that whatever he's going through isn't his fault.

Huck's voice reaches my ears from behind. "What's going on?"

Out of my peripheral, he and Logan round the front of the vehicle, but I don't take my attention off Xed as he blinks slowly, gaze dropping to where he's still pressing me into the jeep. His eyes widen before he lets go, stepping back abruptly. Everyone's watching us, including Matty, and the two share a look before Xed scowls.

"You owe me a new pipe," he mutters, forcing me out of the way when he pulls open the back door, slamming it shut behind him.

"Fuck you." Pulling out my wallet, I slap some cash into Christian's hand, telling him to buy something for Xed as I move around to the passenger side. Huck and Logan slide into the back next to Xed while Matty and Arya wait for Christian near my truck since he's been driving it.

"Are you okay?" Salem asks gently.

I can feel Huck's eyes on the back of my skull. Xed scoffs, making me grit my teeth, and I pull open the glove box to rummage for my smokes.

"Just peachy. Let's get this shitshow on the road." Four more hours. Just four more hours.

After Christian returns to toss a new pipe at Xed through the open window, we take off again for the interstate. I connect my phone to the Bluetooth while I puff on my cig, throwing on some Lamb of God because I'm pissed off. The first six hours, we vibed to Salem's reggae music and Xed's techno, but now my bad mood is about to be everyone's problem. I don't give a fuck.

After a while of stewing, my phone vibrates on my lap.

> Huckleberry: What was all that about?

I almost smile when I see his contact name, recalling our conversation where I called him my Huckleberry. He had no clue what I was talking about because he's uncultured and has never seen the movie Tombstone.

> Me: With Xed? Fuck if I know.

> He's been in a shitty mood ever since Matty dropped it on everyone that he and Hannah are leaving.

> Huckleberry: Did he hurt you?

Me: Nah. Nothing I can't handle. I'm tough.

Huckleberry: Maybe on the outside. Tell me what's going through your head.

Me: ...are you saying my insides are nice and soft? ;)

Huckleberry: You're impossible.

And yes, they are.

And tight.

And warm.

Shifting in my seat, I lift my knee onto the dash to hide the chubby he just gave me. Every time we've been together, he's had his fingers inside me, slowly stretching, hitting that spot that has me coming like a geyser in under two-point-five seconds flat. In anticipation for tonight, I purchased a butt plug online which I may or may not be wearing right now, as a surprise for him. We both got tested last weekend, and I'm excited to take him bare.

Me: I bet they'd feel great around your cock.

Huckleberry: Do NOT give me a boner back here, it's impossible to hide.

Me: Your fault for mentioning my insides.

> Huckleberry: Can we tone down the screaming music a little? I have a headache.

> Me: You are a headache.

But I switch it to Post Malone because I know how much Huck likes him even though he pretends he doesn't.

> Me: Better?

> Huckleberry: I guess. Now tell me what's wrong.

> Me: Why do you think something's wrong?

> Huckleberry: Because you haven't smoked in over two weeks, and you only do that when you're upset.

Fuck, he's got me there.

> Me: Just something Xed said.

> It's fine. I'll get over it.

> Just let me be a dramatic bitch for a bit.

> Huckleberry: Okay, princess.

> Me: Fuck off.

Really, though, I am bothered by Xed's words. What the fuck was he trying to say? My life is far from miserable. Maybe it was at one point...but things got better, even before Huckslee returned. Am I where I want to be in life? Not particularly, but I'm no longer where I was either, and that's what matters. And what's so wrong with me wanting to help my friends figure out their bullshit? Isn't that what you do for the people you love? It's what they would have done for me, I'm sure, if they'd known about my dad. It's what I wish someone had done for me. What I should have done for Huck.

So Xed can fuck off outta here because I'll never stop caring about the shit he's going through or any of them. I just wish he'd talk about it. Xed's home life was almost as bad as mine when Matty's parents took him in. Like Christian and I, the two have spent nearly every minute together since elementary school, and I know their bond only grew stronger when Hannah was born. Hell, Xed's helped raise that little girl so far. It must be eating him alive that he's losing them, but the asshole won't speak up about it. He's as stubborn as I used to be before Doctor Hart got me all up in my feels and cracked me wide open.

Shit, maybe that's what he needs. A good crack on the fucking head to knock all that shit inside his mind loose.

Metaphorically, obviously.

...or is it?

My phone vibrates again, distracting me.

> Huckleberry: You're thinking so hard I can smell the gears turning from back here. Please tell me?

> Me: Can't talk.

> Planning operation 'Get Xed To Open Up About His Feelings Without Hopefully Resorting To Violence But We'll See.'

I hear him snort over the music.

> Huckleberry: Bit of a mouthful, if you ask me.

> And do not turn that into a dirty joke, Logan's trying to peek at my phone.

> Me: The urge to send a random dick pic just now was so strong.

> Really, you should be proud of my restraint.

> Huckleberry: You already scarred my best friend for life by kissing him. Let's not traumatize him with your dick, too.

> Me: Worried he might see it and fall in love?

> Huckleberry: I mean, I did, so yeah.

Whoooosh and there goes the fucking air out of my lungs. Goddamn, he has a way of leaving me breathless and speechless with just one text.

> Me: Aw, shucks.

> Thanks, bud.

Huckleberry: Annnnd I take it back.

Me: No take backsies. It's in writing now.

And just for the record, I'm in love with your dick too.

Admitting that in text is so much easier than telling him I love him in person, and I wish it wasn't. We already admitted our feelings to each other, so why must those three words be so hard? I do love him. I have for years. But despite his words, there's still that nagging voice telling me that my feelings aren't reciprocal. We only have until the end of July, and all of this is temporary. Maybe Huck was right when he said it might hurt less if we end this before it even begins. Though the last month with him has been easy and fun, my gut tells me that something is brewing on the horizon that has my heart bracing for a crushing blow.

The hours crawl by as we make our way toward Greeley. Christian's uncle owns a plot of land in the wilderness that he lets us camp on for free, and we make this trip yearly. In the past, it was always an excuse to get as shitfaced as possible and just vibe, but last year was my first time being sober, so in support of it, Christian and Salem were sober as well. We still had fun, but now that I've had time to adjust and we've brought a whole gaggle of friends along, I told them I didn't mind if they let loose.

Eventually, Huckslee and Logan make a game of coming up with names for license plate numbers they spot, Salem and I joining in while Xed dries out with a nap. It's surprising, at first, to see Salem actually speaking to Logan, but I try not to make a big deal out of it. We stop one more time for Christian to fill up my gas guzzler, and then finally, after the longest day of driving in my life, we're pulling off the road and into the trees.

His uncle's property is marked by bright green flags tied around trunks of tall pines, and Christian leads the way to the usual spot we camp at, our bikes and Logan's uncle's four-wheeler bouncing in the back. Our spot is a small area that we fenced in with logs a few years back, complete with a raised cinderblock firepit that Christian and I built ourselves. We picked the flattest part of the five acres with the best tree cover for shade.

"Some ground rules for you fucks who haven't been here before," Christian starts when we all exit our vehicles, "my *tío* marked his property line with bright green flags, do not go beyond those flags. They also glow in the dark."

Logan groans as he stretches his long legs. "And what happens if we do?"

"You will be shot on sight," I deadpan. Everyone except Christian and Salem stops to stare at me.

"F-for real?" Logan glances at Huck nervously, who blinks several times, and I smile grimly.

"Yep. There's an old man who lives in a camper on the property next to us, and he likes to use his shotgun."

"Found that out the hard way," Salem mutters, opening the back of the jeep to start unloading our camping gear.

Xed grunts, rubbing his eyes as he helps her. "I remember hearing this story the summer before junior year."

Huck cocks a brow. "What story?"

"This asshole," Matty throws a sweaty arm around my shoulders, shaking his head, "decided to sneak over there and steal the guy's propane. Needless to say, he was *not* happy."

With a snort, I shake him off. "Understatement. I almost took two buckshots to the ass."

"Good thing you're a squirrelly motherfucker who can run." Christian lowers the tailgate to grab out coolers of food. We set up camp, placing our chairs and supplies around the firepit. Salem starts to pull the tents out of the back of the truck when she stops short.

"Uh, guys? We have a problem." Turning around, she dangles two bags from each hand. "There's only two tents."

"What? No, no." Stepping up next to her, I peer into the back to see for myself. Sure as shit, it's empty, other than the dirt bike. "What the hell?! Who was supposed to pack the other tents?"

"Three guesses." Matt crosses his arms, throwing a look at his best friend, who groans and covers his face.

"Guys, I may have fucked up," Xed mumbles into his palms, and I growl in frustration.

"You *are* fucked up, dude! Seriously? What are we supposed to do with two tents?"

The truck door opens as Arya steps out dressed in a sports bra and leggings. "Hmm, I think since Christian and I are the only couple here, we should get a tent to ourselves."

No. This is not happening, goddammit.

Huckslee and I had a plan. We were going to force Logan and Salem into their own tent and have Matty and Xed share so that we could finally be alone somewhere other than the bed of my truck. This is bullshit.

*There's a plug up my ass!*

"I'll fight you for it." Lifting my fists, I advance toward Christian. "Square up."

He jumps back as I aim for his stomach, putting me in a headlock, both of us scrambling until we fall to the ground, dirt and rocks digging into my back when we roll around.

"Ah...shit...Huckslee, get your bro off of me!"

That comment earns him a kidney punch, and then his hand comes down between my legs.

"Ouch, fuck! Did you just flick my dick, dude?"

"Accidentally on purpose."

"Fuck you."

Matt grabs an ice-cold water bottle from the cooler and dumps it on us. "That's enough, you two."

"Daddy Matty's been activated," Salem laughs.

Shaking out his wet hair, Christian pins me beneath him while he hisses in my ear. "You're just desperate to get dicked down."

"No fucking shit!"

"Christian and Arya get the extra tent. That's final," Matt barks, and I shove my best friend off me as I roll to my feet, shooting him a glower. Huck shakes his head, rolling his eyes even though he flashes me a sad smile.

"Where the hell are we supposed to sleep?" He takes a tent from Salem and stares at it like it has the plague. "All six of us have to squeeze into this?"

Logan studies Salem from his peripheral. "What's the placement going to be? Like, who sleeps where?"

"Doesn't matter." I grab the tent, walking it over to a spot near the log fence. "We'll figure it out later. Let's just fall where we fall tonight."

"Of course, *you* would say that," Xed mutters darkly, and I throw him a wink over my shoulder.

"If you want to snuggle me, Xed, all you have to do is ask."

Christian smacks the side of my head. "Can we get this shit set up so that we can ride the bikes already?"

That shuts me up quickly.

Nearly an hour and several arguments later, both tents are erected, and we're peeling off into the trees on our bikes—which honestly is a terrible idea because I'm fighting a boner the entire time with the plug vibrating against my prostate. Matthew follows on the four-wheeler with Salem sitting behind him, her camera pointed at us to capture footage for our socials.

My jump at the qualifier earned me a new sponsorship, and I'm repping them with their brand on the side of my new helmet. Part of our contract entails daily social media updates from me with their company logo in the post; in return, I receive free gear. As someone who's pretty illiterate when it comes to this kind of shit, I'd be lost if Salem wasn't managing my online presence for me. She's a saint, and we should honestly start paying her soon.

Once the 'work' is done, we have the fun, racing each other and jumping off small mounds while everyone else takes turns on the four-wheeler. I even let Huckslee have a ride on my bike, reminding me how fucking good he looks when he's racing. Ten out of ten. He needs to get back into riding because my mind is conjuring up all kinds of devious things I can do to him on a bike. The way his eyes heat with desire when I whisper that into his ear has my own blood running hot.

Christian was right about one thing, I'm fucking desperate for him. It's driving me crazy not to be able to touch him like I want, to run my hands over the hard lines of his shoulders and arms on full display in the sleeveless shirt he's wearing. He cut his hair again the way I like, short on the sides with longer curls on top falling over his brow, and I want to mess it up. Tug my fingers through it while he deepthroats my cock. At one point, he pulls his shirt up to wipe the sweat off his face, flashing glistening abs, and I almost drag him behind a tree right then and there to have my way with him; consequences be damned.

"You're drooling, Taytortot," Salem snickers, passing over her camera to show me the photo she snapped of him, and you can bet I'll be adding it to the album on my phone of Huck that I shamelessly jerk off to.

When the sun eventually starts to descend below the treeline, we put the bikes away to get a fire going, all eight of us surrounding the pit to roast some shitty hotdogs and marshmallows. I'm about halfway through my fourth smore, enraptured with the sight of Huck licking melted white goo off his lips, when Arya pulls a baggie out of her bra.

"Who's ready to get this party started," she sings, holding up a plastic bag full of mushroom caps.

"Oh, hell yes." Xed is the first one out of his seat, reaching for the bag, but I snatch it before he gets a chance.

"Nuh-uh, nope." Pointing a finger at him, I shake the baggie. "You lost your party privilege by being a dick earlier. And

I'm not about to babysit seven tripping assholes by myself. You and I aren't taking any."

His jaw drops, eyes widening as he glares at me incredulously. "Who the fuck died and made you king?"

"I did." Christian raises his hand, taking the shrooms from me. "My family's property, my rules. I ain't about to have anyone wander off where they shouldn't and get eaten by bears or some shit. Two of us need to stay sober to watch."

Logan's head snaps up from where he was skewering a marshmallow next to Salem. "Did you say bears?"

"Why does it have to be me?" Xed growls, flinging out his hands. "Why can't it be Matt?"

"Matty and Huck are leaving soon. They deserve to let loose one last time before training camp."

"And I don't deserve to let loose?"

A snort leaves my throat as everyone passes the bag around, pulling out caps. "You've let loose like every single day for a month. Give someone else a chance. If you wanna smoke, go for it."

Xed plops back down into his seat, seething in my direction, but I ignore him as I grab bottles of orange juice out of the cooler and hand them out.

Huck looks down at his drink with a raised brow. "OJ?"

"Helps hide the bitterness and enhances the trip," I answer, grinning. "You ever used magic mushrooms before?"

Logan answers with an uncertain *no* while Huckslee nods. "Once, a few summers ago, but we didn't drink juice."

Matt opens his bottle, popping the mushroom cap into his mouth before taking a few gulps with a grimace. "The citric acid helps break down the psilocybin, so the effects hit sooner and harder."

"Bottoms up." Salem does the same, her eyes narrowed challengingly at Logan as if daring him to follow suit.

Christian downs his whole bottle before slapping Logan on the shoulder. "No one's forcing you, *hermano*. If you don't wanna do 'em, you can babysit with Tay."

"Please, *please* chicken out," Xed begs, sliding off his chair to his knees. "Come on, Logan. You're a better man than this."

Arya rolls her eyes, smacking her plump lips. "You just want him to say no so you can take some yourself."

"I never said *I* was a better man. And no one asked you."

"I've just about had it with your attitude." Christian shoves him over sideways, the two arguing while Logan deliberates. He glances at Huck, who shrugs before swallowing his cap with a giant swig, and excitement lances through me. I've never seen him high before, but I can't wait to experience it firsthand. After a few more moments, Logan meets Salem's gaze and takes the mushroom, not breaking eye contact while he swallows. A slow, dangerous smile spreads on her face, like a cat who just caught a mouse.

Yikes.

"Best of luck, buddy." I pat his arm with a snicker before scooting my chair closer to Huck, wanting to watch his eyes to catch the exact moment the trip hits.

Everyone bullshits around us for a while, but my focus is on him. The way his lashes fall over his cheekbones when he blinks, that husky tone to his voice when he laughs at something Matty says, the shadow of his jawline against the fire glow. When he notices my staring, he turns and raises his brows, amusement dancing across his features.

"What?"

*You're beautiful.*

"Nothing," I reply instead, resting my cheek in my palm. "Just waiting for you to freak out."

His eyes drop down to where my teeth sink into my bottom lip. "Why would I freak out? I've done this before, remember?"

"With caps?"

"No," he frowns. "What's the difference?"

"Oooh, boy," Matt laughs, shaking his head. "You're in for a wild night, man."

Logan's eyes jump around nervously. "What, why?"

Xed rolls his eyes. "There's a mass theory that the shroom caps are more potent than the stems, but it's all bullshit, in my opinion. It's all the same."

"Agree to disagree." Christian pulls Arya onto his lap. "Stems just make me chill. Caps make me contemplate life and the existence of outer space and shit."

"It's all in your head, dude."

Salem puts a hand on Logan's erratically bouncing knee. "Don't get anxious. You'll have a bad trip if you're anxious."

"I'm not," he says quickly, glancing down at where she's touching him, and Arya giggles.

"I have an idea," she announces, shooting a glare at Xed and me as we groan simultaneously. "Who wants to make this night even more fun?"

"We are *not* having an orgy, Arya," Xed grumbles, scrubbing his face. "Not everyone wants to see you naked."

Christian grins widely, nuzzling his face into his girlfriend's neck. "Well, they should. I love showing her off."

"That's not what I meant," she protests, and I scoff as I lean back in my seat.

"Been there, done that. Literally. Hard pass."

There's a brief silence while everyone gapes at me before Arya jumps angrily off Christian's lap. "You guys are such fucking dicks!"

She hops the log fence and makes for the trees, disappearing into the dark before anyone can stop her.

Salem throws me a deadly look as she takes off, too. "Nice going, asshole."

"Hey! Salem, get back here," Xed shouts as Christian shakes his head at me and rises from his seat as well.

"Not cool, Tay."

*Ah, fuck.*

He goes after the girls, and just when I think things can't get any worse, Matty hops to his feet and runs in the complete opposite direction as everyone else.

"Every man for himself," he hollers, laughing maniacally when I call after him to stay put. "Catch me if you can, fuckers!"

"Goddammit." Xed sprints after him in a heartbeat, barely tossing me a glance.

Before I know it, I'm alone with Huck and Logan, both gazing at me wide-eyed. One look at their pupils tells me the shrooms have started to hit.

Fucking great.

"You two stay here," I growl firmly, heading toward where Christian, Salem, and Arya disappeared. "I mean it. Hold hands, sit on each other's laps, whatever you gotta do to stay in your damn seats. Do not go anywhere, or I swear to fuck, you'll be sorry."

Neither of them responds, and the way Logan's lid twitches gives me bad vibes, but I have three dumbasses to wrangle, so I can only hope that the two of them can hang on for the ride until I get back.

Because it's going to be a long fucking night.

# TAYLOR

"**I**f I get eaten by a cougar because of you asshats, I'm gonna be *so* pissed."

Using the flashlight on my phone, I sweep the beam over the trees, searching for signs of anyone. A breeze has picked up, sending a shiver down my spine, the sound of my feet treading dirt unusually loud. The crackle of the fire fades in the distance as I walk farther away, calling out names, straining to hear over the rustle of trees.

No one answers back.

Of course, because why would they make this easy?

"Come on, guys, I'm sorry. I'm an ass with no filter. Arya can punch me in the face."

Still, only silence answers back. A prickling sensation on the back of my scalp has me turning around, twigs snapping somewhere in the dark, and my stomach knots uneasily as I walk toward the sound. It takes me even further from Huck and Logan than I intended.

Usually, I love being in the woods at night, but something about how the full moon casts shadows through the canopy of leaves above gives me the creeps. Any minute now, I'm expecting to find a serial killer in a hockey mask jumping out at me. Another twig snaps, followed by the scrape of something against a tree trunk to my left, and I can't help the undignified yelp that comes out of me.

"Christian, Salem, cut it out!"

A soft laugh in my ear takes me by surprise, and I whip around with a very unmanly scream before losing my balance. Hands try to keep me steady, but I only end up pulling whoever it is down on top of me, the air leaving my lungs when my back connects with the dirt.

"Oh, shit." a familiar voice grunts next to my face. "My bad."

"Goddammit, Huckslee." Catching my breath for a second, I roll us over, pinning him beneath me while I straddle his hips. "I told you to wait at camp, motherfucker."

He smiles broadly, his hands coming up to cup my face. "I tried."

"You tried? For all of five seconds?"

"But then I had to piss, and I feel so good, Tay. I pissed on a patch of flowers, and they were dancing like they enjoyed it."

"You're trippin'," I laugh, rubbing my palms over his chest and stomach. "Go back to Logan, baby. You left him alone."

"Mm." He pulls me down, nuzzling his cheek against mine. "I love it when you call me baby. I saw your light out here and had to follow because I'm a satellite."

"A satellite, huh?"

He nods, wrapping his arms around me. "Yeah, and I fell out of orbit. Can't have me doing that. So I came to you because that's where we belong. In each other's gravity."

A warmth spreads throughout my limbs at his words. I should try to get up. Really should. But laying on him like this feels too damn good. "If you're a satellite, am I your moon?"

"We're just floating through space, getting closer and closer to the sun until we burn."

My warmth turns ice cold. "Lucky for us, the sun is pretty far off. Huck, you need to go back to camp. Logan's probably freaking the hell out right now."

"Let's fuck, Tay, right here," he whispers, thrusting his hips up into me for good measure, and a laugh bursts out of me because he's not even hard.

"You wouldn't fuck me in a bathroom, but you'll do it on the forest floor? You animal."

A hum leaves his lips as he starts singing some song about doing it like mammals.

"The fuck is that?"

"Bloodhound Gang. You really need to expand your music tastes."

Extracting myself from his arms, I lean on my elbows as I squint down at him. "Listening to Post Malone is enough expansion for me."

"He's just so sweet and talented," Huck sighs, and I can't hold back anymore. Don't even know why I tried in the first place.

With a chuckle, I softly place my mouth against his. "You gonna leave me for Posty, baby?"

Something like a purr rumbles out of his throat at the sensation of our lips brushing together, my head slowly moving from side to side. It probably feels fantastic to him right now. Shrooms aren't as potent as psychedelics like ecstasy, but they still enhance your senses. He opens for me, and I slip my tongue inside, groaning as his cock starts to thicken against my ass. God, I've been needing this all day. All week. All my life.

But goddammit. Logan. And everyone else. I'm a terrible babysitter.

"We gotta get up," I murmur in between kisses, rubbing the crease of my crack against him. "I'm supposed to make sure no one wanders into a cave, and you're distracting me."

"Please don't go." His arms crush me against his chest. "I've grown roots, and I can't move. Don't want to be here alone."

"Huckslee, come on." Yet I'm still moving on top of him, my own dick straining against my sweats.

"The forest has claimed me, my love. Let me be a tree. Or a weed."

*My love.* Fucking hell.

"How about a sunflower." I bite along his neck as his nails graze my back. "Like that Posty song you like."

Bringing my lips back to his, I kiss him deep, scooting down lower so that our cocks are rubbing against each other. My fingers tangle in his curls, his hands touching me everywhere while he moans into my mouth, and I'm about to tell him to hush when Christian's barking laugh breaks through the lust clouding my brain.

"Hell yeah, get it, *cariño!*"

I snap my head up to yell at him, but my eyes find who he's standing next to in the dark, and I freeze.

"Shit." Wriggling out of Huck's hold, I try to lift off of him, but his grip is tight. "Hey, let me go. We need to get up." I can feel eyes on my face, which has now turned several shades of bright ass red. Thankfully, it's dark, so I'm sure they can't see it because being caught dry-humping my stepbrother with my tongue down his throat is compromising enough.

Gripping Huck's shoulders, I try to stand when he lets out a painful yelp.

"No, Taylor!" Real fear flashes in his eyes as he fights me. "If you rip me from the ground, I'll bleed out."

*Jesus.*

"Hey, it's okay." Cupping his face in my palms, I search his erratic gaze, hot breaths coming quick from his heaving chest. His trip is starting to turn. "You're alright, baby. I won't let that happen. You can stay here."

Footsteps draw closer, Xed's combat boots coming into my line of sight.

"I've got him," he says gently, Christian tied to his wrist by a belt. "You go get Arya. She's up a tree, and I ain't climbing that shit."

"Don't let me bleed out, Tay," Huck whispers hoarsely, clawing at my arms, and for a second, all I can do is gaze down at him, momentarily unsettled, throat working to swallow as memories from four years ago flash before me.

"I didn't. I won't. Xed's gonna keep you planted, okay? I gotta go."

He brushes my lips with his fingers. "You'll come back for me?"

"Always."

Not caring about being seen anymore, I lean over to kiss him before tugging his shirt down, covering his hard-on. Since I'm still shirtless, I have nothing to hide my own, so I just awkwardly cover my junk with my hands when I stand.

"She's over there." Xed jerks his thumb in Arya's direction, a calculating spark in his eyes as he studies me. "I put the others in the tent and turned on a light show with my phone. They'll be occupied for a while."

"Alright." Clearing my throat, I hesitate before turning away. I really don't want to leave Huck like this, but I don't have a choice right now.

When I'm a few steps away, Xed calls my name, drawing my attention back.

"I'll take care of him," he promises, holding my gaze as Christian tugs him down next to Huck.

"I know you will."

Adjusting my deflating dick, I make my way over to the tree he pointed out and stand below it with my arms crossed. A shadow moves on the branches above.

"Arya, get down here. Now."

There's a rustle of leaves before she fucking caws at me like a damned crow or some shit, and something hard bounces off the side of my face.

"Ouch! Did you just throw an acorn at me?"

She giggles, scrambling further up the tree, and I curse under my breath as I jump up to grab onto the lowest branch, pulling myself up and over. I haven't climbed a tree in years, but it doesn't take long before I'm closing in on where she's perched, her face turned upwards. The hem of my sweatpants snags, ripping the leg, and when I growl in frustration, she lets out a screamed cackle as she turns and tries to get higher.

"Oh, no, you don't."

Wrapping my arms around her waist, I yank her down against my chest. We fall against the trunk when she struggles, laughing like this is a damn game, and then she gasps with a finger pointed up above.

"Look, Tay Bae! Look at that!"

Following her finger, I let out an exasperated sigh. "Yes, I've seen the sky before. Fascinating. Will you get down?"

"I wish I were up there," she responds dreamily, both arms lifted above her head as she smiles and relaxes in my hold.

"In the sky? Or space?"

"Wherever isn't here."

The way she says that makes me pause.

"What—" Exhaling sharply, I let my head fall back against the tree. "What do you mean by that? Goddammit, Arya, I want to get back to my...Huckslee."

*Boyfriend* almost falls from my lips, but something holds me back.

She hums, going limp in my arms until I'm forced to slide into a crouched position. "I was watching you two, you know."

Shit. "That's not creepy at all."

"I wish I had that." Her fingers lace through mine as she settles in between my legs on the broad branch. Normally, I'd be shaking her off, but the melancholy in her tone is setting off alarms.

"Had what?"

"Love."

My mouth falls open and shuts, momentarily at a loss for words. I'm still antsy from leaving Huck, but his laugh carries over the breeze, telling me he's fine, so I lean back against the trunk and get comfortable, tightening my arms around her.

"You've only been with Christian a few weeks. Love doesn't grow on trees."

Is that how the saying goes?

Her head rolls to the side, cold cheek pressed against my shoulder. In the dim light of the moon, tears glisten on her face. "He loves what my body can do for him, but I don't think he'll ever love *me*. As a person. No one ever does."

Fuck. I am such an asshole.

"That's not true," I say firmly, thumbing away the tears. "Salem loves you. Owen loves you. And trust me, Christian wouldn't be spending all his time with you if he didn't care about you."

"But you don't like me." She pokes my peck, sniffling. "And I don't even know what I did to make you hate me. Or Xed."

It's official. I am worse than scum.

"I don't hate you, Arya. I..." What am I supposed to say here? The truth? "I can't say I particularly like you, but I guess I don't really know you all that well, either."

Which is a super messed up thing to say to someone you've fucked more than once.

Her lips shake with a tremble. "Because you've never tried. I just wanted to be part of the group."

Gum on the bottom of a shoe. Dirt underneath fingernails. Weeks-old rancid bacon grease. That's how I feel right now.

"You're right. I never did, and I'm sorry." The side of me that wants to problem solve kicks into gear, cogs turning in

493

my mind for ways to make this better. "Tell you what, I'll stop ragging on you all the time if you stop calling me Tay Bae. Deal?"

I'll also make an effort to include her more. As Christian's girlfriend and Salem's best gal pal, she really deserves nothing less, and I should have realized that sooner.

A bright smile forms on her lips. "Deal. Is Taytay still okay?"

"I'll allow it."

She giggles that high-pitched screech, and honest to God, I try not to cringe. I really do. I'll try to work on it. Baby steps.

We sit up there a bit longer while I ask her questions, like what she's getting her degree in (cosmetology) and her favorite food (pad thai). It's a mediocre attempt, at best, but I'm trying. Her fingers dance above our heads the whole time like she's playing with the stars. Since she's tripping, she probably thinks she is. We slowly make our way down when I've calmed her down enough to leave our little tree spot. The hem of my pants catches again on the lowest branch, and I slip with her in my hold, causing her to knee my nuts when she lands on top of me.

"You deserved it," she cackles while I wheeze, hopping off to run toward Christian, and I can't disagree.

By the time we all trudge back to the campsite, Huckslee's finally free of his dirt bed, and everyone's starting to come down. The fire is practically out, but we pour water on it just in case. When I unzip the tent, I find Matty and Logan lying side by side in a pile of blankets, Salem on the farther side against the wall, while Xed's phone flashes lights and colors on the ceiling.

"This shit was bunk," Salem grumbles, glaring at us when we start to pile in. "I didn't feel anything."

Matty agrees. "Same."

"Ditto." Christian unzips his own tent and pulls Arya inside while I snicker, kicking off my shoes.

"Tell that to Huckslee. He turned into a plant."

Logan groans, covering his face. "All I did was puke. I'm never doing this again."

Huck laughs, falling beside his best friend while I crawl next to him. Behind me, Xed squeezes in, shutting off his phone to cover us in darkness. The rain-fly is off, stars shining through, giving just enough light for me to see Huck's bright gaze as we face each other. Under the blanket, his fingers find mine, and I smile, closing my eyes.

After a long while, when I think everyone's asleep, Xed's arm snakes around me, pulling my back to his chest.

"Is this you apologizing for shoving me earlier?" I murmur, cracking open a lid to find Huck watching us curiously.

A grunt is my only response; Salem throws her leg over him, and Matt shoots into a seated position.

"Huckslee, switch me," he says quickly. "Please."

"No. And why?"

With a snort, I answer for him. "Matty wants to snuggle, too."

"Please?"

Huck's palm tightens around mine. "You are the weirdest group of friends."

"Nothing weird about platonic cuddling." Xed's forehead presses into my back. "Society just says there is."

"Please, Huck?" Matt continues to whine, and Logan sighs heavily.

"Just throw an arm over me, and let's go to bed. My head hurts."

Matt seems to deliberate for several seconds before he lays back down, doing as he's told, and a grin pulls at my cheeks.

Finally, it seems like we're all going to get some sleep.

Until the sounds of Christian and Arya fucking in their tent cut through the silence.

Every single person, including myself, groans simultaneously.

"You've got to be kidding me."

"Really, guys, come on!"

"First one to get a boner loses," I snicker, and Salem reaches over to smack my arm.

"I have an unfair advantage!"

"So does Huckslee," Logan yawns sleepily. "Unless, like, he thinks Christian's moans are sexy or something."

Huck looks absolutely offended at that, and I burst into laughter, mouthing '*you better not*,' earning a death glare in response.

Admittedly, cuddling gets a little awkward for the next fifteen minutes or so until the finale, and when they both finally finish, I begin to clap loudly.

"Stunning performance. Ten out of ten. Can we go the fuck to sleep now?"

"Fuck off, asshole."

I fall asleep with a grin, my fingers entwined with Huck's, surrounded by the only family I've ever wanted or needed.

# HUCKSLEE

A six-mile hike after a night of tripping was not high on my list of fun things to try before the sun is up, but apparently, Taylor and his friends are a bunch of masochists—and sadists.

Seriously, who hikes an uphill trail for fun every single year? I'm a trained athlete, and even I'm struggling. Matt, too, dirt crunching under us as we pass beneath the trees and over hills, crisp Colorado air filling my lungs.

"Keep up, bitches!" Salem laughs as we all huff and puff at least twenty steps behind her and Christian. Taylor's been trying to hang back for my sake, but I can tell he's getting frustrated. The only good thing about this hike so far is that I've spent the last few hours staring at his luscious ass in those tight joggers, imagining all the ways I'm going to fuck it. Secretly, I think he's been positioning himself in front of me on purpose because he knows how much I like to watch him walk.

It's making me sweat, and not because of the temperature today. Though honestly, it's also hot as hell outside.

He turns around, walking backward to whine at us for the tenth time in the last half hour. "Come on, guys. And girl. At this pace, it'll take us until nightfall to reach Ouzel Falls."

"How long does it usually take you guys?" Logan asks in between breaths, pausing to dump some water over himself. We've passed a few bodies of water, and he's dunked his head into them every time. I'm tempted to do that myself the next one we get to.

"Usually three hours," Christian calls back. "But we've stopped so many times that it'll likely take us six."

All of us complain. This is torture. Arya sags against Xed, who looks too tired to push her off as she cries for him to carry her.

Pumping my screaming legs forward, I catch up to Taylor. "How can you do this every year when you don't even go to the gym?"

"Who says I don't?"

I lift a brow at him because really?

He throws me an equally incredulous glance. "Do you know how heavy a dirt bike is, Huck? How much stamina is needed to throw that thing around? Guarantee my core strength is ten times stronger than yours."

"Yeah? You wanna test this theory?"

"No need," he grins, flashing his crooked incisor before speeding up. "I'm not the one falling behind!"

Dammit. He has a point.

Coming to a halt, I rest my palms on my knees and breathe. Admittedly, I've been slacking a bit in my training regimen, but this is embarrassing. Xed stops beside me, letting Matty, Arya, and Logan get ahead of us. When I finally straighten, his light brown eyes meet my dark ones.

"So, you and Taylor, huh?"

Right. And there's that. He caught us making out last night.

"So, you and Matt, huh?" I counter, narrowing my gaze. I've never brought up what I saw that night at the Prospector, but if he wants to go there, we'll go there.

He shrugs a leather-clad shoulder before glancing away, sweat dripping from his brow. I don't know how he always wears that jacket, especially in this heat.

"Not anymore." Swallowing hard, Xed keeps his voice low as he stares at the ground. "He wants to try and work on things with Valerie, even though it's never worked before. Guess he thinks he owes it to Hannah to have her mother in her life. I'm not enough."

"That's..." I trail off momentarily, glancing at Matty's broad back, unsure what to say. Being a father is something I have no experience in, nor do I think I ever will. But still. Something about the situation feels so wrong. "I know I haven't been around long, but from what I can see and what Taylor's told me, you've practically been another parent to Hannah. She's lucky to have you."

"For now. I'm really going to miss her. Miss him. It's not fair." Xed's eyes are also on Matt, shining under the midday sun with unshed tears, and I clear my throat against a swell of emotion.

"This probably doesn't make it any better, but Taylor might be in the same boat as you come August. I don't know if this is just a summer fling or not."

That surprises him, his brows rising. "And does he know that? How long have you two been a thing?"

"It's...complicated." My attention shifts forward when Arya shrieks in delight, Taylor tossing her over his shoulder as he laughs. Seeing them get along is new. "Our history goes back to the eighth grade, with bits and pieces in high school. We didn't officially start anything until a month ago. There's a lot of shit between us that we're still working out. And you know how Taylor is, how much he needs to touch and be touched. I don't think forcing him into a long-distance relationship is fair, but I can't ask him to wait."

"Is it forced, though, if he agrees to it?"

Sighing wearily, I shake my head. "I don't know. It feels like it is. He already waited so long for me to pull my head out of my ass while I was in California, and this just feels like going backwards. Relationships are supposed to move forward."

"You're going into the NFL, and he's working on his motocross career," Xed scoffs. "That's the definition of moving forward."

Yeah. It is. I'm just worried we won't be able to do it together. Because even though we're new to this, I've come to understand that Taylor needs someone he can feel in his life. And no matter how you slice it, loving someone from a distance goes against his human nature. Even if he had spent the last four years wanting me, he hadn't spent them alone and single. I'd never ask that of him. He can't even go for a week without showing up to drag me out the front door, aching for contact, and who am I kidding? Neither can I. We crave each other. Two thousand miles of distance between us will make seeing each other every weekend impossible. In the back of my head, I can hear the clock counting down as our time slowly runs out.

*Tick, tick, tick.*

Xed and I fall silent as we try to catch up, lost in our own thoughts. When we return to the group, everyone is standing on the side of the trail, watching a small waterfall cascade down the mountain into a clear lake. It's not the one we're trying to hike to, but this entire trailhead is littered with smaller falls and rushing rapids. Taylor shoots me a questioning look when I step up beside him, but I just flash a soft smile and brush my hand against his, wishing I had the guts to claim him in front of Logan, who's currently barreling toward the lake like he's on fire.

"Jesus, slow down," I holler, laughing as he strips off his shirt and dunks his head into the water.

"I could go for a swim myself, it's hot as fuck." Matt begins to undress when Christian slaps him in the chest, halting him.

"How about a cliff dive?" He points up to the top of the waterfall. "Should be an easy climb. Not too high, and the water looks deep enough, yeah?"

Taylor bounces up and down, ever the adrenaline junkie. "Hell yeah, let's do it!"

Xed sits down near a tree, crossing his legs as he pulls out his pipe. "I'm good, I'll watch the packs. You kids have fun."

"We're the same age, you goofy fuck."

The rest of us spend the next twenty minutes clambering up the small cliff, my muscles screaming at me for help. Once up to the top, I take a minute to admire the beauty of the Colorado wilderness, lush green trees, and clear blue skies. All of us strip down to our underwear, even the girls. I try to keep my eyes off Taylor, but he looks so damn good in his red boxer briefs, dick perfectly imprinted in the crotch. He catches me ogling and winks, wiggling that ass like he's asking me to smack it, which I almost do.

At the last minute, Salem whips off her sports bra and jumps topless, cackling at the shocked look on everyone's faces. Arya follows suit, tits bouncing as she runs to the edge, Christian and Matt cheering after her when she careens down to the lake below. Logan's got a dopey smile on his face, and I pat his cheek before taking off, too. My stomach leaps into my throat when the ground leaves my feet, my body spinning through the air for far too short a time until it smacks into freezing water.

When I come up for air, there are two more splashes, Christian and Matt surfacing next to me with choked laughs and curses at the tepid temperature. Logan follows soon after, and I watch for my stepbrother to make his jump. Of course, in true Taylor fashion, he leaps off the cliff completely nude, cock and balls fucking flapping in the wind while his friends hoot and holler. He hits the water just as Logan covers his eyes, screaming.

"You're such a dumbass," I shout when he comes up, shaking hair out of his eyes with a grin.

"Now everyone here has seen my junk! You're welcome!"

"I could have gone my entire life without that image, thank you." Logan swims over to the shoreline to pull himself out, teeth chattering, while the rest of us swim around to get used to the water. Knowing he's naked under the surface has me swimming close to Taylor, wanting to cop a feel.

Christian moves to the shallow side of the lake, pulling Arya onto his shoulders as he stands. "Topless chicken! Matty, put Salem on your shoulders. Xed, keep an eye out for people."

Making sure Logan's back is turned, I tread over to Taylor and lightly brush my fingers over his ass, making him shiver. His eyes reflect dark green against the water as he peeks up at me beneath his dark, dripping strands, a sensual smile curling his lips. Feeling a little bold, I reach down again to grip one of his cheeks in my palm and squeeze, causing him to squeak in surprise, my dick immediately going rigid when I touch something in between his crease.

Yanking his back to my chest, I place my lips next to his ear as I grind my hard cock against him. "Did I just feel what I think I felt?"

"Yep." He grins sheepishly over his shoulder, pushing his ass back against me, and I curse roughly under my breath.

While everyone is distracted with the show Arya and Salem are putting on, I grab Taylor's wrist and pull him away toward the waterfall, needing to get my hands on him before I implode. The cascading torrent is surprisingly warm when we slip beneath it, albeit loud, and behind it, we're greeted by a small alcove in the cliffside, just big enough to give us some privacy.

Spinning around so that my shoulder rests against the rough, moss-covered stone, I wrap my arms around him and claim his mouth in a sweltering, consuming kiss. There's enough of a ledge jutting out underneath for me to stand on.

"How long have you been wearing the plug?"

"Since yesterday," he moans against my mouth, wrapping long legs around my waist. "Took it out for a few hours this morning, but I wanted to be ready for you."

"Fucking hell, Taylor." Licking along the dragonfly tattoo on his throat, my fingers trace down his sternum, barely touching the tip of his hard dick before I bring them around to his ass. The plug sits firm in his hole, and I put pressure on it, causing Taylor to groan as he bucks his hips, fingers tangling in my damp curls, thighs tightening.

"I need you so bad, Huck."

Twisting the plug around inside him, my free hand moves to wrap around his cock. He clings to me, whimpering as I work him, teeth sunk into that plump bottom lip. Reaching between us, he pulls out my own length underneath the water, and for a moment, we gaze at one another while we stroke each other slowly. He's so beautiful it breaks my damn heart.

"Huck, please." His plea is a soft whisper on my lips, thick with need. "I want you. Right here."

My gaze flicks over his shoulder, beyond the falls, where I can barely make out everyone still engaged in their game. Between the rippling water and darkness of the alcove, I know it's too dark for anyone to witness what we're doing. "This is probably not the most sanitary place."

Taylor chuckles against my neck, biting hard enough to elicit a hiss. "Don't care. It's romantic as fuck."

"Relax for me," I murmur after a snort, kissing along the wet skin of his jaw while I slowly begin to remove the plug. He moans into my shoulder the entire time, body vibrating from the force of keeping still. Once it's out, I tuck it inside the waistband of my underwear so as not to lose it before replacing it with my fingers. Two of them sink inside his slick hole easily, and we both groan in unison as my teeth find his earlobe.

"Someone's been a good boy."

Gently, I insert a third finger, the whimpers clawing out of his throat so fucking sweet, his fist still pumping me while I finger his ass. When he's nice and prepped, I lift him slightly so that my cock hovers over his entrance, my muscles screaming, but I don't really give a shit at the moment.

"Water makes terrible lube." Pausing to give him a warning, our lips find each other again. "If it gets to be too much, tell me. We can stop."

He shakes his head, holding my gaze intently. "It won't, I used silicone-based stuff. Please, baby, I've been dying for this."

God, I love hearing him beg.

Positioning my tip against his hole, I tell him to exhale deeply and bare down while I slowly push myself inside. Sparks ignite behind my eyes at how good he feels, so fucking warm and tight. The plug helped, but I'm still met with a bit of resistance, and I freeze when Taylor cries out.

"Doing ok?"

"Yeah, just..." His arms tighten around me as he buries his face in my neck. "Just give me a minute."

So I do. The urge to thrust into him is so strong that it takes everything I have to remain still while I rub circles around his lower back. His cock has started to soften, so I use my free hand to stroke it softly, feeling his breaths brush my collarbone. Beyond the waterfall, I can tell that no one is in the lake any longer, and they're probably wondering where we went, but I won't rush this. He deserves better than that.

Lifting his head, Taylor captures my mouth in a deep, heated kiss. "Ok. I'm good."

"Sure?"

"Y-yeah. Move. Please."

"So polite." My chuckle breaks off into a moan when he clenches around me, and I shoot a glare at his smirking face. Pushing in a little more, my hips rest against his ass as I seat myself fully inside him, the angle nudging his prostate enough that his length jerks to full attention.

"Mhmfuuck." His lids sink closed when I grip his hips to lift him up before bringing him back down, gently fucking into him so that he gets used to the feeling. Every muscle in my body is wound tight as a bowstring, the feeling of him on my cock unlike anything I've ever experienced. I want to pound into him, own him, make him feel what no other man ever could.

"More," he whimpers, planting his feet on either side of my hips against the cliff wall. "I need more."

"You feel so good, Tay." My speed picks up, water sloshing as I begin to fuck him faster. "God, you're taking me so well."

Our little alcove fills with the sounds of pants, moans, and grunts. His eyes roll into the back of his head every time I peg his prostate, slamming into him with just enough force that his moans grow louder. My name falls from his lips along with a string of garbled words I can't make out when his nails bite into my shoulders, the pain so pleasurable it nearly sends me over the edge. Using his stance on the mossy wall for leverage, he lifts himself up and down, meeting my pace beautifully.

"That's it. Help me fuck you, make yourself feel good."

"Huck, I can't..." His teeth are biting his bottom lip so hard I see indents. "C-can't last. Gonna come."

Wrapping my fingers around his shaft, I jerk him hard while continuing to pound into him. "Come for me, baby. Come on my cock so I can fill you up."

That's all it takes. His hole clenches around me, and he cries out, echoing in my ears, dick twitching his orgasm against my palm in the water. I thrust deep one last time before my own climax overtakes me, spilling hot cum inside his ass, marking him forever as mine. My vision turns white from the exertion of it, blissful static momentarily filling my ears when Taylor breathes a contented sigh, dropping his forehead to my shoulder while I thrust through my orgasm, slowly coming to a stop before slumping back against the wall. Our chests heave against each other.

"Holy shit," he hums after a few minutes, voice hoarse. "That was..."

"Amazing?" I kiss his damp strands, a sated smile pulling at my lips. "Earth shattering? Mind-blowing?"

He lifts his head, cracking open one eye to squint at me. "Those are my lines. What have you done with my Huckslee?"

"I think he got lost somewhere in your ass." Flexing my softening dick, which is still inside of him, a chuckle leaves my throat when he whimpers. "Fuck, I never wanna leave. You're incredible."

Those gorgeous eyes roll, but a satisfied smirk pulls at his mouth.

"I'm serious. I think you ruined me. I'm gonna need you stuffed with my cock daily from now on."

"Jesus," he coughs, a faint flush on his cheeks as he squirms, and my hands fly to his hips to hold him in place when my dick jolts at the movement.

"Unless you're ready for round two, which you're not, I'd stop moving if I were you."

A challenge flashes across his features, but just as the damn brat rolls his hips, Salem's voice has us both freezing.

"Alright, coming in! My eyes are closed!"

We turn to watch her tread underneath the waterfall, bright red hair catching in the sun as her hands cover her eyes, causing Taylor to bark out a laugh.

"Hey guys, Christian and I stalled for as long as we can," she says, parting her fingers to peek at us. "Xed already climbed up to get our clothes, and everyone's waiting. Logan's getting concerned."

"Shit. What'd you tell him?"

She smirks. "That you both needed some brotherly bonding time."

"Be gone, she-devil!" Taylor smacks the water to splash her, and she dives away, tossing a *hurry up* over her shoulder as she leaves the alcove.

"They're not exactly making it any easier for me to tell him about us," I mutter, dropping my head to his shoulder, and he hums in agreement.

"Yeah...speaking of, when do you plan on doing that, by the way? Because everyone knows now except Matty and Logan."

The idea of telling my best friend that I'm dating my stepbrother raises a panic in my throat, and I exhale slowly.

"Soon."

That's all I can say. Because I really do plan on telling him...I just don't know how or when.

Pulling out of him slowly, my fingers replace my dick, a soft gasp leaving his lips as I gently prod his hole, wishing I could see the mess leaking out of him. "If I wasn't worried about trapping lake water inside of you, I'd put the plug back in and make you walk around full of my cum all day."

"Fuuuck." He snags my bottom lip in between his teeth. "You're gonna make me horny again, and I'm naked."

"Like nearly everyone here hasn't seen your boner before." Drawing back to cup his cheek, I search his eyes. "Was it good for you? Did you like it?"

His expression softens as he steals a light, sweet kiss. "I didn't like it, I *loved* it. I'm dickmatized. One hundred percent can confirm I'm switching teams. Don't think I've ever come so hard in my life."

"Good, because you're mine, and I fully plan on fucking you again."

Taylor laughs, shaking his head as he turns away to swim toward the waterfall. "This is the third time we've fooled around in water, you know. I think it's becoming our thing."

That comment has me going still.

Images from the pool in high school flood my brain, the way he held me under, stealing me of oxygen before breathing it back into me with his kisses. How, at first, I fought before letting go in more ways than one. That night symbolized so many things for me. It was the pivotal moment I'd decided to stop holding back, to acknowledge my feelings for him and give up control. The first time in years that I actually felt free. But then the morning after...waking up to Taylor in my bed...

I have so many regrets. There were about a hundred different ways I could have handled that situation. Part of me wonders if I'd given him the grace he deserved to figure things out in his head, maybe he wouldn't have stolen my car, and maybe his dad wouldn't have put him in the hospital. Hindsight's a bitch.

For the last four years, I've done my damndest not to think about the pool, him, or anything that transpired between us because of how my lungs would seize and my chest would burn. It used to fill me with anger and hate. Now? All I feel is a deep sadness and shame, wishing I could turn back time. Wishing I could have loved him sooner. Because it feels like all I'll get is months when I could have had years.

*Tick, tick, tick.*

"Huck?"

My attention snaps to where he's watching me with uncertainty, eyes half hidden under his lashes as if he senses the sudden shift in my mood. And I want to take it away, all of it. Every negative emotion that ever came between us, every bruise and every scar. All of his guilt, all of mine. If I could, I'd crawl inside his brain and change the story, perhaps make it one where our friendship morphed naturally into love over time instead of the twisted monster it became.

Water laps against my chest as he paddles over, wrapping his arms around my waist. "Don't let them win."

"Hm?" My brows furrow tightly as he presses a wet thumb between them.

"The bad thoughts. Don't let them win. I'm here now. *We're* here. How we got to this point doesn't matter. Delaware, remember?"

Taking my hand, he lays my palm on the tattoo over his heart before pressing his lips to mine. And just like that, everything...calms. The gentle yet firm way he's holding me is enough to still the chaos, anchoring me to this moment. I let his soft kisses ground me, losing myself in his fingers, tracing my spine. Xed's holler is what eventually has us pulling apart.

"Ready?" Taylor gives me a reassuring smile, and I nod reluctantly.

"Yeah." *No. I don't want this to end.* "Let's go." *Let's stay and never leave this cave.* Alcove. Whatever.

Something settles over me that I can't quite place as we swim beneath the waterfall and tread toward shore, a melancholic weight pressing on my chest. It isn't until I'm pulling myself up onto the bank that I remember Taylor is naked. And there's a butt plug tucked into the hem of my underwear.

Logan's eyes narrow as I pull on my clothes, but I avoid his glare. A storm of emotions flashes across his face—disbelief, then incredulity—and I silently curse myself. Disappearing with a naked Taylor for over half an hour wasn't exactly subtle. Even Matt's eyes dart between us, his lips pursed, the silence hanging thick and heavy.

Once Taylor is fully clothed, he clears his throat, running a hand through his hair. "I'm kinda beat. Think I'm gonna head back to camp and take a nap."

Salem snickers with Arya, and Christian slaps a hand across his back.

"I bet, bud. You just got a good workout in."

Fucking hell.

"Seriously, big mouth?" Xed shoves him in the shoulder while Matt's eyes widen to saucers, and Logan turns away before I can judge what else he's thinking.

Taylor stays uncharacteristically silent, his teeth worrying his bottom lip. He glances at me briefly, grabbing his pack from Xed before taking off downhill the way we came. The sight of him walking away raises my hackles worse than Logan knowing about us, and I find myself heading after him without so much as a goodbye to the group.

"Taylor, wait. I'm coming with you."

He stops in his tracks, throwing me a guarded look over his shoulder. "What about Logan?"

"What do you mean?"

"You can't ditch your best friend for me, Huckslee."

Rearing back, my mouth opens to refute that ridiculous statement when Salem scoffs loudly behind me.

"He's a big boy, he'll be fine." She tugs Logan into her side, throwing an arm around him. "Won't you?"

He blinks down at her for several seconds. "Y-yeah. Sure."

"See? You two run along. I expect dinner to be ready for us by the time we return."

Taylor rolls his eyes before continuing downhill. "Yes, Mommy."

Salem turns Logan around as she mouths something like *you owe me* and I flash her a thankful smile before taking off after Taylor.

"You didn't have to come with me, you know," he says, taking my hand.

"Yes, I did. This is probably the only time we'll be alone this weekend, and you also wore me out. I want to nap with my boyfriend somewhere other than the bed of his truck for once."

A bright grin spreads across his face. "Boyfriend, huh?"

"Yep. I'm yours, and you're mine, remember?"

He's quiet momentarily, focusing on the dirt path ahead of us. "And Logan? What's going to happen now that he knows?"

"Good question."

Would he judge? Be disgusted with our relationship? Kick me out of his apartment? Would I have to move back in with my dad and Maisie until the end of July? A tendril of panic swells in my throat, but it disappears when Taylor squeezes my hand.

"Whatever happens, we'll face it together," he states firmly, holding my gaze, and I swear the sun shines a little brighter inside his smile.

"Yeah. Together."

Everything about this feels so right. Our palms fit perfectly together, his steady voice a comforting hum as we head back to camp, pausing periodically to make out against tree trunks. When we finally collapse into our tent, too exhausted for anything but sleep, his body fits mine like a puzzle piece I didn't know was missing.

It's perfect.

He's perfect.

*Tick, tick, tick.*

I just wish we had more time.

The rest of the trip flies by awkwardly, but not because of anyone else.

Because of Logan.

He only speaks to me for the remaining two days of our little vacation if he absolutely has to. It might have been worse, but Salem is a certified saint and keeps him occupied so that no one notices except us and Taylor. She even opts to sleep next to him in our cuddle pile, and for that, I could honestly marry her. Platonically, of course. Pretty sure platonic marriages are a thing.

Like I predicted, Taylor and I hardly get time to ourselves, and Matthew has about a bazillion questions to ask us. Like when did we realize we were into each other? (Nearly a decade ago, technically.) Have we told our parents? (No and never, ever, probably.) How long has Taylor been into men? (That one was fun to watch him answer; his bright red face and explanation that he's only into me were cute as hell.) At one point, Xed and Taylor disappear on a long walk together to discuss things, but when they return, I can't tell if he knows about them or not.

Eventually, we pack up camp and load everything into the vehicles to return home. This time, Taylor gives Logan the front seat, opting to sit between Xed and me so that we can hold hands. Xed shakes his head and rolls his eyes at the sight, but Taylor simply flips him off with a smirk, and I admit it feels good to finally be out in the open with our relationship.

As fleeting as it might be.

Logan barely utters a word the entire trip, his phone blasting country music too loud for anyone to hear each other speak. Two hours into the ride, Taylor finally has enough and leans forward to switch on some alternative rock station, muttering something like *better than that twangy shit* under his breath. I know that Logan's pissed because his ears turn red, but still he says nothing.

The closer we get to home, the more my apprehension spikes. After a few games of I Spy, my boyfriend falls asleep with his head on my shoulder, and Xed does the same on his other side. The weight of both of them smashes me into the door, but it calms my erratic heartbeat.

Salem meets my gaze in the rear-view mirror, chewing her lip as she glances sideways at the stoic figure in her passenger seat. Of all our years as friends, I don't recall ever seeing him like this. I can tell she hasn't, either. Even after I OD'd, he wasn't this angry at me.

Night falls by the time we pull into the parking lot of our apartment complex, clouds rolling in to block out the moon. Logan is out of the passenger seat once the jeep barely stops on the curb, yanking his bag from the back without a farewell to anyone. He slams the trunk down hard, causing all of us to wince, and Salem turns to me after watching him disappear inside the building.

"You gonna be ok?" She asks softly, gray eyes wide with concern, and I nod quickly.

"Yeah. I'll talk to him."

I say goodbye, and Taylor exits with me as his truck pulls in behind us. With Salem moving in, it makes more sense for Matt and Taylor to switch rides. He grabs my bag from the back, slinging it over my shoulder before wrapping his arms around me and pressing his chest to mine.

"Call me if you need me to come get you," he murmurs, making me dizzy with a sloppy kiss.

"I will. FaceTime later?"

Grinning crookedly, he winks. "Always."

My chest tightens as it warms at how far he's come. At first, he was awkward about being on the phone, but not a day has passed that we haven't called or video chatted, and if I forget, he makes sure I know.

Reluctantly, I let him go, checking out his ass when he climbs into his truck with Arya and Christian. Shooting them a casual wave and shaking my head when Taylor makes a heart at me with his fingers, I make my way into the building toward the elevator.

Logan's already in the bathroom showering when I step into the apartment, so I flop into my desk chair, not wanting to crawl into bed before I shower myself. He takes his sweet time, so I work on some sketches for *T.O.T* while I wait. Christian and Taylor finally agreed—albeit begrudgingly on Taylor's part—to let Royce print some samples with his machines.

The shower finally turns off, and I exhale deeply before standing to knock on the door softly.

"Logan, we need to talk."

Silence meets me on the other end.

"Come on, don't ignore me. You haven't spoken to me in like three days."

"Go away, Huck."

My head thumps against the door as I lean back with an exasperated sigh. "I don't even know why you're mad. You hid an entire relationship from me for two whole years."

He yanks open the door, and I huff as I nearly fall backwards into the bathroom.

"Two years? Really?" He eyes me incredulously, brown hair still damp, pajamas clinging to his lanky frame. "As opposed to eight?"

"None of that really counts. We only officially started this thing a month ago."

His lips tighten. "But you had history, and you didn't tell me. I wondered why it bothered you so much when he crashed your car."

"You really wanna talk about things we didn't tell each other?" I cross my arms with a glare. "Taylor talked to Salem during the hike, and she told him that your dad threatened to cut off college funding unless you married her. And you said nothing."

"Why would I? You disappeared for four years!"

"You know why I had to do that, but I still kept in touch, asshole. You were the first to know about every relationship I ever had."

He plants his hands on his narrow hips. "And now you're with the person who made you run away in the first place? How does that make sense?"

"You literally told me to give him another chance when I came back in January," I nearly shout, jabbing a finger in his direction. "Remember?"

"Yeah, another chance at being a *brother*, not...whatever you guys are doing."

His lip curls as he spits the words, and I immediately go on the defensive, my back snapping straight as my chest constricts.

"I'm sorry, does the fact that our parents are married to each other bother you? Is that what this is?"

"I don't know," he states after hesitantly pausing, leaning against the doorframe. "I don't know how I feel about it, Huck. I just wish you'd told me."

A sigh gunshots from my lungs as I run a hand through my greasy curls. "Look, Loge, Taylor had a pretty shitty upbringing. His dad wasn't a good person. It doesn't excuse what he did to me, but it explains a lot. I don't...I don't blame him anymore. Like you said, he's not the same person he was in high school. We're working through things."

Logan is silent for a long moment, his eyes narrowed, jaw tight.

"You didn't tell me when your father left the priesthood either," he says quietly, dropping his gaze to the floor. "I had to hear about that from my parents. Or that you used to bartend. Or that you've apparently done shrooms before this weekend. We've been friends for over fifteen years, and I feel like I hardly know you."

"Yeah, well, the feeling is mutual." My reply comes out slowly, almost guttural, as I swallow around the emotions clogging my throat. This is the exact reason why I wanted to wait to tell him. But, like my entire life, things never go as planned. "I knew you'd react this way."

His honey-colored eyes flash as they snap up to mine. "My reactions are valid. You never tell me anything about your life. Even before you left. In high school, I didn't know that you were—"

He cuts himself off, face blanching.

"That I was what?" I raise my brows when he doesn't respond. "Gay? Suicidal? Go on, Logan, you can say them. They're not dirty words."

"I was going to say having issues."

"That's even fucking worse!" With a groan, I rub my palms into my eyes until I see stars. "This is why I don't say anything. Why I never said anything. Mental health is such a taboo subject that everyone tip-toes around it. Especially the church. And when you consider the reasons I felt the way I did, do you really think I could have talked to anyone about it? Without being told I was a sinner and going to hell?"

"The fact that you think I would judge you on anything you're dealing with just shows me how far apart we've grown." He reaches up to rub the back of his neck, chewing on his cheek. "Huck, I...I think I need some space. To process things."

It's on the tip of my tongue to say you're *judging me right now*, but I don't. Instead, I moisten my lips and nod despite the painful thumping in my chest.

"Fine. I can stay with Taylor for the next week until I leave for Cali."

He nods as well, avoiding my gaze, so I head to my room to repack my bag and grab my suitcase, ensuring I take my laptop, school stuff, and sketchbook. When I return, Logan is still in the doorway, clutching the sleeves of his sweater tightly.

I pause midway to the front door, uncertain. "Can I still stay here when I get back, or should I make other arrangements until August?"

He's silent for a moment before clearing his throat. "I-I'll let you know."

Fine. Whatever.

Let him have his moment to consider my life decisions, but maybe while he's preoccupied with my choices, he can reflect on his own.

Before I shut the apartment door behind me, I glance over my shoulder to find him staring after me.

"I know you didn't ask, but here's some relationship advice. I spent years being afraid to love who I love because of what others think, and so did Taylor. I'd hate to see you lose something good just because your parents disapprove. Choose Salem, Loge. That's all she wants."

And with those words, I leave my best friend behind, feeling like I've just lost a vital piece of myself.

# TAYLOR

## JUNE

"I swear to God, if you bring me any more dishes, I'll cut your shoelaces."

Slamming down the lever on the small industrial dishwasher, I turn to glare at my coworker Eliza as she piles another tub of dirty cups and cutlery into the large sink. Her dark cheeks redden as she glances down at the Balenciaga sneakers on her feet in horror before meeting my gaze.

"You wouldn't dare."

"Fucking try me." Reaching into the drying rack, I pull out a pair of clean scissors, waggling them at her shoes for emphasis. Not in the mood tonight. Or any night until my boyfriend comes back.

With a huff, she turns on her heel, tightening the dark bun on the top of her head as she pushes open the swinging door that leads out into the bar from the kitchen. "Christian! Come get your boy. He's threatening violence!"

*I'll show you violence.*

Muttering under my breath, I dunk a bundle of dirty spoons underwater, pretending to drown them slowly. Out of my peripheral, Gale, the cook, shakes his large head at me from over the grill, but I just throw him a sour look. Usually, I enjoy being on dish duty more than cleaning tables, but honestly, the last few days have been rough without Huckslee.

That whole week before he left was a dream come true, having him all up in my space and in my bed. Crawling in next to his sleeping body after a long night at work, waking up every morning to my cock in his mouth. Showering with him. My ass twinges when I think about the amount of sex we had. Even though I knew he was trying to distract himself from his fight with Logan, I loved every minute of it. Now he's been gone for an entire seven days, and I'm fucking miserable.

One more long week to go.

I don't know if I'll make it.

"Why you being a moody bitch, *pendejo?*" Christian smacks my back, causing me to pitch forward, splashing nasty ass sludge water onto my jeans.

Grabbing the sprayer, I squeeze the trigger, hitting him directly in the face. "Fuck off."

He shouts, raising his arms to shield himself against the stream. "Hey, Juanita! Did you see that shit? Taylor assaulted me."

Through the open office door in the back, our boss glances up from behind her desk with a smirk. "*No hablo inglés.*"

"Why does she only pretend not to understand English when it involves you?" Christian clicks his tongue in mock offense.

"Because I'm a delight and her favorite."

He shoves me again, and I take aim, spraying the front of his pants this time before he wrenches the damned thing from my hands.

"Okay, killer, put down the deadly weapon, and let's go smoke."

Letting him guide me toward the employee entrance, I spot Eliza bringing in another tub of dishes, her eyes narrowed in my direction. She's a sweet girl, and we get along great, but I scissor my fingers at her and mouth *snip snip* as I follow Christian outside. He pops a cigarette into my mouth and lights it for me, then one for himself, as we both lean back against the building.

I didn't need a single smoke while I was with Huck. Now, I'm almost up to an entire pack a day. I hate this. My lungs hate this. So does my wallet.

"You know," Christian starts slowly as he exhales, "it's only been one week, man."

My head thumps back against the wall, eyes on the dark sky. "I know."

"He'll be gone much longer when he leaves in August."

No shit, asshole. "I know."

We smoke in silence for a while, low bass of the music inside mixing with the traffic on the street. I've almost finished the entire cig when he finally speaks again.

"If you miss him so much, why don't you visit?"

"You don't think I want to? Almost didn't stop on the way here tonight. Just wanted to keep driving until I got to Cali."

"So why didn't you?"

I start to respond but stop, realizing he has a point. Why am I still here when my boyfriend is eight hundred miles away? He didn't explicitly invite me, but maybe he wasn't sure if I'd want to come. Chewing my bottom lip, I consider his words. "I can't exactly afford a plane ticket on such short notice, and the drive is like fifteen hours."

"So?" Christian shrugs, putting his cigarette out on the ground before tucking the butt behind his ear. "We've gone on longer trips. Remember when we drove to Portland for doughnuts?"

"Those were Voodoo Doughnuts, and they were totally worth it," I argue, tossing the rest of my snuffed-out smoke into the dumpster. "Plus, I had you and Salem with me. I'd have to make this drive alone."

"You can do it, *cariño*, I have faith."

Well, yeah, I probably could, but...

I hate being alone. And I've never gone anywhere outside of Utah by myself before. Not to mention...

"I don't even know where he's staying."

Christian's brows jump at that. "He didn't tell you?"

"He told me that he had an apartment off campus with a roommate, but I don't actually know the address, you know?"

"And you can't ask him for it because...?"

I shift my head from side to side, debating whether to voice my concerns. "What if he doesn't even want to see me? Like, what if he's happy with the space?"

"Taylor. My man." He grasps my shoulders, shaking his head with a grin. "You FaceTime every night, and when he stayed with us, you were practically joined at the hip. Or should I say ass? By the sounds constantly coming from your room, I'm pretty sure he lived inside your butthole."

"Shut the fuck up, dude." I slap his hands away from me, face heating and his laugh echoes around us.

"My point, nympho, is that Huckslee can't get enough of you. I'm sure he'd be thrilled if you showed up."

Yeah, maybe. But there's still that nagging voice of doubt in my head, telling me he's glad for the time apart. He probably has friends out there he's been missing, and he needs to say goodbye to his grandparents before leaving for training camp. What if I show up and mess up all his plans?

And then there's an even darker thought: what if he's using this separation as a test to see how we deal without each other? Does he miss me as much as I miss him? Is this as hard for him as it is for me? Hell, we've only been together a short time, but I'm already fucking gone for this man. The moment he kissed me again, I was done for. Can't be without him, don't even want to try. But what if—

Christian snaps his fingers in my face, cutting off my thoughts. "Taylor, just go. It'll be fine. I'll smooth things over with Juanita, and you can get some dick so that you stop being an asshat."

God, some dick sounds so good right about now. But not just any dick. Huckslee's dick.

With a snort, I drag my best friend back inside by the arm. "We both know Juanita lets me do whatever I want, anyway."

"Don't I fucking know it."

The rest of the night has me in a better mood as I plan out what I'm going to do, and when I talk to Huck upon returning home, I try to get as much information out of him as possible without making him suspicious.

Like what's his schedule for the week? Where will he be? Who is he going to be with?

Somehow, I manage to gather as much information as possible without sounding like a jealous househusband, and the following morning, I'm filling up my gas tank to head out. As I return the pump, my fingers shake with nerves and anticipation.

After hanging up with Huck last night, I called Logan on a hunch. He wasn't thrilled to get a call at two in the morning, but he did have the address to Huck's apartment in Berkeley. Taking a deep breath, I plug the address into my phone's GPS and start the long, lonely journey to surprise my boyfriend.

And I do mean long.

And lonely.

Three hours into it, I debate turning around to drag Salem with me, or at least Xed but decide against it because their lives and jobs aren't as flexible as mine.

Five hours go by, and I'm so bored that I pick up a hitch-hiker at a gas station, agreeing to take him as far as Carson City, Nevada. He's a pretty chill older guy, kinda odd. We chat and jam to Pink Floyd and The Rolling Stones for four hours. When I drop him off, he offers me a baggie of coke or a blowie for the ride, which I quickly decline but thank him anyway—what else do you say when someone offers you free drugs and a blowjob?

The next seven hours are pure torture. Just red dirt and cacti for miles. I call every person I know, even Huckslee's dad, which made for a weird five-minute conversation. I asked how he was; he said fine. He asked how I was; I said fine. When he offered to put Maisie on the phone, I quickly ended the call because nope. I'm good.

Only person I didn't call was Huck since that would ruin the surprise.

By the time I pull into Berkeley, it's night again, and I'm exhausted. My eyes are burning, my collarbone aches like a motherfucker from the gear shift, and there's a cramp in my thigh. Road-tripping alone is not for the weak, and I won't be doing it again. Zero out of ten stars; do not recommend.

Huck's apartment complex is just a few blocks from his university, which honestly looks like an old cathedral, complete with pristine white columns and a steeple, the San Francisco Bay visible in the distance. The Bay is probably a breathtaking sight in daylight, but right now, I can only see dark, rippling water. As I step out of the truck and stretch, the smell of sea salt mixed with weed is so strong it nearly makes me cough. I'm hit with a bit of culture shock when I see a group of people lighting a bong in a nearby stairwell.

Right. Definitely not in Utah anymore.

Glancing down at the address Logan gave me, I wander around the complex, taking in the carefully landscaped rocks and tan stucco buildings until I find the one I'm looking for. His unit is on the second floor, and as I make my way up the stairs and down a breezeway, uncertainty starts to settle in. My breath comes out in short gasps when I find his door, and I raise my hand to knock.

Fuck, what if this is a mistake? What if he... isn't alone?

The door swings open, and I blink at the guy on the other side. He's a bit taller than I am, tan, with long blond waves tumbling over his shoulders. A loose button-up shirt reveals lean muscles, paired with board shorts—a typical surfer dude if I ever saw one. But damn, this guy is pretty. Big blue eyes and long lashes. From what I've been told, this must be Huck's roommate, Shawn. I'm slightly jealous.

"Can I help you?" He asks with the voice of an angel, and I frown.

Okay, I'm more than slightly jealous.

"Uh, yeah." Clearing my throat, I glance over his shoulder. "I'm looking for Huckslee Davis. Is he here?"

He eyes me cautiously, shaking his head. "Not currently. Sorry, man."

Wait, what? Fuck. He told me he had no plans other than packing up his stuff tonight.

"Do you know how long he'll be out?"

"Probably not until tomorrow, honestly."

"Tomorrow?" My voice breaks with rising panic. "Are you sure?"

Hot surfer Shawn gives me a nod. "Yeah. He's at Greg's place."

I stare at him, utterly baffled for a moment. "Who's Greg?"

"His boyfriend."

My heart drops so far into my stomach that I swear I feel it crack. The ground shifts beneath my feet, and I have to lean against the doorway to keep myself from tumbling over my unsteady feet.

His...boyfriend.

Huckslee has a boyfriend? Has he had one this whole time? Did he cheat on me? Am I...am I the side piece?

Was this the reason he wanted to end things?

"Do you happen to have the address?" I croak, my throat feeling like gravel, and my lungs seize when Shawn shakes his head again.

"I don't. Sorry, man, wish I could help."

I'm full-on freaking out now, hyperventilating, fingers shaking as I lift my snapback and tug on my hair. I knew this was a mistake. I shouldn't have come here. And now I just wasted fifteen hours of my life driving out to a state and city I've never been to before, completely alone and nearly broke, if I'm being honest.

God, I'm a fucking idiot.

Shawn eyes me with concern the longer I stand at his door, and he places a hand on my shoulder when small choked noises start to claw from my throat.

"You okay? Do you need me to call him for you?"

"No!" Jerking out of his touch, I shake my head quickly, turning toward the stairs to run back to my truck. "I-I'm fine. Sorry to bother you, forget I was here."

He calls after me, but I run faster, reaching the cab and collapsing against the steering wheel, trying not to throw up all the junk food I've eaten. Jesus, I haven't felt this way in years—not since Huckslee first left to come here. It feels like I'm splitting in half. My head is throbbing, blood roaring in my ears, and my chest is so heavy it feels like I'm being crushed. Without thinking, I pull out my phone and dial Logan's number. He answers on the first ring.

"Hey, what's up? Did you make it?"

"I fucked up." It comes out as a strangled whisper, my throat too tight to speak louder, and Logan pauses momentarily.

"What do you mean? What happened?"

I lick my chapped lips, mouth dry. "He's not here. I showed up, but he isn't here."

"Well, where is he?"

"I don't know." I'm so stupid. "I don't know where he is, Logan, and I'm by myself and freaking out. I don't know what I'm supposed to do."

Fuck, look at me. I'm twenty-two, and I'm having a meltdown like a child, but I'm powerless to stop it. Can't even remember the last time I did anything alone like this before. Don't think I ever have.

"Do you want me to call him and find out for you?"

"Please, don't. I don't want him to know I'm here."

More silence greets my ears, his steady breaths calming me a fraction. "Okay. Okay, I think I have an idea. This app lets us track each other's phones in emergencies. I can get his location and send it to you. Would that help?"

That's actually super smart. Should look into something like that for Salem, Arya, and the guys.

"Yeah, man, that'd help a lot."

Part of me doesn't believe what pretty boy Shawn said; I want to see what Huck is up to.

*Could just call him and ask*, says a voice in the back of my head that I should probably listen to, but I ignore it, misinterpreting the alarm bells ringing in my gut.

My phone pings a second later as Logan speaks once again. "I just sent it, but I really think one of us should call him. You've got me worried."

"No, no, I'm fine. I'll be fine. Promise. Thanks, Loge. I appreciate it. I'll text when I find him."

He says something else, but I miss it as I hang up and check my texts for Huck's whereabouts. Entering the coordinates he sent me into the GPS, I'm relieved to find he's only a few blocks away as I throw the truck into gear and peel out of the parking lot, speeding back the way I came. Pulling up to the address, I gape out the window at a large two-story brick frat house. A giant, hand-painted banner hangs from the balcony reading **CONGRATS GRADS**, and vehicles are parked all up and down the street.

What the hell is he doing here?

Luckily, there's a spot nearby, so I parallel park the truck before making my way up the sidewalk toward the house. Music is bumping so loud that I hear it from down the street, empty cups and trash littering the front yard. A wide porch leads to two double wooden doors thrown open, and groups of people enter and exit. Some are smoking outside, others already passed out in the bushes. This is obviously a graduation party, judging by the homemade graduation caps people are wearing. As I step onto the porch, I scan faces for Huck but come up empty.

A few ladies near the entrance eye me with interest, but no one stops me as I step into the house and take in what I can only describe as utter chaos. People are *everywhere*, wall to wall, bass pounding so loudly from massive speakers that I can feel it vibrating through my feet. The crystal chandelier above my head even shakes, and I step to the side in case it detaches and crushes me. My body accidentally collides with someone playing beer pong near the entryway, causing them to spill their drink down their front. Before I can shout an apology,

I'm shoved back so hard that I trip over a twisted rug and fall on my ass with a wince.

No one helps me up. No, these people just step on my fucking fingers where I sit on the ground in front of a sweeping staircase, and I scramble to my feet as the crowd forces me into a living room. More tables are set out for pong games, strobe lights blinking while couples make out on the couches, and I have to do a double take because did I just see what I think I saw?

Yep. Totally did. There are two women literally fucking each other on the coffee table while bystanders cheer them on. Holy hell. And I thought the parties Christian and I used to throw were wild. This is on a whole other level.

Still no sign of Huck. I start asking around, tapping people on the shoulder to shout in their ears if they've seen him, but I'm either met with blank looks or head shakes. One guy mistook me leaning in for an invitation and planted a kiss on my cheek, prompting me to quickly run in the opposite direction, wiping his spit off my skin. Desperation claws at me as I continue searching, feeling disoriented and fucking exhausted from the long drive.

Tears prick the corners of my eyes as I step into the kitchen, blinking them away while I rest my aching shoulder against the wall to catch my breath. I'm about to pull out my phone to call him when a loud laugh draws my attention. I turn toward the back door and see a group of guys gathered around a firepit in the backyard, Golden Bears colors adorning their varsity jackets.

Football players. I recognize them from the games I watched Huck play. Shoving off the wall, I weave through the crowd and head outside. As I make my way over, a few of them raise their brows at me when I enter their circle, but luckily, the music is muffled enough out here for them to hear me speak.

"Hey guys, I'm looking for Huckslee Davis. Anyone seen him?"

A player to my right flicks his gaze over me with a smirk. "Maybe. Who's asking?"

Some teammates snicker, one rolling his eyes, and I scrub a hand down my face.

"I'm his, uh...stepbrother. I drove in from out of town to surprise him, but I don't know where he is."

"Oh, shit. My bad. Never knew he had a brother. He's upstairs with Greg."

Seriously? He...never told his team about me?

One of them points toward the upstairs balcony, and relief floods my system when I spot Huck's familiar form leaning against the railing. A smaller guy stands before him, a dark brunette wearing a polo. When he turns slightly, recognition hits me like a punch to the gut.

The boyfriend from his FB profile picture last year.

Huck's arms are crossed, but the guy has a hand resting on his bicep, standing too close for comfort. My whole body tenses as that asshole stands on his tiptoes and places a fucking kiss on my boyfriend's mouth. I hold my breath, waiting for something to happen—for Huck to shove him away, to shout, to at least wipe the damn kiss off. But what he does instead has me seeing red.

He smiles.

A bright, luminous grin lights up his handsome face as he reaches out and touches the other guy's shoulder. Suddenly, I can't breathe. My vision swims, eyes stinging from tears that threaten to spill over. I bite my lip so hard that the metallic taste of blood assaults my tongue. The roaring in my ears drowns out the thumping music, and I drop my gaze, causing a single tear to leak down my cheek.

He's never smiled at me like that. Not that I can remember.

And now it all makes sense—why he was so hesitant to pursue anything with me, why he never invited me to come here for his graduation. Because Greg was waiting for him at home. He never planned on this relationship going any further than July.

In a daze, I stumble back into the kitchen, where I find myself standing before the counter cluttered with liquor. A bottle of Kraken Rum catches my eye, jumbled thoughts and feelings swirling around my head. What even was I to him? Just something to pass the summer away? All of the things we said to each other, all of the bullshit we worked through...was it even real?

Did I mean anything to him at all?

My hand slowly rises to the bottle, wrapping around its neck, testing the feel of it as memories flicker behind my eyes.

Harsh words snarled after bruises, my father's voice inside my head synchronizing with my own, saying things to Huck-slee that I never should have said.

The feeling of my bones snapping against my father's hands, followed by Huck's arm breaking.

Holding him underwater while he drowned.

The look on his face when that curtain opened right before I almost lost him.

But I did lose him, didn't I? I never even had him.

*Blood, so much blood.*

*"Stay with me, baby."*

How could I ever believe he'd love me after everything I've done?

I don't deserve it. I don't deserve him.

Before I can even process what I'm doing, the lid is off the bottle, cold glass pressing to my lips. Spiced liquid slides down my throat as I sip something that I haven't tasted since the night I went to jail for beating up Huckslee's dad.

And I sip again.

And again.

Until I'm

Fucking

*Gone.*

# HUCKSLEE

G oddamn, Greg talks forever.

My foot is tapping while I listen to him drone on, my phone burning a hole in my pocket. It's getting late; Taylor is expecting my call soon. Between packing up the rest of my shit from the apartment and preparing for the graduation ceremony at the end of the week, I've had no time to talk to him all day. I'm fucking dying to hear his voice, see his face. But of course, the minute I pulled out my phone to text him, I'd seen the message from my ex asking if we could meet to 'properly' break up face to face. And I'd felt like such an asshole for ending our relationship through text that I agreed, but only because I thought I'd be here twenty minutes max.

Greg's been talking for forty-five minutes about the new guy he's dating, and I don't know if he's trying to make me jealous, but I brought up Taylor and how great we are together just to shut him up. It worked for all of two seconds until he asked if he could give me a goodbye kiss. I don't know why I was expecting a peck on the cheek, but I nearly gagged when his lips touched mine. The minute he pulled away, he mentioned how much happier and healthier I looked, and I couldn't help but smile, knowing that Taylor was the reason.

I harbored a lot of anger and guilt when I lived out here and held on to too much hate. It's crazy how much five months can change a person.

My ex continues talking for another ten minutes before my phone buzzes for the umpteenth time, so I decide against being polite and pull it out. First, I check the Delaware chat, where Taylor's been sending me weird pictures and random street signs all day that make no fucking sense. Still, I grin because he's an oddball, but I like it. Actually kind of love it.

After sending him every color of heart emoji, I pull up a missed text from my old roomie and frown.

> Shawn: Hey man, some guy came to the apartment looking for you. Told him you were at Greg's, but he looked super strung out.

> Just letting you know.

Well, that's...strange. Everyone I know from school is at this party except for Shawn. But I shrug, figuring maybe it was some college football fan who found out where I lived and wanted to talk. Believe it or not, that used to happen a lot over the last four years.

Swiping away the message, I pull up the ones from Logan and notice I also have a few missed calls from him. The moment I read his texts, I go rigid against the railing.

> Logan: Did Taylor find you??

> Answer, please. I'm really worried about him.

> Pick up the phone. Taylor isn't answering either and he sounded agitated when he called me because he couldn't find you.

> He's out there in Berkeley. I sent him your location.

Wait, *wait*, hold up.

Taylor is *here?*

My head snaps up, heart in my throat as I look around the balcony expecting him to materialize right in front of me where he belongs. Worry begins to gnaw at my gut when I don't see him.

"I have to go find my boyfriend. Apparently, he's here." Cutting Greg off in the middle of whatever he was saying and not caring in the least, I make my way back inside. Logan's messages have me alarmed, and I press my phone to my ear to call Taylor, cursing loudly when it goes straight to voice mail. So I send him a text.

> Me: Baby, where are you? Logan said you're here.

> Why didn't you tell me?

Looking over his earlier messages, all of the random photos now make sense. He was sharing his trip with me.

Panicking, I search the house from top to bottom, finding the few friends I know scattered throughout to show them his picture and ask if they've seen him. They all say no. I even check the rooms where super nefarious shit is going down, but I don't find him in any of those, either. I'm nearly pulling my hair out on my third sweep of the house when Greg finds me again.

"Hey, what's going on?" He grabs my arm, brows pinched in concern when he sees the frenzy I'm in. "Thought you were with your man?"

My voice cracks when I answer in his ear. "I can't find him, I've looked everywhere. And his phone is off."

"I'll help you look. Have you checked outside?"

Frantically, I shake my head, and we search the front yard, coming up empty. When we step into the backyard, one of my teammates, Robbie, calls me over to the firepit.

"Yo, Davis! Did you find your bro?"

"Huh?" I gaze at him with wild eyes, probably looking like a psycho from the look he exchanges with some of the other players.

"Guy was looking for you. Tall, dark hair, lots of tattoos? Eyebrow piercing?"

A sharp gasp escapes my lips. "That was my boyfriend! Did you see where he went?"

His eyes widen, jaw dropping slightly. "Oh. He said he was your stepbrother. Saw him disappear with a bottle of rum, but I didn't see where. Sorry, dude."

*What?!* Why the hell would he do that?!

"Goddammit," I shout angrily, causing Greg to wince as he follows me back into the house. That familiar feeling starts to squeeze up my spine, my neck tense as the bodies around me close in. But I can't lose my shit right now, not when Taylor has clearly lost his mind, and I can't fucking find him.

Shoving through the crowd until I'm back on the front porch, I rub my eyes and try to breathe. Greg traces circles on my back like he used to when I'd get this way, and admittedly, it's helping, even though I wish it was my boyfriend doing it and not my ex. Once I've calmed down enough to think clearly, I rack my brain, trying to figure out what to do.

"Is there somewhere he might have gone to stay?" Greg asks.

"He doesn't know anyone out here. He's never even been here before." That gives me an idea. "I'm going to drive around and look for his truck, search all the nearby hotels to see if I can find it."

"I'll come with."

I raise a brow at him, wondering why the hell he's helping me, but I don't push the issue. Greg's always been a good guy, and I didn't treat him very well. He follows me to where my red Audi is parked—a graduation gift from Grandma and Gramps—and I start it up before heading down the road. I barely get ten feet before a flash of yellow has me slamming on the brakes.

"That's his truck right there!"

I'm out of the car in seconds, leaving it in the middle of the street as I sprint to where the truck is parked on the curb. Terror claws up my throat when I glance inside the window.

Taylor is lying face down on the seat, bottle clutched in his hand where it dangles on the floor. Music screams over the speakers, but the door is locked when I try to pull on the handle. Fuck.

"Taylor! Open up, baby." I bang on the window, trying to rouse him, but he doesn't move. My knuckles split when I start punching the glass, cursing to high heaven for it being so strong, and Greg grips my wrist before I can land another blow.

"Huckslee, stop, stop. You're going to break your hand before training camp. Do you really want that?"

"I don't give a fuck right now. I need to get to him."

Shaking Greg off, I pull back to launch another hit, but he steps between me and the truck, palms on my chest.

"I know you're upset, but you need to calm down. I have an idea, alright? His back window is cracked. I can probably shimmy through and unlock the door."

Shit, he's right. It is. I hadn't even noticed.

Blinking the tears of frustration away, I frown down at him. "You'd do that for me?"

"Duh." He clucks his tongue, rolling his eyes as he walks around the truck to the back. "For someone so smart, Davis, you're really dense."

Well, fuck. I don't even know how to respond as I watch him hop into the truck bed and slide open the window on the back of the cab above the seat. He's barely tiny enough to squeeze through, and he leans over Taylor to unlock the door. He tries to open it from the inside, but it gets stuck because this truck is a piece of shit, and the door only opens from the outside. I yank it open, causing Greg to nearly fall forward, and I wrap my arms around Taylor, pulling him up to my chest.

"Baby, it's me. It's Huck. Wake up."

His lids flutter but don't open, lashes crusted, and the tears streaking down his cheeks set me off instantly. I've never seen him cry before. Why the hell was he crying? He mumbles incoherently, breath rank with alcohol, and I shake his body firmly, gripping his jaw.

"Come on, Tay, open those pretty eyes. I need to see that you're okay."

Glancing at the bottle on the floor, I notice it's empty, and my breath leaves my lungs. God, please don't tell me that bottle was full when he took it. The keys dangle in the ignition, and I grab them, stuffing them into my pocket with his phone. Greg appears next to me again as I throw one of Taylor's arms over my shoulder and lift him out of the truck. His dead weight almost takes me down, but Greg presses into his other side, helping me lift.

"I think I need to get him to the hospital," I grit out as we drag him to my car, managing to slide him into the backseat. When Greg jumps into the passenger side, I glance at him in surprise. "You don't need to come with."

He flicks his hand at me, buckling his belt. "I don't mind. Just drive."

So I do. Within ten minutes, I'm pulling into the emergency lane of the nearest medical center, and we both heft Taylor through the automatic doors. We barely make it past the entrance when my boyfriend turns his head, and projectile vomits all over himself and Greg, whose face turns green as he begins to gag.

Shit.

"I am so fucking sorry."

A nurse behind the counter glances up in surprise as we approach, wrinkling her nose when she takes in our appearance. "Can I help you?"

"I think he has alcohol poisoning. He won't wake up," I babble desperately, my arms tightening around Taylor. She stands quickly, coming around the counter with a wheelchair, and we get his limp body into it. When he slumps forward, she holds his shoulder, instructing us to stay where we are as she wheels him away behind a set of double doors. Greg spots a trashcan and makes a beeline for it, unloading his stomach while I wince. Feeling bad, I rub his back as he pukes.

What a hell of a first impression for Taylor.

The nurse returns with a clean sweater folded in her arms and offers it to Greg, who wipes his mouth and takes it with trembling fingers. Then she's behind the counter again, handing me a clipboard with papers attached. "Your friend is being checked out now. In the meantime, please take a seat and fill out these forms for him."

I sit in the packed waiting room and answer what I can, listing myself as his stepbrother. Greg opts to take an Uber home instead of sitting here with me, and I don't blame him one bit. I owe him lunch or something for helping me with this.

With nothing left to do but stare at the clock, anxiety begins to settle in. I clasp my hands behind my neck and lower my head between my knees, willing myself to breathe. What the hell just happened? I am so damn confused. Did something happen at home to set him off?

Pulling his phone out of my pocket, I search for some kind of clue. Normally, I don't condone going through a partner's personal shit, but seeing how he almost fucking died, I think an exception can be made. His texts give me nothing, but his call history makes me pause. Jesus. He literally called everyone on his contact list, including my dad, which is worrisome all on its own. Why was he calling my dad?

Ringing him up on my own phone, I realize too late that it's after midnight by the time he answers.

"Son? Is everything okay?" He sounds groggy, and I mentally kick myself for waking him up so late.

"Yeah, sorry pops. I just, uh...had a question. Did Taylor call you today?"

"He did earlier this afternoon. Why? What's going on?"

Swallowing hard, I try to keep the tremor out of my voice. "Nothing, I'm just curious. Did-did he sound alright?"

There's a brief pause. "Yes, he seemed like himself, though I admit the call was out of the blue. He wouldn't talk to his mother. Are you sure nothing is wrong, Huckslee?"

"Yeah. Yep, all good. Thanks, Dad. I'll talk to you later. Love you."

I hang up before he can answer, leg bouncing erratically, and send texts to all Taylor's friends, asking if anything happened that made him drive out here. They all respond the same, Christian saying he's been down since I left and wanted to surprise me for graduation. So what the fuck is going on?

"Huckslee Davis?"

Glancing up, I see the doctor gesture for me, and I stand quickly to follow her back.

"How is he?"

"Luckily, he's fine. The alcohol in his system didn't warrant a stomach pump, but he is very dehydrated. We're giving him fluids now, you should be fine to take him home in a few hours."

My shoulders sag with relief as she leads me to a large room with several beds, all divided by curtains. She slides one out of the way to reveal Taylor, still passed out, lying on his back with tubes in his arms. I freeze for a moment, blinking away memories of my mom in her hospital bed.

*Not now, Huckslee. We can freak out later.*

The doctor continues, checking his vitals. "You're free to sit with him until he wakes up. When he does, alert one of the nurses so they can give him a once over before discharge."

Sitting down next to the bed, I take in his still form as the doctor shuts the curtain and leaves us alone. They've exchanged his soiled shirt for a light blue smock, the color making his sallow cheeks look even paler than usual. His hair is a greasy mess, hanging in strings around his face, with dried vomit on his chin. Fuck, he looks nothing like he did when I last saw him at the airport a week ago when he dropped me off.

This does not bode well for August. Not at all.

With a heavy sigh, I grab a water bottle from a table near the bed and dampen the edge of my shirt before wiping his face clean. My fingers thread with his, carefully avoiding the tubes sticking out of his veins.

And then I wait.

# TAYLOR

A three-ring circus elephant is stomping around my head. At least, that's what it feels like.

The pounding is so bad I can feel it behind my eyes, against my eardrums. Is Christian blasting his music again? Groaning, I try to turn over but flinch when a burn scorches through my throat. Fuck, why does that hurt so bad?

A hand tightens around mine as I slowly try to open my eyes. They feel swollen and gritty like sandpaper. Bright light hits my corneas, sending shooting pain through my temples, and I hiss as I lift an arm to block it out. There's a horrible taste in my mouth, my tongue drier than the Sahara. A wound on my bottom lip splits and starts to bleed.

"Hey, easy. You're okay," whispers the voice I constantly dream about, "don't hurt yourself."

Blinking rapidly to relieve my eyeballs, I turn my head to take in the man sitting next to me. Huckslee gazes down, his dark eyes glittering with concern as his brows crease. A stray curl falls over his forehead, the rest of his hair looking wild as if he's been running a hand through it. Or someone else has...

The thought makes me cringe.

"What happened?" Wincing at the roughness in my voice, I eye the small tubes taped to my arm and the curtain surrounding us.

"I found you passed out in your truck with an empty liquor bottle, and you weren't responding," he answers accusingly, holding on tight when I try to pull my hand free from his. "I thought you had alcohol poisoning. They needed to give you fluids. Baby, what were you thinking? What happened?"

*Baby.*

I yank my hand away, feeling a painful twist in my chest. As I open my mouth to tell him what I saw, a nurse pulls back the curtain, interrupting us.

"Mr. Tottman, it's good to see you awake," he says with a smile, oblivious to the chaos in my head. "How are you feeling?"

Like my heart just got thrown in a blender.

"Fantastic," I snap, avoiding Huckslee's gaze as the nurse chuckles and nods.

"Oh, I bet. Let me just get your vitals real quick. As long as everything looks fine, we'll get these tubes out, and you can be on your way."

The entire time he checks me over, I keep my eyes down. When he's satisfied, the nurse removes the tubes and wraps my arm with a strip of gauze. It isn't until he leaves to get my discharge papers that I finally look Huck in the eye and hate what I see. He looks absolutely gutted.

"Why are you here?" I rasp, touching my tender lip as his jaw tightens.

"I could ask you the same thing."

His response pulls an almost manic laugh out of me. "Wanted to drive up and surprise you. Didn't mean to ruin your date."

"Date? What do you mean?"

"With Greg." My lips twist as I glance away, hating myself for throwing away two years of sobriety, for turning into *him* again.

Huck's eyes nearly bug out of his skull as he sputters momentarily. "What the fuck are you talking about, Taylor? I wasn't on a date. Greg asked me to meet him so that we could talk. I broke up with him through text on the plane in January, and he needed some closure. That's all."

"Please don't," I whisper, fisting the sheets at my sides. "Don't lie to me. Give me that courtesy, at least. I saw the kiss."

His lips part, and I catch the flash of guilt that crosses his face. "It...that wasn't what you think, I swear–"

"You *smiled*, Huckslee. Afterwards. I watched you smile."

"Baby. You have this all wrong." He pinches the bridge of his nose, lids sliding shut. "He asked for a goodbye kiss and I thought he meant on the cheek. I didn't know he would go for the lips, though I should have. And after, I smiled because–"

The nurse returns with my release papers before he can get another word out.

"Alrighty-roo, you're all set." Nurse dude smiles impatiently, clearly wanting us to hurry for bed space. "Do you need a wheelchair?"

"I'm good." Swinging my legs to the floor, I fight the nausea as I try to stand. Huck reaches out to wrap his arm around my waist, and despite the shredded feeling inside my chest, I let him steady me. Every nerve lights up at his touch, goosebumps spreading across my flesh, the intoxicating scent of his aftershave surrounding me in a cocoon of warmth. I cling to him shamelessly as we hobble out. My feet grow more stable the further we go, and by the time we reach a shiny Audi, I'm walking on my own.

Sliding into the passenger seat, I scrunch my nose at the new car smell and pull my seatbelt on as Huck gets behind the wheel.

"You can probably drop me off at my truck," I tell him, honestly feeling better since they pumped me full of electrolytes. Still obviously buzzed, but I can at least sleep in the cab until tomorrow morning.

"Shut up, Taylor," Huckslee snaps through his teeth, putting the vehicle in reverse. "Just shut up."

I shoot him a glare. "Look, I appreciate you helping me, but I'm fine now. Seriously. You can go back to your boyfriend."

He exhales sharply as he merges onto a freeway. "*You're* my boyfriend."

"Not according to Pretty Boy Shawn, I'm not."

"I swear to God, if you say another word, I'll pull over and stuff you in my trunk."

I'm not even gonna analyze why my dick jumps at that threat.

*We're supposed to be mad at him, motherfucker*, I think, seething down at my crotch as Huck takes an exit onto some quiet, empty road. I don't know where he's taking me, but I'm clear-headed enough to know it's not back to the frat house. We drive silently for a while, and I lean against the window, taking in the moonlit coast, feeling like my insides have been scooped clean. A pit of self-loathing yawns within, consuming me. Why the fuck did I grab that bottle? Why did I turn into my dad again? If Christian or Salem had been here, this never would have happened.

Eventually, he pulls into a suburban neighborhood, the streets lined with cute houses that all look the same, with terracotta shingled roofs and palm trees in the front yards. The homes become older and further apart as we drive until Huck pulls into the driveway of a ranch-style rambler at the end of the road, parking under a carport before shutting off the engine.

"Where are we?" I ask, peering out into the dark and grimacing at a grease mark on the window from my hair.

"My grandparents."

Without another word, he exits the car, slamming the door before going over to a back gate, where he disappears. For a minute, I contemplate sitting here in solidarity because I'm mad at him, but then the Audi begins to honk as he locks and unlocks it with his key fob, clearly demanding I follow. And, of course, I do because the scent of the fresh leather seats only makes my headache worse, and I hate the silence. Plus, my phone is missing, so that sucks.

Slamming my own door with a huff, I make my way through the gate into the backyard, squinting my tired eyes at the sight of a large in-ground pool glowing a soft hue of blue. Fairy lights twinkle above, lining the yard from a covered back porch to the roof of a guest house where Huckslee stands waiting.

"In," he commands, pointing to a set of French doors, his delicious jaw set firmly.

Muttering under my breath, I brush past him inside. He's close behind, flicking on a switch as he shuts the doors, and the sudden flood of light makes me hiss as I squeeze my eyes shut. It takes a second for the sharp pain in my temples to dissipate, but when my lids peel open, I slowly take in the room we're standing in.

A soft-looking queen bed with a wrought-iron headboard sits against the far wall, flanked by two nightstands. To the left is a desk piled with boxes, and to the right sits a mirrored dresser holding a flatscreen. An ornate rug covers the tiled floor, and shelves line the walls with various books and figurines I remember from his room at our parents' house.

"This is where I stayed during the summer and weekends when I wasn't in school," Huck explains softly, kicking a cardboard box out of the way as he walks toward an adjoining bathroom. "I've been moving shit back and forth from the apartment all day. Come on."

My eyes fall to the swell of his ass while I watch him walk away, those hard muscles flexing in his tight jeans, and I follow him with a scowl. Why? Out of all the men I could have been attracted to, it had to be Huckslee Davis. Honestly, I don't know if my heart can take it anymore. It feels like a dirty rag that's been used and wrung out too many times.

He stands above a jetted tub and turns on the shower, testing the temperature with his back to me. "Take off your clothes."

His bossiness has my cock perking up, but I cross my arms. "No. You don't get to tell me what to do after today."

"Taylor." The low timbre of his voice and the dangerous undertone send a shiver through me. "Undress, or so help me, I'll rip that hospital gown off you myself."

The what? Oh, yeah.

I frown down at myself, examining the light blue smock covering me over my jeans. Where the hell did my tank top go? How wasted was I? Fuck, I hate this side of myself. I vowed two years ago that I'd never be here again, yet here I am. Falling right back into old habits. Because I'll never be anything but my father's kid. Bad genes all around.

Gentle fingers brush the bottom of my chin, tilting my face up to meet Huckslee's concerned gaze. "Baby, please. Let me take care of you, and then we can talk."

Goddamn, the way he makes me melt when he begs. I'm so deep in it for him that I'd give him anything he asks for, even if it hurts me. Even if it kills me.

He turns me around to face the double-vanity sink, his eyes holding mine in the mirror as he unties the gown, letting it drop away. Then his shirt comes off, and the warmth from his bare chest seeps into my back. Wordlessly, he opens the cabinet and hands me a toothbrush and a tube of paste, watching me as I scrub my teeth and rinse.

When I'm finished, his arms encircle my waist, undoing my jeans as he trails kisses along the side of my throat, burning my flesh when I remember where those lips were earlier. Still, I tilt my head to the side, giving him easier access when he slowly slides my pants and briefs down until they fall to the floor. My hard cock springs up to slap against my lower abs, hard and aching to be touched.

"So fucking beautiful," Huck murmurs, his own stiff length resting against my crease beneath his jeans. I press back into him, his hands roaming everywhere on my body except where I need them.

Gripping the edge of the counter, my hips rock back and forth as his teeth sink into the sensitive junction between my shoulder and neck, pulling a whimper from me, our gazes still locked. I missed the feel of him, even if it had only been a week. Even if he didn't miss me.

Each sweep of his fingers on my skin sends a shock wave of heat to my balls, precum leaking from my swollen tip when I turn my head to claim his mouth. His nails scrape across a nipple as he licks into me, our tongues fighting for control, the wet sounds of our kisses and heavy moans mixing with the shower running behind us. When I can't stand it anymore, I wrap my hand around my cock to pump myself, but he grabs my wrist and stops me.

"Shower." His teeth nip at my earlobe. "Now."

Fuck me, but I love when he tells me what to do.

Pushing my bottom lip out, I obey, smirking when his eyes darken. Hot water cascades down my body as I step beneath the spray, eliciting a deep groan at how good it feels against my sore muscles. Huck steps in behind me, as nude as I am, massaging my shoulders and expertly digging those magic thumbs into my tendons and ligaments. The ice that had built up around my heart chips a little.

He leans forward to grab a bottle of shampoo off the shelf, his cock sliding against my ass, and his free hand holds my hip in place when I try to rub against him, jerking myself.

"Stop moving, Taylor. Put both hands on the wall."

"Fuck off." I stroke even faster, balls painfully heavy as I flex my ass cheeks, squeezing his length between them.

With a muttered curse, he sets down the shampoo before wrenching my arms behind my back, careful not to hurt my collarbone.

"You're such a brat." He licks at the water on my neck. "You want me to fuck you, baby?"

"Yes. Please?" I'm humping the air like a slut, desperate to come, and he hums into my skin.

"Then be good and do what I say. Let me wash you, and if you behave, you'll get what you want." He leans me forward, taking my hands until my palms are flat against the tile. "Do. Not. Move."

Over the next five minutes, he tortures me, cleaning every inch of my body, from my hair down to my toes. Kneeling behind me, he spends extra time stroking my cock while his thumb rubs teasing circles around my hole. He presses the tip inside of me, smiling against my lower back when a choked moan leaves my throat, and then he's standing to rinse me off. When he turns me around, I meet his mouth with a heated kiss, needing to feel his tongue on mine, sucking on it greedily while I grab the body wash and flip open the cap. Pulling back, he lifts a brow in question as I flash him a wicked grin.

"My turn."

And I return the favor, washing him like he did for me. When I get to his dick, I line it up with mine, whipping us both into a lust-fueled frenzy as we devour each other, whimpers and groans echoing off the shower walls. Pressing my back against the tile, he lifts one of my legs, setting my foot on the lip of the tub. Two soapy fingers tease my sac before massaging my hole, and then he slips them inside of me.

"Oh, fuck," I breathe, nipping at his throat when he's seated up to his knuckles. He pulls them out before sliding back in, fingering me slowly.

"God, you're perfect."

Biting down onto his skin when he hits my prostate, I pump us faster, feeling tears prick my closed eyes at his praise. I want to believe it, to believe him. But the image of his lips on someone else and that fucking smile still burns my mind like a brand, so all I can do is cling to him while he stretches me so deliciously, my cock throbbing for relief. Removing his fingers, he turns me back around, rinsing off the soap before grabbing a bottle of lube on the shelf. Generously coating his length, he bends me forward and positions himself at my entrance.

"Breathe out."

My lips part right as he presses into me, the burn so good, his hard cock filling me until the sting morphs into pleasure.

"Why do you always feel amazing?" He groans, thrusting into me, emphasizing every word with each punch of his hips. "Every. Single. Time."

"Mmfuck, right there." My eyes roll back as he pegs that spot inside of me that makes my legs shake and my dick leak. "Please, Huck, don't stop."

"Christ, I want to be inside of you constantly. You're the only one who makes me feel like this, do you understand? Only you."

Pounding into me, he reaches around to slap my hand away from my shaft so that he can jerk me himself, teeth marking my shoulder, flooding all of my senses.

"Tell me you're listening," he pleads desperately. "Say it for me, baby. There's only you."

But I'm too wrecked to speak. Everything is Huckslee, in the relentless way he fucks my ass, coaxing me closer to orgasm with his cock and his fist. In the euphoric pain of his bite, skin sliding against skin as he moans my name, the scent of sex mingling with the body wash we just used. When he shoves his fingers inside my mouth and commands me to suck, it's all over.

I come hard, nails digging into the back of his neck where I'm holding him, my strangled cries reverberating as my cum shoots onto his hand and the wall. He follows shortly after, spilling inside of me, fingers digging into my hip with bruising force.

"Mm, the way you feel when you come on my cock." His thrusts slow as he works himself through his orgasm, nuzzling into my neck, and if it wasn't for his strong arms holding me up, I'd be a puddle on the floor, swirling down the drain.

He holds me for a long while, our breaths growing steady. The shower water has grown lukewarm but feels good as it cools my heated skin. Huck's fingers gently grip my jaw, turning my face up to capture a sloppy kiss. When he pulls back, his starry eyes hold mine intently.

"I meant what I said, Tay. There's no one for me but you. Nobody I want but you."

I lick my lips, still heartsick and feeling like a petty bitch. "Did you say the same thing to Greg, too?"

His forehead falls to my shoulder as he releases a ragged breath. "You're so fucking stubborn. What must I do to make you believe me, baby?"

I already do. Huckslee is many things, but a liar isn't one of them. It's that smile afterwards that's tearing me up.

Pressing between my shoulder blades, he pushes me forward and drops to his knees, palming my ass cheeks to spread them wide. "Stay still."

"What are you doing?" I gasp, looking at him over my shoulder as he gazes at his release dripping out of me in rapt fascination.

"Something I've never done for anyone."

Warm breath hits me first, and the minute his tongue flicks out to run over my hole, I jerk forward on reflex.

"Huck, you don't have to–*oh*, fuck, goddamn."

His tongue enters me, cutting off my words as he swirls it around, lapping at the cum he just filled me with moments ago. The act is so filthy that my cock swells again, growing heavy with each lick. My head tilts forward to rest against the wall, soft whimpers leaving my throat from the sensation of him. Gripping my length, I stroke myself lazily, still hypersensitive, and it only takes a few pumps before I'm coming again, moaning his name when I spill over.

As soon as he stands, I spin around, throwing my arms around him as I crush my lips to his, not even caring where his mouth had just been. His cock presses between us, and I wrap my hand around it, our tastes mixing on his tongue as it dances with mine, melding our very molecules until every part of him makes up every part of me. He fucks my fist, chasing his own second release. By the time we're clean again and out of the shower, I can't believe I ever let my insecurities make me doubt his love for me.

Because he does love me. I can feel it in the way he dries me off, careful not to rub the towel too harshly because I have sensitive skin. I can feel it in the way he dresses me in his clothes, his eyes darkening possessively at the sight of his football jersey on my body.

When he tucks me into his bed, he puts on the Sci-Fi channel because he knows how much it calms me, holding me close while I doze off until our food delivery arrives. He ordered my favorite without even asking, a smothered chili verde burrito, even though I always complain that it's never as good as Christian's mom's cooking.

"We still need to talk," he whispers against my hair when we're curled up after eating.

I nod into his chest. "Tomorrow."

For now, I just want this bubble of bliss—the feel of his warmth beneath me, his steady heartbeat in my ear. I want to pretend that tonight is our normal.

Because tomorrow, I'll have to face the fact that I made a huge mistake.

The next morning, I wake up slowly to fingers trailing down my spine.

Sometime in the night, I must have gotten hot and taken off Huck's jersey because it's cradled in my arms under my chin. Soft blankets are coiled around my feet, a strong leg thrown over mine, and I nestle back contentedly into the warm chest against my back.

"You should check your phone," Huck says groggily, continuing his exploration of my back. "It's been buzzing like crazy since I plugged it in last night."

"I was wondering where it went." Cracking open an eye, I spot it on the nightstand and reach over to read the notifications. There are about a dozen missed calls and texts from Logan, Salem, and Christian. Guilt renders me fully awake as I type out quick responses, assuring them that I'm fine and that I'll call them soon.

Then I steal a deep breath before facing the man I love.

His dark eyes are bright and clear, searching my face as he wraps an arm around my waist, tugging me closer. For a moment, we just gaze at one another, breathing in each other's air. A stray curl falls over his brow, and I reach up to coil my finger around it, biting my lip.

"What happened to my shirt?"

"You threw up all over it. And Greg."

I can't help the smug smirk that stretches my lips. "Serves the asshole right for kissing you."

"That asshole helped me save you last night," Huck argues. "Crawled into your truck to unlock it so that you didn't drown in your own puke."

"I..." Well, shit. I really am a fucking asshole. Grabbing his hand, I raise his battered knuckles up between us. "Did you do this trying to get to me?"

He nods and brushes a thumb over the wound on my lip. "You do this when you saw me last night?"

My lack of response is enough of an answer.

"Why didn't you just talk to me, Tay?" There's pain in his voice as he gently palms my throat. "You made it clear that we can figure shit out together, but you were so quick to believe the worst..."

"I know, *I know*." Squeezing my eyes shut, I cover my face and exhale into my palms. "I just...it was that smile. After everything we've been through, all the shit I've done, I never got that smile. It made me jealous. And I've never done this before."

"Dated exclusively."

"Yeah. I don't like other men touching you. And I handled it all wrong."

He's silent for a moment before his fingers pry my hands away from my face, forcing me to meet his steady gaze. "Greg said he could see how different I was right after he kissed me. How much happier I'd become, and the reason is you, baby. That's why I smiled. Because you've made me happier in the last few months than I've felt in years. I was smiling because I was thinking of you."

Emotion clogs my throat as I shake my head. "I don't deserve you. Sometimes I think you're too good for me." At the stiffening of his body, I move in quickly to press our lips together. "But I'm selfish and never want to let you go. So you're stuck with me."

He sighs softly into my mouth before pulling back with a severe look. "You drank last night, Taylor. Downed a whole bottle of rum."

"It's..." Swallowing hard, I glance away in shame. "It's not the first time it's happened. I struggled a lot with staying sober after my dad died and fell off the wagon a bunch. It's why

Christian and I moved in together two years ago. Before then, I lived in my dad's old trailer by myself. Having someone around helps me stay accountable."

"But you work at a bar?" His brows jump up, and I laugh.

"Yeah, with *Christian*. Everything I do is with him. Or Salem. They keep me straight." A snort leaves my nostrils as I grin. "Okay, maybe not *straight*, but you get what I'm saying."

He rolls his eyes but pulls me in for a deep kiss. "I'm glad they have your back like that. After the childhood you had, you deserve people in your corner."

"But what about you?" I ask breathlessly, breaking away from his lips and fighting the urge to rut my hard cock against him. "Who's in your corner, baby? Have you talked to Logan?"

"No, but I don't want to talk about that." He nuzzles into my neck, running his tongue along my tattoo like he loves to do. "Right now, we're discussing you and how you drove out here alone without telling me."

"As a surprise. And I wasn't alone the whole time. I picked up a drifter at one point."

Inhaling sharply, he rears back to grip my jaw. "You did fucking not."

"Did so. His name was Don, he was pretty cool. Used to own a petting zoo down in Florida, but his wife took it in the divorce along with the house and kids."

"I don't know whether you're joking or not." His eyes dart between mine, and when I smile innocently, he rolls over with a growl, pulling me on top of him. "Seriously, Taylor, he could have been a serial killer!"

His thick length presses against me as I roll my hips, loving the way he feels beneath me. "In my defense, I was left unsupervised. You can blame Christian for that. The whole thing was his idea."

"Oh, I'll have words with him when we get home." He cups the back of my neck, prompting me to lean forward so that our lips collide, and then we're moving against each other, his cock rubbing along mine as he fucks into my mouth with his tongue. We do this for a long while, panting and groaning as we kiss each other dizzy, and then Huck suddenly grips my hair roughly, yanking my head back so that his teeth graze my throat.

"Next time something like this happens, when you feel like drinking, you come talk to me," he demands, placing his free hand over the outline on my heart. "Delaware doesn't just apply to our texts and the track, it's our whole fucking lives. Understand?"

"Yes." My own palms run down the hard planes of his chest, nails scraping his nipples. "I will. I promise."

I'll promise anything as long as he keeps touching me like this.

Humming in approval, he releases my hair and tugs down the waistband of the sweats he dressed me in, freeing my cock. "Now fuck my face like you're still mad at me, baby."

And so I do.

Gripping the rungs of the headboard, I slam into his throat until I'm spilling on his tongue, leaning down so that he can kiss my cum into my mouth. It's becoming one of my favorite things that he does. Then after, we strip ourselves bare before he grabs a bottle of lube from the nightstand, and I sink down onto his cock, riding him while he guides me by the hips. My second release coats his chest and abs when he hits my prostate just right, and I swipe my fingers through the mess, bringing them to his lips so that he can lick them clean.

After he pumps me so full it's dripping around his length, I collapse onto him, and he holds me while our bodies are still joined. Another favorite thing of mine that he does. Like he doesn't want to lose our connection just yet. We lay like that for a bit, the stickiness drying between us as he rubs my back. I'm so worn out between the drive yesterday, the drinking, and the sex that I don't even protest when he reaches over into his nightstand and produces the butt plug I'd worn on the camping trip.

"Stay still," he murmurs as if I could even move, and he uses his arm to lift me off of him before replacing his cock with the silicone plug. "You're going to spend the rest of the day filled with my cum, since, apparently, I need to remind you that you're mine."

All I can do is quietly hum and nuzzle into him, loving the possessive tone of his voice and the feel of a part of him still inside of me. I'm almost passed out again when his palm gently smacks my ass.

"Come on, baby, we need to get up and shower."

A whine leaves my throat as I wrap myself tighter around him like an octopus. "Why? So comfy. So tired."

"Because I want to do something else with you that I've never done with anyone," he chuckles into my hair, and I look up at him suspiciously.

"Like what?"

A slow smile lights his face as he kisses me softly. "I want to introduce you to my grandparents."

# HUCKSLEE

Taylor is freaking out. I can tell.

He was silent the entire time we showered, those ocean eyes distant as if lost inside his head. And now, as we stand before the French doors of the guest house, he's gnawing his lip while his fingers twist the bottom of my jersey nervously. The sight of him wearing my college number, combined with the knowledge that my cum is in his ass, has my cock half-hard, and I have to adjust it before throwing open the doors.

"What's going on up there?" I ask, tapping the side of his temple, and his apprehensive gaze flicks up to mine.

"I'm just...I'm not really the 'bring home to mom and dad' type," he says anxiously, making my heart lurch.

"Do you not want to meet them?"

His response is quick. "I do. Of course, I do. I'm just not so sure they'd want to meet *me*."

564

"They'll love you as much as I do." Taking his face between my palms, I give him a chaste kiss, feeling his smirk against my lips.

"You saying you love me?"

That makes me lift a brow. "You know the answer to that. Do I need to say it out loud?"

"Maybe." His smirk turns into a shy smile as he tries to duck his head, but I hold him in place so he can't hide from me.

"Taylor, I love you. I'd be a fool not to."

He searches my gaze for several seconds before grinning widely. "I am quite the catch, huh?"

"Damn straight. Now, come on."

Grabbing his hand, I go to pull him outside, but he tugs me back.

"I love you, too, Huck."

"I know."

He's loved me for a long time, and all I've done so far is put doubts in his head about how I feel. So now I need to ensure that my man believes our feelings are aligned, starting with this.

We make our way out into the backyard, hot California sun already baking the pavement. There's not a cloud in sight, miles of blue sky as far as the eye can see, and a slight breeze rustles the palm trees. Perfect surfing day, if I ever saw one.

"Nice pool," Taylor comments as we pass it, and I glance at the rippling water thoughtfully.

"I've never been in it."

But maybe that's something we can rectify...

Later. Definitely later.

When we reach the sliding glass door under the back porch, he tries to free his hand from mine, but I hold fast, not letting him get away. I know my grandparents are right on the other side because my grandma texted me this morning about breakfast. Sliding open the door, I pull him into a cozy kitchen with hardwood floors and yellow-painted cabinets.

My grandma stands at a gas stove, her back turned to us as she cooks and jokes about something with my gramps, who's sitting at a round table watching the news. Both are already dressed in their Sunday best, having been to church hours ago. I've always been thankful that they've never forced me to attend while I stayed with them.

Gramps is the first to notice us, his eyes widening when they drop to where Taylor's sweaty palm clasps mine.

"Well, hello," he says lightly, salt and pepper mustache twitching as he sits back in his chair. "What do we have here?"

His tone causes Grandma to turn around, and she freezes momentarily before a warm smile lights up her fair complexion.

"Good morning, you two. Breakfast is almost ready, please have a seat."

There's a knowing spark in her green eyes, so different from the dark ones that Mom shared with Gramps and I. Honestly, the only trait I share with my Grandma is the light hair, which I also get from Dad. Even my skin tone is deeper, though not as dark as Gramps and Moms.

"Grandma, Gramps." Drawing their attention, I pull Taylor in front of me. "I'd like to introduce you to my boyfriend, Taylor."

They know who he is, though they've never met him. Back in high school, I'd phoned them multiple times about the bully who never gave me a break. Recently, I'd informed of his past with his dad, to some extent, though I didn't go into detail about a lot of things, like what he'd done at prom or the fact that we're dating.

Raising a shaking hand, Taylor waves awkwardly. "Hi, Mr. and Mrs. Jones. Nice to meet you."

"Oh, sweet boy." Grandma wipes her hands on the apron she's wearing and crosses the small kitchen, pulling Taylor in for a hug. "It's so nice to finally meet. Huckslee's told us so much about you."

Gramps rises to his full height of six foot seven, towering over everyone as he reaches out to shake my boyfriend's hand. "This is long overdue, but welcome to the family, son."

Taylor's back stiffens for a second before he relaxes, arms slowly coming up to return my grandma's hug, and I have to clear my throat at the emotion swelling from the sight. I will always love my dad and be thankful for everything he did for me, but no one in the family has ever been as supportive as my mom's parents. They understand discrimination themselves, having been an interracial couple in the nineteen-sixties, and they welcomed me with open arms when I fled Utah after coming out. Taylor asked me earlier who I had in my corner. I can easily say without a doubt that Grandma and Gramps are there for me one hundred percent.

We sit at the table as Grandma goes back to cooking, shaking her head at me when I ask if she needs any help, and Tay's hand finds mine again. I squeeze it, flashing him a smirk when he squirms on the chair, no doubt due to the plug. A gorgeous pink blooms on his face as he kicks my leg under the table and avoids my gaze.

We spend the morning chatting and eating massive amounts of pancakes while they engage him in conversation about motocross. And they're *actually* interested, not just pretending for my sake, because they were the ones who bought me my first dirt bike. Gramps used to race back in the day, though far from the professional level.

Grandma tells the story of how they met; Gramps, the bad boy next door, rode a motorcycle that her parents disapproved of. When she gushes about how hot he was as a teen, Taylor bursts into laughter, the darkness in his eyes slowly dissipating. I can't help but lean in to kiss his cheeks, which puff up with every smile.

It hits me then, this sense of rightness in the moment. How normal it feels to have him here, sharing a meal with my grandparents like the last eight years were nothing more than a fever dream. And maybe they were. Because I'm finally awake for the first time in what feels like forever. I've come home.

We're in the Audi heading back to pick up his truck a few hours later, and Taylor faces me thoughtfully.

"Your grandparents are cool. I think they like me, but honestly, they aren't what I expected. I thought they'd be, like, super rich."

"They aren't millionaires or anything, but I know they have money." My hand reaches for his as I switch lanes, not even caring that I'm being clingy. "Gramps is retired from the state, and my grandma still trains horses at her ranch just like my mom did."

He hums, running a thumb over my knuckle absently. "And you never brought a guy over to meet them before?"

"Nope."

"Why not?"

Lifting a shoulder, I glance at him sideways, weighing my words carefully. "Nobody ever felt permanent enough to bother. If that makes sense."

"It does, I think. Like, I get it. Why go through all the effort of introducing someone to your family if you aren't even sure they'll be around long enough to really appreciate them?"

"Exactly." My heart warms as I take an exit toward the coastline. "So, I have an idea for today. How about we get your truck later, and I can show you some of my favorite things about the city instead?"

A grin spreads across his features, flashing that crooked incisor and brightening those blue-green eyes. "Fuck, yeah. I'd love that."

So I take him everywhere—or at least try to, with the hours we have left in the day. He's here for the week, and I know we have time, but I try to stuff as much as I can into our minutes together, regardless.

We visit my favorite coffee spot, which has a perfect view of the Bay. Sitting in my usual spot, I order him the best raspberry cream latte he's ever had, guaranteed.

Next is the bar I worked at, although I was initially unsure about bringing him inside. But we had a conversation about trusting one another that made me realize I can't treat him any differently just because he relapsed. Just like I hated being treated differently after I overdosed. He proves my point further by turning down the free shots one of my old co-workers offers us, but thanks her anyway.

There's a surf shop Shawn owns with his dad that I drag him to if only to set the record straight that Greg is, in fact, my ex. Despite the confusion, the two hit it off and Shawn offers to give Tay some surfing lessons later in the week. It's nice of him, but if anyone is teaching my boyfriend how to surf, it'll be me, though I'm not all that great at it.

Finally, I show him the little cantina just off the beach that serves the most delicious tacos al pastor—which, of course, aren't as good as Christian's mom's—and we end the day by sitting in the sand, watching the sunset. It's his first time seeing the ocean, and I want to make it memorable for him.

There's so much more I want to show him, but we have time. I have to keep reminding myself of that. We still have two more months.

The thought hits me as I wrap my arms around him, pulling his back to my chest while the waves lap at our feet. When all of this started, I wasn't sure how we could make it work with so much bad blood between us, but now...now, that's all I want to do. Make sure that this works so I can keep him, even if we'll be separated again in August.

"So, what's the plan for the rest of the week?" He asks, grabbing a handful of sand before letting it slip through his fingers.

"Well, the graduation ceremony is in a few days, and I have a few things to prepare for. I'm packing up the rest of my stuff so that..." I trail off but clear my throat to continue. "So that once I find a place in Baltimore, my grandparents can ship everything to me."

He goes still, tensing slightly. "Have you started looking?"

"Here and there, yeah. My new agent has been sending me some listings, but I don't need to make a final decision until next month."

A few of the players on my new team have also been helping out to break the ice. So far, they seem nice and easy to get along with, and they send me suggestions on which areas are good and which I should avoid.

Taylor grows quiet, eyes on the setting sun reflecting over glittering waves. I wish I could crawl inside his head and look around.

Grabbing his chin, I tilt his face up to mine. "What are you thinking?"

"I can come visit you whenever I want, right? And we'll still video call as much as we can?"

"Yeah. Of course." I give him a small smile, knowing it doesn't reach my eyes. "I just wish we'd had more than one summer."

*Tick, tick, tick.*

"We'll make it work. You'll have plenty of free time in the off-season, and I can fly to games. It'll be fine."

Nodding, I press my lips to his, noticing how he shuts his eyes to hide his thoughts from me. Like he's hearing his words but doesn't truly believe them. And as much as I want to accept them, I'm also worried that I'll give him empty promises if I agree. It'll take both of us putting in the effort for this to work, but what if he can't? What if he doesn't want to?

What if I just gave my heart to someone who broke it once before already?

"Hey." Taylor turns slightly, trailing kisses down my jaw. "I can tell we're both in our heads about this, so let's get out of them. Show me something else you like."

My arms tighten around him involuntarily as I stare at the rolling waves. "You want to go for a swim?"

He eyes the ocean suspiciously, eyes narrowed. "I'm good."

"You afraid of the ocean, baby?" I grin at how adorable that is, my self-proclaimed badass afraid of a bit of water. It's a complete juxtaposition to the guy from high school who laughed in my face and called me a sissy for being scared of spiders.

"Hell yeah, I'm afraid. Literally, everything out there can and will eat me."

Pressing my lips to his ear, I sweep my tongue against the lobe. "Why don't we go back to the house and swim in the pool so I can eat you instead?"

I've never seen him run to the car so fast in my life.

# TAYLOR

M y lungs burn, chest spasming for air as I take Huck's cock to the back of my throat again and again.

The pool lights cast an ethereal glow, everything hazy as he uses my mouth like his own personal Fleshlight beneath the water, and I've never been more turned on. I'm hard as steel, my own cock straining between my legs as I fuck my fist to the taste of his precum on my tongue, free hand rolling and gently tugging on his sac.

It took a lot of convincing to get Huck to agree to this.

Ever since what happened at the cabin, he's made it his mission to be gentle with me whenever I go down on him. While I appreciate the sentiment, I'm done with that shit. He has nothing to fear. When he admitted that he hadn't been in a pool since that night in high school, I knew this was the perfect opportunity for us to take back some power. At first, he was adamantly against it, worried he'd traumatize me, which broke my heart to pieces when I realized the damage I'd done all those years ago.

No more. No more living in the past, regretting the choices we made. If we're going to move on with our lives, it has to end at some point. And that point is now, with Huckslee gripping my shoulders beneath the cool water, thrusting down my throat while the world fades to black around me, my dick leaking as I pump myself.

Lack of oxygen combined with rough fingers pulling my hair has my orgasm slamming into me, bubbles forming around my face when I moan through my nose and swallow Huck's length, sending him over the edge himself. Thick ropes of cum slide down my constricting throat, salty warmth that I've become addicted to. By the time he pulls me to the surface, I'm almost ready to pass out, my lips parting to suck down air as he crushes me tightly to his slick chest.

"Goddamn, Taylor," he cries into my skin, sounding as wrecked as I feel. "That was...Jesus. Are you ok? Did I hurt you?"

I shake my head because that's all I can do while I catch my breath, fingers and toes tingling. Rivulets of water run down my cheeks, lids too tired to keep open, and my body suddenly feels lighter than air, so I just float there and let Huckslee keep me from drifting away. Like an anchor holding me steady.

He gently cups my face, searching with those eyes that remind me of the constellations inked down my back. "I need words, baby. Are you ok?"

"Fucking fantastic," I rasp, sagging against him with a sleepy smile. "Five minutes, and we can go again."

"Oh, hell no. The only thing we're doing in five minutes is going to bed."

A hoarse chuckle leaves my throat as I kiss his collarbone. "You're such an old man. It's barely ten-thirty."

"We all can't be pretty like you, I need my beauty sleep. Come on." He walks us up the stairs and out of the pool naked, my legs wrapped around his waist.

"What the fuck ever. You're the most beautiful person I've ever met."

"Stop trying to kiss my ass."

"But it's such a nice ass." I squeeze his cheeks when he sets me down in front of the shower, shaking his head with a grin before turning away.

Once we've washed away the chlorine off our skin—and the plug is removed from my ass—Huck leads me back out onto the deck, where he plops into a lounger in his boxers, arms open for me to crawl onto his lap. We sit like that for a long time, his fingers massaging my neck while I run mine across his abs. Silent but content. Mind empty of anything but him and this moment.

"I can see why you blacked out all those years ago," I murmur eventually, exhausted. "After the pool, I mean. I'm completely zonked."

He hums softly against my temple. "Breath play will do that to you. I was also on some meds back then that I think had some weird side effects."

Jesus. And I had no clue. Shit could have gone down differently, and that fact scares the hell out of me. A world without Huckslee is a world I don't want to be a part of.

"Is that something you've done often with past partners? Breath play?"

"Uh," he coughs, cheeks turning red. "Sometimes."

"Aw, are you blushing, Huckslee?" His scowl makes me laugh. "That's cute. No need to be shy, baby, I've told you tons about my sexual history."

He shifts uncomfortably beneath me. "I don't kiss and tell."

"Uh-huh, sure." Leaning down to kiss his throat, I feel his Adam's apple bob under my lips. "Can I ask you one question?"

"Just one."

Inhaling deeply, I pause for a moment to gather courage. "Why don't you ever bottom?"

I've been dying to know since the never-have-I-ever game at the cabin but haven't had the balls to ask.

He's quiet for so long, I worry I've upset him, but then he lifts a shoulder and threads our fingers together. "I like being in control. There's a certain power imbalance that comes with bottoming that I've just never been comfortable with. Growing up, I never had a lot of choice, so I'm sure it stems from that."

"Yeah, that makes sense." Nuzzling into him with a yawn, I shut my eyes. "Odd thing for me to enjoy it, though, considering my own childhood."

"I don't think it's odd at all. You also didn't get a lot of say when it came to your dad, and now you can *choose* to give up choice. For a lot of people, that's very freeing."

*Well...shit.* I've never thought about it that way before. And yet, what he's saying makes so much sense when I remember all of the ways I lashed out growing up as a way to feel some control.

"Daddy issues for the win," I mumble, feeling his chest shake as he snorts into my hair.

"What made you ask?"

"No reason. Was just curious."

It's true, for the most part. Do I ever think about topping him someday? Hell fucking yeah, I do. But I also know that it's not something he likes, and I'd never push him to do what he won't enjoy. The dynamic between us right now is perfect as it is; I'm one hundred percent happy taking his cock in my ass for the rest of our lives if that's what he wants.

He runs his fingers through my hair until I doze off, waking only when he leans down to kiss my lips softly.

"I love you, Taylor."

Those words light me up, spreading warmth from my head to my toes. I'll never get tired of hearing them.

"I love you too, Huck."

With every atom and every breath. Whatever happens in August, nothing else matters.

Just him, me, and whatever life we can carve out for ourselves.

# TAYLOR

## July

**"I** don't think this is a good idea."

Standing on the porch of our parent's house, I eye the front door like it just offended my great ancestors. Music and laughter filter through the open windows, the smell of roasted meat wafting from the backyard. The Davis Fourth of July annual barbecue is in full swing, and only one of us got an invite.

Bet you can guess which one isn't on the guest list.

"I think it's a great idea." Huckslee bumps my shoulder, hands stuffed into his pockets to keep himself from reaching for me. "You're a part of this family, too. You belong with me."

Those words send a flutter through my stomach, but the butterflies are quickly squashed by the wave of nausea rampaging through my gut. This is a terrible fucking idea.

Honestly, this last month has been a dream come true. We spent that whole week together in California, and Huck showed me so many new things. The Golden Gate Bridge, Alcatraz, Six Flags. Somehow, he still found time to take me surfing—which I will not be doing again, because sharks. I even went to his graduation ceremony with his grandparents, where he officially introduced me to his college teammates as his boyfriend. A few of them seemed weirded out that I was also his stepbrother, but fuck 'em. We had the time of our lives.

Upon returning home, Logan made it clear that he and Huck should get some distance for a while. I know it hurts Huck more than he's letting on, but he refuses to discuss it. In the meantime, he's been staying with me for the last few weeks, and I've let him know that I'm here when he needs to talk. But integrating him into my life has been so fucking easy.

During the day, Christian and I practice our routines on our bikes while Huck gets into shape for training camp and Arya cuts hair at the salon she just started working for. By night, we're at the Prospector, with Christian and me managing the dishes while Huckslee bartends, thanks to Juanita giving him a temporary job until he leaves—I batted my pretty lashes until she said yes. On our days off, we all come together, making dinner and cuddling on the sectional while Baby Bones hops all over the four of us. Huck is one hell of a cook; who knew?.

Just...living. Existing, enjoying each other's presence. For the first time, it's made me see what life with Huck could really be like, and I don't want to give it up. I don't want to rock the boat. Which is why, I repeat, him bringing me here is a *terrible fucking idea*.

"Maybe I should change," I mumble, staring down at my shirt of Venom with his long tongue obscenely wrapped around a melting ice cream cone. It's one of the samples for *T.O.T* that Huck and Royce worked on. Even though I love the design, it's highly inappropriate for a family barbecue. Why the fuck did I wear this? I should swing by Christian's mom's and borrow a t-shirt from his little brother.

"Absolutely not." Huck sweeps his gaze from side to side, ensuring no one is watching, before pulling me in for a quick kiss. "I like my artwork on you. And besides, why should you hide yourself from them?"

"Isn't that exactly what we're doing?"

My question has him stepping back with a frown, sadness flashing in his eyes. "Yeah. You're right."

Disappointment claws at my throat, but I swallow it down because, honestly, neither of us is ready to come out to both our parents about our relationship. I don't know if we'll ever be. He already told me how Aaron has never asked about any of his relationships over the last four years, so it's safe to assume that he already disapproves of Huckslee's sexuality. It's always been a sore spot between them, and the last thing I want to do is make things more strained. I couldn't care less what Maisie thinks, but family is important to Huck. Always has been.

"Stop that." He reaches up to thumb my bottom lip out from between my teeth. "It's going to be fine. I promise."

"Okay."

It will not be fine. Ever since the night I nearly beat Aaron unconscious, the entire family has been against me, and I don't blame them. Not that they were ever on my side. Pretty sure I don't even know the names of half the people here.

*Why did I come again?*

"If it makes you feel any better, this is my first Independence Day here since I left for Cali." Stepping up to the door, Huck glances at me over his shoulder. "Ready?"

*No.* "Yep."

As soon as he pushes open the front door, he's immediately swarmed by three boys who look no older than nine or ten, all identical, their arms hanging off of him as they jump all over. From their features, I'm pretty sure they're Logan's siblings.

"Huckslee!"

"I brought a football. Can we go play?!"

"Who's that?" One of them glances under Huck's arms at me, shyer than the other two, and Huck grins down at them with a laugh.

"Holy crap, look at you three! When did you grow so big?"

They pull him toward the backyard, leaving me awkwardly in the entryway. Without the grounding presence of Huck, I can sense a heavy silence. Glancing into the living room, I find a bunch of eyes on me. Some are wide, some squinted, and I recognize a few, like Maisie's sisters' haughty gaze.

Lifting my hand in a half-hearted wave, I follow Huck, ignoring the prickling, itchy feeling as I pass the staircase leading up to the bathroom. Too many bad memories up there.

When I step into the kitchen, Maisie and a few other women who must be from Huck's side of the family are in there. I don't miss the disapproving sweep of her gaze when she spots me.

"Taylor? What are you doing here?" She sounds polite, but I know what that sickly, sweet tone of her voice hides, so I just lift a shoulder as I pass out the backdoor.

"Huckslee invited me."

I get no response, but I wasn't expecting one anyway. Stepping onto the deck, I arrive just in time to watch Huck get tackled by one of the triplets into the grass. Well, *pretend* to get tackled because he's incredibly muscled, and they're all pretty scrawny. Aaron is standing around a smoker with a few people, unaware of my intrusion. I take the time to study him now that I've met Huck's grandparents. I can see the resemblance in hair color and facial shape alone, but overall, he definitely takes after his mother's side.

"Hey, man," comes a voice to my right, and I spot Logan sitting on a patio chair at the end of the deck. His brows are raised as if surprised to see me. "Didn't know you were coming."

"Yeah...me either until this morning. Huckslee dragged me along."

He studies my clothes as I take a seat next to him. "Nice shirt. That Huck's work?"

"Yeah, how'd you guess?"

"I know his style." Logan glances toward the lawn, watching Huck throw the football for a few other kids who have joined in, a flash of hurt still prominent in his eyes. Something twists in my gut, feeling slightly responsible for the rift between their friendship.

"Look, Logan, about Huck and I—"

He cuts me off before I can get any further. "It's fine, Taylor. Really, it wasn't your responsibility to tell me anything."

I stay quiet, thinking through what to say as I meet Huck's gaze. His eyes flick to Logan and back to me in question, and I flash him my stomach. It distracts him enough that the football hits his cheek with a loud *smack*. The small girl who threw it giggles as I burst into laughter, which earns me a dark look from my boyfriend, promising retribution later. I'm tempted to blow him a kiss or flip him off, but I refrain, choosing to sit back and smirk instead.

*Do your worst, baby.*

His tongue darts out to wet his lips, eyes trailing down my body as if he can read the challenge in my features. When he turns back to the game, I feel the loss of his attention immediately, like a blanket being ripped away in a cold room. And damn if I don't want it back.

"Word of advice," Logan says slowly, a small smile on his lips. "You both might want to stop looking at each other like that if you're trying to keep things under wraps because I saw *everything* just now."

Ah, shit.

I open my mouth to respond when a deep voice startles me from behind.

"Keep what under wraps, son?"

Logan visibly winces, and I turn to see a man I'm sure is his father, if I remember correctly. He was Aaron's best man at the wedding. We both flounder for an answer until Huckslee steps onto the deck, saving us from looking like fish out of water.

"I've started making concept art for Taylor and his friend's stunt bike act," he explains as Aaron studies us from the smoker. "Like the picture on his shirt. I drew it."

Cold eyes take in the shirt in question as I lift my hat to nervously run a hand through my hair. "Yeah, we're in the process of creating a business. Kinda was thinking of asking Logan again to be our business manager now that he has his degree."

Logan's brows jump at that, but his dad shakes his head.

"My boy is far too busy at work for your little side hustle."

*Oh, fuck you, old man.*

"With all due respect," I drawl, my cheeks heating at the dismissive tone of his voice, "your *boy* is an adult and can decide for himself."

He rears back, sucking his teeth while Huck gapes at me. Before he can respond, Aaron calls us over by the smoker.

"Boys, come get these steak burgers and bring them inside."

Huck, Logan, and I make our way over, and I can feel his dad's seething gaze on the back of my head. We each grab a plate stacked with meat and take them inside to the kitchen, where Maisie stands at the stove. The room falls heavily quiet, like everyone hushed as soon as we walked in, and the shifty glances from people tell me they were probably talking about me.

Sweat breaks out on my neck under their scrutiny, making me feel like a bug under a microscope or a fish in a bowl. Huck starts a conversation with some family members in the dining room, chatting about football and graduation, entirely at ease in the environment. All the while, I can feel gazes prickling my skin, some more hostile than others. Whether the stares are coming from Huck's side of the family or Maisie's, I can't be sure because I know nobody here, and they don't know me.

*I don't belong here.*

The thought has me mumbling to Huck that I need some air, ignoring the concerned pinch of his brows as I make a beeline for the front. Eyes follow me the whole way, watching, analyzing, and I suck in a deep breath when I make it out onto the front porch. Leaning against the door, I finally feel like I can relax. My lids sink closed momentarily as I inhale, shaking my shoulders to rid myself of the crawly feeling of everyone's judgment.

A deep chuckle draws my attention, and my eyes snap open to spy a figure sitting on the steps, studying me over his shoulder. He's got unkempt brown hair, a sleeve of tattoos, and a lip piercing. I've never seen him around; his appearance is totally out of place with the crowd inside, much like mine.

"I know the feeling," he says, something familiar about his honey-colored eyes taking me in. I just nod because I have no clue what the fuck he's talking about.

Moving past him down the steps, I walk across the lawn to Huckslee's Audi, my attention lingering on a sleek black Ducati parked behind it. Reaching into the glove box, I pull out a pack of cigarettes and light one up, swinging my gaze back to the stranger watching me with a smile.

"Mind if I bum one of those off you?" he asks. "I'm dying for a smoke."

I wave him over, too irritated with the people inside to form a complete sentence at the moment.

There is something so reminiscent of how he unfolds himself to a stand, significantly taller than Huck or me. As he stalks over with long legs, it finally registers who he reminds me of.

"You related to Logan?"

He huffs, taking a cigarette and my lighter from me. "Yep. I'm his uncle, Devon."

"Ah, I've heard about you."

Logan mentioned an uncle numerous times over the two years he dated Salem and how he doesn't come around much because he doesn't get along with Logan's dad. I didn't expect him to look so...young. But what do I know?

"All bad things, I hope." Devon winks, puffing on his smoke, and I kick the curb with my Doc.

"I don't think Logan has it in him to talk bad about anyone. I'm Taylor."

His eyes widen a fraction, sweeping down my frame. "The stepkid who beat up Aaron?"

"Uh...yeah."

*And the stepbrother's boyfriend.* But I don't say those words out loud.

"No shit?" He matches my stance, leaning a hip against the Audi while he takes me in with renewed interest. I squirm under the attention, feeling slightly uncomfortable. "Well, would you look at us. Two peas in a pod."

I raise my cigarette in mock cheers. "Here's to the black sheep."

His eyes snag on my arms. "Nice ink. Mind if I take a look?"

"Sure."

I expect him to just step closer, but he surprises me by reaching out to grab my wrist. Lifting my arm to his face, he turns it over to study my skin. While he examines my tattoos, I glance again at the beautiful piece of machinery parked behind Huck's car.

"That your bike?"

"Yep." His eyes flick up to mine. "Do you know anything about bikes at all?"

My lips twitch. "A little bit, yeah."

"Wanna go for a ride?"

The question takes me off guard, and I tamp down the immediate response of 'fuck yes' that wants to barrel out of my mouth. Honestly, I've wanted a motorcycle for years but never had the funds. Plus, the cigarette isn't cutting it; I'm itching for some kind of rush after dealing with the dumpster fire that is Maisie's family inside, but...

"I better go let Huckslee know first," I murmur, more to myself than anything.

Devon's brows lift amusedly. "Why? Is he your keeper?"

"He's..." No, but something about taking off without telling him seems wrong. "He's my ride. I'll be right back."

"I'll be waiting," he breathes as I step away, the flirty tone of his voice making my steps falter.

It's not like men haven't flirted with me before; it used to happen constantly at the Prospector when Christian and I shot some pool. And though I was never interested, I played into it because that's just who I am—a major flirt. But something about it happening now that I'm with Huck makes me feel icky, and I'm not sure I like it.

When I step back in, the house has the same tense vibe, and I try my best to ignore the looks as I search for Huck, my jaw tight.

"Huck in the kitchen?" I ask Logan when I see him coming into the dining room. He nods, opening his mouth to say something, but the curt tone of Maisie's voice cuts him off.

"Really, Huckslee, what were you thinking, inviting him? After what he did to your father?"

Logan and I both freeze, our wide eyes meeting as we stand hidden just beyond the archway, out of sight.

"He was going through a rough time," Huck answers placatingly. "That was years ago. He's changed."

"And that's an excuse to lay hands on someone?"

I flinch at her words as I hear him sigh. "No, of course not, but he's better now. Sober. He's been through therapy for the stuff that happened with his dad."

"What stuff?"

My heart starts to pound rapidly in my chest, both Logan and I as still as stone.

"The abuse."

Maisie huffs, lips smacking in protest. "Is that what he told you? Taylor is a compulsive liar, Huck. He has been since he was a child."

I don't even hear his response over the roaring of blood in my ears, breaths coming out in ragged, short gasps. White-hot rage licks up my spine, my hands fisting at my sides to keep from punching the drywall.

Compulsive liar. That's a new one, I'll give her that. As if she had ever paid enough attention to me to tell if I had lied while growing up. Things didn't even get bad for me until *after* she left.

Logan places a hand on my shoulder, eyes filled with sympathy, but I shake him off, backing away toward the door.

"Tell Huck I'm going for a ride with your uncle," is all I say before turning on my heel to exit the house, blood boiling. Devon is waiting on his bike, head bent while he scrolls through his phone, and he smiles at me when I approach.

"Your babysitter give you permission?"

I grit my teeth, choosing not to respond as I climb on behind him, just wanting to get away from this fucking house and this fucking family. They aren't mine, not truly. Never have been. Salem and Christian are all I need. Matty, Hannah, and Xed, too.

"Grab on," he says before starting the bike, and my arms wrap around his thin waist. He feels wrong against me, nothing like the man I really wish I could hold right now, but I can't make Huckslee choose between me and his family. I can't. I won't.

So I hang on tight, craving high speed as Devon peels out, taking me away from the other half of my heart.

# HUCKSLEE

My jaw clenches so hard at Maisie's words I swear I hear a molar crack.

I've never hated her more than I do at this moment.

"I just don't understand why you'd think this was a good idea. He's violent and unpredictable, just like his father was."

But he's not. And I can't believe my ears are even hearing a mother talk about their child this way right now. Over the last few months, I've grown to know Taylor better than I know myself—all his scars, hopes, and dreams. He's beautiful, inside and out. It took me far too long to realize that, and it eats me up that his own mom can't even see that about the human she brought into this world.

"Now, Mais, let's just catch our breaths." Dad tries to calm the storm brewing in the room, but his wife is having none of it.

"I do not want him here. Not after what he did to you, Aaron. And Huckslee, have you forgotten that he wrecked your car? You boys never got along, I don't know what's changed—"

The anger inside me bubbles to its boiling point, and finally, I snap, unable to stand her vitriol any longer.

"Taylor and I are dating."

I shout it out loud enough for the whole house to hear, cutting off her words. A shocked silence permeates the air, my dad and Maisie wearing matching expressions of astonishment. When Dad's features morph into appalled, I speak again, feeling like I've just been shot in the chest.

"I love him. I have for years, and I won't stand here and listen to you break him down when he's already been broken enough by one parent. We all make mistakes and do things we regret, but people can change. He's the one for me, and if you can't accept that, then this is the last time you'll see me."

Without a backward glance, I exit the kitchen, intending to find Taylor so that I can kiss him breathless. It's dead quiet in the house, aunts, uncles, and cousins gaping at me, but I don't give a fuck. My feet barely make it through the dining room when Logan pulls me back by my arm, an odd look on his face. I'm surprised to have his attention on me, seeing as we haven't talked in weeks.

"Taylor's gone," he rushes out, eyes like saucers, and my brows slam together.

"Gone? What do you mean, gone?"

"He heard everything Maisie said and got upset. Said he was going for a ride with my Uncle Dev before your big announcement."

*What the hell?*

"Your uncle's here? I didn't even see him."

We both hurry to the front door, my gaze sweeping over the porch and lawn, hoping to catch them before they leave, but they're nowhere to be found.

Logan rubs the back of his neck. "He must have shown up shortly after you did because I didn't see him either. I don't think I told you this, but things between him and my family have been bad ever since he came out as bisexual."

My stomach drops, my mind racing with all kinds of scenarios, jealousy simmering deep in my gut. What the fuck is Taylor thinking? He doesn't even know Devon; why would he go off with a total stranger instead of talking to me? Pulling out my phone, I thumb over to the group chat, finding a message from him already sitting in the thread. I only smile slightly at the contact name he made for himself after I showed him the movie *Superbad*:

> McLovin: Sorry, Huck, I can't be there anymore.

> Met Logan's uncle, he's pretty chill. Offered me a ride on his motorcycle.

> Stay as long as you need, there's no rush. We'll be at Flytrap when you're ready.

A muttered curse leaves my throat. Flytrap is a gay bar in the next town over, about ten minutes from here. Why the fuck would he be going to a bar? *With a strange bisexual man he's never met?*

Goddammit, Taylor. God-fucking-dammit.

"I gotta go." Shoving my cell into my pocket, I march toward the Audi, seeing red. I'm about to shift into drive when the passenger door opens, and Logan meets my bewildered gaze with a half-smile as he slides on his seatbelt.

"I've seen you two fight; someone's gotta be there to limit the bloodshed."

"Oh, trust me," I growl, taking off down the road, "you don't want to witness the things I'm gonna do to him. Not unless you want therapy afterwards."

He only shakes his head, saying nothing during the drive while 'Blackout' by Breathe Carolina blasts through my speakers. We're almost to the bar when he turns to me thoughtfully.

"Did you mean it? What you said to your dad and Maisie about Taylor?"

"What? They'll never see me again if they can't accept Taylor and I?" At his nod, I give him one of my own. "I meant every word. The way I feel about him, Loge...it's everything. They've got him all wrong, and if they won't take the time to understand him, then I want nothing to do with them. He's my priority. I won't lose him because of what they think."

He's quiet for a long time, processing my words, and I have a feeling he's thinking about his own issues, but I'm too anxious right now to ask him about it. I definitely will later, after I've taught my boyfriend a lesson about getting into vehicles with strangers since he didn't learn when I bent him over my knee for picking up a hitchhiker.

Seriously, this motherfucker is going to make my blood pressure higher than it already is.

The parking lot is packed by the time we pull in, sunset on the horizon. Flytrap is on the smaller end, but as the only gay bar in the surrounding rural areas, it draws quite the crowd. I've never been inside, but Royce mentions the place from time to time. People exit and enter the front wooden door in all kinds of attire, ranging from patriotic body suits for the holiday to leather halters and platform boots.

Music thumps from the sound system when we step up to the large bouncer at the door, giving him our IDs, and as we make it onto the dance floor, I search the space for my man. It's not lost on me how similar this is to the frat party, how much our stories intertwine like the universe is trying to find our perfect balance. Like finding Delaware.

We saddle up to the bar, pushing between people to get the bartender's attention. He's wearing nothing but a pleated skirt and a bow tie, bare torso on display, and his eyes light up when he catches me waving at him.

"What can I get for you, sweetheart?" He leans an elbow on the countertop, a seductive smile playing on his lips. I pull up a photo of Taylor on my phone that I took at the San Diego Zoo back in California.

"Have you seen this guy around?"

He briefly eyes the picture, rolling his lips between his teeth. "That cutie? Yeah, he's here with Devon. Booth in the other room, far back corner. Why? There's no trouble, I hope?"

"Oh, there will be." My teeth are clenched, so I don't think he can hear me, but his wary eyes follow Logan and me as we push through the dance floor into the second room where the tables are. Following the bartender's directions, I spot Taylor huddled in a corner booth with an older-looking Devon than I remember.

Logan's uncle has my boyfriend's hand in his, holding it up to his face while he studies the markings on his knuckles, and

I cross my arms to watch. I'm sure he's asking what the four Japanese symbols tattooed there mean, and I hope Taylor tells him that it's my name forever inked into his skin. I fucked his brains out after he admitted to me what they meant.

Taylor pulls his hand away, looking slightly uncomfortable as he lifts a drink to take a sip, and I tense. It's a clear glass with dark brown liquid. Is it whiskey? Rum? Beer? Devon reaches out to touch the dragonfly on Taylor's throat, causing my hands to flex with the urge to break his fingers, which shocks the hell out of me. When did I get so violent? My boyfriend backs away, his gaze bouncing around the room uneasily, eyes darkening when they land on mine. He visibly swallows, and I know he can feel the rage radiating off of me.

Logan follows silently as I stalk over to them, Taylor's attention holding mine the entire way. His teeth sink into his bottom lip as he tries to hide his smirk.

*Oh, you're in so much trouble.*

My cock swells with ideas about what I'm going to do to him, and I mentally thank whatever higher power is out there for choosing to wear a long enough shirt today to hide it. When we step up to the side of the table, Devon whips his head around before flashing us a wide grin.

"Well, if it isn't my favorite nephew and his best friend, the football star. Made a break for it, too, huh?"

I ignore him, focusing on Taylor instead as I point a finger at his drink. "We're doing this again? I thought we agreed that you'd come to me the next time you felt like drinking?"

Devon looks peeved as Taylor leans back in his seat, eyes like green pools of fury when he flicks a wrist at me. "Why don't you take a sip, asshole, and see what's in the cup before making assumptions?"

With nostrils flared, I do as he says, tasting nothing but Dr. Pepper on my tongue as I glower at Taylor's smug face.

Devon scoffs, glancing between us. "I don't know what I'm missing, but your stepbro can make his own decisions."

Logan chokes on his spit, coughing into his arm as I raise a brow at Taylor expectantly.

"That so?"

He swallows again, the column of his throat flexing, and I catch how he subtly shifts in his seat to adjust himself. "Yup. I'm a big boy. I can do what I want."

"Hmm," I hum, tapping my chin. "You're right. And so can I. I'm going to find someone to dance with."

"Wait, what the fuck—"

Without giving him a chance to finish, I stride toward the dance floor, knowing full well I won't get far. I've barely entered the crowd when a hand grips my arm, spinning me around, and I grin down into Taylor's blazing eyes.

"Got you."

He jabs a finger into my chest, lips curling into a snarl. "First off, fuck you. And second off, why are you mad at me?"

"*Me?*" Wrapping my arms around him, I grind my hard cock against his thigh as I yank his head back by the hair. "Why am I mad that you took off with a stranger without a word?"

His breath hitches, pupils blowing wide with desire as he licks his lips. "Devon's not a stranger, and I told Logan where I was going. Plus, I texted. Those are words."

"But he's a stranger to *you*," I growl as I capture his bottom lip between my teeth. "You can't just take off on bikes with men you don't know."

"I...I couldn't be in that house anymore, Huck," he breathes, matching my thrusts as we rut against each other on the dance floor. "The shit Maisie was saying, everyone's judgment. I don't belong there but I didn't want to ruin your holiday. They're your family."

"You're my family, too. And if you're ever in a situation that makes you uncomfortable, communicate, and we'll leave. Understand?"

He nods, small whimpers of pleasure working his throat as he clings to me.

I grip his jaw firmly. "Words, baby."

"*Yes*, goddamn. Now, can we go? Everyone's at Christian's mom's, and I want to get off before we go blow shit up. Plus, we didn't get to eat, and I'm starving."

*Ah, that's cute.* He thinks he's off the hook for ditching me, but I'm not easily distracted.

Spinning around, I yank him toward the back, where a sign hangs from the ceiling pointing toward the bathroom. There's a dimly lit hall and, thankfully, no line, so the toilet is empty when I pull him inside and throw the lock. As soon as I turn around, he's on me, clawing at the button on my jeans while our mouths crash together, sucking, biting, a mess of spit and teeth.

He practically climbs me like a tree, wrapping his thighs around my hips to writhe against my cock, desperate and needy for me. I fucking love it when he's like this. Taylor has an insatiable sex drive, much to my delight. Every morning over the past few weeks has been spent with his cum on my tongue, some days swallowing, some days feeding it back to him, and I've come to crave it more than caffeine.

But my baby is in trouble. He has a lesson to learn, and I'm going to make sure I get my point across.

"Turn around, hands on the sink," I command, reveling in the shiver of anticipation that visibly shakes him. He bites his lip, letting go of me as he obeys, eyeing me in the mirror with a mixture of lust and defiance. Pressing my chest to his back, I hold his gaze as I slide my tongue along the side of his neck, tasting the salty sweat on his skin as I push his pants and briefs down just past his ass only, keeping his hard cock trapped.

"Bend forward."

That gorgeous face of his twists into a sneer. "Hmm...nah."

"That wasn't a request." Biting down on his ear until he hisses, I lick the sting away, unsure of when this kinky game between us started but loving it all the same.

His eyes flash, ass pushing back against my bulge. "Make me."

Placing my palm against his back, I hook an ankle around his leg and roughly force him down until he has no choice but to brace his forearms on the counter or risk smashing his face.

"Jesus," he chokes, a flush blossoming on his skin as I lightly trail a finger through his crease. That tight, pink hole puckers under my touch, begging to be filled.

"Remember what happened in Cali when we talked about going on rides with strangers?" I ask softly, gently rimming him as he moans softly.

"Y-yeah. I remember."

"Obviously, someone wasn't listening." Reaching into my back pocket to grab my wallet, I pull out a packet of lube and rip it open with my teeth, squirting some down his crack while he whimpers. My finger slips right in up to the knuckle, soft heat surrounding it as I fuck into him.

Taylor rocks his hips back, groaning. "More. Please."

He's pressing his groin against the counter, seeking friction, but he knows better than to try and touch himself before I let him. That knowledge makes me heady with power, and I add another finger while my free hand whips the belt out of my pant loops.

"You need to learn not to talk to strangers."

Folding the belt in half, I drag it down his ass cheek before meeting his wide gaze in the mirror. His eyes are nearly black, lips parted as he pants from my fingers still inside his body, sweat beading on the back of his neck. Suddenly, I'm unsure, not wanting to hurt him. This dynamic between us is still uncharted.

I tap the belt gently on his ass. "This okay?"

Swallowing, he fucks himself on my fingers. "Yeah. I can take it."

*Oh, my god.*

Taking a deep breath, I raise the belt, keeping my gaze on his. "If it becomes too much, tell me to stop."

The belt comes down against his flesh with an audible *crack*, leaving a bright red welt in its place. Taylor cries out, jerking forward on my fingers, his yelp morphing into a moan of pleasure, and I add a third digit while I bring the belt down again.

"Oh, shit," he whimpers through clenched teeth, meeting my thrusts as I massage his skin before whipping him two more times.

"Take out your cock and stroke it, baby," I tell him, pulling mine out as well to relieve the pressure in my jeans.

He complies, an almost painful sound coming from him when he wraps his fist around his length and begins to jerk. I get one more smack in before I can't stand it anymore, and I pour more lube on my dick before lining myself up with his hole. Grabbing his throat, I pull him up against me as I thrust inside, feeling his muscles clamp onto my cock like a vice.

Someone chooses to bang on the door at that exact moment, hollering at us to hurry up. We both freeze, meeting each other's gazes in the mirror, and my hand moves from his throat to cover his mouth.

"Shh..." Biting down on his neck, I pull out slowly before slamming back in, his own teeth sinking into my palm to stifle a moan. Pounding on the door continues, nearly in sync with the pounding I'm giving Taylor's ass as I take him over and over. A single drop of moisture drips from his lashes, and I catch it with my tongue, feeling him shake when I hit his prostate just right.

"Mmfuck, fuck, *fuck.*" He explodes into the sink, spurting cum all over the counter and mirror, cries of pleasure barely muffled by my hand. As always, the sight of him losing control and his ass spasming on my cock sends me right there with him, coming so hard I nearly blackout as I pump him so full, he'll feel it for days.

Taylor collapses forward, his legs giving out, but I wrap my arms around him to keep him steady. My forehead drops to his back, both of our breaths ragged, and his trembling hand lifts to pull my face in for a searing kiss.

When we pull apart, our eyes find each other, emotion passing between us, making my heart skip a beat. He smiles, a sight so beautiful that I realize I'd burn the world down just to keep it on his face, and I have to clear my throat before I end up doing something stupid. Like dropping to one knee and proposing.

"Are we going to communicate now like a normal couple, or do I need to worry about you running off with hot guys on bikes next time you're upset?"

His grin turns wicked, a chuckle brushing against my lips. "Well, I mean, if you're willing to chase me down, baby." When I growl in response to that, he bursts into laughter. "I'll come to you first, I promise. I just couldn't go in there with Maisie talking shit, and I didn't want to make everyone suspicious by pulling you away, so...yeah."

Oh, which reminds me.

"There's no need to worry about that. If you'd stayed just five more minutes, you would have heard me announcing to the entire house that we're together."

"Y-you *what?!*" His jaw drops as he pulls himself off my dick, turning around in my arms. "Are you fucking for real?"

"Yep." Lowering my gaze, I wet some paper towels to clean him up. "It kind of just came out. You mad?"

"The fuck? Hell no, I'm relieved. Lying makes me gassy."

A choked snort makes me cough as I wipe off my dick and wash my hands. "That's a very odd reaction."

The banging on the door starts again, someone on the other side shouting angrily, and I holler at them to hold up while we quickly clean up the mess. With our clothes righted and junk tucked away, I grab Taylor's hand, kissing his knuckles before opening the door.

Angry eyes of the bartender in the skirt greet us on the other side, surrounded by two bouncers. "Seriously? Can't you two read?"

He points to a neon sign hanging on the wall that reads '*no fucking in the bathroom*,' and we share a baffled look as the bouncers walk us to the door. A few people clap when we're marched out, but I can't even find it in me to be embarrassed. Not when Taylor squeezes my hand and gives a princess wave to the crowd, hair a mess, lips swollen from my kisses, a hickey forming on his neck where I bit down.

*Mine.* Absolutely mine, and I wouldn't have it any other way.

"Why do they even need a sign like that?"

"Right? Are people getting fucked regularly in the bathroom at this place?"

As we cross the parking lot toward my car, I spot Logan and Devon standing near the motorcycle several spaces over. A sensual smirk rests on Devon's pierced lips when he flicks his gaze over Taylor before dragging it to where our hands are clasped.

"Ah, young love," he sighs, straddling his bike, and I turn to where his nephew stands with his hands on his hips.

"Well, I see no blood, so that's a good sign." Logan checks us both over with an assessing gaze. "No bruises. I think it's safe to say everything's sorted?"

"Yep," Taylor grins, jabbing a thumb over his shoulder. "Though, I wouldn't be so sure about the bruises. My ass is so sore, I won't sit right for a week."

Logan sputters while Devon throws his head back to laugh, and I pull Taylor against me, resting my chin on his shoulder.

"We're going to light some fireworks at Christian's mom's if you both want to come," he says, his gaze bouncing between them.

Devon angles his head. "Will there be booze?"

"Oh, yeah. And the best *pozole* you've ever tasted."

"Shit, I'm in."

My brow lifts at my best friend. "What about you, Loge? Salem's gonna be there."

He deliberates for a moment, chewing on a cheek. "Thanks, but I should probably head home. I've got work in the morning."

My shoulders sag slightly with disappointment, but I offer to drop him off at his car because I won't make him pay for an Uber. Doubt there's one this far out from the city, anyway.

As the three of us pile into the Audi, Devon calls to Taylor from his bike.

"You sure you don't want to come with me? I'll even ride bitch."

Taylor freezes, eyes brightening with excitement. I glare at Devon, knowing precisely what he's doing, preparing to begrudgingly watch my boyfriend drive off with another man because I can't say no, but Taylor surprises me when he shakes his head.

"Nah, man, I'm good. Thanks for the ride earlier, though. I need to invest in one of those."

As we're buckling in our seatbelts, I throw him a curious look. "You could have gone with him if you wanted to. I know you're dying to drive a motorcycle."

"Yeah. But I'm dying to be with you more." He throws me a cheesy grin, which I roll my eyes at, even though I'm secretly pleased with his answer.

Because honestly, I've been dying to be with him, too. For a very, very long time.

# TAYLOR

"**F**uck yeah! Happy fucking birthday, America!"

Christian makes a run for it after lighting a monster of a firework, barely escaping before it erupts, shooting balls of flame high into the air. They explode above us, blooms of light booming loud enough to echo off the surrounding mountains. Hannah and Christian's siblings cheer, screaming in laughter while his brother prepares the next one. Huck holds me on his lap as I finish my fourth bowl of *pozole*, Matty pressing in next to us, and I sigh contentedly.

This is where I belong. This is my real family.

"I still don't understand where you put all that food," Huck laughs, running his hands over my abs until I squirm.

Christian wiggles his brows. "Probably his dick."

He whispers low enough that no one could possibly hear, but Devon must have superhuman senses because he swings his head our way from where he sits across the lawn with

Salem and Xed tucked under both his arms. He sucks his piercing in between his teeth, eyes glinting as he winks, and Huck's arms tighten around me.

"Dev sure seems to have hit it off with those two," he comments, and Matty scoffs, scowling in their direction.

"They look ridiculous."

"I dunno." Studying them, I watch Devon rub a hand over Xed's chest while he plays with Salem's hair. "I think they all look kinda hot together." Huck grabs my jaw, turning my face to his with a raised brow, and I bite back a grin. "Subjectively speaking, of course. Like, from a purely platonic standpoint."

"You don't think it's a little messed up that Salem's flirting with her ex's uncle?"

I shift uncomfortably, not wanting to get in the middle of it. "She's a big girl, and Logan can handle himself."

That makes him narrow his eyes. "You are the meddler of all meddlers but you're choosing *now* to turn a blind eye?"

"I mean...yeah. We tried, right? It's been six months. Maybe we should just let them move on. If it's meant to be, they'll find their way back to each other."

"Like me and you?" He asks softly, lips pressed against mine.

"Yeah, Huck. Like me and you."

We're splashed with ice-cold water from the hose a moment later as Christian's mom sprays us down.

"N*o besos delante de la mamá, cariño!*"

"Aye, friendly fire! I wasn't involved!" Matty jumps out of the way while I laugh, shaking my damp hair onto Huckslee like a dog.

"Sorry, ma. Won't happen again."

Another firework goes off above, brightening the sky as it cracks under the stars.

Huck's eyes sparkle when he grins and wipes the water from his face. "What did she say?"

"No kissing in front of her," I pout, batting my lashes.

"I didn't even know you could speak Spanish."

"I can understand it from being around Christian my whole life, but I can't really speak it."

My best friend snickers, reaching over to ruffle my dark strands. "Yeah, fucker can't roll his r's. Sounds like a gringo."

Hannah gasps, holding her palm face up, and Christian winces when he pulls a dollar bill out of his wallet and hands it to her for swearing.

"Did you guys really jump off that thing?" Devon asks, pointing up to the ramp bolted to the roof we never took down. Christian, Matty, Xed, and I all answer *yes* simultaneously. He whistles, looking impressed. "I'd like to see you ride."

"That can be arranged." Christian turns to call for his little brother, who's in the middle of lighting another firework. "Yo, Carlos! Where's your dirtbike? In the garage?"

"Yeah, dumbass."

"Ah, ah!" His mother sprays him off, too, as he yanks out a few dimes and some lint from his pocket, passing them off to Hannah. The toll was never discussed; she just marched around one day demanding money for bad words, so she got what she got.

A few minutes later, Christian wheels his brother's bike to the backyard, where a few other ramps are set up while we follow. Before he climbs on, Salem gasps dramatically, falling into manager mode.

"Wait! This is the perfect photo op. Let me grab my camera from my car. I want a shot of both of you in the air while fireworks go off in the background."

"Aw, come on Sally, no working. It's a holiday."

"It'll only take a sec, quit bitching."

It did not 'only take a sec.'

Thirty minutes later, after Christian and I did jumps while Carlos lit fireworks, we were finally back to having fun, switching off as we rotated between doing tricks on the dirt and our old foam pit. Each landing makes me wince with my smarting ass cheek. Devon seems super into it, commenting on our form as Xed slams beer after beer, still hanging off him. Matty doesn't seem pleased but chills with Hannah and Christian's sisters, keeping them entertained. Huckslee even gets in on the action, taking a few jumps with a finesse that surprises me, considering he's pretty rusty. I'd be lying if I said my cock didn't perk up at the sight of him in a helmet.

"Kinda wanna ride you while you straddle a bike," I whisper to him after he lands in the parking lot behind the house, and he has to take a moment to get his boner under control.

Everyone begs me to show them the trick I'm doing for the competition next month, even though they saw it at the qualifier, so I give them a show. None of our ramps are high enough for me to do the backflip, and I don't feel like climbing onto the roof, so I keep it minimal. I can't fucking wait to show it off to all of them again. Well, other than Huckslee. Because he won't be here...

The thought drops my mood for the rest of the night.

I do a pretty good job of hiding it for a while, but eventually, Huck catches on because he's become so attuned to me and my emotions. Pulling me aside, he gently grips my chin, lifting my face up to his while he searches my eyes.

"What's wrong?"

I shrug, smiling sadly up at him. "Just wish you could be here for the competition, that's all. But I understand why you can't."

He exhales slowly, dropping his face to my neck without responding. Christian does a few tricks, drawing hollers from Devon, who convinces my best friend to teach him the basics. All the while, I'm holding Huck and rubbing my palms over his tight back muscles. When he raises his head, he brushes a kiss against the corner of my lips.

"Wanna get out of here?"

His thoughtfulness makes my chest ache.

"Yeah. I wanna show you something."

We say our goodbyes and slip into the Audi after I hug everyone tight, especially Hannah, because I don't know when I'll see her again. I'd like to think I'll be able to say goodbye next month, but plans don't always go how they're supposed to. As we pull away, I give Huck the address to my dad's old trailer. I need to check on it anyway since I haven't driven by in a few months, but also because...something in me just wants him to see it. To show him this part of my past.

He eyes the metal arch of Arbitrary Hills as we pass beneath it, pulling into the trailer park slowly because of the speed bumps on the cracked asphalt. "This is where you grew up?"

"Yep. This one on the right." I point out the trailer, noting the weed-filled yard and tire tracks permanently etched into the dirt from peeling out on my bike as a teen. It looks super rundown, worse than when I was growing up–the front wooden stoop is sagging, the siding is falling off in places, and some shingles are missing from the roof. Out of all the units on the street, mine is definitely the worst.

Unbuckling my seatbelt to get out, I throw Huck a pained grimace. "Come on, let's make sure no one's squatting."

"Do you own this place?" He follows me up to the splintering front door, and I nod as I search through my keys.

"My dad gave it to me in his will. I lived here for a while after he died, but when things started getting bad, and I moved to the city with Christian, I kind of let it fall apart. Can't decide if I wanna fix it up to sell or rent it out."

Once the door opens, I flick on the living room light and immediately yelp as a large black ball scurries into the kitchen. "*A fucking raccoon!*"

The most unmanly shriek leaves my throat as I jump into Huck's arms, the vile creature causing chaos as it bounces off the cabinets like a basketball.

Scrambling around Huck's body, I climb up his back, pointing to the old broom leaning against the closet. "Get it out! Get it out!"

He jumps into action, grabbing the broom and chasing the hissing raccoon all over the living room like a hockey puck, shouting curse words that would probably make his grandma's hair curl.

"Go on, git!" With a shove from the broom, the filthy animal rolls out through the open front door and shuffles away, its claws scraping on the wood, making me shudder.

After it's gone, I climb from Huck's shoulders while we watch it leave momentarily, catching our breaths. Then the asshole throws back his head and laughs, a loud guffaw barreling out of his mouth as he holds his stomach and crashes to his knees, his whole body shaking.

"You screamed like a girl," he chokes, eyes watering, and I seethe at him.

"Those things have rabies, Huck!"

"You're scared of a little trash panda?"

"That thing was far from little. Fucker looked like he eats all the trash in the trailer park like some raccoon kingpin."

That only makes him laugh harder, doubling over. "But they're so cute!"

"No, they're creepy. They have thumbs, and they eat cats."

"They do not," he gasps, gaping at me.

Yanking the broom from his hands, I nudge him with it. "Do so. I read it somewhere."

"Sounds legit."

"Stop being a dick," I grumble, despite the smile pulling at my lips, and Huck grins as he wipes his eyes.

"Payback for putting that spider in my locker sophomore year."

My gut twists at the memory of how awful I treated him, causing my smile to immediately drop.

"Guess I deserve that." Turning toward the kitchen to hide my face, I spot an empty bag of cat food on the ground, probably left over from when Lasagna was alive. "Guess we know what he was living off of, that fluffy fuck."

Huck's arms envelop my waist as he holds me from behind, his stubble brushing against my cheek. "I forgive you, you know."

"You shouldn't." My throat tightens as tears sting my eyes, my lashes fluttering to blink them away.

"I do anyway." He pulls back after a quick kiss, turning with his hands on his hips. "So, this is where you grew up. Give me the tour."

"Not much to see." I clear my throat, spinning to focus on the broken window above the peeling leather sofa where the raccoon must have gotten in. "We need to board that window up before the rodent mafia makes this their base."

"We can figure it out before we leave."

Thankfully, all doors were closed when we dealt with the raccoon problem. I walk down the short hallway to my old bedroom. "This was my room. I used to sneak in and out of the window at night to hang with Christian and the gang. That one across the way was my dad's, and here's the bathroom."

I open doors as I go, showcasing the empty spaces because I sold almost everything once my dad died—not that there was much to sell. All that's left in the trailer is the sofa, my old mattress, a dresser, and a TV stand. The bathroom is the last room I stop at, turning to see Huck standing in the hallway, studying various holes in the drywall. His eyes flicker over to me, and I smile tightly, leaning against the doorway.

"Most of those are from his fist. A few from mine. Couple of the lower ones happened when he shoved my body into the wall."

Stepping back into the bathroom without looking at him, I gaze down at the porcelain sink and run my finger over the chunk missing from the corner, wincing at the phantom pain that shoots through my temples. "That night I stole your car...this came from my head when he slammed me down. It's why I had the concussion. That's where I got the scar."

Lifting up the side of my hair to show him, I find him closer than he was a moment ago. He wraps himself around me, pulling us flush as he buries his face in my neck.

"I'm so sorry I wasn't there," he whispers against my skin, and I quickly shake my head.

"It's okay. I forgive you, too."

Honestly, there's nothing to forgive, but I hate the thought of him feeling guilty about anything. I was the one who screwed up, not the other way around.

Huck's lips gently trace around the tattoo on my throat. "He should have gone to jail for what he did to you."

With a shaky inhale, I pull away, licking the dryness from my lips. "Jail sucked, to be honest. Did he deserve it? Yeah, probably, but it's all in the past now. No use dwelling on it, you know? He's dead."

The words stick in my throat and I cough around them, unsure of what's come over me. It's been three years, and it's not like I didn't mourn—if you can call it a month-long bender and then three months of forced sobriety mourning. I'm fine. I've moved past it. And I lived here after I got out of jail, for fuck's sake. It's not like I didn't see the evidence of the abuse day in and day out. But something about being here with Huck, having him see it for the first time, see me...

"My mom called me a compulsive liar," I blurt out, my voice cracking to my horror. We gaze at one another for a few moments. When my jaw quivers, I clamp down on my molars, and the shock on his face quickly hardens.

"She doesn't know you like I do," he says firmly, pulling me into his arms again. "You didn't need to bring me here to prove anything, baby. Those that matter know the truth."

His words settle something deep inside of me, easing an anxiety I didn't know was building until this moment. Emotion tightens my chest, skipping a heartbeat, and I force a chuckle to hide the relief washing over me.

"But if we didn't stop by, Al Capoon would still be living on the sofa."

His lips twitch. "Capoon?"

"Yeah, tried to mix Capone and raccoon, but that just sounds dirty, huh?"

"You're ridiculous." Our lips find each other, and he gently pushes me against the wall.

"You know...we could always replace the bad memories with new ones. Better ones."

"Yeah?" I'm suddenly breathless. The hard lines of his body press into mine, and the scent of his aftershave floods my senses. "What did you have in mind?"

"Hmm..." He sinks his teeth into my shoulder, sending a jolt of heat straight to my groin. "I have a lot of things in mind, but what do you need, Taylor?"

"I..." The feeling of his cock rutting against mine short-circuits my brain, a hiss rolling off my tongue when he pinches a nipple over my shirt. "I just need you."

Always. Forever. In every way.

He growls softly, kneading my welted cheeks. "Is your asshole sore?"

I clench it and wince. "I'll be okay."

Fuck, I want him. I don't even care how much it hurts.

"Nope, not happening. You need to heal." He nibbles on my bottom lip when I pout before dropping to his knees and reaching for the button on my jeans.

"Huck, this place is filthy."

"Maybe I like it filthy. Already fucked you in a bar bathroom. How much worse could this be?"

"Considering that bathroom probably gets mopped way more often than–" I'm cut off by a sharp inhale when he takes my semi-hard dick in his mouth, swirling his tongue over the tip until I'm rock solid. "God, you're so good at that."

He gives me his all, letting the spit drip off his chin while swallowing around my shaft, but I don't want to be the only one feeling this way. Want to touch him, feel him inside me.

"Come on." Pulling him to his feet, I tug him toward my room, shoving him backwards onto my old bed. He bounces with a grunt, dark eyes glittering when I quickly shed my clothes and practically tear his off. Once we're both naked, I climb on top, spinning around so that my ass is in his face while his cock juts up toward my lips.

"Mm, what a view." Huck flicks his tongue out, licking a wet-hot line from my balls up to my tender hole. "I love the way your pretty ass gapes for me, baby. All sloppy and used, with my cum still dripping out of you."

I groan as I take him to the back of my throat, immediately gagging but loving every second of it. Ever since that night in the shower in Cali, Huck's been obsessed with rimming me, and I'm not complaining. Never thought I'd enjoy getting my ass eaten, but apparently, I love everything he does to me.

Gently, almost reverently, he circles and prods my hole, occasionally breaching it with his tongue in a way that feels too fucking good. My cock slides between our writhing bodies, slick with precum, as I ride his face, and he thrusts into my mouth. Feeling a little brave, I take his sac in my hand, lifting it to massage a finger against his taint, causing him to gasp sharply.

His orgasm comes quick and unexpected, flooding my mouth with so much cum that it drips from the corners of my lips, his loud moans sending me free-falling into my own release. I unload between us, a sticky mess coating our abs, as I continue to suck and wring him completely dry.

Afterward, we lick each other clean before collapsing side by side, my muscles aching but content. As he catches his breath, Huck's head rolls sideways to gaze at me, brows raised, curls disheveled in a way I love.

"Where did you learn that little trick?" he breathes, dark eyes narrowing. "I've never come so hard in my life."

A hoarse laugh bursts from my throat as I close my eyes, grinning smugly. "You're supposed to be the gay one. I did research."

"Research?"

"Mm-hmm."

The bed shifts as he moves closer, running a hand over my jaw while he nips at my earlobe. "Did this research include watching gay porn?"

"Uh..." Shit. "I plead the fifth?"

He snorts, shaking his head as he moves to his feet. "You know, if you ever have any questions or want to try something, you can just ask me, right?"

"Really?" Lifting up onto my elbows, I watch him slide on his underwear and jeans. "Anything?"

That makes him pause, and he crawls on top of me. "Anything, baby. There's no judgment here. If it's something I don't know a lot about, we'll look into it together."

"Oh. Okay." I bite my lip, searching his open expression, words on my tongue I'm dying to speak but too worried to say out loud. He notices my apprehension because, of course, he does and leans down to brush his lips against mine.

"Just say it, Taylor. Whatever it is you're thinking so hard about, let it out."

"I want to fuck you." The words tumble out in a breathless rush, and when he goes still above me, I turn my head into the mattress, losing my nerve. "I-I mean, I know it's not something you're into, and I'd never...never force you to do something you don't like, Huck. I just... I'm really attracted to you, and your ass is so damn hot. I think about it all the time, and just...fuck, but it's not a big deal if we never do that because I really like having you inside of me, too, and–"

He cuts off my rambling by biting down on my nipple, causing me to yelp, my still-naked cock twitching.

"You're fucking cute when you're flustered," he chuckles, licking away the sting with a grin, and I cover my face to hide the redness on my cheeks.

"Like I said, it's not a big deal."

"Baby. Look at me."

Lowering my hands, I tilt my head down to look at him where he rests his chin against my sternum.

"Not gonna lie, I've never been interested in bottoming before." His thumbs run calming circles over my inked ribs. "But the thought of trying it with you is... I'm not entirely against it."

"Yeah?" My dick jumps at the possibility of being deep inside his tight hole. "You think you'd like that?"

"Maybe. Probably. When it comes to you, it seems I like everything."

"God, me too," I laugh, lifting my hips to press my hard-on into his hip as he rubs his stubble against my stomach, making me squirm.

"Can I think about it?"

"Of course you can. Take all the time you need, baby. Like I said, I'm happy with what we've been doing. Really happy."

As our lips meet again, I try to forget that we only have about a month left until he leaves. There's only this moment, with Huckslee in my arms, and there's no rush for us to do anything tonight other than just be. Even though we're currently in my childhood home, where so much went wrong, it feels lighter.

His very presence seems to strip every negative word and action from the walls, replacing them with his touch, his scent, the way he looks at me like I hung the moon. He's the love of my life, and he's slowly healing me, making me whole.

I just hope I can still remain in one piece when he's gone.

# HUCKSLEE

"Already, I can tell this one is better than the last. The open concept brings in a lot of natural light. Plenty of cabinet space, a double wall oven, and an island for more cooking room. Honestly, Mr. Davis, this place is just beautiful."

Blowing a stray curl out of my face, I slump back in my seat and let go of Baby Bones to rub my palms into my eyes. I'm so damn tired. I pushed myself hard in the gym earlier this morning and then immediately jumped onto a video call with Randy, my agent, while he and a realtor spent the last four fucking hours showing me places to rent in Baltimore.

One week to go, and I still haven't signed a lease. There were talks about buying a place instead, but...that felt too permanent. I'll just pay rent a year in advance at a time.

"So, what do you think?" Randy turns the camera toward his face, running a free hand through his light beard. "I like this one. Good neighborhood, too. Secure. No one's allowed in without a code for the gate."

"I guess."

Really, they're all beginning to look the same. Why do I care about shit like double wall ovens and cabinet space? Who will I be cooking for once I'm out there? No one. Me, myself, and I.

Randy frowns at my lack of enthusiasm and takes off his thick-rimmed glasses. "Huckslee, can I be candid with you for a moment?"

*Please, don't.* "I'd appreciate that."

He waves to the realtor, letting her know he'll be back before stepping onto a back balcony. "Look, son, I can tell that your heart isn't in this. And while I know it will be a big change for you, and that can be scary, time is running out. You need to decide on a place by the end of the day so we can get this ball rolling."

"I know, I know," I sigh, looking over at the rumpled, empty bed in Taylor's room that we've been sharing. "I just...I have a lot on my mind."

"Want to talk about it?"

"Eh..."

What can I say, exactly? That I'm less than thrilled about an opportunity most people only dream of, with more money in my bank account than I know what to do with and more on the way? That I spent the last four years as a shell of a person, revolving my life around something that didn't even set my soul on fire because it was the only thing I could think of to fill the void? That I'd rather live in this small duplex with my boyfriend and two other people plus a rabbit, bartending and creating art for his dream?

As much as I want to, I'm contractually obligated to be in Baltimore. There's no way around it. And though I'd love for Taylor to move with me, his life and his career are here in Utah. So, instead, I just shrug and give some vague excuse about missing my friends and family, even though I haven't heard a word from my dad since I walked out on the Fourth of July three weeks ago. No response to my texts or calls, and not gonna lie; it hurts. More than anything. Logan, at least, has been a little more chatty, but I haven't seen him since then, either. He's agreed to be Taylor and Christian's business manager, though, so that's something.

"If you want time to think it over, I can give you until five," Randy continues sympathetically, his eyes crinkling at the corners. "The realtor can have the papers drawn up by tomorrow morning."

Well, shit. This is really happening. As much as I'd tried to put it off and forget it all summer...our time is just about up. What good would waiting until later do? There really isn't anything that could change the situation.

"No, it's fine. That place is fine. She can get the paperwork started now."

Randy blinks at that, bushy brows furrowing. "You sure? I have no problem waiting for you to make a decision."

*Except you've been waiting a month already.*

"Yeah, I like that one. Like you said, lots of natural light. An extra room for a home gym. Checks all my boxes."

"Alright, if you're certain. I'll send everything to your email by the end of the day, and then we can talk tomorrow about getting your things shipped."

"Sounds good, thanks, Randy. Talk to you later."

Once the video call goes black, I feel all the strength leave my body, and I let my head fall to the desk, gathering my thoughts. There's still so much to do and so little time. Never enough time.

I stand with a sigh, heading over to the dresser to grab a pair of briefs, my throat closing at the sight of Taylor's folded pairs next to mine. He hates folding his laundry, so I've been doing it for him. That man would live out of the dryer if he could—and he did until I started staying here. I'm really going to miss putting his clothes away for him, strange as it sounds.

After putting BB in her cage, I head into the bathroom for a quick shower, scrubbing off all the sweat from the gym that I didn't get a chance to do earlier. Everything aches. I'd gotten lost in my head this morning, thinking about the seven days I have left while on the weight bench, and my shoulders are screaming.

Throwing on some clothes, I roll my stiff joints and wave to Arya on the couch before heading outside, where Christian and Taylor are tuning up their bikes in the driveway. Loud, thrashing music thumps from a portable speaker while my boyfriend kneels, bent over, focusing on putting back the skid plate, dark hair falling into his face. It's getting longer now, the dyed tips faded and touching the collar of his tank top. He's so fucking gorgeous, it takes my breath away. How did I get so lucky?

Sensing my presence, his head snaps up, and he smiles over at me leaning against the porch railing, his color-changing eyes lighting up. When he sees the expression on my face, though, the smile drops, making my heart lurch. I only ever want to make him happy, always. And it kills me that I can't.

"How did it go?" he asks, setting down a screwdriver.

I shrug with a wince. "Alright, I guess. Finally picked a place. Everything should be official by tomorrow."

His gaze drops as he nods, wiping the oil off his hands with a rag. "That's good."

We both fall silent, the space between our words heavy. Christian shoots me an annoyed look over the seat of his own bike, choosing this moment to gather up his tools and take them to the shed. Wandering from the porch, I stuff my hands in my pockets and watch Taylor work, taking in his graceful fingers and toned, inked arms. My back twinges, causing me to grunt, and his eyes meet mine before he gets to his feet.

"Turn around."

When I do, his hands find my shoulders, kneading and pressing into my sore muscles in a way that has me groaning. He works his way down my spine, thumbs moving in circles down to my obliques, and I wish we could just forgo work tonight to lay in bed, watching movies and holding each other. I don't feel like we did that enough. I want more.

"I hate this," he whispers softly, leaning his forehead against my shoulder blades as he continues to massage me.

"Hate what?"

"*This*. The silence, the broken look in your eyes. Feeling like everything's about to change. I don't like it."

Reaching up to rub my aching chest, I clear the emotion clogging my throat. "Everything is about to change, though."

"Yeah, but...we'll be okay, right?"

My mouth falls open to respond, but it shuts when I can't think of what to say. Because I want us to be okay, I really do, but what if we aren't? What if the distance becomes too much, and we drift apart? There's no use in bringing it up because we've already had this discussion numerous times over the last few days. Instead, I turn and pull him against my chest, kissing him gently.

"We need to leave soon."

Those eyes I love so much darken, something akin to hurt flashing across his features before he nods and steps away. "Yeah. Let me get my bike in the shed, and then we'll go."

"Taylor, wait–"

He cuts me off with a shake of his head, wheeling his bike away. "It's fine. We knew this had a time limit when we started it."

*Fuck*, but I don't want it to. I want to continue as we have been, but it's impossible. And even though I know I should go after him, drag him back, and reassure him that everything will be alright, I can't. Because how can I give him something that I can't give myself? Giving him hope feels like a lie. Will I do everything possible to maintain this relationship from across the country? Of course, but...sometimes, love isn't enough.

We all pile into Christian's Bronco, none of us speaking, as he drives us to the Prospector for work. I can feel his judging eyes from the rearview mirror, but I keep my focus out the window, every desolate thought crushing me like an anvil. If it wasn't for the medicine I'd taken earlier during the call with my agent, I'm pretty sure I'd be in full panic mode right now. Thanks to Taylor making life so much better, I haven't needed to take it in a few months, but with my impending departure...I couldn't help it. I caved.

When we pull up to work, Taylor gets out and enters the building without a word or glance back. Before I can follow, Christian grabs my arm.

"Hold up, *hermano*," he leans against the door of the Bronco, pulling out a pack of smokes. "Let's talk."

Sighing heavily, I fold my arms, raising a brow at him to continue. He takes a moment, lighting his smoke and inhaling deeply before he speaks.

"What are your intentions with my boy?"

"Really?" A snort leaves my throat, nose scrunching. "You're giving me the dad talk? *Now?*"

"Well, his own dad ain't around to do it, so someone's got to."

"Christian, the apartment is small. You've walked in on us a time or two. I'm pretty sure you know my intentions."

"I don't mean with his body, Huckslee." Smoke curls around us when he exhales, hazel eyes narrowing. "I'm talking about his heart."

That hits me like a kick to the gut, and I flinch. "I'd never hurt him."

*Again.*

"Maybe not intentionally."

"What is that supposed to mean?"

"Just a little observation from an outside perspective." Finishing up, he leans down and puts the cigarette out on his tire before tucking it behind his ear. "Either you're all in, or you're not. You've had one foot out the door since the beginning, and even if Tay hasn't noticed, I have. Don't string him along only to break him later because then I'd have to break your face."

I gape at him for a moment, unsure how to respond. My initial reaction is to *deny, deny, deny*, but deep down, I know he's right. I began this whole thing unsure if it would even work, and somehow, along the way, I just decided it probably wouldn't.

"It's not fair to him," Christian continues in my silence. "Like I said, all in or nothing. If you don't think you'll last, break it off before you go."

I recoil from that, rearing back with my lips curled. "You want me to break up with him?"

"No, *culo*, I want you guys to live happily ever after, but I'd rather help him pick up the pieces sooner rather than later. You feel me?"

Goddammit. And suddenly, I feel like the worst boyfriend on the face of the planet.

"Yeah. I feel you."

He slaps my shoulder before heading inside, leaving me to my thoughts, and all I can do is pace with my hands in my hair. I don't want to break things off with Taylor. *I don't.* I want to spend the rest of my life separating his laundry and bickering over me using his face moisturizer.

I want to wake up to the scent of his body wash and morning breath and fall asleep with his naked body on top of mine. How the fuck did we get here? Four short months ago, I never would have dreamed that the source of all my pain could bring me the most happiness I've ever known. And I don't want to give it up. I can't. I won't.

But how do I show him? What can I do to lessen the blow of my absence while still making him feel like he's wanted and loved? Because that's what my baby needs; to be needed in return. But how the fuck am I supposed to do that from miles away?

With that thought weighing heavily on my mind, I head inside to do my prep work before the bar opens, setting up and ensuring kegs are full. Once we open, it gets busy, as usual, for a Friday night, and I don't see much of Taylor between making drinks and taking food orders. The few times I spot him running dishes to the back, he refuses to catch my gaze, twisting my stomach into knots. A few hours into the night, when we reach a lull in business, Juanita steps behind the bar and tugs my earlobe painfully hard, making me yelp.

"What did you do to my Taylor, hm? He's being more bratty than usual!"

"I didn't do anything," I refute, yanking myself out of her grasp to massage my ear, and she points a gnarled finger at me.

"*Pinche mentiroso*, you fix it! Now!"

With an iron grip, she shoves me through the door into the kitchen, where I stumble over the floor mat and slam right into Taylor's back. He drops all his dishes with an *oomph*, glass shattering all over the tile.

"Are you fucking kidding me?!" He whirls around, mouth open to shout, but slams it shut when he sees me standing there like a deer in headlights.

"Sorry...Juanita pushed me. I'll clean it up."

His eyes follow me as I grab the broom and dustpan, sweeping the sharp shards into a pile. "And why is Juanita pushing you?"

I shrug, depositing the mess into a trash can. "Because she thinks I pissed you off and wants me to make it better."

Christian smirks over his shoulder from the sink, shaking his head before returning to what he's doing. When I notice Gale glaring at me, I lift my chin and mouth *what?* He doesn't break his stare or respond, which isn't surprising because I don't even think he talks. Taylor crosses his arms, drawing my attention back to the matter at hand.

"She's such a mama bear," my boyfriend huffs, rolling his eyes. "I'm just in a shitty mood."

"Because of me?"

He drops his head, letting dark strands fall into his eyes as he kicks the trash can. "No...the situation, yes, but not you."

"Baby," I sigh, pinching the bridge of my nose, "we both knew that I'd be leaving toward the end of summer."

"Yeah, I know," he turns away, the defeated tone of his voice making my heart crack. "I've got more dishes to grab, Huck. I'll see you later."

That's how the rest of the night goes; Taylor ignoring me and being a beast to everyone else. And because Juanita thinks I'm the reason, so does the whole staff, which means they're all giving me the cold shoulder, too. I'm not particularly close with most of them, but it still stings.

Two in the morning comes and goes for last call, and once the bar shuts down, I stay behind to help close up like usual. As I'm mopping the front, I hear pounding on the front door, and Salem's face appears through the glass, scowling at me. I tip-toe over the wet surface and unlock the door, raising a brow at her when I pull it open.

"What are you doing here?"

"Picking up Taylor," she brushes past me, leaving footprints all over my clean floor as she marches toward the kitchen.

"What the fuck?" My brows slam down as I follow on her heels. "What do you mean, picking him up? It's the middle of the night."

Christian and Taylor are putting everything away when we step through, and Taylor's eyes briefly meet mine before he gives his attention to Salem. "We're almost finished. Ten more minutes, and we can go."

"Go? Go where?" I block his path on the way to lock up the walk-in freezer. "Tay, what's going on?"

He licks his lips, looking everywhere but at my face. "I'm going to stay at Salem and Xed's tonight. Matty's gone with Valerie and Hannah, so I'll chill with them while they get high."

My jaw tightens painfully, blood pulsing in my veins. "Why?"

"I just...need some space," he mumbles with his back to me, finishing his work tasks, and it feels like my heart just dropped to the ground. Christian and Salem watch me closely as if waiting for me to react poorly. All I can do is gaze at the ground, feeling like my walls are closing in.

When everything is finished, and we shut off the lights, I trail after them out the employee exit, waiting until Taylor veers off toward Salem's Jeep before speaking.

"Why are we always running away from each other?"

His steps falter, and he stops, turning his head slightly. The fingers at his sides flex before he continues on, sliding inside the vehicle. They pull out onto the road, and I watch him slip away from me bitterly until he's nothing but a speck of light against the night sky.

# TAYLOR

Two days pass without me coming home, and all of my
texts to Huck are short and clipped.

> Huck: You gonna be home today?

> Me: No.

> Huck: Okay...when will you be?

> Me: Dunno.

I'd be a nervous wreck if it wasn't for Salem and Xed. After
spending weeks sharing space with Huck, the nights are lonely
as fuck on the couch, missing the safety of his warm body
pressed against me.

Thankfully, I spend all weekend clear-headed and in prob-
lem-solving mode, coming up with ideas to convince him that
we can make this work. I get it, I fucked up by leaving. But I

needed reassurances from him that he couldn't deliver, which hurt. He's scared; that much is obvious. So, I need to take away that fear.

It took all day Sunday, pacing around the townhome and driving Salem and Xed insane, but I have a plan. And they're both on board with it, which means I just have a few more people to convince—including Huck's dad.

Early the following day, I take off for Gville, knowing from past conversations between him and Huck that Aaron telecommutes on Mondays. As I pull into the driveway, apprehension licks up my spine, and I wipe my damp palms on my jeans. Every time I come here, I leave with a bad taste in my mouth. Some of the worst memories of my life happened inside this house. But this needs to be done because even though I know he'd never hold it against me, I'd hate for Huckslee to always harbor resentment toward his father. It's time to clear the air.

With a deep breath, I get out and walk up to the porch, pausing briefly before ringing the bell. It only takes a few seconds, and then Aaron pulls open the door, dressed in a pair of slacks, blue eyes wide as he takes me in.

"Hi, Mr. Davis."

"Taylor?" He glances over his shoulder. "Your mother is at work right now. Do you want me to let her know you stopped by?"

"I'm not here for Maisie," I gesture inside, heart pounding. "I actually wanted to speak with you. Can I come in?"

There's a moment's hesitation before he nods and steps aside, letting me pass. He shuts the door behind us and turns toward the living room, crooking his fingers for me to follow. "I have a meeting in a few, but we should have some time."

"This won't take long."

He chooses the chair, and I settle into the sofa, glancing around the familiar space that hasn't changed much over the last four years. That creepy picture still hangs over the television, maybe a few more photos of family, a couple of Huck in his college football uniform. None of me, of course, but I wasn't expecting any. An awkward silence permeates the air, and Aaron shifts in his seat, making it squeak.

"Would you like something to drink, son? Tea, juice, beer?"

Uh...huh? My brows shoot up, but I quickly decline. "Oh, uh, no thanks. I don't drink. And I'm not thirsty."

He seems surprised at that, nodding as he smooths out the wrinkles on his pant leg. "What did you need to discuss with me?"

Well...here goes.

"You haven't spoken to Huckslee since Independence Day." My tongue darts out to moisten my dry lips. "And I wanted to ask why?"

His gaze drops, head hanging slightly, and he reaches up to remove his glasses. "I... I'm not sure what to say to that."

I adjust my snapback, gathering strength. "Okay. That's fine. You don't have to say anything. Just listen. Huckslee loves you, Mr. Davis, but your silence is hurting him. I think he doesn't show it, doesn't show a lot honestly because of how much he had to hide himself growing up." Aaron's brows crease, but I continue quickly. "We both grew up hiding ourselves. Despite what Maisie thinks, my father really was a piece of shit. I bullied Huck to try to hide the evidence, and as a result, I hurt Huck. A lot. I'm sure you remember when I broke his arm...I think we just made things worse for him between you and me."

Aaron shakes his head. "I don't understand. I did my best. I raised my boy to be a good man."

"You did," I agree, "but the pressure he was under...this expectation of him to be and act a certain way, it was a lot. All he ever wanted was your approval and acceptance. That's what he still wants. I..." My throat closes, and I swallow hard, trying to get the words out before I lose my nerves. "I don't know if Huckslee ever told you this, but the night of prom...when everything went wrong, and he attempted suicide, my actions were the reason. See, I've known that Huck is gay since the end of eighth grade when I kissed him for the first time, and even though I felt the same way about him, I treated him like shit for it because I was scared of my dad.

I knew he was behind the curtain, kissing Royce, and...well, my feelings don't really matter because what I did that night is something that I can never take back. I was the one who opened the curtain and exposed him to everyone, including you. Took something from him that wasn't mine to take, and I'll spend the rest of our lives together making it up to him. Because that's what I intend to do, Mr. Davis. I'm in love with your son. I have been for years, and I plan on growing old together. With your blessing, I hope."

A choked gasp shoots from my lungs as I inhale deeply, finally getting it all out. Aaron says nothing for a long while, his eyes taking on an almost dazed glint as he gazes around the room. I give him time to process everything I've just said. There's more I need to say, but I don't want to bombard the poor man, so I just sit in silence and pick at a loose thread on the arm of the couch.

"You love each other," he murmurs thoughtfully, rubbing a thumb over his chin. I clear my throat as I nod.

"Very much. Think whatever you want about me, Mr. Davis, but please don't push him away. He's leaving on Friday, and it would mean the world to him if you would speak to him by then."

His attention shifts to mine, brows creasing even more dramatically. "I've only ever wanted the best for you, Taylor."

"I know." I really do. "I never got a chance to thank you for allowing me into your home when you married Maisie. Living with my dad was...not great, but you did me a kindness by taking me in, and you didn't deserve how I treated you. What you did for me, choosing not to press charges when it would have served me right, is something I'll never forget—"

"No, no," he holds a hand up to stop me. "I should be the one apologizing for that night. You were lost, in pain, and I let my anger get the better of me. I want you to know that my words were never how I truly felt. As the adult and your stepfather, I was appalled at myself for acting that way."

I lift a shoulder, offering him a sad smile. "We both were in pain. Almost losing Huck affected us all."

"Yes, it did," he sighs, tapping a finger on his knee before setting his glasses back on the bridge of his nose. "I can't say I understand or completely agree with the relationship between you two, but... I'm willing to try. I never wanted Huckslee to feel like he couldn't come to me when he struggled. Or you, either."

"I can appreciate that. Thank you."

Another silence fills the space between us, and he flicks his gaze absently to the photo of Huck's team holding the championship trophy from his win in January. "It seems I have some more apologies to make."

"Yeah, about that." Straightening up, I scoot to the edge of my seat. "I have a plan. Something I want to do for him before he leaves, but I need your help to do it."

"Whatever you need, son. What can I do?"

Every ounce of unease leaves my body, anticipation taking its place as I relay my idea to Aaron. From the look on his face when I'm finished, it seems that he's excited about it as well. We part on better terms. He goes to make a few calls, and I pull everyone besides my boyfriend into a group chat to let them know what's happening. Once everyone is on board, I begin to set it all in motion.

One last move to mend everything that was broken between Huck and me for good.

# HUCKSLEE

F our days. Four fucking days Taylor's been gone, and I'm losing my mind.

> Me: Today is Tuesday.

Tay: Yes, I know how a calendar works.

> Me: Oh, good, I was worried. Since, you know, I haven't seen you since Friday.

Tay: You missing me, baby?

> Me: What the hell kind of question is that, Taylor?

> Obviously, I miss you. And I leave in three days, you know that, right? Am I going to see you before then?

My text goes unanswered, and the rest of the day is met with complete radio silence from him. The amount of anguish

I feel is unhealthy and downright toxic, but I couldn't care less. We've spent so much time together over the last few months that I feel his absence like a missing limb, the cold sheets on his side of the bed every morning instantly bringing moisture to my eyes. I hate this. Maybe Christian was right—cutting things off would be easier than feeling this way. Only, I don't want to. I just want Taylor.

But as much as I want to mope around the apartment and fall apart, my dad reached out today, inviting me over for dinner. So reluctantly, I drag myself out of bed, throw on some clothes after putting Baby Bones in her cage, and drive down to see him. I'm not a hundred percent in the mood to talk, but I know I need to smooth things over between us before I leave, or it'll eat at me every day that I'm gone. I wish I could do the same with Logan, but he hasn't responded to my texts or calls. I just feel like a lumpy sack of shit.

The house is dark when I pull up, and my gaze snags on a shiny black limousine parked on the curb next to the drive, which has my head tilting. Maybe it belongs to one of the neighbors? As I park and exit the Audi, the driver of the limo exits as well, moving to open the back door, and my jaw drops when I see Logan step out onto the sidewalk, dressed like fucking James Bond.

"What are you doing out here in a limo?"

He only smirks. "Get in, Huck."

I shake my head, feet stepping toward him of their own accord. "But I have to meet my dad for dinner."

"He's not here," Logan's grin grows wider. "Now get in, we're already late."

What the fuck?

"Late for what?"

Huffing in frustration, he grabs my arm and yanks me toward the limo, forcefully shoving me into the backseat while the driver just stands there and watches what is essentially a kidnapping in progress. Logan climbs in after me, slamming the door shut, and the next thing I know, a garment bag is being tossed over my lap.

"You're going to want to put this on."

"Whoa, hold up a damn minute." The limo lurches forward, causing the bag to slide off my lap. "What is going on here, Logan? What do you mean my dad isn't home? He invited me over just an hour ago."

He grabs the bag off the floor and throws it at me again. "Would you just put on the suit and shut up?"

"I swear, this exact scene happened in a Marvel movie once," I snort, unzipping the bag to find a sleek-looking tuxedo inside instead of a superhero costume, much to my disappointment. "Are we going to a wedding?"

"You'll see," he says, zipping his lips, pretending to lock them and pitch the key over his shoulder. Despite the heavy ache in my chest, his antics get a choked laugh out of me. I wish Taylor were here to witness whatever weird fuckery is happening right now.

Peeling off my clothes, I do my best to slide into the tux, but I'm not exactly having an easy time with it, seeing as I'm over six feet tall. Logan's eyes widen when he spots the new tattoo on my chest, sputtering slightly.

"D-did you just get that?"

I nod, buttoning up the white undershirt. "Yep. He hasn't seen it yet, though. I... I think he's mad at me."

There's a slight pause before Logan shrugs, reaching up to rub the back of his neck. "I'm sure he'll come around."

Something odd catches in his voice, and I narrow my gaze at him, immensely suspicious. He just smiles and shrugs far too innocently. Before I can pry any more information out of him, we're pulling into the parking lot of our old high school. A frown tugs at my mouth as I glance around, finishing up getting dressed.

"What are we doing here, Logan?"

"It's a surprise." He climbs out once the driver opens the door and offers me his arm, which I scowl at before exiting without help. Glancing down at my feet, he scoffs.

"You didn't even put on the nice shoes that came with the tux."

"These are brand new Astro Grabber's, Logan. They're the nicest shoes on the market right now. Got them with my signing bonus."

With an eye roll, he turns toward the steps leading to the school's front doors. "Okay, Mr. Football Star, let's get a move on."

"Hey, I can buy you a pair if you want." I follow after him, trying to shake the itchy feeling that arises from being here again after all these years. "Maybe for your birthday."

"I'm holding you to that. It can be your apology gift to me." He leads us through the dimly lit halls, which is creepy as hell, and I grab his arm just before we get to the gym.

"If you get one, where's mine?" Raising my brows, I drop his arm when he faces me. "We both hid shit from each other and for my part in that, I'm sorry. I should have been a better friend and trusted you with everything."

His honey-brown eyes soften as he nods slowly. "Yeah. Me too."

"So, are we good? I don't want to leave with any bad blood between us on Friday. I love you, man. You're my best friend."

"Yeah, Huck. We're good. And I love you, too, or whatever." He shifts on his feet awkwardly, looking uncomfortable as hell, and I chuckle at the sight. This guy literally cuddled with Matty in a tent back in May but can't even handle a few words of affection.

"You need to be more open about your feelings, Loge. It's okay to tell your friends you love them."

"I just did, didn't I?" He glares at me as I continue to laugh, a small smile curling his lips. "Asshole. Anyway, we're here."

I glance over his shoulder, my grin fading when I take in the double wooden doors behind him. "The gym?"

Just being back here after what happened is like a lightning bolt to my nerves. The last time I stood here, I was with Royce, preparing to break it off with him while feeling like my life was ending. And it almost did. All because of what took place inside this gym, among other things.

Music filters through the door, hitting my ears for the first time, and Logan grins as he slowly pulls on the handle. "Surprise."

The lights are what I notice first, balls of color bouncing off the walls, ropes of twinkling lights strung from one end of the room to the other. Paper streamers hang from the rafters, fluttering gently, glowing balloons covering the entirety of the gym floor. And standing in the middle of it all is Taylor, stealing my breath away in a fitted tux matching my own, looking so beautiful it hurts. He's frowning down at his phone, typing furiously, and relief washes over his features when he glances up to find us standing there.

"About damn time, Jesus," he mutters irritably, gazing over my shoulder at Logan, who smacks his lips in response.

"Not my fault Huckslee drives like he's eighty. Or that he was less than enthused to get into the limo."

"Yeah, yeah, thanks for getting him here." Taylor moves his sparkling eyes to me, a smile lighting up that gorgeous face as the doors shut behind me. "Hi."

"What..." I swallow, sweeping my eyes over the decorated space. "What's happening right now?"

His grin turns shy as he follows my gaze, taking in the flickering tea lights and confetti joining the balloons on the ground. "I'm calling it prom two-point-oh. Or, prom as it should have been." Turning to me, he holds up a plastic box I hadn't noticed with two matching boutonnieres inside. "If you'll be my date?"

A tingling warmth blooms inside my stomach, spreading to my scalp and the tips of my toes, rendering me awestruck and speechless. I search his face, completely at a loss for words. His eyes soften as he takes out one of the boutonnieres to pin it on my jacket, making me tense when the material of the dress shirt scrapes over the sore spot on my left pec.

"Now you put this one on me," he says, grabbing my hand to set the box in my palm. I oblige, sticking it to his lapel before running my hands down his chest and wrapping my arms around him, loving the feel of this man against me after four long days.

"You did this for me?" My voice is hoarse, nearly silent under the music, but Taylor hears me just fine. He nods, licking his lips, which I capture with my own, greedily licking into his mouth. After a few heated moments of sucking on each other's tongues and pulling hair, he breaks away breathlessly, lips red and swollen from my teeth.

"We can revisit this later," he groans, grinding against me, "I have plans."

I nuzzle into his neck, kissing along the dragonfly tattoo covering his Adam's apple. "Four days, baby. I've been without you for four days. I need you."

God, I need him so bad. Need to be inside him, filling him up, claiming him.

A raspy chuckle vibrates against my lips on his throat. "We'll have plenty of time for that, trust me. But right now, I want to dance with you."

Reluctantly, I pull away and let him drag me by my hand through the sea of balloons swirling around our feet. A few of the words on some of them catch my eye, and I choke out a laugh.

"*'Just Divorced'? 'Aging Like Fine Wine'?*"

Taylor kicks at a balloon that says *'Best Bitches'* with a smirk. "The party supply store didn't have a lot in stock. We grabbed what we could last minute."

"We?" I come to a halt, tugging him around to face me. "Who's we? Is this why my dad wasn't home? Why you were gone all weekend?"

"Huckslee," he whines, sighing in exasperation. "Would you just let me surprise you without trying to ruin it?"

I lift a brow at him. "No."

With a light scoff, he turns away. "Come on. I'll explain while we dance."

I let him continue to pull me through the gym, expecting us to stop in the middle of the room. But when he changes direction and leads me to the stage in the corner, my feet slowly come to a standstill. Ghosts of memories replay in my head, my heartbeat kicking up to flood my ears as feelings of shame and fear squeeze my throat. When Taylor turns around, though, and looks at me with those eyes glittering like the ocean under a summer sun, all my thoughts cease.

It's just him and me, surrounded by soft lights, speakers softly playing 'i apologise if you feel something' by Bring Me The Horizon. His hand is warm in mine, thumb sliding over my knuckles in a calming caress, the familiar scent of his shampoo like a blanket over all my doubts.

"Do you trust me?" His gaze is intense, imploring, digging underneath the surface, and I don't even need to think about my answer.

I don't hesitate. Don't think twice.

"With my whole heart."

And I do. Unflinchingly, fiercely, with every ounce of my soul, I know that Taylor would never break me. Not like before, when we were young and naive, still too far under our parents' thumbs to be anything to each other than what we were.

Now, we're just Taylor and Huckslee. Two men who fell for each other despite every reason not to, every odd stacked against them. And if this love between us could blossom despite all of the bullshit, how could I have ever questioned that it wouldn't survive a few months of separation out of the year? Our bond is stronger than that. I see it now. I feel it.

We slip behind the curtain, stepping onto the stage, which is as dank and musty as I remember. Band equipment still litters the space, along with a few props from old plays and stacked plastic chairs. Taylor spins around to face me when we reach the middle, still cautiously searching my face as he wraps his arms around my neck, and my hands instinctively find his waist.

"I promise I'm not going to freak out," I whisper against his mouth, not thoroughly kissing him, lightly pressing our lips together.

He shakes his head, brows furrowing when we sway to the music. "I'm not worried about that."

He says it with conviction, as if his faith in me is unshakable, and I have to clear out the emotion clogging my throat.

"Then what's the face for?"

"I just..." He pulls his head back slightly, teeth sinking into his bottom lip as he glances away. "I went and saw your dad yesterday. We had a long talk. Well, I mostly talked, and he listened. You and I lost so much time because of what I did to you and speaking with Aaron made me realize that I don't want to waste a single second more."

Gently cupping his cheek, I drag his gaze back to mine. "Is that what this is, Tay? Making up for what we missed?"

"Partly. I can never change what I did, but I hoped we could do the same thing you did for me in my father's old trailer. Replace the bad with something good."

The weight of his words makes my chest tighten, moisture stinging my lids, and I quickly burrow into his shoulder to hide the obliteration I feel. It's nothing like the last time I stood here–this is dismantling in all the best ways, letting every piece of armor that I'd built to protect myself fall. It leaves me raw, like an exposed nerve, tender and aching, but...I love it.

"You saying you want me to fuck you on this stage?" I deflect, still hiding my face because even though it feels so right to be cracked open like this with him, I still have my dignity to maintain.

Taylor chuckles softly, twisting his fingers through my curls. "As fun as that sounds, it might get awkward with everyone watching."

My brows jump to my hairline as I lift my head, giving him a questioning look because we're alone, and the smile on his face turns wicked. Glancing over my shoulder, he motions at something behind me.

"Ready?"

"Oh, yes."

I spin around in time to see Royce toss me a wink before he pulls on the rope, opening up the curtain. My eyes widen as I gaze out into the completely filled gym.

Wall to wall, it's packed; some faces I know, and some I don't. Christian and Arya are dressed in formal attire near the middle, with Salem and Logan beside them. Xed is pressed against a smirking Devon, and Matty stands with a dark-haired woman holding Hannah. There are quite a few people I recall from school, ones that had been in this very gym four years ago and had witnessed one of the worst moments of my life. Old church members, too, and coworkers from the Prospector. Juanita, Eliza, Gale.

And standing smack in the front, in a tailored suit and smiling with so much pride in his eyes, is my dad.

Everyone begins cheering, hollering, and clapping their hands when I turn to Taylor with my mouth agape, eyes burning.

"What...how...I don't..."

He grins, flashing that crooked incisor I love so much as he leans close to repeat the words I said to him on the Fourth of July, ones he told me a lifetime ago when we watched my mother's favorite movie. "You're so fucking cute when you're flustered."

All I can do is stare at him, completely astonished. "I don't understand. What is this?"

"This is me coming out." Our fingers entwine in front of our bodies, connecting and grounding me to this moment while his eyes hold mine steady. "About how I feel for you, to all our friends, family, and whatever random ass people responded to the online invite Salem may or may not have posted to the high school's social media pages."

That gets a watery laugh out of me, the tears I'd been battling finally spilling onto my flushed cheeks.

His thumbs brush away my tears as he continues, "It's unfair that I should get a choice in coming out when you didn't." I open my mouth to tell him for the umpteenth time that I've forgiven him, but he holds up a hand to stop me. "I know we've already said our sorries and moved past it, so I won't apologize again. But I want everyone to know I'm in love with you, Huckslee Davis. And I'm proud to call you mine."

My hand raises to grip the back of his neck before I crash my mouth to his, kissing him with every ounce of love and passion I can muster. A roar comes from the crowd, but I barely register their presence, every synapse and neuron entirely focused on the man in my arms, kissing me back with so much fervor and reverence that I nearly drop to my knees.

Which, in fact, is exactly what Taylor does. Well, he drops to *one* knee in particular. The entire gym goes silent with a gasp. He looks up at me from under his lashes, and my stomach drops into my ass right before this motherfucker giggles. Actually giggles.

"I'm just tying my shoe. What the hell are you all thinking?"

Relief crashes into me as a few laughs and groans come from the people watching, none louder than our best friends and my dad, who are gaping at him as equally horrified as I am.

"*Taaaylor-uh!*"

"For real, what is wrong with you, fool?"

"I was about to be *so* pissed that I didn't bring my camera for this!"

He snorts, pushing to his feet with his hands raised. "It was a joke. *A joke.* Calm the fuck down."

I haul him to my chest, nuzzling my nose into his hair while I will my heart to slow down. "I seriously almost shit myself, Jesus Christ."

"Don't worry, I'm not ready to be a football wife yet," his shoulders shake with laughter, and I pull back to squint at him. "Yet?"

He sobers quickly, realizing the slip as his cheeks pinken. "I-I mean, not right now, obviously, because we're only like twenty-two, almost twenty-three. That's super young for marriage, you know? If we even want that. Like, maybe in ten years? Unless...unless that's too long for you–"

"Just shut up, Taylor." I pull him in for another kiss, smiling against his lips when he sighs. We melt into each other, intertwining until the very imprint of his spirit becomes forever entangled with mine.

# TAYLOR

"**M**mm, fuck, I'm gonna come."

Huckslee slurps off my cock at the last minute, grinning wickedly from his place between my legs in the back of the limo, and I slump against the seat with a whine. My tuxedo jacket is crumpled in a ball next to me, sweat dripping down my neck and forehead from the edging he's been giving me the entire ride back to the city. I feel like I'm on fire.

"Baby, please," I beg, lifting my hips like the needy slut I am. "God, I need to come. Please make me come."

He only snickers, holding my hard dick but not stroking it as he runs his lips over my hip bones. "Do you really think you deserve to come after ghosting me for four days?"

"That's not fair. I threw you a party and everything!"

A party, I might add, that we spent hours hanging out and dancing at, sipping sparkling cider until we couldn't keep our hands off each other any longer. If it wasn't for how keyed up he's made me, I'd be falling asleep from the exhaustion of putting the whole thing together. Granted, everyone had pitched in to help, including Aaron, by pulling some strings with the school district, but still. I want to shower, orgasm, be fucked into the mattress, and then pass the hell out. Not necessarily in that order.

"Hmm, that is true." Giving me what I want, he jerks me slowly. "And it was amazing. You're amazing. I love you so much."

I thrust up into his fist with heavy breaths, balls painfully tight. "Yeah? How much?"

"Not enough to let you come yet."

He releases me, leaning back on his heels as the limo starts to slow, and I cry out in frustration. I'm tempted to get myself off, but I know the minute I try to touch myself, he'll force me to stop. Make me wait longer just to torture me. Fuck, he's trained me to be good for him, and I am one hundred percent on board with it.

The back door opens seconds after Huck tucks me away, and the limousine driver drops us off at the duplex. Christian offered to drive my truck home, and tomorrow, I'll take Huck to get his Audi when we go for lunch with his dad...and Maisie, much to my disappointment. Aaron pleaded with us to go, and even though I'm not interested in fixing something I didn't break, I can at least try to talk with her as a thank-you for what he did today.

Even if nothing comes from it, because honestly? I came to terms a long time ago with the fact that sometimes we won't get closure from the people who hurt us, and that's okay. I learned that lesson when my father passed away, and I had to accept an apology that I'd never get. At the end of the day, so many other people in this life love me and are there for me. They're the ones that matter. Those who show up and put in the effort matter.

We're barely inside before Huck is ripping off my shirt, buttons littering the floor at our feet, and I gasp in mock outrage as he pins me against the wall.

"Guess I'm not getting my security deposit back for this tux."

"Guess not." His tongue traces a wet line down to my nipple, and I nearly come from that sensation alone. We kiss our way toward the bedroom, my clothes peeling away until I'm standing next to the bed, fully nude, hard as steel.

"Better get this off before I lose the deposit on both suits," I laugh, making quick work of his jacket. But he stops me when I undo the top button on his shirt.

"Hang on," he wets his raw lips. "I have something to say."

The waver in his voice makes me drop my hands, stepping back slightly. "Okay."

His eyes shine in the room's dimness, reflections from the lava lamp on my desk swirling in their dark depths like a nebulous cloud. "Taylor, these last few months have made me the happiest I've ever felt. I thought I had a life in Cali—football and superficial friendships that never went deeper than the team or the parties. But being here with you, getting to know your circle, and growing closer to Logan, I've realized that the life I was living out there was a lie. It wasn't me or the person I wanted to be. I've never been more myself than I have with you, and I don't want to lose that."

"You won't," I say, touching him again, cupping both hands on either side of his face. "I promise, Huckslee, I'm not going anywhere. Even if it means going without seeing you for months at a time. We can make this work."

He leans into my palm with a smile. "I know that now. I just wanted you to know, too. Know that I know. You know?"

With another laugh, I pull him in for a kiss, my cock pressing into his beneath the seam of his pants. "Yes. I know. Now, will you please fuck me?"

A contemplative look passes over his features, his throat flexing as he swallows audibly. He searches my gaze for a few moments before speaking.

"Actually...I was kind of hoping you'd fuck *me*."

My brain must have blown a fuse because I blink at him for several seconds, unsure if I heard him right. "...what?"

"You heard me." Desire has his pupils expanding, nostrils flaring when he grabs my length and strokes it slowly. "I want you to fuck me, Tay. Stick this big cock in my virgin ass."

"*Holy shit.*" I have to stop his hand from moving, that filthy mouth of his seconds away from making me bust. "Baby, are you sure? We don't have to do that. I'm perfectly fine being your bottom."

He nods emphatically, reaching up to unbutton his shirt. "I want this. I want you and everything that implies."

"I don't want to hurt you, though, and I had weeks to prep myself for..." I trail off when his shirt slips off his shoulders, revealing what he has inked on his left pec. It's in the exact same spot as mine, right over his heart. Only the outline of Delaware on him has my fucking name scrawled inside of it in elegant, curling letters. "Is that a tattoo?"

"Yep," he grins, looking down at it with pride. "Got it on Saturday when my boyfriend was busy ignoring me."

I lick the pad of my thumb, moving toward him to erase it, and he laughs as he bats my arm away.

"It's not going to come off, Taylor."

"Huckslee," my jaw drops, eyes near bugging out of my skull as my heart implodes. "That's permanent. As in, my name will be inked on your body forever!"

"You're already in my soul. Now the outside just matches," he says simply, fingers trailing down his abs until they reach the button on his pants. I watch in awe as he slips them off achingly slow, standing before me completely bare, all soft bronze skin and hard-earned muscle. He's the most exquisite thing I've ever had the pleasure of laying eyes on. It doesn't matter how many times I've seen him naked; the sight always manages to make me speechless.

With one sweet, breathtaking kiss, he backs us toward the bed, crawling onto his back and spreading his legs before reaching for me. "Come here."

Settling between his thighs, we rut against each other until Huck reaches into the nightstand, pulling out the lube.

"Get me ready, Tay."

*Oh, fuck yes.*

I take it from him and lather my fingers, placing a kiss on the underside of his cock. "Last chance to back out."

He only rolls his eyes and hooks a hand behind his knee, spreading wider for me. When my gaze runs over his puckered hole for the first time, I have to pinch the base of my dick to keep from blowing my load all over him.

"Goddamn, that's hot." Circling it slowly, we both gasp when he clenches and nearly sucks my finger inside.

"Fuck," he moans, head dropping back onto the pillow.

"Feels good, huh?"

"Mmm."

He jerks himself lazily, lips parted with soft pants, and I slip inside of him the minute his hole relaxes for me, the sight of my finger sliding in and out of his ass making my cock drip.

"Jesus, you're tight. I don't know if I'll fit."

His laugh has his walls clenching. "You'll fit. Add one more finger, scissor them inside of me."

Doing as he instructs, I gently massage his balls when I feel some resistance, catching his gaze as I lean forward and spit directly onto his hole for more lubrication. His loud groan vibrates the bed when I twist my fingers and hit a raised bump.

"Shit, that's...fuck." His own length is leaving a puddle on his stomach as he strokes it, his face flushed red from pleasure.

"That the spot, baby? Right there?"

He curses and writhes beneath me when I nudge it again. Wonder if I can make him come this way, hands-free. I know I probably can. He's made it happen for me countless times by just milking my prostate, but Huckslee doesn't give me a chance.

"Fuck me, right now," he demands, hauling me up to nip at my throat like a damn vampire, "unless you want me to come on your fingers instead of your cock."

"Fucking bossy." I slide in a third finger without warning, loving the strangled cry that leaves his lips. "Just a bit longer. Don't wanna split you in half."

Moving back down his body, I lick the precum off his abs before sucking his dick into my mouth, teasing at the tip with my tongue. He slowly unravels under me, sweat beading on his skin as he moans and thrusts his hips. It's only when I feel him start to tremble that I pop off and pull my fingers out, positioning myself between his asscheeks. At the last second, I pause, my nerves getting the better of me.

"S-should I get a condom or something?"

He lifts a brow, reaching for the bottle of lube beside us. "Not unless you did something you want to tell me about over the last four days?"

"What the fuck? *No*. I just... I've never done this before."

"You've done anal before, Tay." He squirts lube onto his palm and reaches down to slick me up in long, hard pumps.

"Yeah, but not with *you*," I argue, losing myself momentarily to the feeling of him working me. "And I've never fucked anyone without a condom before. Not even Salem."

His movements falter slightly. "If it makes you more comfortable, you can wear one."

Ah, hell, this isn't coming out right.

Placing my hands on his chest, I gently push him back until he's lying flat on the bed. "No. I want to feel you. All of you."

From the way his breath quickens, that was the correct answer. Lifting his knee, I move my hips forward slowly, filling him one inch at a time. The intention here is to let him adjust to my size, but Huck shocks the hell out of me by grabbing my waist and forcing me forward.

"Fuck, *fuck*, oh my god." I bottom out in one quick thrust, pelvis hitting hot skin, his asshole strangling my cock so tight that I lose strength in my arms and collapse on top of him.

"Move, goddammit," he barks through clenched teeth, and I lift my head to glare at him.

"If I move, I'll come. Jesus Christ, Huck, what the fuck was that?!"

Instead of responding, he wraps his arms around my middle and rolls his hips, crushing me to his chest while he fucks himself on my dick. I'm so gone to the pleasurable heat that all I can do is bite down on his shoulder and try to fight for control. It's frenzied and desperate, both of us battling to dominate the other with each thrust and groan, bodies gliding together.

With a growl, he flips us over, pinning my arms above my head while he rides me into oblivion, the feel of his heavy cock slapping against my abs sending me over the edge.

"God, Huck, I'm gonna..."

He takes my bottom lip between his teeth as I come with a shout, pumping him full of cum. Once I go limp, he lifts himself off and turns me onto my stomach, diving his face between my cheeks.

"Mmm, I missed this ass," he moans, tonguing me open while I whimper into the pillow. A cold sensation slides down my crease as he coats my hole with lube before pushing his cock inside, leisurely fucking me while he gently wraps a hand around my throat. I'm so overstimulated that I mumble incoherently and try to squirm away when he pegs my prostate, but Huck is having none of that. He presses me into the mattress as he moves in and out, torturously slow.

"I'm so close, baby. You're taking me so good." His lips trail the back of my neck and shoulder blades, adding to the sensations sending my nervous system into overdrive. "Just a little longer."

"Huck, I-I can't—"

"You can. Such a good boy for me."

The sounds coming out of my mouth are fucking feral, something between a whine and a snarl clawing its way out when another orgasm rocks through me, spilling in between my body and the sheets. Huckslee shudders, groaning as he finds his own release, slowing while his cock pulses inside of me. He collapses once he's spent, rolling us to the side without pulling out so that we're spooning, and I swear we both pass out for a solid thirty minutes.

It's not until BB honks for food from her cage that we eventually stir, and I languidly stretch out my sore legs with a sigh. "Well, that was..."

"That was flip fucking," Huck breathes drowsily into my hair, slipping out now that he's gone soft. "I think I see the appeal now."

"We're definitely doing that again. Once I can move." At his responding snort, I twist around to crack open an eye at him. "Are you feeling okay?"

He nods, humming contentedly as he snuggles closer. "Your big dick made my ass hurt."

"Hey, I wanted to take it slow, but *someone* got impatient."

There's no answer, only loud snores in my ear, so I roll around to shake him awake.

"No sleeping. We need to shower and feed the bunny. And change the sheets."

"Too tired," he mumbles, his curls a sexy mess as he turns his head into the pillow. "Give me a sponge bath."

"Like a nurse?"

"Mmm, you would look pretty hot in a nurse's dress."

With a scoff, I open my mouth to deny it, but why the fuck is my dick twitching at the idea?

"Yeah, we can unpack all of that later, but I really want a shower right now."

Reluctantly, he lets me tug him off the bed, grabbing food for BB while I get the shower going. Once we're both under the spray, we scrub each other quickly, too exhausted to do anything more than kiss, and then we're crawling back into bed under the fresh sheets.

Laying on our sides, we face each other as I trace the skin around his tattoo. "I can't believe you did this."

"Why not? You have my name on you already."

I scoff as he kisses my inked knuckles. "Yeah, but I usually just tell people it says 'fuck'. There's no hiding yours."

"I don't want to hide you," he says softly, searching my face. "I'm going to love you loud, Taylor."

My stomach flutters as I drop my gaze. "And when everyone finds out that the new lineman for the Ravens is dating his stepbrother?"

His thumb brushes my bottom lip. "'Step' being the keyword, there. And I've loved you since before that happened, so I don't give a fuck what they think."

"Yeah?"

"Yeah. It's me and you, baby. Has been since the moment we kissed beneath the bleachers in eighth grade, and it will be for the rest of our lives. I'm not afraid of what the world thinks about us. I love you, and nothing they do or say can change that."

Our lips meet in a gentle caress full of future promises as we quietly kiss until our eyes close. I murmur his name into the dark just before we drift off in each other's arms.

"Huck?"

"Yeah?"

"I love you, too. Always."

"I know, Tay." His forehead rests against mine, fingers cradling the back of my neck with care as if holding something precious. "I know."

# Epilogue One

## Huckslee

"Am I on screen? Can you see me?"

I bring my phone closer to my face, resting against the sofa cushions in my new apartment. "Yes, Arya, I can see you."

She smirks at the camera, the stadium's bright lights illuminating her blonde hair like a halo. "Do I look hot?"

Christian and Salem step into the frame as I roll my eyes, both grinning at me over Arya's shoulder. "Hey, *hermano*, how's Baltimore?"

"Not too bad. Different."

Different is an understatement. Going from California back to Utah and then Maryland in eight months has definitely been a culture shock. I've been here for three weeks, and I'm still settling in. The coach and my team have been really accepting, though there are a few I can tell are uncomfortable with me being openly gay. I'm trying not to let it bother me, though. Our first preseason game is happening next weekend, so I'm focusing on training for it.

"Our baby boy's up next." Christian takes the phone from Salem and turns it around to face the stadium, giving me a front-row view of the competition grounds. It looks just like it did for the pre-qualifier; instead of one ramp, there are several, along with a dirt track complete with jumps. The stands are packed, cheers from the crowd cutting through my phone speaker, luckily not too loud with whatever noise-dampening mechanism Salem has on her phone for filming.

I know this event is a big deal. Nitro Fuel hosts talent from all over the country; only the best in action sports earn a spot. If Taylor were to win Best Trick, it would open so many doors for him. Their *T.O.T* brand would grow, and a win would guarantee him a place at this championship every year and possible X Games invites in the future. It's everything my boyfriend ever dreamed of as a kid, and even if he doesn't win, I'm so proud of him for making it this far.

Who would have thought? Taylor fucking Tottman, the kid that tormented me in high school daily, who constantly had me coming home covered in bruises, the boy who stole my first kiss and outed me to the entire community, would be mine? What's even crazier is that I still fell in love with him despite it all.

Salem's shout snaps me out of my thoughts, and I focus on the screen when the rev of a dirt bike engine cuts through the stadium. The announcers say his name just as he appears, dressed in new gear, making my heart hurt with how much I miss him. He'd already competed earlier in the FMX comp, coming in seventh place, but I'd missed it due to my training schedule. We FaceTimed last night, like always, but I still can't help the empty feeling that settles in my bones when I wake up every morning alone.

Just one more month, and then I'll see him at our game against the Raiders in Vegas. And then again in Phoenix a month after that, along with Matty, when our teams go head to head. I only signed a six-month lease since Taylor decided that I'll live with him in Utah during the off-season, and I can't tell my baby no.

I can do this.

We can do this.

He lines up his bike as they finish setting up, each rider needing a specific ramp for the type of jump they want to do. Taylor's trick, a repeat of the Captain Morgan backflip, requires launching himself off the Moon Booter, which will send him fifty-five feet into the air.

I'm a fucking nervous wreck as he takes off down the strip. His front wheel hits the ramp, and he jumps onto his seat, soaring high into the sky above the stands. The bike flips back, his legs extending to complete the trick, but...

Something's wrong. He's way too high. None of the ramps he practiced on over the summer were as tall as this.

Gravity takes over, and his bike falls away from him, along with my heart, as he plummets back to earth. Arya's scream nearly blows out my eardrums as his body hits the ramp, bouncing before sliding away, the bike narrowly avoiding smashing him to pieces. I'm on my feet in seconds, pulling on my shoes and grabbing my keys, every thought focused on somehow getting to Utah and Taylor, even if it ruins my career.

I'm about to yank open the front door when Christian's voice breaks through the panic icing my veins.

"He's getting up! He's fine, Salem. Stop being a crybaby. The landing ramp is cushioned, *tonta*."

Fuck. That's right, I forgot. It's a country-wide competition. They wouldn't let people fall from five-and-a-half stories high without ensuring they were as safe as possible.

My eyes fly to the screen, a shaky breath shotgunning from my lungs as I see him walk toward his bike, picking it up to try again. Each rider gets two attempts, luckily, and as he shakes his head before getting back on, I slump back into my seat, legs feeling like jello and visions of a broken, bloody Taylor in my brain.

He lines up again, flying down the strip, and this time, when he flips back into the trick, it goes just as it's supposed to, his hands on his hips while he lifts a foot onto the bars. Both wheels stick the landing, roars and shouts erupting from the crowd, and I blink away the moisture that had formed as Taylor lifts his hands in triumph.

"Let's fucking goooo!" Christian shouts, the camera bouncing as he jumps around, throwing his arms over both girls.

My phone drops to my lap as my head hits the back of the couch, my heart thumping so hard I can feel it in my fingers. Jesus Christ. I know dirt biking is dangerous, especially combined with freestyle motocross, but goddamn. I don't know if I can ever watch another one of these again. My nervous system can't take that shit, especially knowing where every scar on his body comes from. He's such a daredevil that it's only a matter of time before it happens again.

"Baby, are you there?"

Taylor's voice echoes from the speaker, and I quickly pick up my phone to gaze at his grinning face. Dark, sweaty strands stick to his forehead, the tips now an electric blue. His smile slowly fades when he sees the look on my face.

"Scared you, huh?"

"Terrified. I was almost halfway across the country when I realized you were fine."

A smug smirk pulls at his pouty lips. "A few bruises won't keep me down. I'm a badass, remember?"

"Bruises?! Show me," I demand, sitting up straight. Taylor chokes out a laugh.

"Considering they're on my ass, I'll show you later. Unless flashing the judges would help me win?"

"Well, it *is* a magnificent ass..."

Heat sparks in the green of his eyes, but Salem steps into view before he can respond, her bright red hair piled high.

"If you two are done flirting," she snickers, throwing me a wink, "they're about to announce his score."

We all hold our breaths, waiting for what feels like ten minutes, but it's probably only two. Finally, the judges score his performance, technique, and originality.

Eighty-four.

Eight points less than his qualifying score, and two points less than the lead, putting him in second place.

His shoulders visibly slump on screen, his smile growing tight, and a spark of anger ignites in my gut.

"That's fucking bullshit," I shout, jumping to my feet. "You should have been first! No one else has even been able to do that move other than you!"

"Huck, it's okay," he chuckles, running a hand through his hair while Christian and Arya sandwich him into a hug. "Second place is fine. It's good. There are still a few more competitors to go, but even if I make the top five, I'll be happy."

My brows raise at that. "You will?"

"Are you kidding? Some of these riders have been doing tricks since before I was born. Of course, I'll be happy." A grin spreads across his cheeks, beautiful and genuine, lighting up my entire world. "Honestly, as a rookie rider, just getting the chance to be here is enough. More than I ever thought possible."

For a moment, I'm breathless, seeing the joy on his face while he laughs at something Arya says. My throat tightens as I think about the boy from high school who lost the scholarship race, the boy he used to be, and more tears threaten to spill. Fuck, he's so different now. In all the best ways. And though I can't take credit for being the reason, I'm incredibly thankful to Salem and the guys for sticking by his side through all the shit he went through, for pushing him and believing in him to be better. They saw his worth when no one else did. Not even his own parents.

Not even me.

And I'll never make that mistake again.

"I'm so proud of you, baby," I whisper, though he can't hear me over the chatter coming from his friends. And it's okay because I could sit here and look at him all night if he let me. Which he would. He'd probably like it, too.

Smiling broadly, I settle back into the couch and watch the love of my life shine.

# EPILOGUE TWO

## TAYLOR - ONE YEAR LATER

"Y ou gonna tell me where we're going?"

Huckslee smiles amusedly over at me from the driver's seat of the Audi, squeezing my hand tightly. "Why? Don't you trust me?"

"No." Yes. "Not at all." With my life.

He snorts as if reading my mind, shaking his head while he turns up the radio. "Relax and enjoy the scenery. We'll be there soon."

Huffing dramatically, I fold my arms and lean back in my seat, watching Maryland's coast fly by while 'Royal We' by Silversun Pickups fills the silence. The Chesapeake Bay yawns in the distance, the clear, shimmering waters of the Atlantic kissing the horizon. I've only been here a week, and I love it already.

The temperatures are milder than in Utah, the summer heat taking a break every few days with lightning storms that crack open the entire sky. We'd spent some time last night laying on Huck's balcony, letting the raindrops soak us as we kissed and held each other. It was easily the most romantic moment of my life.

Well, maybe second. The first would have to be riding Huck's cock on his bike, parked on a secluded beach while the waves rolled in. I still can't get over how sexy he looks in a motocross helmet. Honestly, when his NFL contract is up, I might try to persuade him to join Christian and me now that our brand is taking off, thanks to my competition results last year. Our latest show at the monster truck rally helped, too.

We partnered with Royce full-time just to keep up with the clothing production, and Salem's getting paychecks now, so that's a plus. So is Logan. We want to start branching into motocross gear. I'm trying to find a way to involve Xed since he hasn't taken Matty and Hannah's absence very well, but...more on that later.

Huck squeezes my hand again, drawing me out of my thoughts. "What's on your mind?"

"Just you," I smile coyly, throwing him a sideways glance, "and the sounds you made when I toyed with you last night."

"Don't distract me," he groans, letting go of my hand to adjust himself. "I might drive us off a cliff, I swear."

But I'm already distracted. Remembering how he came apart for me when I fucked him with a vibrator has my dick hard.

Reaching over the center console, I run my hands along his muscular thigh. "You know, no one's around...the road is quiet."

He scowls even though his eyes heat up. "Taylor, no. We already chanced getting caught on the beach."

I push my bottom lip out, pouting while my hand climbs higher, and his eyes drop to my mouth as he shifts in his seat, widening his legs.

"Such a needy brat."

"Only for you." Humming triumphantly, I unbutton his pants, reaching under the hem of his briefs to pull out his thick cock. "And when I go back home, it'll be months before I see you again. Gotta make sure my man is satisfied until then."

I wait for the thought to drop my mood, but surprisingly... I'm alright. As much as I miss him during the season, it's gotten easier. Come summer, he'll be all mine, and I get him to myself. Plus, it's only for a few more years. All these months apart hasn't dampened our feelings for each other one bit. If anything, not seeing him every day has only heightened our insatiable need.

"Like we don't jerk off on FaceTime nearly every night," he laughs, moaning when I spit into my palm and stroke him.

"That's different. Not to brag, baby, but your hand has nothing on mine."

"Needy *and* cocky. It's a wonder I put up with you."

Releasing my seatbelt, I lay my stomach over the console, smirking up at him while I flick my tongue over his crown. "You love it."

"I don't know about love, but I tolerate—oh, shit, do that again."

He bucks his hips when I take one of his balls into my mouth, gently sucking as I work his shaft. The car starts to slow, gravel crunching beneath the wheels, and he throws us into park before shoving his jeans down. "Don't stop, Tay."

Oh, I don't plan on it.

Using my saliva as lube, I slip a finger inside his hole, fucking into him as he fists my hair and brings me back to his cock. I take it all the way to my throat until I'm gagging, the sound alone driving him wild. When his warm cum hits my tongue, I savor it, loving the way he pulls me up for a filthy kiss, desperate to taste himself.

I'll never get enough of Huckslee Davis. No matter how much time or distance we spend apart, I'll always come back for more. Out of all the addictions I've had in my life, his presence is the most potent. The one habit I can't kick and I never want to try.

"Fuck, I love you," I murmur, climbing over to straddle his lap, but he holds me back with his palms on my chest.

"Hang on, we're here," he grins, laughing when I cup my hard-on with a whine. "I'll take care of that in a minute. Close your eyes."

The idea of refusing hits me hard, but the promise of an orgasm has me throwing that thought out the window and obeying him instead. My lids sink shut, arms folded while I wait for him to straighten up his clothes.

Humid air hits us as he opens the door and guides me over soft grass with his hands on my shoulders. A car whizzes by, indicating that we must have pulled over on the side of the highway.

"Okay. Open."

As soon as my vision adjusts, a gasp fills my lungs, followed by a laugh as I read the state sign standing tall before us.

**Welcome to Delaware. Endless Discoveries.**

Turning around, I raise my brows at him despite the tightness in my chest. "Really? You took me to Delaware?"

"Yep. Who knew it was so close to Maryland?"

"I did. We really need to get you a map, Huckslee."

He simply smiles, reaching out to cup my face as I wrap my arms around him. "Looks like it's real, after all."

"The people who live here are thrilled to hear that." Tears prick my lashes, spilling over when I try to blink them away, and I bury my face into his broad chest, feeling every ounce of the love he has for me. "Thank you. For bringing me here."

He delicately lifts my jaw, those dark, starry eyes searching as he presses his lips to mine. "Is it everything you hoped it would be?"

Clearly, he's not talking about the state of Delaware but rather the state of *us*—Taylor and Huckslee.

"No." Deepening the kiss, I jump up to wrap my legs around his waist, trusting his strength to catch me if I fall. "It's so much more, baby. So much more."

The End

# Afterword

If you've made it this far, thank you from the bottom of my heart!

Finding Delaware is my debut novel, and I hope you loved reading it as much as I loved writing it. Huckslee and Taylor's journey is a testament to the power of secrets and their toll on our lives. I wanted to dig deep into the messy struggle of hiding who you really are—the kind of pressure that eats you alive, leaving you with this gnawing shame that whispers you're never enough. Both characters are trapped: Huckslee, choking on the weight of perfection everyone expects from him, and Taylor, haunted by trauma that just won't quit. Together, they reflect that never-ending battle between who we are on the inside and who we show the world. But there's always light at the end of the tunnel.

This story is about finding the guts to stare down your demons, forgiving yourself for the things you thought could never be forgiven, and realizing that redemption isn't just possible—it's *worth* fighting for. It's about loving yourself despite your scars, and most importantly, it's a reminder that no matter what you've done in the past, you can always change.

If you've ever been crushed under a secret, suffocated by the weight of expectations, or burned by desires you've kept hidden, I hope Huckslee and Taylor's story hits you right where it matters. Writing this has been just as messy and vulnerable for me as it was for them, and honestly, I'm honored that you're here for the ride.

Remember, we all wear masks, but it's the moments when they fall away that we find our true selves. Embrace those moments, no matter how terrifying they may be.

With love always,
Bree Wiley

P.S. For those of you interested in Xed and Matty, you can read the first chapter of their story, Crossing Arizona, by subscribing to my newsletter at www.authorbreewiley.com

# Acknowledgments

To my wonderful partner, Joe, thank you for being so supportive over these months while I lost my mind. You're the best in the west, babe.

A huge shout-out to my sister-in-law, Jessicka, for putting up with my constant late night messages and mental breakdowns. Love you so much!

Last, but not least, to my beta readers who gave me honest opinions and feedback; Giselle, Cici, Kimberly, Sayward and Lavender, y'all rock!

# CW List

The following list contains spoilers, so if you're the type that prefers to go in blind, please skip to the first chapter.

- Struggles with mental health, anxiety and depression

- Prescription drug abuse

- Child abuse

- Neglectful parents

- Mentions of domestic violence

- Mentions of parental death by cancer and a parent having cancer

- Drug addicted parent, mentions of parental death due to overdose

- Suicidal ideations and attempted suicide

- Violence between the MC's

- Internalized and external homophobia due to a bigoted parent

- Homophobic slurs

- Struggles with alcoholism

- Loss of faith

- Underage drinking and drug use

- Cheating—not between MC's

- Forced outing

Graphic sexual situations not intended for readers below the age of 18 such as:

- Mild breath play

- Cum play/snowballing

- Dubious consent

# About The Author

I'm a Utah native who can be found cuddled on the couch with my partner and our black cat, Norman Bates. Mostly, I'm a homebody but I do enjoy getting lost in the woods. I love romance, fantasy, science fiction, and every horror video game ever made. Finding Delaware is my first novel.

Let's be besties!

instagram.com/authorbreewiley
facebook.com/authorbreewiley
www.authorbreewiley.com

Printed in Great Britain
by Amazon

53390244R00384